A SAILOR OF AUSTRIA

A SAILOR OF AUSTRIA

In which, without really intending to, Otto Prohaska becomes Official War Hero No. 27 of the Habsburg Empire

By John Biggins

McBOOKS PRESS, INC.
ITHACA, NEW YORK

PUBLISHED BY MCBOOKS PRESS, INC. 2005

Copyright © 1991 by John Biggins

First published in Great Britain
by Martin Secker & Warburg Limited

Cover Design: Michael Rider, Rider Design, Ithaca, NY

ISBN: 1-59013-107-X

Library of Congress Cataloging-in-Publication Data
Biggins, John.
   A sailor of Austria / by John Biggins.
      p. cm. — (The Otto Prohaska novels ; #1)
      ISBN 1-59013-107-X (trade pbk. : alk. paper)
      1. World War, 1914-1918—Naval operations,
Austrian—Fiction. 2. Austria—History, Naval—
20th century—Fiction. I. Title.
PR6052.I34S25 2005
823'.914—dc22
                                        2005007282

Distributed to the trade by
National Book Network, Inc.,
15200 NBN Way, Blue Ridge
Summit, PA 17214
800-462-6420

Additional copies of this book may be ordered from
any bookstore or directly from McBooks Press, Inc.,
ID Booth Building, 520 North Meadow St., Ithaca,
NY 14850. Please include $4.00 postage and handling
with mail orders. New York State residents must add
sales tax to total remittance (books & shipping). All
McBooks Press publications can also be ordered by
calling toll-free 1-888-BOOKS11 (1-888-266-5711).
Please call to request a free catalog.

Visit the McBooks Press website
at www.mcbooks.com.

Printed in the United States of America
9 8 7 6 5 4 3 2 1

This book is dedicated to all those whose stories were never told

Österreich, du edles Haus,
Steck deine Fähne aus,
Lass sie im Winde wehen.
Österreich soll ewig stehen!

Austria, thou noble house,
Raise thy banner high,
Let it wave in the wind.
Austria shall stand for ever!

Patriotic verse
Anon
Vienna, 1915

Ganzes Dasein ist ein Schmarren,
Freunderl sei gescheit!
Heute über fünfzig Jahren
Leben and're Leut'.

Everything is just a mess,
Friend, be clever!
Fifty years from now
Other people will be alive.

"Die Csardasfürstin"
Emmerich Kálmán
Vienna, 1915

ABBREVIATIONS

The Austro-Hungarian Empire set up in 1867 was a union of two near-independent states in the person of their monarch, the Emperor of Austria and King of Hungary. Of these two only Hungary had formal status. The rest of the Monarchy was loosely referred to as "Austria," a kind of mental shorthand for a collection of provinces extending in an untidy half-circle from the Ukraine down to Dalmatia, but to the very end it never had an official title.

In this way it came about that for fifty-one years, almost every institution and many of the officials of this composite state had their titles prefixed with initials denoting their status. Shared Austro-Hungarian institutions were Imperial and Royal: "kaiserlich und königlich" or "k.u.k." for short. Those pertaining to the Austrian part of the Monarchy were designated Imperial-Royal: "kaiserlich-königlich" or simply "k.k.," in respect of the monarch's status as Emperor of Austria and King of Bohemia; while purely Hungarian institutions were Royal Hungarian: "königlich ungarisch" ("k.u.") or "kiraly magyar" ("k.m.").

If readers find this complicated they may draw some comfort from the fact that it seems to have been equally bewildering to contemporaries.

The Austro-Hungarian Navy followed contemporary Continental practice in quoting sea distances in nautical miles (6,080 feet), land distances in kilometres, battle ranges etc. in metres and gun calibres in centimetres. However, it followed pre-1914 British custom in using the twelve-hour system for times. From 1850 onwards its surface vessels had been designated "Seiner Majestäts Schiff"—"S.M.S." Submarines were officially "Seiner Majestäts Unterseeboot" or "S.M.U.," but in practice this was nearly always shortened to "U-," as in the Imperial German Navy.

PLACE NAMES

A glossary of place names is attached since border changes between 1914 and 1947 have altered many of those used in this story beyond recognition. The list merely records Austrian official practice in 1914 and implies no endorsement whatever of any territorial claims past or present. Where there was more than one alternative name for a place (as was often the case, for instance, in Transylvania) the German-speaking Austrian usage is given first.

Abbazia	Opatija, Yu.	Comisa	Komiža, Yu.
Adelsberg	Postojna, Yu.	Curzola I.	Korčula I., Yu.
Agram	Zagreb, Yu.	Dignano	Vodnjan, Yu.
Breslau	Wroclaw, Po.	Divacca	Divača, Yu.
Brioni I.	Brijuni I., Yu.	Durazzo	Durrës, Al.
Brünn	Brno, Cz.	Fáno I.	Othonoi I., Gr.
Budua	Budva, Yu.	Fiume	Rijeka, Yu.
Budweis	Budějovice, Cz.	Gjenović	Denovici, Yu.
Cazza I.	Sušac I., Yu.	Gravosa	Gruž, Yu.
Castellnuovo	Herzegnovi, Yu.	Hermannstadt	Sibiu/Nagyszeben, Ro.
Cattaro	Kotor, Yu.	Incoronata I.	Kornat I., Yu.
Cephalonia	Kefallinai, Gr.	Kaschau	Košice, Cz.
Cerigo I.	Kythira I., Gr.	Klausenburg	Cluj/Kolzosvár, Ro.
Cerigotto I.	Antikythira I., Gr.	Kronstadt	Braşov/Brasso, Ro.
Cherso I.	Cres I., Yu.	C. Laghi	Kep i Lagit, Al.

Lagosto I.	Lastovo I., Yu.	Punto d'Ostro	Oštri Rt, Yu.
Laibach	Ljubljana, Yu.	Ragusa	Dubrovnik, Yu.
Leitmeritz	Litoměřice, Cz.	C. Rodoni	Kep i Rodonit, Al.
Lemberg	L'vov/Lwów, USSR	S. Giovanni di Medua	Shëngjini, Al.
Lesina I.	Hvar I., Yu.	San Pedro	Sv. Petar, Yu.
C. Linguetta	Kep i Gjuhëzës, Al.	Santi Quaranta	Sarandë, Al.
Lissa I.	Vis I., Yu.	Saseno I.	Sazan I., Al.
Lussin I.	Lošinj I., Yu.	Sebenico	Šibenik, Yu.
Marburg	Maribor, Yu.	R. Semani	R. Seman, Al.
R. Maros	R. Mures, Ro.	Sissek	Sisak, Yu.
Medolino	Medulin, Yu.	R. Skumbini	R. Skhumbin, Al.
Meleda I.	Mljet I., Yu.	Spalato	Split, Yu.
Merlera I.	Erikoussa I., Gr.	Strachnitz	Strchnice, Cz.
Oderberg	Bohumin, Cz.	Teodo	Tivat, Yu.
Olmutz	Olomouc, Cz.	Traü	Trogir, Yu.
Oppeln	Opole, Po.	Troppau	Opava, Cz.
C. Pali	Kep i Palit, Al.	Valona	Vlorë, Al.
Parenzo	Poreč, Yu.	Veglia I.	Krk I., Yu.
Paxos I.	Paxi I., Gr.	Zanté I.	Zakynthos I., Gr.
Pilsen	Plzen, Cz.	Zara	Zadar, Yu.
Pola	Pula, Yu.	Zengg	Senj, Yu.
Porto Rosé	Rose, Yu.		

MAP OF AUSTRIA-HUNGARY
WITH INSERTS OF THE BOCCHE AND POLA

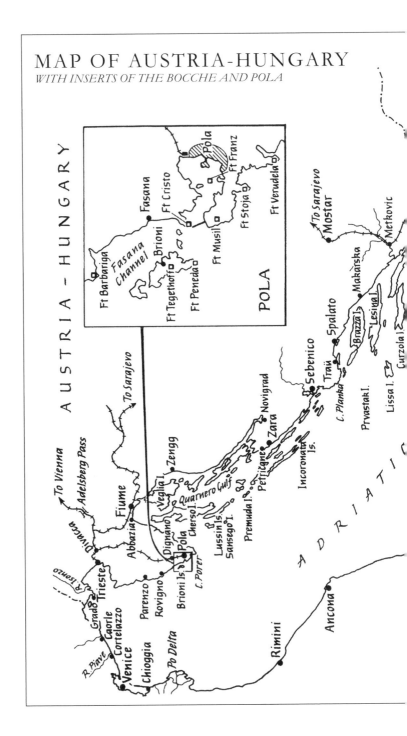

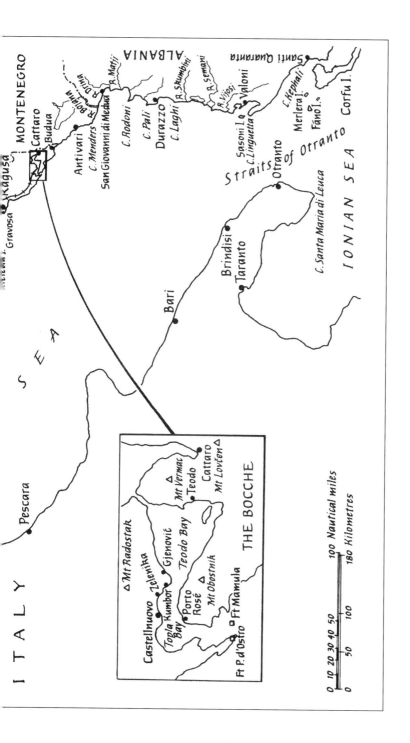

MONTENEGRO

Cattaro
Budua

ITALY

Pescara

S E A

Bari

Brindisi
Taranto

C. Santa Maria di Leuca

I O N I A N   S E A

Antivari
C. Menders
San Giovanni di Medua

R. Drina
R. Bojana
R. Mati

ALBANIA

R. Skumbini
R. Laghi

R. Semani
R. Vijosi

C. Rodoni
C. Pali
Durazzo
C. Laghi

Sasoni I.º
C. Linguetta
Valoni

Straits of Otranto

Otranto

C. Kephali
Merlera I.
Fáno I.º

Corfu I.

Santi Quaranta

Ragusa
Gravosa

THE BOCCHE

Castelnuovo
Zelenika
Gjenović
Togla Kumbor
Bay
Porto
Rosé
Mt Obostnik
Ft Mamula
Ft P. d'Ostro

△ Mt Radostak

Teodo Bay

Mt Vermac
Teodo

Cattaro
Mt Lovćen △

0 10 20 30 40 50   100 Nautical miles
0   50   100   180 Kilometres

SUBMARINE DIAGRAMS

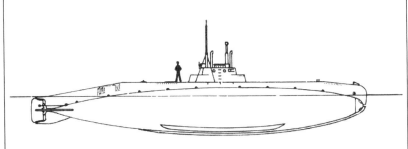

U8 (1915)

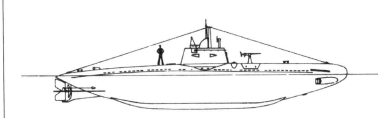

U13 (1915)

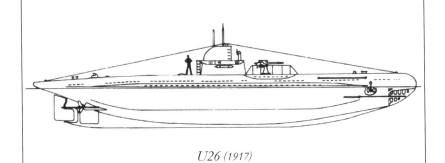

U26 (1917)

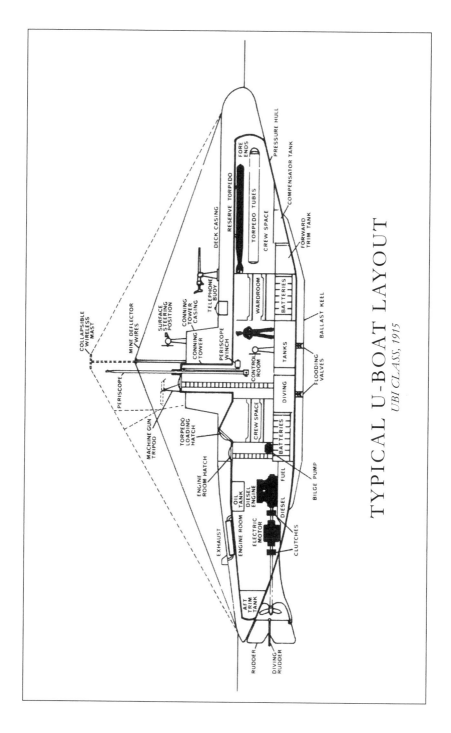

TYPICAL U-BOAT LAYOUT
UBI CLASS, 1915

1

WHY I AM TELLING YOU ALL THIS

PLAS GAERLLWYDD

PENGADOG

NEAR LLANGWYNYDD

WEST GLAMORGAN

SEPTEMBER 1986

I IMAGINE THAT MANY OF MY LISTENERS will take the view that if a man has to wait until his hundred and first year before committing himself to posterity, then what he has to say cannot really have been very important in the first place. I am afraid though that I cannot help this. Please understand that I am sitting here now, speaking into this little machine, as much for my own benefit as for yours. Naturally, I hope that these ramblings of mine may be of some historical value; perhaps also divert or even amuse you. But my main purpose in committing all this to record is to try and make some sense of it all to myself: to carry out, if you like, a sort of final audit of the accounts before they tow me away on my long-overdue voyage to the breaker's yard.

I think that I may not have much time left now. This, I appreciate, hardly sounds a very remarkable statement, coming from a man who celebrated his hundredth birthday nearly six months ago; but the fact of the matter is that the ghosts have been hovering about me night and day these past few months, ever since the reappearance of the album and my arrival here in this place whose name I shall not even attempt to pronounce. But no, "ghosts" is not the right word, I think: there is nothing at all threatening or sinister about these sudden, vivid, quite unpredictable incursions of the people and events of seventy years ago into the world of here and now. Quite the contrary: now that I have got used to them they leave me with a curious feeling of peace. Nor are they transparent or insubstantial in any way; in fact they seem far more real than the events of a few minutes ago—or what pass for events in an old people's home full of decrepit Central European émigrés. Do they come to me or do I go to them? Or have they been there all the time? I really cannot say. All I know is that time is falling to pieces now: day and night and past and present all shuffled together like a pack of cards as I drift into eternity.

We had a storm last night, with a good deal of that loud, ill-tempered thunder that seems to go on above the clouds. I was lying half-asleep, half-awake in the fitful way that you will doze if you ever live to be as monstrously old as I am. Then suddenly, for no reason that I could think of, I was back there with them aboard *U26* that morning—it must have been May 1917—when the British destroyers were depth-charging us off Malta. It was no dream, I can assure you: I was present again among them in that cramped, stuffy little control room as we turned and dived and doubled our course down there in the crashing green twilight, sixty metres below the ultramarine waves, thrown about like frogs in a bucket as each brain-jarring concussion shattered the electric lamps and brought flakes of white paint showering down from the deckheads. No, it was no dream; they were all there exactly as they had been that morning: my Second Officer Béla Meszáros, his brow beaded with sweat and his knuckles clenched white as he gripped the edge of the chart table to steady himself. And our helmsman, the Montenegrin Grigorović, huge and impassive as ever, with his egg-brown face and his little waxed moustache, wedged into his chair behind the steering wheel and gyro compass card, repeating my helm orders as calmly as if he were piloting a steam pinnace at a regatta in Pola harbour—except that I could just hear him mutter to himself: "Hail Mary, full of grace . . . Starboard ten points Herr Kommandant . . . Pray for us sinners . . ." CRASH! ". . . now and at the hour of our death . . ."

Well, even as a lifelong sceptic I have to admit that the Blessed Virgin's intercession on our behalf was efficacious that morning. We all lived to die another day, for I suppose that they must all be dead now, many years since, except for me: the thirty-one-year-old whom they called "der Alte"—"the Old Man."

But this is unforgivable, to ramble on like this without introducing myself. At your service: Ottokar Eugen Prohaska, Ritter von Strachnitz, sometime Senior Lieutenant in the Imperial and Royal Austro-Hungarian Navy, sometime Commander-in-Chief of the Czechoslovak Danube Flotilla, sometime Admiralissimo of the Paraguayan Republic, Commodore in the Polish Navy and Attaché Extraordinary to the Polish and Czechoslovak Governments-in-Exile, holder of the Knight's Cross of the Military Order of Maria Theresa, the Gold and the Silver Signum Laudis, the Knight's Cross of the Order of Leopold, the Order of the Iron Crown First Class, the Military Service Cross with Laurels, the German Iron Cross First Class, the Ottoman Liakat Order with Crossed Sabres, the Order of Polonia Restituta, the Silver Virtuti Militari, the Order of the White Lion, the Paraguayan Golden Armadillo with Sun Rays and the Distinguished Service Order with Bar.

However, if you care to strip away the fake title of nobility and the encrustations of metalware, like layers of paint and rusted drawing-pins off the back of an old door, you may think of me as Otto Prohaska, which was my name during my years in the Austrian service. Or if you prefer it, as plain Ottokár Procházka, the square-faced old Czech peasant who looks at me out of the mirror each morning: a wrinkled Bohemian village elder with high cheek-bones and a bristling white moustache, just like his grandfather and the preceding forty or so generations of Procházkas who goaded their plough-oxen across the fields around the village of Strchnice in the district of Kolin, about sixty kilometres east of Prague. They certainly built us to last. My grandfather lived to be ninety-seven, while as for my father the Imperial-Royal Deputy District Superintendent of Posts and Telegraphs, he would probably have made the century as well if he had not been run over by a railway locomotive.

As for myself, I passed my hundredth birthday back in April. I didn't receive the customary telegram from your Queen. But please don't think that I am complaining about this: I gather that the telegram has to be requested on behalf of the recipient, and the Mother Superior did write to Buckingham Palace on my behalf. Her Majesty's secretary was very polite, but said that they have to abide by certain rules, and require a birth certificate as evidence. And of course, as to my birth certificate, who can say? Perhaps it lies mouldering in some cellar in Prague or Brünn or Vienna; more likely it was burnt and scattered to the winds in 1945. No, I am more than grateful enough to Queen Elizabeth and her father for having given a penniless old refugee somewhere to rest his bones these past forty years. Beyond that, why should I be any concern of hers? I was born a subject of the Emperor Franz Josef, and I have served a dozen states since without ever having sworn allegiance to any of them. No, the only oath of loyalty that I ever took was as a pink-cheeked young Seefähnrich that morning in 1905 on the quarterdeck of the old *Babenburg,* swearing lifelong devotion to Emperor and Dynasty as I tied on for the first time that sword belt of black-and-yellow silk, like a nun taking the veil. Since then it has all been one to me: Austria-Hungary, Czechoslovakia, Paraguay, Poland, The United Kingdom of Great Britain and Northern Ireland; Empires, People's Republics, thousand-year Reichs, all of them as insubstantial as smoke and transient as hailstones on an August afternoon, those huge Central European hailstones that smash roof-tiles and kill animals and flatten hectares of rye, then vanish before your eyes as the sun comes out.

That was what they used to drum into us cadets at the Imperial and Royal Marine Academy in Fiume: "Whoever puts on the tunic of a Habsburg officer puts aside his nationality." The only snag for me and for a generation of my brother officers was that there would come a day when the tunics would be rudely stripped from our backs and we would have to don our old nationality again—if we could remember what it had once been. Most of us found that they fitted indifferently on middle-aged bodies, while as for myself, I never really found one that suited me. I have been a

Stateless Person these past thirty-five years, ever since the Poles took away my passport and the Czech regime sentenced me to death in absentia, and I must say that this citizenship suits me as well as any other. A good joke really, if you think about it: the man without a country who doesn't know his own name, born in a town without a name and brought to die in a place whose name he can't even pronounce. When young Dr Watkins came to see me a few weeks ago I asked him if he would consider making out my death certificate in advance, so that I can have at least some official evidence that I exist. He smiled evasively and pretended not to have heard me.

Anyway, I am wandering away from my task, which is to tell you why I am putting my recollections on record. So really I suppose that I have to start with Sister Elisabeth—or Elzbieta, to give her her on-duty Polish title. She arrived at the Convent in Ealing about the middle of last year, on secondment from the Mother Convent of the Sisters of the Perpetual Veneration at a place called Tarnów in southern Poland: a dull little town which I remember quite well from my youth when some cousins of mine lived near by. Now, I will say nothing against the Sisters: they took me in, free of charge, ten years ago when my wife died and I could no longer look after myself, and since that time they have been very good to me in so far as they have been able, with ninety or so other aged, sick and cantankerous Polish refugees to look after. In fact I feel a perfect fraud for having lived so long and been such a burden on their generosity. They are all very sweet and kind. But even so these have been lonely and trying years for me. For one thing, being a sort of Czech has set a certain gulf between me and the other "pure ethnic Polish" residents (I must try not to call them inmates) of the Home. My mother was a Pole, I speak the language better than many of them and I think that my record of service to the Polish state speaks for itself. But still there has always been a certain reserve and awkwardness between me and them. And there is the matter of age, now that I am "Our Oldest Resident" (Mother Superior's sickly sweet way of addressing me— "And how is Our Oldest Resident this morning?"—as if I had forgotten my name during the night). I am now nine years older than the next most senior resident Mr Wojciechowski (who is completely gaga) and thirty-eight years older than the eldest of the Sisters. Perhaps this might have been tolerable if my brain had turned to soup, but I'm afraid that it remains as sharp as ever, though sadly lacking in stimulation these past couple of years now that the cataracts prevent me from reading very much.

But Sister Elisabeth is not like the rest of them. It must be admitted that she is not much to look at: a drab, mouse-like little woman with wire-rimmed spectacles and a mouthful of stainless steel teeth to replace the ones lost through scurvy and beatings in a Soviet labour camp in 1940. But for me she has been a spring of crystal water in a ten-year-wide wilderness of dust and stones: someone who talks with me about things that we both know and understand, someone who treats me as an intelligent human being rather than a near-imbecile. Also she is great fun to be with: a natural anarchist with a deadly talent for mimicry and a charmingly irreverent attitude to the Church and all other purveyors of received truth. I believe that her father was a senior civil servant in the old Imperial-Royal Ministry of Education, in charge of middle schooling throughout Austrian Poland: a Regierungsrat, no less. Elisabeth was born in 1924 in the former provincial capital of Lemberg, by that time renamed Lwów. But even though her home language was Polish she was brought up to think of herself as a servant of the now-vanished Dynasty and its scattered peoples: in other words, as an Old Austrian, unencumbered by anything so vulgar as a nationality. One of her first memories, she tells me, is of her father lulling her to sleep by humming the "Gott Erhalte," Haydn's beautiful old imperial anthem with its versions in all eleven official languages of the Monarchy. They work her very hard in the kitchens, but we still find time to sit together and talk about the places we both knew and the people who once lived in them, before the flood came and swept them all away.

It was Sister Elisabeth who restored the album to me one morning early in May, as the lime trees of Iddesleigh Road were breaking into flower and the Heathrow Nightingales were starting to thunder overhead, one every three minutes. It was the day before I was due to set off on my journey down here to South Wales, and I was sitting in my room watching as Sister Anuncja packed my suitcase, kneeling on the lid in an effort to engage the catches. As she worked she talked to me over her shoulder in the way that one would speak to a cat or a low-grade mental defective—someone at any rate who is not expected to reply, or even to understand very much. She was telling me how much I would enjoy my holiday at Plas Gaerllwydd.

"Really," she prattled, "it's so lovely down there by the sea. The beach is all white sand and three kilometres long and the waves are huge and go crash on the beach all day long. You'll really enjoy it. It's nearly as nice as Sopot."

I was just about to enquire whether I would be allowed to go paddling (though I find that, in general, sarcasm is quite wasted on the Sisters) when Sister Elisabeth came scuffling in through the half-open door with that slightly furtive, hamster-like gait of hers. I saw that she was carrying something wrapped in a Sainsburys carrier bag; also that she had about her a distinct air of excitement and conspiracy. She smiled at me from behind her thick, round lenses and gave me a glimpse of the dental catastrophe behind her lips. Anuncja glanced behind her.

"Oh, it's you Elzbieta—been out shopping I see." Then, without waiting for a reply: "Here, look after the old rascal for a few minutes will you, while I pop down to the laundry?"—for all the world as if I, who still read newspapers and am neither senile nor incontinent, would infallibly electrocute myself or drown in the wash-basin if left alone for more than twenty seconds. As Anuncja's busy footsteps receded down the linoleum-covered corridor Sister Elisabeth shut the door gently behind her and came over to where I was sitting.

"Here," she said, "look what I've brought for you. I found it outside a junk shop on Hanwell Broadway and I thought it might be of interest." She fumbled in the rustling plastic bag and produced a large, thick book, bound in mulberry-coloured watered-silk board and evidently much the worse for wear. She placed it on the table beside me, then stepped back with the expectant air of one who has just lit the touchpaper of an old firework without a label and is waiting to see what will happen: whether it will be a shower of blue and orange stars, or a loud bang or simply a damp splutter and then silence.

"Thank you, Sister Elisabeth," I said. "You are really too good to me. I wonder what on earth this can be. Would you be so kind as to pass me my reading glasses from beside the bed?" I slipped on my spectacles and began to examine the volume lying on the table in front of me.

It was certainly an album of some description: a thick, heavy book with tattered morocco leather corners and a broken spine. I could not for the life of me imagine what it might be. But as I touched it, without knowing why, I felt a sudden and disturbing tingle of recognition. I inspected the book more closely, and saw that the lower left-hand corner of the front cover bore a small, round, embossed stamp; and that the stamp consisted of a double-headed eagle surrounded by the legend K.K. HOFRAT J. STROSS-MAYER. FOTOGRAF. WIEN 7. MARIAHILFERSTRASSE 23. My hands trembled as I opened the front cover and my ears began to sing with a high-pitched ringing note. Then my eyes fell on the first page. My mind skated helplessly across the paper, trying to take in what lay before it.

There could be no doubt about it. The photograph was on poor-quality wartime paper and had already turned brown and begun to crumble slightly about the edges. But there was no doubt about it: there I stood, sixty-seven years before, leaning against the gun on the foredeck of a submarine at sea, surrounded by a group of laughing men and holding up a painted egg for inspection. And there at the bottom, written in German in my own once-firm handwriting, was the inscription: *U26*, EASTER SUNDAY 1918, 23 MILES WNW OF BENGHAZI.

It was all there, captured in an instant of a long lifetime ago: myself in seaboots and a shabby grey Army tunic with the Linienschiffsleutnant's three cuff-rings home-made out of sailcloth; the others in the usual Austrian U-Boat mixture of naval uniform and Dalmatian fisherman's rig; the two look-outs up on the conning tower—Preradović and Souvlička by the looks of it—sweeping the horizon with their binoculars; and our helmsman, Steuerquartiermeister Alois Patzak, standing behind the surface steering wheel, gazing sternly into the distance in a manner appropriate to a man on watch with no time for any of this off-duty skylarking.

Perhaps you may imagine what a shock it was for me, to come face to face with myself as I was nearly seventy years before, looking out from the pages of a photograph album which I had last seen in my lodgings in the Romanian port of Braila one day in 1922. I was quite unable to speak for some time, and thinking that perhaps her little gift had done for me at last, Sister Elisabeth rushed out of the room in alarm, to return a minute or so later with a tooth-glass full of water laced with spirit wheedled out of the duty cook downstairs. This brought me out of my state of shock—largely because I detest vodka. But as I returned to my senses the memories came surging through as if a dam had burst: a dam so old and overgrown that everyone had forgotten the existence of the weed-covered lake behind it.

I have the album on the table in front of me as I speak to you now, open at that photograph. Yes, we are all there: healthy, cheerful young men in the full exuberance of life that spring morning off the coast of Africa, sailors of an empire already tottering its last few steps to the grave. But the picture has a good deal more than sentimental or documentary worth for me, since it was very nearly our tombstone. I well remember how, about five seconds after the shutter clicked, a yell from the port look-out had turned our attention to the track of a torpedo, streaking towards us from the submerged submarine that must have been stalking us unobserved for the past hour or so. Luckily for us, Patzak had the presence of mind to put the wheel hard down without waiting for an order, so that the torpedo hissed past our stern, missing us by a couple of metres. We did not stay around to congratulate ourselves though: only tumbled down the hatches one on top of the other to execute what must have been one of the fastest dives on record, then, once we had sorted ourselves out, set off in search of our would-be assassin intending to return the salute. But an hour's zigzagging to and fro at periscope depth produced not even a glimpse of our attacker, so we surfaced and resumed our previous course. Our enemy had failed to kill us: we would certainly have done the same to him, given the chance, and there was no more to be said about it, other than a terse entry in the log that evening: "9:27 a.m., 32° 24′ N by 19° 01′ E; single torpedo fired from unidentified submarine. Missed." We had survived yet again, perhaps only to be blown up on a drifting mine half an hour later. In those days, who could tell?

Looking now at that laughing group of young men I think to myself how little I have ever wanted to know the future, ignorance of which seems to me to be one of the few anaesthetics administered by Providence to us mortal men. Poor Patzak, so strong and confident-looking up there on the conning tower: he could not know that he had less than a week to live. And there at the back of the group, grinning broadly in shirtsleeves and a fisherman's woollen cap, my young Third Officer Fregattenleutnant Franz Xavier Baudrin de la Rivière, Graf d'Ermenonville, mercifully unaware of the Gestapo cell and the loop of wire lying in wait for him a quarter of a century into the future. In fact, as I turn the dog-eared pages of the album I cannot help reflecting on the sheer whimsicality of Fate, that a whole continent should have been devastated and tens of millions perished while such an insignificant piece of flotsam should have survived; and not only survived but been carried back to its owner sixty-odd years later by God alone knows what strange currents and eddies. Sister Elisabeth went back to the shop next day of course, at my request, but the proprietor remembered little of how he had come by the album. All he could tell her was that he had been over to North Acton about three weeks previously to clear out a bed-sitter whose tenant—an elderly Russian or Ukrainian or something like that—had been felled by a stroke. No, he couldn't remember which house or even the street; only that it had been filthy dirty and had contained nothing much except girlie magazines and empty bottles. The only items of value had been an old cavalry sabre, which someone had bought the following week, and a shoe-box with some coins and postcards. He had considered flinging the album into the skip with the rest, but on reflection had put it out in a cardboard box on a broken-legged table in front of the shop since (he said) you never knew what people collected these days. There it had lain in the traffic fumes and the summer drizzle until Sister Elisabeth had chanced that way, drawn towards it by a loathsome oleograph of the Sacred Heart which now hangs in the residents' lounge.

The previous owner had left few traces of his possession of the book, apart from a few photographs of heavy-featured women in late-1920s hair-styles and a picture postcard of Marseille harbour, posted by one "Volodya" to a certain M. Dushinskyj at Antibes on 20 June 1932. Otherwise, what moved him to acquire the volume, keep it for perhaps half a century and carry it with him to the other side of Europe is a complete mystery. Certainly the album has some good ship photographs in it. I was always interested in photography and took one of the early Joule-Herriot box cameras to sea with me on my first ocean voyage as a cadet aboard the *Windischgrätz,* back in 1901. The keeping of diaries was of course forbidden during the war—though Austria being Austria, this ban was generally ignored. But I had special permission to keep the album since it was the War Ministry's intention to publish a book entitled *The Wartime Career of an Imperial and Royal U-Boat.* The book never appeared of course, but I kept photographs for it, and not only photographs but a great many sketch-maps of engagements, log excerpts, notes of positions and so forth. Perhaps a quarter of the pictures had fallen out and been lost, their positions marked by oblong dark patches on the faded brown pages. But enough remained to hold me a prisoner for most of my first fortnight down here in Wales, until Sister Elisabeth arrived to distract my mind a little from the flood of memories from out of that forgotten world.

No, "forgotten" is not the right word: I very rarely forget things even now, far gone as I am in bodily decay. I always had a retentive memory and would learn whole navigational exercises and pages of Italian irregular verbs by heart when I was a cadet at the Marine Academy. No, the truth is that in the years after 1918 I made an almost conscious effort not to think about my eighteen years' service in the now vanished Navy of Imperial

Austria. That part of my life was never forgotten, only rolled up like some unwanted, moth-eaten old carpet and locked away in a remote lumber room at the back of my mind. This was not duplicity on my part: at least I never denied my past or—like some of my contemporaries—concocted half a dozen fraudulent and contradictory life-histories for myself. But there I was, a thirty-three-year-old career naval officer in a miserable, defeated, poverty-stricken little country which no longer possessed either a navy or a coastline for it to defend. Unlike Sister Elisabeth's poor father and thousands of others like him, I neither believed nor even hoped that the Habsburgs would return. I had seen far too much of Old Austria's decay ever to imagine that a restoration of the Dual Monarchy was any more likely than an Egyptian mummy getting up and dancing the polka. No, like tens of thousands of other ex-wearers of the black-and-yellow sword belt, I had to make my way as best I could in that harsh new world of defeat and hunger. What was past was past, and there seemed little sense in dwelling upon my glorious deeds in the service of the Noble House of Austria— not when the ministerial corridors in Prague and Belgrade were crowded with once ultra-Kaisertreu former officers, all brandishing pre-1914 police dossiers (usually forged) in an effort to prove that they had been secret nationalists all along. Then in later years, in England, there were the feelings of my second wife Edith to be considered. She had lost an adored elder brother to the U-Boats in 1916, a Third Engineer on the liner *Persian;* and although she knew that I had been in the Austrian fleet and had served aboard submarines, she was a tactful woman and never enquired too closely into what I had been doing in those years.

But this is all becoming unbearably sentimental, and if I am not careful it will end up like one of those touching little patriotic stories that we used to be set in German classes at the k.u.k. Marine Akademie: I am sure that you can imagine the sort of thing—the broken-down old ex-cavalry horse, wearing out his days dragging a Viennese coal-cart, but still pricking up his ears and breaking into a trot when he hears a band playing the "Lothringen March." So let us get on with the story.

In the normal course of things not even the near-miraculous restoration of my old photograph album would have induced me to sit here boring you with my memoirs. Like most seafarers, I have always appreciated a good yarn; but I have never been one of nature's diarists and certainly not one of those (of whom this place, unfortunately, holds many) who consider it their duty to relate their life-histories and accumulated wisdom to anyone unable to escape. No, some last safety catch had to be released, and this was done for me early in June by Kevin Scully.

Kevin is about twenty-five years old, I should think, and works here as a part-time handyman and jobbing gardener, driving over from Llanelli two or three days each week in his battered Ford Cortina. And there is certainly never any lack of things for him to do about this ramshackle property up here on the headland over the bay, blasted by every Atlantic gale. Gutters fall down, windows leak, roof-slates blow away and drains block: but it is good for him that they do, because it seems that he has no other income apart from unemployment benefit. I have known him now for nearly three months and I must say that he has impressed me very favourably as one of those people, lowly in origin and of little education, who still possess a lively intelligence and sense of curiosity that not even the schooling system has managed to knock out of them. Also I detected in him from the very beginning some remnants of the bearing of an ex-serviceman. It appears that he left the Royal Navy two years ago and has never had a proper job since. He lives on a council estate with his mother and a girlfriend with whom he has an "on and off" understanding.

We first met at the beginning of June, after I had been here some three weeks. The weather had turned unexpectedly warm and the Sisters had allowed me to sit out in the sunshine in a secluded little stone-flagged garden at the back of the house that serves as a drying ground. It is very pleasant to sit there from about mid-morning, when there is no wind, looking out across Pengadog Bay to the pine-clad promontory at the end of the huge whale-backed ridge they call the Cefn Gaerllwydd. Sister Elisabeth had left me there in the deckchair with a rug over my legs while she went down to the post office in Llangwynydd on the Convent bicycle. The Plas is seven kilometres from the village, and five kilometres from the nearest public house, in the otherwise uninhabited parish of Pengadog which gives the bay its name and the house its postal address. This remoteness from alcohol is a particularly sore trial to the residents, several of whom are said to have been ushered out of this world by swigs of metal polish or unspeakable distillations of raisins and mashed potatoes. But there; as we say, it is not permissible to examine the teeth of a gift horse. The property was donated to the Sisters some ten years ago, a deathbed bequest from a local Polish farmer who is said to have murdered his partner, about 1948, then disposed of the body so efficiently that the police were never able to bring charges.

I sat there in the little garden, gazing out across the bay to the great ocean beyond as recollections surged and swirled inside my head. The smallest thing would bring the memories back now: that idiotic film *The Sound of Music* on the television in the residents' lounge, with someone trying to impersonate my old comrade Georg von Trapp; or a whiff of diesel fuel from a delivery van in the driveway; or the wireless playing the waltz from *Where the Lark Sings* and taking me straight back to dying Imperial Vienna in that hopeless, hungry spring of 1918. Even out here there was no escape; not when the blue waters of the bay—calm for once—and the pine trees on the limestone rocks around were so like the sea as I had first set eyes on it, on that family holiday at Abbazia in 1897. What was it all for, this terrible, sad comedy of life? No sense; no order; no purpose: only to live for a century and end up here alone on the edge of nowhere, a bundle of skin and arthritic bones barely distinguishable from the deck-chair supporting me.

Just then my thoughts were interrupted by a discordant whistling as Kevin came into the garden, carrying a coil of thin line slung over his arm. We had been introduced by Sister Elisabeth a few days before, and since Kevin has no manners, and therefore no notion that ancients like myself should automatically be treated as mental defectives, he greeted me cheerfully in his nasal Cardiff accent.

"G'mornin Mr Procházka, lovely day iznit? You out here doin' a bit of sunbathin' then?"

"Yes. As you see, I am taking advantage of this sunny weather and also admiring the view."

"Yeah, not bad izzit—lucky you can see it when it isn't rainin'."

"Is the weather here usually that bad, then?"

He grinned. "Not half—you can only tell it's summer because the bloody rain gets a bit warmer, like. They reckon the sheep round 'ere all fall over when the wind stops blowin'."

With that he turned to set about his work. He was fixing up a new clothes-line for Sister Teresa, who runs the laundry. The new line had turned out to be several metres too short and Kevin was now engaged in joining a relatively sound section from the old line on to the end of the new one, using a simple reef-knot. Knowing that he had once been a sailor I thought I would torment him a little.

"Is that what they teach you in the training establishments these days? When I was at sea you would have been up on Captain's Report for using a hitch like that. A splice is required there. Really. What is the world coming to?"

He turned around and stared at me for some moments as if a snake had bitten him, then guffawed—though good-naturedly, I saw.

"Huh! Fat lot you know about splices an' all. When was you ever at sea then, ey?"

"I was a career naval officer for something like thirty years in total, young man, and trained in pure sailing ships. But if it comes to that, when were you at sea yourself?"

He advanced upon me in mock indignation. "Me?" he said. "'Ere, take a look at that will you?" He rolled up his sleeve and thrust an arm under my nose. It was covered from elbow to shoulder with a baroque riot of dolphins, anchors, mermaids, lions, tritons blowing conch-shells and heaven alone knows what else, all bound together by a tangle of cordage. In the middle of it all sat Britannia with her trident, an English lady staying calm amid these foreigners, while beneath was an ornate scroll with the legend DREADNOUGHT and a list of battle honours. I have seen quite a few tattoos over the years and I must admit that this one was quite pleasingly done: a well-balanced design, and about as finely executed as is possible when drilling pigment into living skin. It was quite clearly the work of a Mediterranean artist: possibly Maltese I thought.

"See that?" he said. "Cost me two hundred and fifty quid out in Gibraltar that did: took him thirty-four sessions too. Swollen up like a bloody black pudding I was for weeks after—used to wake up half the lower deck if I turned over in my bunk at night."

"Yes," I replied after examining the tattoo at suitable length, "most impressive, and I dare say that it cost nearly as much as you say. But not everyone with a tattooed arm is a seaman."

"Lissen, five years' service—left with the rank of Able Rate I did, and two good-conduct stripes into the bargain: Radio Operator Second Class H.M. Submarines, that's me—one year in nukes and two in diesel boats."

This last remark caught my interest. "Ah, Kevin, so we have something in common then. I myself was a submariner once."

He stared at me in puzzlement, not quite sure whether to take me seriously. "G'won then, you wasn't. When was that then?"

"In the World War of 1914 to 1918: I was a U-Boat captain for three and a half years."

Kevin gave me a look of even greater bewilderment and suspicion, though mixed with increasing interest. "You—a U-Boat captain? But I thought you was a Pole, not a German. What were you doing with them?"

"Well, Kevin, it's a long story, but for one thing I am a sort of Czech, not a Pole, and for another they were Austrian U-Boats that I commanded, not German."

He abandoned his work and came over to sit on the low stone wall next to me, entirely baffled by the complexities of European history. He looked me straight in the face with the air of a prosecuting counsel determined to worm out the truth.

"Now, let's get this straight—you're a Polish Czech and you were Captain of an Austrian U-Boat, right?"

"Yes, that is correct."

"Well," (with an air of triumph) "I know that's not bloody well true because, for one thing, you can't be a Polish-Czech-Austrian, and for another, I got a pass in CSE Geography and I know Austria's up in the mountains: me Mam went there last year on a coach outing so that proves it."

"Yes," I replied, rather enjoying this little argument, "I take your point. But you are a Welshman, yet you served in the British Navy, and as for Austria, it may be a little inland country now but in my day it was a huge empire with a coastline and a sizeable navy, including a fleet of submarines."

"Oh yeah? I bet you never sank anything though."

"On the contrary: in three years and seven months in the Mediterranean I sank an armoured cruiser, a destroyer, an armed liner and a submarine. I also sank or captured eleven merchant vessels totalling twenty-five thousand tonnes, shot down a dirigible airship . . ." Kevin stared at me speechless, his mouth hanging open ". . . and damaged a light cruiser, a destroyer, an armed trawler and at least two merchantmen."

Kevin had by now regained the power of speech. "You old liar, you ought to be fuckin' well ashamed at your age, you did."

I felt that this was really going a little too far.

"Young man," I said, trying my best to sound like a newly commissioned Leutnant taking offence outside an ice-cream parlour, "I have to inform you that as an officer of the House of Habsburg it would once have been my duty to draw my sword and cut you down like a dog for so much as suggesting that I was not telling the truth; in fact I would have been court-martialled and cashiered for failing to kill you on the spot. Whoever insulted an officer insulted the Monarchy itself."

To my surprise he became very contrite at this. "No, sorry, I di'n' mean to call you a liar—only it just seems a bit . . . a bit far-fetched like, what you was sayin'." Then, moving up closer to me: "'Ere, how 'bout tellin' me then? Always liked a story I did, ever since me ol' man used to tell me them when I was a kid—before he ran off." Then, in a low conspiratorial tone, fumbling in the back pocket of his jeans: "Wanna fag, do you? That ol' cow Felicja's out for the day so she won't come botherin' us. Always prowlin' about she is." Sister Felicja is a large, ugly nun from Pozna who controls the day-to-day business of the Home with all the tact and charm of an old-style Prussian Feldwebel—except that she seems not to wax the ends of her moustache.

I sensed that the offer of a cigarette (which I refused as politely as I could, not having smoked for many years now) was an outward sign of confidence and esteem on Kevin's part. He rolled up his jacket as a pillow, lit up a cigarette and lay down on the grass beside my chair. He blew out a cloud of smoke and closed his eyes. We were quite unobserved there in the little garden. In the distance pots and pans were clattering in the kitchen, while from an open upstairs window in the house there came the characteristic sound of two elderly Poles arguing—curiously soothing at this distance, like a ball being whacked to and fro on a tennis court. The bees hummed among the flowers in the unaccustomed sunshine and stillness of the air, while from far away there came the sound of the Atlantic waves breaking on the beach in Pengadog Bay and the faint chickering of a tractor working among the bracken on the side of Cefn Gaerllwydd.

"Well, you goin' to tell me about it then?"

I hesitated. What concern was it of his? What possible interest could there be for this child in disinterring the dusty bones of a half-forgotten empire perished a half-century before he was born, in telling tales of dim events that must surely mean as little to him now as the Siege of Troy?

"Aw, c'mon Mr Procházka, tell us about it. You mightn't get the chance ag—" He stopped. "No, sorry, I di'n' mean that . . . only, you know . . ."

"Yes Kevin, please don't apologise. I understand perfectly, and you are quite right of course."

"No, what I meant was, there can't be many of you left now, and when you're all dead it'll have gone with you, like."

Then it struck me for the first time: you are one of the last witnesses. In fact it's quite possible that you are all that's left of the old Imperial and Royal Navy, in so far as you are now probably its most senior surviving officer. The ships that you sailed aboard have all vanished long since into the far blue, while as for those who sailed with you, the youngest Midshipman would now be in his mid-eighties. Was it all such a waste of time though that the very memory of it has to perish?

So I told him, as I am telling it to you now in whatever time is left to me. To my considerable surprise Kevin not only listened to me all that morning, plying me with tea laced with rum stolen from the kitchen when I began to flag, but came back the next day and the day after that, all through this past summer. In the end he and Sister Elisabeth conspired to get me this attic room overlooking the sea and this little machine. So here I am now, reclining in a comfortable if shabby old armchair, with my photograph album open on my knees to remedy the deficiencies of memory as far as possible. I will do my best to steer straight from headland to headland as I tell you these tales; but I am a very old man, and I trust that you will bear with me if I sometimes deviate from my charted course to explore some hidden cove or river-mouth. You may believe what I have to tell you, or you may consider it the most amazing pack of lies that you have ever heard and think it shameful that a man on the edge of eternity should tell such whoppers. It may bore you, or you may decide to stay around for the story even if you consider the history to be doubtful. But in any event, I hope that it will give you some idea of how it was for us all those years ago, fighting for a lost empire in that first great war beneath the waves: of what it was like to be a sailor of Austria.

2
TAKING COMMAND

MY CAREER AS A SUBMARINE COMMANDER began, I remember, one morning early in April 1915 in the Adriatic port of Pola—now part of Yugoslavia, but in those days the principal base of the Imperial and Royal Austro-Hungarian Navy.

It was a glorious spring morning as I stepped down on to the platform at the Hauptbahnhof beside the harbour. A few hours earlier the last of the winter snow had still been lying on the mountain-slopes as the overnight-leave train from Vienna had wheezed and laboured its way over the Adelsberg Pass. Even this early in the war, coal was so short that the Monarchy's railway locomotives were burning lignite, and its sour, tarry fumes filled the commissioned-ranks carriage of the train as we trundled through the tunnels at the head of the pass. But once we were rattling down the opposite slope towards Pola it was clear that we had passed from Central Europe into the sunlit world of the Mediterranean, from the regions of spruce and birch into the land of pine and fig and cypress. Just north of Dignano we had passed the first olive groves and then, suddenly, quite as much of a surprise to me as the first time that I had seen it, a gap opened in the low hills to reveal a straight horizon of cobalt blue. I was nearing home once more: the only true home that a seafaring man can have.

Here in Pola there was no mistaking the arrival of spring. The sun shone warmly, and around the huge Roman amphitheatre the peach and almond trees were already starting to blossom. We got down from the train, eight officers and about forty sailors, and boarded the tram to make our way to the naval base. As we clattered along the Riva Francisco Giuseppe

I gazed out of the window at this peculiar town which had been my home port for the past fifteen years. "The Imperial and Royal Monarchy of the House of Habsburg fills the Danubian Basin," we used to chant in Geography lessons at junior school. Yes, I thought to myself; not only fills it but slops over the edges, and nowhere more incongruously than on these enchanted shores of the Adriatic, where our German-speaking Empire overlay the earlier empires of Rome and Venice. We rattled and banged our way along the Riva, between the great Ringstrasse neo-classical bulk of the Marine High Command building, its pediment a riot of naked females representing "Austria Pointing Her Children Towards the Sea," and the harbour with its rows of lateen-sailed bragozzi moored along the stone quayside. Out there in the harbour lay the Scoglio di Olivi—the Island of Olives, except that it was now joined to the land by a bridge and no longer boasted any olive trees, only the gantries of the Imperial Navy's construction yards. Then suddenly, our destination lay before us: a limestone gate-arch with its black-and-yellow-striped gates surmounted by the double-headed eagle of Imperial Austria and the inscription K.U.K. SEE ARSENAL POLA.

We descended from the tram inside the dockyard walls. I had to wait for a porter to carry my bags, so I stood watching as the ratings were fallen in on the cobbled square by a Petty Officer. They had evidently been making the most of the last few hours of their leave in the station buffets at Marburg and Divacca: caps were at all angles and scarves were being hastily reknotted in a babble of Czech and German and Magyar. All the same though, as the Petty Officer (an Italian by the sound of him) roared out the command "Hab'acht!" the two score boots crashed to the square with quite a creditable precision. I watched them as they stood there, stiff to attention, though some were swaying slightly: all the faces of that sprawling, polyglot Empire of ours—faces from the Tyrolean valleys and the slum tenements of Vienna and the vast expanses of the Hungarian plains; the blond, smooth countenances of Poles and the sharp, dark features of Italians. As I walked past them the Petty Officer bellowed, "Rechts Schaut!" and the heads snapped towards me in salute. But it was not naval discipline or the German language that held so many different races together there that morning; it was a round metal badge on the front of each man's cap, a black disc surmounted by the Imperial crown and bearing the gilt letters FJI—the simple cipher of His Imperial Majesty Franz Josef the First, by the Grace of God Emperor of Austria and Apostolic King of Hungary; King of Bohemia, Dalmatia, Croatia, Slovenia, Galicia, Lodomeria and Illyria; Archduke of Austria; Grand Duke of Cracow; Duke of Lorraine, Styria, Carinthia, Krain, Upper and Lower Silesia and the Bukovina; Prince of Siebenburg; Margrave of Moravia; Count of Salzburg and the Tyrol; King of Jerusalem; and Holy Roman Emperor of the Germanic Nation. We were his men, all of us there that morning, officers and ratings alike; not Austrian patriots but servants of the Noble House of Austria, the venerable dynasty of the Habsburgs. Other countries might be monarchies: only ours was The Monarchy, remnant of an empire which had once stretched to the Philippines and which even now, far gone in decay, still sprawled across a quarter of the European continent west of Russia. The radiance of its black-and-yellow embers would still warm us for another three years, before everything crumbled into grey ashes and blew away on the winds.

At last I was able to find a porter, an elderly reservist, and set off for the Movements Office with the iron-tyred barrow grumbling along on the cobbles behind me. Security was far from rigorous at this stage of the war, and after a cursory, bored glance over my papers the Provost Warrant Officer stamped them, saluted in a perfunctory sort of way and pointed down the quayside.

"I see you're for the U-Boat station, Herr Schiffsleutnant. Quay number five; there's a launch waiting now. It'll be about twenty minutes; they're still waiting for some mailbags."

The U-Boat station tender was an old steam pinnace from a battleship, much eroded at bow and stern by years of bumping against jetties and commanded by a very young Seefähnrich. I had my luggage handed down to me on its deck, then found myself a seat near the stern. My only companions were a naval chaplain, evidently the worse for drink and not disposed to conversation, and a crate of live chickens. I also noticed two or three wooden crates packed with straw and stencilled AUSTRO-DAIMLER GMBH, WIENER NEUSTADT. We had some time to wait, so I lit a cigar and looked about me; not out of any particular curiosity—the town and harbour were as familiar to me by now as the features of my own face—but rather out of a desire to see what had changed since I had last been here over a year before.

It was a curious place, Pola: an Imperial creation even more than most other towns of the old Monarchy. In those days one still met old people who could remember it as it had been back in the 1830s: a dismal hole of a place where a few hundred inhabitants shivered with malaria in their hovels scattered among the ruins of a Roman city; a forgotten fishing village down at the end of beyond, where the pigeons cooed mournfully in the walls of the amphitheatre and the only link with the outside world was the monthly Austro-Lloyd packet steamer, which might stop to deposit a mailbag or two on its way down from Trieste. But this had all changed after the revolts of 1848. Venice was no longer a safe base for the growing Austrian fleet, so Pola was taken in hand. The swamps were drained and sewers were laid; quays and drydocks and repair yards were constructed; and tenement blocks and hospitals were built for the growing population. The town acquired those three monuments of Austrian civilization: the barracks, the coffee-house and the theatre, while all around the naval base there sprang up the taverns and bordellos which I suppose have grown up around naval bases ever since the Greeks rowed out in their triremes. Pola began to count for something in the world.

Looking out over the harbour now though, surrounded by its low, pine-covered hills, the reason for the town's existence was very much in evidence, moored in three long rows out beyond Fort Franz. Always the smallest of the old Great Power navies, the k.u.k. Kriegsmarine was still an impressive-looking force that spring morning: first the three handsome super-Dreadnought battleships of the *Tegethoff* class, with the fourth sister fitting out at the Arsenal quay, then the three *Radetzky*-class battle-ships—rather out-of-date now but still powerful vessels—then the three *Erzherzog* ships out towards the harbour entrance. The Austro-Hungarian battle fleet was a puny affair when compared with the mighty British or German navies, or even with that of France, but it was still a formidable enough force to defend the Monarchy's six-hundred-odd kilometres of salt-water shore, a task which it was to discharge until Old Austria had fallen to pieces behind it.

It was nine months now since the nations of Europe had flung themselves upon one another in murderous fury, and already three million young men were dead. Somehow, though, no decision had been reached. The war that was to have been over by Christmas (everyone said) was now likely (everyone said) to go on perhaps to August or September, and the sun that shone so pleasantly upon me that morning was also dispersing the early-morning mists from those first tentative trench lines that now snaked across the fields of France and Belgium.

Austria-Hungary had already suffered grievously. Up in Poland, the previous autumn had seen the Imperial, Royal and Catholic armies of His Apostolic Majesty executing a great many Orderly Tactical Withdrawals to Carefully Prepared Positions—in other words, running away until they ran the soles off their boots and the Russians nearly came pouring through the Carpathian passes into Hungary. Nor had things gone much better with Austria's other war, the short, sharp little campaign against Serbia that had set off the greater conflict. And this was a matter close to my own heart that morning, for my elder brother Anton, a captain in the 26th Jäger Regiment, had been part of General Potiorek's punitive expedition which had crossed the Drina the previous August, only to cross it again a few days later, running for its life and leaving tens of thousands of dead and missing on the other side. My father had received the fateful telegram the previous morning as I had set out for Pola: "The k.u.k. Minister for War regrets to inform you . . . Exhaustive perusal of the Red Cross lists has failed to reveal . . . therefore presumed dead . . . Personal effects of the deceased may be collected from regimental depot, Leitmeritz, within thirty days of today's date (date as postmark) . . ." The old man had not taken it too badly, I thought: in fact as a convert to pan-German nationalism, his chief grievance seemed to be that his son had been killed in a quarrel between the moribund House of Habsburg and a tribe of Balkan sheep-stealers when he could have been fulfilling the higher racial destiny of the Germanic peoples through getting himself shot by the Russians.

These musings were interrupted by a toot from the steam pinnace's whistle. The mailbags and one or two last-minute passengers had arrived and we were on our way to the Imperial and Royal U-Boat Station, Pola-Brioni, where I was to take up my new command, the submarine *U8*. Once more I took out the Marine Oberkommando telegram from my wallet. Yes, there it was in black and white: "Command effective from time of arrival in Pola." So I was already a U-Boat captain. Somehow, in those early days, that honour did not signify a great deal to me.

There was a great deal of bustle about us as the pinnace hissed smoothly across the waters of the harbour: picket boats and liberty boats and tugs and small craft by the dozen; also a couple of destroyers lying at the oil wharf, even though most of the light forces were now down south at Cattaro. I had been away from Europe when the war broke out, on the China Station with the *Kaiserin Elisabeth,* and it was not until February that I had managed to get home, after many adventures that need not concern us here. I saw that the battleships were now in mobilisation dark grey, and that lines of trenches and barbed-wire entanglements meandered across the hillsides to landward of the town; also that decades of undergrowth had been cut back from the glacis of the forts around the harbour, presumably to give the enemy's gunners a better aim at their poorly armoured casemates and the museum-worthy artillery behind them. Up above Fort Musil on the promontory a kite balloon tugged fretfully at its cable, swaying to and fro in the breeze, while out beyond the harbour entrance a seaplane droned its way southwards to inspect the minefields off Cape Porer. These outward tokens of hostilities apart, though, the war might have been a thousand miles away from Pola that April morning. But in fact, come to think of it, I suppose that it wasn't far short of a thousand miles away. Battles might be raging on the Western and Eastern Fronts, but with Italy still neutral and the British Mediterranean Fleet tied up at the Dardanelles our only effective enemy was the French battle fleet. In the first months of the war the French had made a few half-hearted forays through the Otranto Straits into the Southern Adriatic. But then, just before Christmas, Egon Lerch's *U12* had succeeded in torpedoing a French dreadnought—not fatally, but enough to dampen their enthusiasm for such parades. The French battle-ships had since withdrawn to Malta, nine hundred miles away from Pola, and showed little sign of coming out. It was stalemate: they could not get at us, and we had no intention of going after them. As the tender steered past the stern of the *Franz Ferdinand* we saw about three hundred of its crew engaged in hanging out the great, heavy steel-mesh anti-torpedo nets from the booms along the ship's side. It was back-breaking work, univer-sally loathed and by now utterly pointless, since a modern torpedo would go straight through the nets like an arrow through a rotten lace curtain. No, it was abundantly clear that the nets were being hung out for no other reason than to keep the crew busy after months of swinging at the buoy. The Marine Section of the War Ministry had offered me the choice of a berth as Second Gunnery Officer on one of these ships or command of a submarine. I now blessed the urge that had made me choose the latter. Whatever unknown perils lay ahead it could not possibly be worse than the make-works and enervating routine of a harbour-bound battle fleet. I might end up at the bottom of the sea, but at least I would have some amusement on the way.

The pinnace made her way past Fort Cristo, then out through the mine-fields and anti-submarine nets around the harbour mouth. Ten minutes later we were steering into the miniature harbour of Brioni Island.

It was a mystery why the Naval High Command should have chosen to move Austria-Hungary's meagre flotilla of six submarines out to Brioni when war had been declared the previous July. The most probable reason was that in those days nobody, least of all in Austria, had much idea of how these odd, still half-experimental little vessels would be employed in a real war. In the mean time though there was a great deal to be said for getting the boats and their socially undesirable crews out from under the feet of the surface fleet, where they were always getting themselves run down in the harbour entrance, going aground or otherwise making infernal nuisances of themselves. Brioni answered admirably: three hotels and a small yachting harbour, delightfully located on a group of wooded islands a few kilometres north of the entrance to Pola Harbour. The place had been a rising resort for the wealthy and fashionable of Europe until the previous summer, when the ominous international rumblings had set them packing their bags. Now the trim, snow-white yachts had departed from its stone quayside. Instead the depot ship *Pelikan* was moored at the harbour entrance, and the wooden hulk of an old frigate inside it. As I caught sight of the boat-house in front of the Hotel Neptune I smiled as I remembered the afternoons spent here aboard my sailing boat *Nelly*, a modest craft appropriate to the wretched salary of a Linienschiffsleutnant, but still a fine little vessel for all that. Well, those days were past now, and as the pinnace made her way into the harbour I caught my first sight of the sort of vessel that I would sail aboard from now on: a row of secretive slate-blue shapes lying moored bows-first to the breakwater. Two of them were very similar in size and general appearance, except that their conning towers were of slightly different shapes. Both carried red-white-red recognition stripes painted across their bows and the further away of the two had the large white numeral 8 painted on its conning tower. Two men in very dirty overalls stood on its deck, hands in pockets, regarding us without any particular interest as we passed. So this was the vessel that I was to command, making it perhaps a receptacle for honour, perhaps a sepulchre for myself and eighteen others.

My arrival at k.u.k. Unterseeboot Station Pola-Brioni was not marked by any great ceremony. I stepped up on to the quayside as the pinnace ground to a stop and was greeted by a young Fregattenleutnant with a clipboard under his arm.

"Schiffsleutnant Prohaska?"

"The same."

He saluted. "Fregattenleutnant Anton Straussler, of *U4;* temporarily employed here on general duties while convalescing. Pleased to make your acquaintance. The U-Station Commander wishes to see you in his office at once."

"But I am just off the train from Vienna. I must at least shave and get my bags to . . ."

"Nonsense—we're not a battleship here. I'll take you up to the Old Man's office myself and look after your things. They're berthing you in a cabin aboard *Pelikan,* which is home from home for most of us here. Only Korvettenkapitäns and above get rooms in the hotel."

We walked up to the Hotel Neptune together. I felt that I had better make conversation, since this young man seemed engagingly friendly.

"Tell me, Herr Fregattenl—"

"Oh, none of that nonsense please. We're all very informal out here where the Admiral can't see us. Call me Straussler if you like."

"Very good then . . . Straussler. Please tell me, after what are you convalescing, if I might ask?"

"Chlorine. Some silly idiot left one of the ventilators open when we did a practice dive off Cattaro last month and we took in a lot of water. Some of it got into the batteries and the atmosphere down below became pretty thick before we could get the hatches open. I just breathed in a little too much of it, that's all. I'm hoping that the station doctor will pass me fit this week so that I can get back." He turned to look at me. "But tell me, Prohaska, how long have you been in the U-Boat Service?"

"About ninety minutes, I think."

He looked at me with some pity. "And they're giving you *U8* . . . ?"

"Why, is there something wrong with the boat?"

" 'Der Achtzer'? Oh no, not really . . . Ah, here we are. It's on the second floor, room 203. I hope that we'll be able to talk again in the ward-room this evening, but for the present I trust that you will excuse me." And with this he left me.

The Hotel Neptune was a long, low building constructed in the Vien-nese Jugendstil. The place had evidently not been much looked after since the hasty departure of its guests the previous summer. The ornate plas-terwork friezes in the corridors were grimy, while the carpets were much scuffed by seaboots and grubby with lubricating oil. Boxes of spare parts and stacks of papers stood everywhere. A 45cm torpedo, minus its war-head, lay half dismantled beside the reception desk. Somewhere in the building a gramophone was squawking its way through the "Blaue Adria"; and as I neared room 203 a door opened to let out a din of clattering typewriters and a cheerful-looking Warrant Officer who called back: "All right, on Saturday then," before slamming the door behind him. All in all, I thought, the place had been remarkably quick in acquiring that loud, mas-culine, spit-and-polish-but-slightly-frowsty ambience common to barracks, police stations and naval shore establishments the world over.

I knocked on the door of room 203. A voice from within called, "Come in," and I entered to be greeted by the U-Boat Station Comman-dant himself, Korvettenkapitän Franz, Ritter von Thierry.

"Ah," (glancing at the papers on his desk as he came to meet me) "Prohaska, is it not? Delighted to meet you. Please be seated."

I knew Thierry by sight from before the war: the k.u.k. Kriegsmarine was such a small service that everyone knew everyone else. But this was the first time that I had had any contact with him in the line of duty. He was a moustached man in his early forties, with a vaguely French appear-ance—his family had come from Belgium, I believe, in the days when it had been the Austrian Netherlands—and the mild, slightly retiring manner of a provincial schoolmaster or secretary of a local natural history society. I was to learn later that this unassuming manner masked a core of steel, as had already been proved on many occasions in his battles with the Marine Oberkommando on behalf of the infant U-Boat Service.

"Well, Herr Schiffsleutnant," he began, "I see from your papers that you haven't commanded a submarine before."

"Yes, Herr Kommandant, that's correct. I was aboard *U3* when she was on trials in Germany before the war and I did six months with the Royal Navy submarines at Portsmouth back in 1908. Oh, and I was nearly drowned aboard a French boat in Toulon harbour when they tried to dive with the funnel up. But that's the limit of my experience of submarines, I'm afraid."

"I see. Well, there's nothing out of the ordinary in that I can assure you. You did your torpedo course in 1910 and commanded two torpedo-boats, so as far as the War Ministry is concerned you are fully qualified to command a U-Boat. Anyway, aren't you the Prohaska who got that Russian auxiliary cruiser in the East Indies back in October?"

"Yes, I am pleased to report that I am, though I heard later the ship was only damaged. Why, did the news get back here?"

"Most certainly it did: it was the talk of the Naval Casino. Everyone said that you ought to have got a medal, but the whole thing had to be kept quiet because of Dutch neutrality. Anyway, I congratulate you: that's the sort of spirit that I want in the U-Boat Service—when we've got some decent boats for you to fight in."

"Yes Herr Kommandant, might I enquire how things stand at present? I have been away from Pola for over a year now."

Thierry got up and went to the window, parted the slats of the venetian blind and looked out over the little harbour. It was some time before he spoke.

"Not too good I'm afraid. I have a total of eight U-Boats at my disposal: five here at Brioni and three down at Cattaro. Of these eight *U1* and *U2* are utterly worthless, scarcely capable of getting to Pola and back without an engine breakdown. *U3* and *U4* were built in Germany, as you know, so they are sound and reliable vessels. But they take eight minutes to dive and they have those damned kerosene engines which leave a pretty trail of white smoke and can be heard five miles away on a still night. Then there are the Holland boats with their petrol engines: *U5* and *U6* at Cattaro, *U12* here for the time being, and your own *U8*. Altogether, you will agree, not a very prepossessing collection of vessels—especially now that the Italians are on the brink of coming into the war against us."

"And what about the five boats that Germania was building for us at Kiel?"

"Not a hope I'm afraid, even though they were nearly ready for delivery when the war broke out. The Germans have taken them over for their own navy and won't even pay us compensation." He turned towards me. "Kruziturken, Prohaska! If we could only have got our hands on those boats what couldn't we have done with them? I assure you that the British wouldn't now be parading quite so insolently off the Dardanelles. Here, look at this." He picked up a newspaper cutting from his desk. "'Our Heroic U-Boats Strike Terror Into the Enemy'—some idiot of a journalist in the *Neue Freie Presse* calling for the scrapping of the surface fleet and the money to be used for building submarines. 'The day of the battleship is over,' he writes. And I'll give you a month's salary if he wasn't one of the jackasses who were campaigning three years back for a fleet of Austrian dreadnoughts. If we had spent some of that money on submarines I wouldn't be here now trying to make war with a collection of floating oil drums. But there," (he shrugged his shoulders) "if wishes were horses, beggars would ride. No, Prohaska: we are officers of Austria and our duty is to do the best we can with whatever is to hand—which is where you come into the picture . . ." There was a knock at the door. A short, rather tubby man in dirty linen trousers and a uniform jacket entered the room and saluted.

"You wished to see me, Herr Kommandant."

"Ah, Herr Fregattenleutnant, I would like to introduce your new commanding officer, Linienschiffsleutnant Otto Prohaska. He has just arrived here, and I understand that the new carburettors came on the tender with him."

The man eyed me with no very evident interest or respect. "Excellent, Herr Kommandant. I am glad to hear that the boat brought us something useful."

Thierry turned to me. "Herr Schiffsleutnant, allow me to introduce the Second Officer of *U8:* Fregattenleutnant Béla, Freiherr von Meszáros de Nagymeszárosháza."

So I was to sail with a Hungarian for a Second Officer. Among most Austrians of my generation our Hungarian partners (usually referred to in private as "the Magyar scum") were regarded with at least a certain mistrust as being engaged in a gigantic conspiracy to run the entire Monarchy in their own interests. Now it appeared that I was to have one of them as my second in command. It must be said though that in appearance at least, Fregattenleutnant Meszáros certainly did not conform to the usual stereotype of the descendants of Árpád and his Central Asian marauders. No dark, flashing eyes and curling black moustaches here: in fact at first glance I would have taken him for a waiter in a Prague beer-garden, complete with white apron and three foaming mugs of Pilsner in each hand. He was clean-shaven, with a smooth, rather pudgy face and reddish hair, thinning slightly at the temples. His eyes were small and greenish, expressive of a malign cunning that was to prove extremely useful over the next three years. As he extended his hand to shake mine I noticed that the two tarnished gold-braid rings on the cuff of his jacket were rather higher up than usual, and that below them was a faint, dark band, as if the navy blue cloth had once been protected from salt spray and sunlight by a third ring. He looked me up and down, evidently making a mental assessment of how long I would last in the job, then turned back to Thierry and said in his heavily accented Magyar German:

"Obediently report, Herr Kommandant, that we have dismantled the starboard gearbox and taken out the damaged wheel. The Maschinenmeister and his men are replacing it now, so if we can get the new carburettors in today we should be ready for diving trials by tomorrow morning."

"Excellent. Anyway, I want you to meet with Prohaska some time today to discuss how things stand with the boat. Herr Schiffsleutnant: you will report to me at 10 a.m. tomorrow with a complete working-up programme for *U8.* I want the boat to be fully operational by the 20th of this month at the latest. Our dear Italian allies may soon pluck up the courage to knife us in the back, and I want us to be ready for them when that happens."

With these words the interview ended. Meszáros and I left and made our way down to the breakwater. We walked in silence at first, then he remarked to me, apropos of nothing:

"Did he tell you what happened to the last captain?"

"No, I don't even know who he was."

"Oh, I see. He was a fellow called the Edler von Krummelhausen. Did you know him?"

"Only by name. Wasn't he the Torpedo Officer on the *Babenburg* back in 1908?"

"I couldn't really say."

"Where have they transferred him to, then?"

"To the cemetery: he shot himself in his cabin the week before last."

I cannot pretend that I was not disturbed by this piece of information. Suicide was very common in Central Europe in those days, and whatever the Church might say, spattering one's brains over the ceiling was still widely accepted in the Habsburg officer corps as a fitting and gentlemanly way of resolving life's little difficulties: women, gambling debts, syphilis, falling off one's horse in front of the Emperor, being caught selling mobilisation plans to the Russians, and so forth. Myself, being a plebeian Czech by birth, I had never had a great deal of time for these sub-aristocratic rituals; but even so it was not exactly pleasant to be stepping into the seaboots of a suicide. However, I tried to pretend unconcern.

"Oh, I see. The usual reasons I suppose: pox, roulette and the d.t.'s."

"Not at all. He couldn't handle the boat, and the petrol fumes got into his brain. Anyway, I must leave you here: I have to sign for those carburettors over in the engineering stores."

I made my way down to the breakwater, by now thoroughly depressed. Yes, there she was, half hidden by a battery-charging lighter. Hardly an impressive-looking vessel, I thought, even when one made due allowance for the fact that most of her was underwater.

Well, I thought to myself, feeling rather like one about to mount a particularly vicious and unpredictable horse, there's no sense in delaying things: you had the choice of a nice boring job aboard a battleship and you chose this instead. Let us at least get the introductions over. So I strode along the quayside towards my new command. Three men were tinkering with some unidentifiable piece of machinery on the quayside. Two of them were engine-room ratings, in striped singlets and black up to the elbows, while the third seemed to be an Engineer Warrant Officer. As I neared them I was also able to look around the conning tower of *U8,* and noticed with some disquiet that a man was standing there, lashed to the superstructure with a network of ropes. He was moaning softly to himself and swaying his head slowly from side to side like a bullock with the brain-staggers. I quickened my pace. I might be new to the k.u.k. U-Boat Service and its customs, but cruel and unusual punishment outside the scope of the Imperial and Royal Service Regulations was one thing that I was not prepared to tolerate aboard any ship of mine.

I strode up to the three men, who snapped to attention and saluted as they saw me approaching: the two sailors with blackened hands to grimy caps as per regulation, the Warrant Officer with a flick of the hand, its degree of negligence beautifully judged, I thought, as that appropriate from a veteran submarine engineer to a new and patently inexperienced captain.

"Very good you men, who is in charge here and will you please tell me what that man is doing lashed to the conning tower?" The Warrant Officer stepped forward. He was a sturdy, squarish man in his thirties with an amiable face and twinkling, bright blue eyes. He seemed confident and rather amused by the situation. As soon as he opened his mouth I discerned by his accent that he was a Czech like myself.

"Stabsmaschinenwarter Josef Lehár at your service, Herr Schiffsleutnant. I obediently report that I have the honour to be Chief Engineer of *U8.* As to the man tied to the conning tower, that is Bootsmannsmaat Grigorović. He was overcome by petrol fumes and asked us to tie him up until he recovers, for fear that he might injure his shipmates or damage government property. As the Herr Schiffsleutnant can see, he is a power-fully built man and capable of doing terrible things in a delirium."

This little speech rather took the wind out of my sails, concluded as it was by the most innocent of smiles. Certainly the sailor—Grigorović was it?—looked a pretty dangerous individual: built like a wardrobe on legs and equipped with arms and hands that seemed capable of tying knots in rail-way lines. This, as it turned out, was not a bad guess since it later emerged that Grigorović—a Montenegrin from Perast in the Gulf of Cattaro—had once been a circus strong man. However, I was still a trifle suspicious.

"No doubt, Maschinenmeister. But how is it that this man is affected while the rest of you are not?"

"Ah, Herr Schiffsleutnant, the Benzinschwammer is an artful customer and affects different people in different ways. Poor Grigoriviç may be big, but he is more susceptible than the rest of us. We call him our canary, because as soon as he starts singing to himself we know that we have to get up to the surface quickly and open the hatches."

I did not quite know how to answer this, beyond giving an order to untie the man as soon as he recovered. So I changed the subject.

"Very good. Anyway, I must introduce myself. I am your new Captain, Linienschiffsleutnant Prohaska. I have already met the Second Officer and you men, and I would like to address the rest of the crew as soon as possible. Where are they Maschinenmeister . . . er—"

"Lehár, Herr Kommandant. They're at dinner over there aboard the depot ship. I'll go over and fall them in here at once."

"Thank you, but let them finish their meal first. Once I have spoken to them I shall wish to go below with you and start finding my way around the boat. I hope that my acquaintance with you all will not be as brief as that of my predecessor."

Lehár gave me a look of slightly dismissive amusement. "Yes, Herr Kommandant. And we all hope so too, of course."

3

BENEATH THE WAVES FOR THE HOUSE OF HABSBURG

THE NEXT THREE WEEKS were not among the happiest in my naval career. Taking command of a new vessel is an awkward business at the best of times; all the more so when the crew are old hands while their new Captain is still a novice. But in this case the initial awkwardness was compounded by the fact that my new command was a very inadequate ship indeed: semi-obsolete even by the standards of 1915, and primitive beyond belief when compared with the submarines of today. Even her hull-form was archaic: a streamlined tear-drop shape, like a plump cigar—elegant enough to look at during the boat's frequent drydockings, but already quite outmoded, and destined to remain so until it was revived by the American nuclear submarines of half a century later. She had two propellers, turned by petrol engines on the surface and by electric motors when submerged. There was a vertical rudder for steering and a single pair of diving rudders aft. And the armament? Two 45cm torpedoes in tubes side by side at the bow, their openings covered by a rotating cap which was swung around just before firing so that two holes in it lined up with the tube muzzles, rather like an old-fashioned pepper-pot. Otherwise there was little to remark upon, except by its absence: no wireless, no gun, no rescue equipment, not even bunks for the crew to sleep in. Looking back on it now it scarcely seems credible that we should have been sent to fight in such a tiny, primitive, dangerous contraption. But there: this was seventy years ago, when airmen flew without parachutes and the *Titanic* sailed with lifeboats for only a third of her passengers. Most things are tolerable when there seems to be no alternative.

The truth is, though, that for all her insignificant appearance when

I first saw her that April morning, *U8* had already achieved a considerable notoriety as the centre of a long-standing bureaucratic muddle such
as only Old Austria knew how to contrive. In fact, by the time that I took
command of her, I think it hardly an exaggeration to say that the little
vessel had generated at least her own weight in official correspondence.
And like so many of the great official muddles of the old Monarchy, this
one was rooted in the uneasy relationship between Austria and Hungary.
Now, if you wish to conceive of this, picture to yourself a worn-out old
man, tormented with indigestion and rheumatism, and married to a pretty
wife much younger than himself. The wife is undeniably attractive, and
can be charming when the mood takes her. But for most of the time
she is an insufferable, hysterical shrew: an expert practitioner of every
form of marital blackmail, forever throwing tantrums, smashing china, ill-
treating the servants and flirting with other men. There are constant rows
and threats of divorce, but in the end she usually gets her own way if for
no other reason than that her husband no longer has the energy to do anything but give in.

Anyway, as the tale was related to me, the k.u.k. War Ministry had woken up to the realisation, about 1908, that the Empire's only shipyard capable of building submarines was Whiteheads at Fiume, which happened
to be in the Kingdom of Hungary. Now, the Austro-Hungarian marriage
was going through a particularly rough patch in 1908, so it was decided
that it might be a good idea to have some submarine-building capacity in
the Austrian part of the Monarchy, "just in case" . . . So the Monarchy's
largest shipbuilders, the Stabilimento Tecnico of Trieste, were approached
and asked to build an experimental submarine to the same pattern as those
being built by Whitehead: a design purchased from the murderous American schoolmaster Mr Holland, who was supplying submarines to half the
world's navies at the time. The directors of the Stabilimento Tecnico replied that they couldn't build submarines and had no wish to try. But in the
end the Chief of the Naval Staff intervened and threatened the yard with
the loss of a couple of fat battleship contracts.

The keel of the new boat was duly laid at Trieste early in 1909, several months behind schedule. But the Stabilimento were still unhappy with the project; and their unhappiness increased beyond measure when the Chief of the Naval Staff was unable to get the necessary money from the 1909 naval budget—largely because the Hungarians had learnt of the project and were threatening to block the entire military estimates for the year in the Imperial Parliament. Never mind (he said), just go on building and if the funds can't be found you can always sell it to a foreign buyer, now that everyone is interested in submarines. So, to cut a long story short, during the five years between her launching and the time that I made her acquaintance, *U8* was offered to the Netherlands, Brazil, Portugal, China, Norway, Russia, Turkey and even (I was told) to Bolivia, who proposed using her against the Peruvians on Lake Titicaca—thereby establishing what I imagine would still be a world altitude record for submarines. But petrol engines were giving way to diesels and Mr Holland's designs were rapidly becoming out of date, and in the end the whole project was given up in disgust. The engines (which had given constant trouble) were removed and the boat was left to rust in a corner of the Stabilimento. Then came the mobilisation in July 1914. The hulk was hastily dragged out, towed around to Fiume and fitted out with new Austro-Daimler engines, still petrol-driven, because no diesels were obtainable. Then she was pushed back into the water, commissioned as *U8* and sent to Pola to be turned into a fighting vessel.

The process of working up the newly commissioned *U8* had proved to be far more troublesome than expected. In fact it had already lasted four months and disposed of two captains by the time that I arrived. There was never any shortage of things to go wrong aboard a submarine in those days when underwater craft were still mysterious, half-experimental things, and certainly not with a cobbled-together dockyard reject like ours. Valves leaked, the hull leaked, battery cells leaked, pipes blocked, fuel filters clogged, crankshafts broke and carburettor jets blocked. We toiled day and night to get the boat ready, my crew and I. At first it seemed an utterly hopeless enterprise. But little by little, in those last weeks of April, we sorted out the technical problems to a point where *U8* might perhaps make Venice without having to be towed back.

My crew were an extraordinary collection of men. But then, Austro-Hungarian naval crews were always the subject of amazed comment, recruited as they were from all the tribes and sub-tribes of that black-and-yellow ethnic ragbag of an Empire of ours. At least things were less complicated on land: the overall language of command in the k.u.k. Armee was German of course, but for internal purposes each regiment would use the language of the majority of its men, which all the officers would be required to learn. In the Navy, though, recruits were posted to ships regardless of language, so that even the smallest vessels might hold a complete set of all the Dual Monarchy's eleven officially recognised nationalities. *U8* had (if I remember correctly) representatives of nine nationalities, and when I commanded *U26* in 1917 my crew of twenty men contained a complete set, plus a Jew, a gypsy and a Transylvanian Saxon, none of whom were officially recognised as separate national groups.

Looking back on it now I suppose the wonder is not that the old k.u.k. Kriegsmarine fought well—which it did until nearly the end—but that it managed to fight at all. We used German as our language of command, even though most of us spoke it as a foreign language with odd accents and peculiar grammar. And in between times we got by in k.u.k. Marinesprache, a curious argot compounded of about equal parts of German, Italian and Serbo-Croat.

The backbone of the Navy was the Croats of course: seafaring peasants from the coastal villages and islands of Istria and Dalmatia, often barely literate, but superb natural sailors who could handle a boat almost before they could walk. The technical branches tended to be staffed by German-Austrians, Czechs and Italians, while the chinks and crevices were filled in by the other nationalities. It sounds crazy, I know, but somehow it all worked aboard *U8:* largely because every single one of us had volunteered for the U-Boat Service, and also because we were blessed in particular with two excellent long-service Warrant Officers.

My right-hand man aboard *U8* was our Tauchführer—the Dive Leader, or what used to be called a Diving Coxswain in Royal Navy submarines: the senior Petty Officer who handled the boat's diving rudder underwater and at other times attended to discipline, supplies and the general smooth running of the vessel. This post was filled by Stabsbootsmann Martin Steinhüber. He was the oldest of our crew at thirty-seven years of age, with a total of twenty-five years' service in the Navy behind him; a married man with two children and a cottage just outside Pola. A native of the Tyrol, he looked very much the mountain man of popular legend, with glaucous, pale blue eyes and a head of near-perfect sphericality, "so that he could roll down an Alp without coming to any harm," we used to say. He was rather an oddity among German-Austrians in being a Protestant—this because his tiny village community was located so far up a mountain valley that the Counter-Reformation and the Prince-Bishop of Salzburg had never been able to get at it. Heaven alone knows what urge had prompted him to run away to sea, instead of sitting up there carving wooden toys and developing a goitre, but there is no doubt that we were the beneficiaries. The Tauchführer always knew exactly what to do and how to do it.

Stabsmaschinenwarter Josef Lehár has been introduced to you already, I think. He was a Czech from Olmutz in northern Moravia, not far from my own home town, and while we never spoke anything but German to one another (for an officer and a senior NCO to have conversed in Czech would have been considered most improper) the fact of a common nationality did ease matters between us. He was an excellent man, the Maschinenmeister: far-seeing, endlessly resourceful and unshakeably good-humoured. However disgusting or dangerous the circumstances he always seemed to regard things with ironic amusement, as a succession of jokes in dubious taste played on us by Fate. I believe that he was a distant cousin of the composer Franz Lehár, whose father had come from the same region, but otherwise the coincidence of name was not remarked upon, except that the proprietress of an ironmonger's shop on the Kandlerstrasse, with whom he had an understanding, was known inevitably as "Lehár's Merry Widow." I recommended him for promotion to Engineer Officer on at least three occasions, but nothing ever came of it. Right up to the end the Habsburg armed forces hung on to their antiquated notions about the Imperial officer caste.

• • •

By the end of April, then, things looked far less gloomy than they had done at the start of the month. But even so there remained an indefinable, sullen stickiness about the men as we drew near to the time for starting warlike operations. It was difficult for me to put my finger on it, but there seemed to be a detectable reluctance to try anything risky. Matters finally came to a head one morning during diving trials in the Fasana Channel. Our long labours seemed to be paying dividends at last. The boat had behaved impeccably all morning and we were now submerged at about ten metres just south of Fort Barbariga, cruising at three knots in the deepest part of the channel. Well, I thought to myself, this vessel is rated as safe to forty-five metres' depth, so let's go down to forty metres to see whether the hull leaks at all. I looked over at Steinhüber, controlling the diving-rudder wheel behind the main depth gauge.

"All right," I called out, "go to forty metres." There was a distinct hesitation before the reply came back.

"Going to forty metres, Herr Kommandant."

Slowly, slowly the pointer of the depth gauge crept around: twenty-five metres, thirty metres, thirty-one metres, thirty-two metres . . . then nothing more; the boat seemed to have bottomed at thirty-two metres. I turned round in some annoyance.

"Come on Tauchführer, for God's sake—there's forty-five metres on the chart here. What are you waiting for? Take the boat to forty metres."

"To forty metres, Herr Kommandant."

The pointer started to creep around the dial once more. Then there was a blue flash and a loud bang from somewhere behind me. The inside of the boat filled with acrid smoke as the two electric motors faltered and died. Lehár's voice called out:

"Sorry, Herr Kommandant, but the main fuse in the E-motor net has blown. We'll have to surface!" No sooner had he said this, however, than the boat began to rise of its own accord. Some air had been left in the small regulator tank amidships to give us reserve buoyancy, clean contrary to standing instructions, which were to dive with the tank completely full and the boat slightly heavy by the bow. There was no point in arguing the matter now, when we were coughing and our eyes were streaming from the smoke of burnt electrical wiring, but I was still extremely displeased, and called Béla Meszáros to confer with me as soon as we had got back to the harbour at Brioni.

"Now, Meszáros, will you be so good as to explain to me what happened out there?"

"With respect, I should have thought that it was perfectly plain, Herr Kommandant. The main E-motor net got overloaded and the fuses blew."

"I see. And will you perhaps be so kind as to comment on this, then?" I held out a piece of aluminium wire for him to inspect: about three centimetres long and melted at one end.

"I found this a few minutes ago at the back of the E-motor switch panel, and do you know what, Meszáros?"

"No, Herr Kommandant."

"I suspect that it was placed there deliberately to short-circuit the motors and prevent us from going below thirty metres."

His face was quite expressionless. "That's a very serious accusation to make, Herr Kommandant. Sabotage in time of war carries the death penalty."

"Oh all right: I can't prove it and I don't intend looking for culprits—not this time at any rate. But will you please tell me, as one officer to another, why everyone aboard this boat is so damned windy about going near her maximum diving depth? For heaven's sake, Meszáros, we are all volunteers, and thousands of men are getting killed in the Army every day, so why are these fellows all so careful of their health?"

He was silent for a moment or two, then said:

"I take it then, Herr Kommandant, that you haven't heard what happened last time *U8* went below thirty metres? No, I thought not. Well, we got to thirty-two metres and the hull above the engines collapsed. We blew all tanks and got her to the surface before she sank, but two men got trapped in the fore-ends and were drowned. The boat was raised next day, but the Edler von Krummelhausen shot himself in his cabin that same evening, after writing a letter to the Marine Oberkommando saying that *U8* was hopelessly ill-constructed and not safe at any depth."

I was silent for a while. "I see. So you're telling me that the crew have no faith in the boat's ability to dive?"

"I respectfully report that the crew have complete faith in the boat's ability to dive: what they are less sure of is its ability to come back up again."

"Well Meszáros, so this is the dark secret of 'der Achtzer' that everyone has been avoiding talking about in the wardroom in the evenings. From what you say I begin to understand why you are all so wary of the boat. But what are we to do? My task is to turn this vessel and her crew into an efficient fighting unit, and how am I to do that when I begin to suspect my own men of sabotage? What are you all going to do if we end up out there with half a dozen French destroyers trailing explosive sweeps after us? They aren't going to be sporting and not chase us below thirty metres."

"No, Herr Kommandant."

"It's not good enough Meszáros: something will have to be done."

So back aboard the *Pelikan* that afternoon I sat poring over my charts. Then I requested and got a special interview with the Ritter von Thierry. He was sympathetic when he heard my story, and a number of telephone calls to Pola ensued. When they were over Thierry put down the receiver and looked at me.

"Well, my dear Prohaska, your request is an unusual one but I am glad to say that by going outside the normal channels I have managed to arrange it for you. The *Herkules* will be here at 5:30 a.m. tomorrow. As you say, a demonstration is needed."

The next morning dawned bright and clear, with a light south-easterly breeze rustling the leaves in the lemon trees around the Hotel Neptune. The crew had been turned out of their hammocks aboard the depot ship at 4 a.m., and at 5:30 sharp two siren blasts outside the harbour breakwater announced the arrival of the naval salvage vessel S.M.S. *Herkules*. The crew were clearly in a rather sheepish mood after yesterday's events, and equally clearly were at a loss to understand what was afoot now as *U8*'s engines hummed into life and we set off in the wake of the salvage ship. Good, I thought to myself, dramatic effect is what we are seeking to achieve today, so the longer the audience is kept in the dark the better. Somehow, though, I wished that I felt more confident that the performance would end as set out in the script . . .

The men were even more puzzled when the *Herkules* stopped and dropped anchor about five miles south of Fort Verudela and a mile west of the Cape Porer lighthouse. *U8* came alongside and everyone was ordered off the submarine and up the gangway ladder on to the deck of the salvage vessel: all except Steinhüber and Grigorović, who stayed to arrange a loose strop of wire rope between the lifting ringbolts at *U8*'s bow and stern. Once they had done this one of the salvage vessel's powerful derricks was swung out to port and the crane hook was lowered until it could be engaged in a loop in the middle of the strop. Steinhüber stuck his head up out of the conning-tower hatch.

"Obediently report that everything's ready, Herr Kommandant. I've flooded diving tanks one and two and the trim tanks as you ordered."

"Very good Tauchführer," I called down. "Now come up on deck and join us. I'm going to make a short speech."

The men were fallen in on the fo'c'sle deck by Lehár and Steinhüber, Fregattenleutnant Meszáros standing off to one side. There they stood, rigidly to attention in their blue jerseys and striped singlets, cap-ribbon tails fluttering in the breeze. Their faces were parade-ground blank, but I could sense a powerful air of expectancy. I jumped up on top of a capstan to address them.

"All right, stand easy." (Crash of boots on the wooden deck.) "Now, my men. No doubt you are wondering for what purpose I have rousted you out of your hammocks and brought you out here on this fine spring morning. So I shall keep you in suspense no longer. The truth is that I have noticed a certain timidity among you these past two weeks, and in particular a strong reluctance to take this boat of ours below thirty metres even though you know damned well that she is safe to forty-five. Now, this is the twentieth century and I am no wooden-headed martinet. But there is a war on, we are expected to become operational by the end of this month and we're certainly going to have to go below thirty metres when we get into action. I quite understand your hesitation after what happened in March; also that you don't feel totally confident with a new captain. But there we are: we are all sailors of Austria, we all volunteered for the U-Boat Service—in respect of which, I might add, many of you receive allowances that practically double your basic pay and I could send any or all of you back to sandpapering the anchor on a battleship if I felt like it. We can't choose what boats we are going to fight in, so" (working up for maximum effect here) "I am going to show you that I at least have faith in the ability of *U8* to reach her designed maximum depth intact. And I shall do this by going down in her on my own. If you were right and I was wrong I shall pay for it with my life. But if I was right all along I shall expect you in future to show as much faith in this vessel as I have shown myself. Now, first I shall demonstrate that there is no trickery involved. Tauchführer, choose a man to take a sounding."

Steinhüber called out: "Elektromatrose Zaccarini—step forward!" Electrical Artificer Ottavio Zaccarini stepped out of the front rank and saluted: a tall, thin Italian from Zara, with a lugubrious black moustache like two grease-brushes. "Zaccarini, take that lead over there and make a sounding to port." Zaccarini walked to the rail, swung the lead with effortless ease and sent it curving gracefully out to plump into the water just ahead of *U8*'s bows. There was a pause, then a call of "Forty-five metres exactly, Tauchführer."

"Good," I said, "then if you will excuse me I shall leave you for a while. I shall stay down for precisely ten minutes. You may smoke if you wish."

As I made my way aft to climb down the ladder I was accosted by my Second Officer and by Steinhüber and Lehár.

"Herr Kommandant," said Meszáros, catching my sleeve, "we're going down with you."

"Oh no you're not."

"But Herr Kommandant . . ."

"That's an order," (lowering my voice): "if this doesn't come off then I want the U-Boat Service to have lost only one officer, not two officers and two long-service NCOs. Now if you will excuse me . . ."

I climbed on to the submarine's narrow deck and up the ladder on to the conning tower, then lowered myself into the hatchway. Once there I paused and turned to look up at the row of expectant faces lining the rail. What were they really thinking, I wondered? Bluster and moustache-twirling might have worked with Radetzky's dumb peasants, but somehow I suspected that it might not cut much ice with graduates of the Prague Technical Academy. No one was smoking. Just as well, I thought to myself, perhaps they're witnessing a burial at sea. I signalled to the winch man on the *Herkules,* and the derrick swung out, dragging *U8* sideways until about ten metres separated the two vessels. Then as I stepped down the steel ladder and prepared to close the hatch behind me the craziness of it all struck me forcibly, despite myself. Here am I, I thought, twenty-nine years of age, in the prime of health, quite possibly taking my last look at the sun because my government couldn't be bothered to provide the money to build anything better than this miserable dockyard abortion. Yet my officer's oath still obliges me to commit suicide in an attempt to deceive other poor fools into thinking that I believe our rulers.

But the code of the Habsburg officer corps was a very powerful one, so I waved as nonchalantly as I was able, closed the hatch and turned the wheel to lock it shut. Then I climbed down into the control room and opened the valves to let the remaining air out of the diving tanks. It escaped with a soft roar until the water bubbled up into the glass indicator tubes, then I shut the valves off again. The boat was now in slight negative buoyancy, supported by the steel wire strop and the derrick of the salvage vessel. All I had to do was to flash the navigation lights twice and the winch man would start to lower *U8* towards the sea bed at a rate of ten metres per minute, stopping only when the boat touched bottom. There was nothing left for me to do now but sit in my canvas folding chair in the middle of the control room, watch the depth gauge . . . and wait.

It was a curious feeling, to be sitting there alone under the soft, white glow of the electric lamps after weeks of being accustomed to seeing the little submarine's single deck crowded with humanity, of always having the throb of the engines and the gurgle of water and the hiss of compressed air as a background to one's thoughts. Now there was only myself, and perhaps the dead captain . . . No, best to keep away from idle thoughts of that kind. I watched the pointer of the depth gauge and checked it against my wristwatch. Ten metres, fifteen metres—the hull was beginning to groan and creak a little now as the water pressure increased. The only other sound was the soft whirr of the electric bilge pump, which was running to deal with the inevitable seepage of water. Thirty metres. By now the groans had turned into sharp little cracking noises, like an old man snapping his knuckles. Thirty-five metres, thirty-seven metres, then a bang like a pistol shot. I closed my eyes and held my breath, but nothing further happened. We were getting near the bottom now. One way or another, I would soon know. Forty metres—then five or six plates fell with a crash from a wooden rack and shattered on the linoleum-covered deck. Evidently the hull was being squeezed out of shape by the pressure. More creaks and snaps, then blessed relief: the depth gauge had stopped at forty-five metres. Now would be the moment of truth, I thought: when the tension of the wire-rope strop was relaxed, for I had an unpleasant suspicion that perhaps it was the upward pull on its two ends that had kept the hull from collapsing this far, rather as a bowstring gives rigidity to a bow. I need not have worried though: the vessel gave an agonised, grating squeal, then settled on to the sea-bed level, with about five degrees of list to starboard.

So we had made it. All that remained for me to do now was to wait for ten minutes as arranged, then be winched up again. I sat back in my chair, trembling slightly. I had a great urge at that point to light up a cigar, but no smoking below was a strict rule aboard this petrol-engined vessel, so I resisted the temptation. Well, I thought, this will show that collection of old women up there: nothing to it rea . . . There was a loud PWOOSH! noise as a violent explosion of spray erupted in the fore-ends. I ran forward into the hissing storm and saw that a pipe joint between the two torpedo compensator tanks had burst under the pressure: a pencil-thin jet of water was hissing upwards with such force that I later found it had actually stripped a patch of white paint off the deckhead above. Without thinking, I tried to staunch it with my hand—and pulled it away again with a yell after it had all but broken the bones in the palm. After a few seconds though I had found the valves to isolate the section of pipe. The jet of water faltered into a sullen dribble, then died. I made my way back to the control room, wet through and shaken but otherwise none the worse for the experience.

As I reached the control room, wiping sea water from my eyes, I felt the deck move slightly beneath my feet. I looked at my watch: thank God, the ten minutes were up and I was on my way back to the surface. The succession of groans and cracking noises was endured again, this time in reverse order as the hull expanded once more. The depth-gauge pointer swung around quite quickly this time, and gradually the water began to lighten outside the thick little glass bull's eyes in the conning tower. Soon we were back at the surface. I ran a comb through my hair and adjusted my bow-tie—appearance, I felt, would count for a lot at this juncture—and climbed the ladder to open the conning-tower hatch. As the sunlight and fresh air burst in upon me a wild "Hurrah!" greeted my ears: not the regulation parade-ground cheers appropriate to an archduke's birthday but a quite unexpected and oddly moving cry of relief from eighteen men who (I was later informed) had stood at the rail for the entire twenty or so minutes in dead silence, eyes riveted to the water and expecting any moment to see the eruption of air-bubbles that would mark the end of a promising young officer's career. But here I was, back again. As I reached the top of the gangway aboard *Herkules* the men crowded about me, clean contrary to all order and discipline, to touch me or try to shake my hand.

"There," I said, with as much swagger as I could muster, "an officer of Austria never requires his subordinates to do anything that he wouldn't do himself. I told you it would be all right, so perhaps you'll do me the honour of believing me in future." But we all laughed together that morning, rather than being scolder and scolded, and from that day until the last day of the war there was nothing that we would not have attempted together.

Shortly after the touching little scene that I have just related, Béla Meszáros took me to one side.

"Herr Kommandant, there's something I must tell you."

"Speak, Meszáros. What is it?"

"That demonstration dive of yours—you didn't go to forty-five metres."

"But surely, the depth gauge read . . ."

"The depth gauge bottoms at forty-five metres. I checked with the winch operator afterwards, and he paid out fifty-two metres of wire."

"But the lead sounding?"

"The sea bed around here must have a good many bumps and hollows in it; and anyway, the *Herkules* was swinging at her anchor as the wind changed."

My jaw fell on to my chest. "You mean to tell me that I went six metres below maximum depth in that cabbage barrel . . . ? Why didn't you stop him?"

"I didn't know about it until afterwards. You had just told him to go on lowering until the boat touched bottom. As you observed, a demonstration was required. And I think the men were suitably impressed."

4

LOOKING FOR TROUBLE

U8 WAS DECLARED FULLY OPERATIONAL in the last few days of April 1915. This did not mean that the boat's technical problems had been solved, of course: merely that they had now abated to a point where we could be sent out on patrol with some small prospect of returning.

It was not that *U8* was without her good points: the little vessel handled well underwater and she was reasonably seaworthy on the surface. Her two six-cylinder petrol engines gave her a surface speed of nearly twelve knots—faster than any other submarine I commanded in that war—and they were very quiet when compared with the later diesels, a source of considerable solace to us when we were nosing about in enemy waters on those still Adriatic summer nights, when the noise of a pencil dropped on the deck seemed to travel for miles across the luminous sea. But these little advantages were quite outweighed by the boat's crippling deficiencies.

For one thing, she was extremely wet in a sea-way: that is to say, anything above Force 4. It required the skill of a tightrope walker to negotiate the narrow deck when a sea was running; while as for the "conning tower," so grandly entitled, it was nothing more than a bad joke, with barely enough room for two men to stand behind a waist-high canvas screen, in imminent danger of being washed away and never seen again. The lookout would be lashed to the periscope standard at the start of his watch and left there, like Saint Sebastian tied to his tree-trunk, until the time came to bring him down and empty him out, soaked through to his underwear despite a double layer of oilskins. Nor was there much space for the crew inside that sleek hull, since they had to share it with diving tanks, batteries, engines, torpedoes, fuel tanks and everything else. The vessel had a single, long deck, open from end to end, which served as control room, engine room, torpedo compartment and living quarters rolled into one. There was no telephone system, and no need for one since both ends of the boat were visible from the control position. When I wanted full speed all I had to do was turn around and shout to the motor machinist. My method of giving the order to fire torpedoes was to stand behind the periscope holding one of those red and white table-tennis bats used by station masters in Central Europe. I would raise it above my shoulder for "Stand By to Fire," then drop it for "Fire!"

Firing torpedoes was a delicate business aboard *U8,* as we discovered in the course of a week of practice attacks out in the Fasana Channel. There was a system of tanks and valves to compensate for the weight of the torpedoes leaving their tubes, but these worked with a considerable delay, while the boat's underwater trim was very delicate. The method that we evolved in the end to prevent the bows from breaking surface at firing was to station eight men some way aft of the torpedo tubes. As each torpedo was discharged a party of four men would run forward to balance the boat, count up to five as the compensator tanks filled, then run back again.

But merely to fire torpedoes is not enough: they have to be fired at something, and there was constant debate aboard *U8* in those spring months of 1915 as to what chance we stood of ever getting close enough to the enemy to risk a shot. The boat had two periscopes: one a Goertz instrument with a head the size of a coffee-pot, to be used for search; the other a much better, German-made Zeiss attack periscope, about the thickness of a hoe-handle at its top end. The system for raising and lowering these instruments was also most unsatisfactory: pneumatic jacks which vented into the boat's interior when the periscope was lowered. The effect of this was that after a couple of hours of up-periscope and down-periscope a considerable over-pressure would build up inside the boat. We found this out one morning when we surfaced and Béla Meszáros opened the conning-tower hatch. There was a loud bang and an agonising stab in our ear-drums, accompanied by a howl as the Fregattenleutnant (who was rather stout in build) was ejected through the hatch like a cork from a champagne bottle. Fortunately he was not hurt, once we had got him back on board, only wet and very annoyed. But after that I made it a practice to take the boat deep rather than lower the periscope; also that whoever opened the hatch after a long dive should have someone else with him on the ladder, hanging on to his ankles.

Navigation aboard *U8* also left much to be desired. But then, "navigation" is altogether too grand a word for the methods by which we got our boat from place to place, either beneath the sea or upon it. Apart from a sextant, our sole navigational instrument was a magnetic compass; I will leave you to imagine how well a magnetic compass functions inside a steel boat packed with electrical cables and with a powerful field surging about each electric motor. At any rate, twenty or thirty degrees' deviation either side of magnetic north was nothing out of the ordinary. It was indeed fortunate that *U8* was operating for most of the time in home waters, well known to me and my Second Officer from our mandatory years of commanding torpedo-boats, and that where our own knowledge of local landmarks was deficient we always had the experience of our Dalmatian sailors to draw upon. There was always someone who recognised that island over there; in fact usually had aunts and cousins living on it. And of course if all else failed we could always hail a fishing boat and ask for directions.

The greatest problem with *U8* though was her surface engines; or, to be more precise, not the engines themselves—though goodness only knows, they were troublesome enough—but the petrol that drove them. Petrol fumes were a constant background to our lives, soaking into our clothes and hair and skin, eventually (it seemed) saturating every fibre of our bodies. Try as we might, we could never make the fuel lines and the carburettors absolutely leak-proof, and it needed only the smallest dribble of petrol vaporising into the already foul and stuffy air inside the boat to produce the most alarming and dangerous effects. The peril was not only that of fire and explosion: it was the insidious menace of petrol sickness, the Benzinschwammer, which would creep up on us unawares and suddenly have half the crew falling asleep at their posts or babbling like imbeciles.

The trouble with petrol sickness was not only its stealthy approach; it was that the symptoms varied so widely, and that we all succumbed at different rates. I remember that for me it usually began with a sweetish taste in the mouth, rapidly followed by drowsiness, then by a throbbing headache and a feeling of wanting to go at once and hang myself from the nearest hammock hook. With others it was sudden nausea; or a wild, hysterical elation accompanied by a pounding heart, shining eyes and shortness of breath. In its extreme form it would manifest itself as delirium tremens, for which the only cure was to surface at once, bind the victims hand and foot and lay them out on the deck to recover in the fresh air while they raved the most bizarre nonsense: chapters from scientific textbooks jumbled up with bits of operetta and decades of the rosary. I recall how, one morning off the Italian coast south of Pescara, acute petrol sickness forced us to the surface in broad daylight—almost under the keel of a small Italian trading schooner. The crew were terrified out of their wits and surrendered at once—luckily for us, since only three of us were able to stand on our feet at the time. We towed the vessel back to Lissa as a prize, and I shall always treasure the memory of the looks of wonder on the Italians' faces as no less than eleven men were laid out on the deck, babbling to themselves and trussed up like chickens.

The only one of us to show any resistance to petrol poisoning was Fregattenleutnant Meszáros. He was usually the last to fall unconscious, and he attributed this partial immunity to his habit of taking a swig from a hip flask just before diving. I was not at all pleased when I saw this for the first time: in my opinion diving aboard *U8* was quite hazardous enough already without having my Second Officer under the influence. However, he assured me that the flask contained only a specific against petrol poisoning: namely an infusion of red paprika in báráck, a vicious Hungarian brandy made from apricots. I took a mouthful myself, by way of a trial, and swore—once I had recovered my breath—that nothing on earth would ever induce me to try a second. After this I allowed him to carry on taking his home-made prophylactic on the grounds that no one would ever drink anything so awful except as a medicine.

The constant inhaling of petrol vapour had other, more unsettling effects on some of us. One day early in May I was conducting the daily Captain's Report on board the *Pelikan,* where we lived when we were not at sea. It was the usual business of assigning duties, hearing complaints, receiving requests for leave, settling pay allowances and deductions etc., etc.: all the fiddling minutiae of shipboard life, much the same in wartime as in peace. One man waited until last to speak with me. It was Seaman Second Class Demeter Horoczko: what we used to call a Ruthene, or what you would now call a Ukrainian. He was a reserved, rather morose man with a face like an unbaked loaf. But today he was lit up like a pumpkin lantern with the inner light of a grievance. He stepped up and saluted. It was a strictly observed rule of the Imperial and Royal armed forces that every enlisted man should have the right to be heard by an officer who spoke his own language. I spoke seven of the Monarchy's eleven languages, but my Ukrainian—although I understood it well enough was exiguous. However, it appeared that Horoczko wished to lend authority to his complaint by speaking in German.

"Herr Kommandant, I wish to speak with you privately."

"Really Horoczko, can't we discuss it here?"

"Respectfully not Herr Kommandant—it is the very personal matter."

"Oh all right then, let's go to my office." So we went to the cubbyhole that I shared as an office with two other U-Boat captains. I shut the door behind us.

"Well, Horoczko?"

"Obediently report, Herr Kommandant, that I wish to claim damages from Treasury because the petrol vapour it damages my health."

"Damages eh, Horoczko? All I can say is that you'll be damned lucky with a war on. But what sort of damage has your health suffered and what sort of sum had you in mind as compensation?"

"Obediently report that the petrol it makes me—how do you say?—impotent and for this I claim four Kronen."

Despite myself I was intrigued. "Tell me more, Horoczko. How did you discover this . . . condition and where do the four Kronen fit in?"

"It happens last night in Pola, Herr Kommandant. I give the girl four Kronen, then I cannot get it up. So I ask for the money back, but she just laughs and says Gésu Maria Giuseppe, what is the Kriegsmarine coming to? I call the gendarme, but he laughs as well and says shove off quick or I call navy police and you fetch up in Marinegefangenhaus."

I sympathised with poor Horoczko: it must have been deeply wounding to his personal honour and that of the Imperial and Royal Fleet. In the end though the only solace that I could offer was to tell him that I doubted whether the condition were permanent, and that at least while he served aboard *U8* he would be in no danger of falling into the hands of the venereal diseases section at the Pola Naval Hospital: a fate which (I assured him) was to be avoided at all costs.

I cannot say that I noticed the petrol fumes having a similar effect in my own case, nor did I hear any other member of *U8*'s crew complain of diminished libido. And certainly there was no lack of opportunity for experiment in that direction in those spring months of 1915. Quite the contrary: the ladies of Pola fairly hurled themselves upon us, now that the exploits of Lerch and Trapp had turned us "U-Bootlers" almost overnight from the Navy's disreputable poor relations into heroes. I suspect also that the very shape of submarines and torpedoes may have had some powerful subconscious attraction in what was, after all, a very repressed age. I believe at any rate that Professor Freud had arrived at very similar conclusions about that time with regard to Zeppelin airships.

Anyway, there we were, she and I, after dinner one warm early May evening, alone in a secluded bower in the gardens of the Naval Casino in Pola. She was a certain Ilona von Friedauer, Hungarian wife of a boring Colonel in the Fortress Artillery who had now spent nearly nine months on a barren rock down Zara way, polishing the guns and scanning the horizon for the arrival of the French battle fleet, an event by now about as likely as a raid by Polynesian war-canoes. Frau Oberstin von Friedauer was certainly a very fine-looking woman in the Magyar fashion: dark brown hair, smouldering eyes and a statuesque figure of the kind that they don't seem to make in this country, or perhaps anywhere else nowadays, a figure that not even the loose-fitting fashions of 1915 could entirely disguise, and which I hoped to inspect more closely in due course. I had just remarked to her that she was worthy of modelling for a sculptor in the character of Aphrodite. She had fluttered her eyelashes, blushed most prettily and asked me how I imagined that any respectable woman could expose herself naked to the gaze of a man other than her husband. In a word, things seemed to be going nicely, and my arm was creeping around her shapely waist as I whispered something about taking a fiacre down to Medolino, where I knew a small pension whose proprietor was very understanding about letting rooms by the hour. As I uttered these words, though, I felt a sudden stiffening and a shudder. Then my hand was removed and placed very firmly on the stone bench as Frau Ilona got up, drew herself up to her full height, rearranged her by now rather disordered dress and flounced away towards the lighted windows and the music and the hubbub of voices.

"But Ilona . . ." I called after her. She stopped, half turned and addressed me in her sing-song Magyar accent:

"Herr Schiffsleutnant, while it may be true that my dear husband has been away a long time and that I am desirous of male society, I still trust that I have not yet fallen so low as to be seduced by a man who drinks petrol. I bid you good evening."

"Ilona, for heaven's sake . . ."

"Good night, Herr Schiffsleutnant. If I were you I would take that trip to Medolino on your own. Perhaps the sea air will help cure you of your unfortunate addiction. Auf wiedersehen . . ."

I suppose, looking back on it, that Frau Ilona had got the idea into her handsome head that petrol was methylated spirit or something of the kind. Anyway, I got up, mightily annoyed, and made my way to the main entrance of the Casino. A sentry stood guard with rifle and fixed bayonet. He snapped to attention as I approached, looking straight ahead.

"Sailor, tell me something."

"Herr Schiffsleutnant?"

"Does my breath smell of petrol?" I breathed over him. The man winced visibly.

"Obediently suggest that Herr Schiffsleutnant would be unwise to light a cigarette for the next hour or so."

But war is war, petrol vapour or not, and our erstwhile partner Italy was expected to come in against us as soon as the Allies had offered an attractive enough bribe. This meant that our miserable fleet of submarines was now to be stretched even further, guarding not just the Gulf of Cattaro against the French but the entire coastline of the Dual Monarchy: six hundred kilometres of it and (if I remember rightly) 727 islands, ranging in size from ones like Lussin, which could boast several large towns, to tiny, waterless, often nameless outcrops of pale grey limestone, barely able to support a few tufts of thyme and a couple of half-starved lizards. This whole intricate coast was to be patrolled by two or three U-Boats whose task—so far as any of us could make out—was to wander wherever their captains' fancy led them or wherever there looked like being some chance of action.

There was certainly not much prospect of the latter, so far as anyone could see that morning at the beginning of May when I was called to the Hotel Neptune at Brioni and handed a set of sealed orders marked TOP SECRET—NOT TO BE OPENED UNTIL AT SEA. Well, I had served long enough in the k.u.k. Kriegsmarine not to be unduly impressed by these dramatic flourishes on the part of Staff Officers, so I opened the brown envelope as I strolled down towards the jetty. The single sheet of paper read:

TELEGRAM

k.u.k. Marine Oberkommando Pola
5 May 1915

To: Commanding Officer S.M.U. 8, U-Station Pola Brioni

With effect from 7 May inst. S.M.U. *8* will operate from port of Sebenico in coastal defence sectors Zara, Sebenico and Spalato, extending from mainland coast at Metković to westernmost tip of Meleda Island, and thence to southernmost extremity of Lussin Piccolo and mainland coast at Zengg.

Operational base: S.M.S. *Kaiserin und Königin Maria Theresa* at Sebenico.

Mode of operation: independent, at discretion of commanding officer, subject to orders of Sea Area Defence Commander, Sebenico.

So there we were then: off to Sebenico to patrol (at a quick reckoning) some fifteen thousand square kilometres of sea all on our own, with no detailed directions whatsoever as to what we were to try to do or how we were to do it. As I arrived at the quayside Béla Meszáros, Lehár, Steinhüber and three or four ratings were at work repairing a punctured float valve in the port carburettor. My Second Officer stood up and wiped his hands on a piece of cotton waste.

"Hello there Herr Kommandant. What's the news?"

"Just had orders," I said, holding up the telegram. "We're going to be based at Sebenico until further notice."

"Ah, Sebenico," said Steinhüber, leaning against a bollard and pushing his cap back on his head, "quite a decent sort of place I believe, though the harbour smells of dead fish and there's only one café. I suppose that means we'll be sleeping aboard the old *Maria Theresa,* now that they've made her guardship down there. Did you ever ship aboard her, Herr Kommandant?"

"What, the 'Alte Reserl'? No, I never had that privilege. What's she like?"

"Bug-infested something shocking, Herr Kommandant. I served aboard her as a lad on the West Indies trip in 1898, and she was a floating zoo even then."

"Yes," Lehár added, "I was aboard the old tub myself back in 1902 off Smyrna. We used to sleep with our socks on down in the stokers' flats, because if we didn't the cockroaches would eat our toe-nails away in the night. They used to say that every time she went to the tropics she'd come back with a new species established below decks. It was only the fact that they fought one another most of the time that allowed us to live at all."

"Well," I said, "while I don't doubt what you have to say about the local wildlife, I don't think we'll be aboard her too often. The patrol sector they've given us is 150 nautical miles long by about twenty-five across, so I imagine that we shall have to spend a lot more time at sea than we have done up to now. Anyway, get the men together and tell them to pack their kitbags to set sail at 5 a.m. tomorrow. They can go across to Pola this evening to bid the whores goodbye, but I want everyone back here by 11 sharp. As for you, Tauchführer, if you like you can leave an hour early to say goodbye to Frau Steinhüber and the children. I imagine that we shall be gone quite some time."

"Thank you very much, Herr Kommandant, but my wife and the children are no longer in Pola. There's talk of all the non-combatants being moved inland now that the Italians are likely to come in against us, so we decided that they'd best leave early. My sister-in-law has got a farm near Klagenfurt and they've gone to stay with her."

"Very well then," I said, "let's start packing for our summer cruise along the Adriatic Riviera."

And that is pretty well what it turned out to be over the next two months. A submarine is not generally the most pleasant of craft for cruising—especially a cramped, cantankerous, petrol-reeking little vessel like *U8,* where the temperature below decks was usually in the lower forties Celsius and where engine breakdowns were an almost daily occurrence. But even so, I still look back on those weeks patrolling the Dalmatian coast and islands as a happy time. After all, we were young and healthy, so what did the petty discomforts of U-Boat life mean to us when weighed against the clear blue sky and the ultramarine waves dotted with countless islands: some outcrops of dazzling limestone, jagged as a broken tooth and bare as a picked bone; others almost hallucinatory in their smoothness and clothed in forests of pine and black cypress; still others hidden below the horizon, but detectable miles out to sea by their wind-borne scents of marjoram and lavender. Life resolved itself into a succession of five- or six-day patrols separated by spells of a day or two back at Sebenico to carry out repairs, have a bath and a shave and take on petrol, lubricating oil and distilled water. Then it was off again, purring out among the islands to nose our way into the little fishing harbours, moor at the riva and perhaps go for an evening stroll and a glass of wine at the local café. I was concerned not to make these patrols too regular: the population of this coast was mixed Croat and Italian, and doubtless our movements were being reported back to certain interested parties. But even so, *U8* became a familiar visitor to Makarska and Lesina and Traü and Comisa. The fishermen would pause at their nets to see us come in, and the local urchins would always swarm down to the harbour to watch the arrival of the "sottomarino" or the "podvodnik." My admirable Dalmatian crewmen knew the coast blindfolded, and anywhere we called we were guaranteed a welcome and tables at the local café invariably run, it seemed, by an uncle of one of my sailors, usually none too clean, but still somewhere to stretch our legs and eat a hot meal after the discomforts of life on board.

Discomfort was certainly never in short supply aboard *U8*. Before 1914 very few people had expected that submarines would be used for anything but harbour defence, so no thought had been given to making them habitable for more than perhaps twelve hours at a stretch. In consequence the living arrangements aboard our boat were of the most primitive kind. Cooking facilities consisted of a single electric hotplate, which I disliked using because it drained too much current from the batteries, or a petrol stove on deck, which could only be used in calm weather. As for sleeping arrangements, bedding down when off watch was a matter of drawing lots for the softest deck plate. And washing? Forget it: the best that could be expected was a wipe-down on deck from a canvas bucket, weather permitting.

We did have a lavatory though: a real china pedestal-type toilet just like those on land—except that it stood beside the port engine, visible for the entire length of the boat. The bowl had a rubber lip and a heavy metal lid which fastened down with four large wing-nuts. Once the lid was in place the idea was to force air into the bowl by means of a lever-operated pump. When enough atmospheres had been pumped in for the pressure inside the bowl to be greater than that of the water outside, a valve would be opened and the contents of the bowl would be blown out into the sea. That at least was the theory: the practice was rather less certain. Judging the relative pressures was far from easy, and if one got it wrong the contents of the bowl would be blown back into the boat all over the user: an occurrence known as "U-Boat baptism." For these reasons the lavatory was little used. In fact, to save the already thick atmosphere inside the boat from being made still worse I eventually laid down that it was not to be used except by permission of the watch officer, and only then in the extremest emergencies. Otherwise it was hanging on to the conning-tower rails with lowered trousers, or opium pills if the sea was too rough.

In the end the problem of the underwater lavatory was to resolve itself in dramatic fashion. It happened one morning early in May, while we were sitting peacefully on the bottom off Petrčane, lying in ambush for a prowling French submarine which turned out to be a floating log, aided by a new directional hydrophone which turned out to be entirely useless. All was tranquillity as we lay there, fifteen metres down. The off-duty watch were dozing wrapped in their blankets up in the fore-ends while Fregattenleutnant Meszáros snored fitfully and muttered to himself on top of the firearms locker, which had been reserved as the Commissioned Ranks' sleeping-quarters. The on-duty watch were sitting about reading, writing letters or playing cards under the white glow of the electric lights while Lehár and two engine-room ratings tinkered with the exhaust manifold of the starboard engine. As for myself, I was seated at the chart table, dividing my time between a little half-hearted navigational calculation and watching the hydrophone operator cursing and blaspheming softly as he cranked the handwheels, trying in vain to isolate some recognisable sound from the cacophony of clacks and gurgles produced by the local marine life. I noticed a man stirring among the sleeping forms up in the fore-ends. He was evidently in some discomfort, and after a few minutes he got to his feet and came aft. It was Torpedoman First Class Matasić. He looked rather distressed and saluted hurriedly.

"Herr Kommandant, I obediently request permission to use the lavatory."

"Oh really Matasić, must you?"

"Obediently report that yes, Herr Kommandant. I think it is the *zuppa di pesce* last night. It does not much like me."

"Very well then Matasić, but try not to foul the air in the entire boat, and give it a good pumping before you open the valve: we're fifteen metres down."

Matasić hastened aft to the lavatory and I resumed my navigational scribblings. Before long I heard the regular pssst-pssst of the air pump, then a popping in my ears as the air pressure fell. I was just turning to bleed a little compressed air from one of the flasks when my ear-drums were punched into my skull by a brutal explosion that sent fragments rattling and ricocheting the length of the boat. There was instant pandemonium as the off-duty watch leapt to their feet to get to action stations. Certainly my own first, dazed idea was that we had been attacked with an explosive sweep, a bomb trailed on the end of a line, which was the only effective way of getting at a submerged submarine in those days. I sprang across to the valve bank, intending to blow all tanks and get us to the surface while we still had some buoyancy left. But then I realised that the explosion, violent though it was, had not been followed by any inrush of water. I made my way aft, still half-deaf. Lehár and his assistants were peering nervously around one corner of the engine at Matasić, who stood, trousers around his ankles and hand on the pump lever, chalk-faced and staring in horror at the jagged stump of the lavatory bowl. It seemed that he had interpreted my remark about giving it a good pumping all too literally and that his brawny arm had done the rest. By some miracle no one was injured by the chunks of porcelain; not even Matasić, who was standing right by the thing. But as for the contents, I think that everyone received some of it. After this I had the lavatory pipe blanked off: from now on the underwater sanitary arrangements would consist of two buckets half full of oil.

However, the truth of the matter is that the exploding lavatory was the greatest danger we encountered during those months of May and June 1915. Hundreds of thousands might be dying on the battlefields from Flanders to the Polish plains, but as far as we were concerned our sole casualty during this period was Elektroquartiermeister Lederer, who received a minor stab-wound during an argument over a young woman in a waterfront café at Spalato. Patrol followed patrol, but still there was nothing to be seen except the same islands and the same tranquil blue sea and the same lug-sailed fishing boats going about their business as if the war had never existed. Only on two occasions during those nine weeks did we so much as catch a glimpse of the enemy.

The first of these fleeting contacts took place about the middle of May, on the second day of a patrol out of Sebenico, as we headed westwards from Curzola towards the fortress island of Lissa. The island's main peak, Mount Hum, was visible on the horizon as *U8* puttered along at eight knots. A brisk north-easterly breeze was blowing from landward, tail end of the previous day's bora, and here and there the waves were white-capped with foam. I was down below, off watch but engaged in the endless form-filling required of any k.u.k. warship's captain: leave dockets, sick returns, damage reports and so forth. I was roused from these tedious labours by a shout down the conning-tower hatch:

"Aeroplane in sight—120 degrees port!"

I dropped my pen and scrambled up the steel ladder. In those days no one bothered unduly about aircraft, either friendly or hostile, but any diversion was welcome from filling in forms in a petrol-saturated atmosphere at thirty-five degrees Celsius. Béla Meszáros was perched atop the conning tower while Grigorović steered the boat from the wheel platform behind it. My Second Officer was examining the distant shape through his binoculars. I could see that it was a biplane, and heading towards us, but because of the sun I could not make out exactly what it might be. He lowered his glasses.

"It's one of ours—a Lohner by the looks of it."

It was indeed a two-seater Lohner flying boat of the Imperial and Royal Navy Flying Service. As it drew nearer I could make out the red-and-white stripes beneath its long, curved wings and see the reflection from the waves gleaming on the underside of its beautiful varnished mahogany hull. The machine circled us about two hundred metres up, then swooped down and flew past us, the observer waving to us as they roared by. Something fell from the aeroplane, trailing a long tail of orange ribbons behind it. Within a minute or so the message canister had been deftly fished out of the water with a boat-hook and brought to me. I unscrewed the lid of the aluminium tube and pulled out the message inside. I have it here now, pasted into my album, yellowed with the passage of seventy years but still recognisable as a sheet torn out of a naval signal notepad. It bears a scrawled pencil message:

11:27 a.m.

Large French cruiser, *Ernest Renan* class, landing men S. side of Cazza Island 11:15 a.m. Good luck and good hunting!

Freglt Novotny

L35

I showed the message to Meszáros. He whistled appreciatively.

"How far is Cazza do you reckon, Meszáros?"

"About twelve miles south-south-east I should think."

"How much fuel have we got?"

"The tanks are two-thirds full."

"Good, then what are we waiting for? Helmsman, steer course 170 degrees!"

U8 made a tight half-turn to port, then I pushed the handle of the engine-room telegraph to "Full Speed Ahead." Soon we were racing southwards at nearly twelve knots, throwing up an impressive stern wave as *U8* surged forward like an enraged sea snake in that curious bow-up, stern-down posture of a Holland boat at full speed. If the engines bore up for the next hour or so we might give the French Navy reason to remember us.

We raced along like this for the next half-hour. The temperature below decks rose to a point where the engine-room watch, naked and streaming with sweat, had to be dragged up into the air every five minutes to avoid being baked alive. The whole boat vibrated to the frantic screaming of the engines as our little craft crashed through the waves towards Cazza Island: a small, rocky islet about fifteen miles west of Lagosto, uninhabited, I remembered, except during the sardine-fishing season, when a small wooden jetty and a stone shed served as a collection point for the catch. Except for the engineers, the entire crew of *U8* was now on deck, partly because of the unbearable heat below and partly in order to trim the boat so that we could squeeze the last fraction of a knot out of her. All of us were straining our eyes on the horizon to southwards, urging the boat forward by the exercise of collective will-power and each hoping to be the first to catch sight of the enemy. Suddenly a shout went up simultaneously from fifteen throats:

"Smoke on the horizon, dead ahead!"

Yes, there was a thin darkening of the sky on the horizon about seven miles ahead of us. I yelled down the engine-room hatchway, straining to be heard above the din and wincing in the ferocious blast of heat.

"Lehár, how long can we keep this up? We can see his smoke on the horizon now!"

A voice came back from out of the pit of hell:

"Should be all right Herr Kommandant—the exhaust manifolds are glowing yellow but the engines haven't missed a beat so far."

"Good work—there'll be a Signum Laudis in this for you if we get him."

"Herr Kommandant, stuff the Signum Laudis and buy me a few buckets of cold Budweisser instead!"

I was already working out my plans for closing with the Frenchman. Our underwater speed was about eight knots and we might get to within six thousand metres before having to dive, if his look-outs were not too alert and *U8* kept bows-on. That meant twenty minutes to half an hour of running submerged. We might just do it . . . But it was not to be. No sooner had the cruiser's topmasts and funnel caps come into sight than thick smoke began to pour out of the sternmost pair of funnels. Despite our speed the horizon ceased to creep down the masts, then began to creep back up again. They were under way, damn and blast them, steaming away from us! By the time that Cazza came in sight the mast-tops were disappearing below the horizon. Pursuit, I knew, would be fruitless: French armoured cruisers might look ungainly, but they could idle along at seventeen knots without any trouble at all.

"Curse them, Meszáros, do you think they saw us?"

"No, but I suppose they must have seen the flying boat turn northwards and put two and two together. Since Trapp sank the *Léon Gambetta* they must be heading for the horizon every time they think that a U-Boat's got within a hundred miles of them."

The only question now was at what point I could decently break off the futile chase, now that the French cruiser's mast-tops had almost entirely vanished. However, the matter was soon decided for me: there was a series of jolts and a frenzied clanking from down below, and *U8* lost way so abruptly that some of the men standing on deck were nearly catapulted into the sea. The starboard engine had broken its crankshaft.

"Well," I said, "that seems to put an end to that. Anyway, we've come all this way at the cost of serious damage to one of the Emperor's engines, so we might as well see what brought our French friends to this insignificant island. Steer course to land at the jetty!"

Sidling along on one engine, the boat bumped up alongside the dilapidated wooden jetty in the little bay on the south side of Cazza. We kept a sharp look-out for booby traps in the water round about, but we need not have worried, for when Béla Meszáros and the two sailors of our landing party returned half an hour later from their search of the island they were carrying nothing more warlike than half a loaf of bread, a couple of empty winebottles and the end of a sausage: the remnants of the French raiding party's al fresco lunch.

"Looks as if they were just over for a few hours' jolly," said Meszáros as he climbed down from the jetty on to *U8*'s deck. "All that we found of any military significance was this." He handed me a French matelot's cap, complete with red pompon and MARINE NATIONALE cap ribbon. Inside was written MÉCANICIEN IIÈME CLASSE E. DUCELLIER. We bore this trophy with us back to Sebenico, and that same evening the wireless station broadcast a message in French: "Would Mécanicien Second Class E. Ducellier of the French Navy care to collect his cap from the Imperial and Royal Naval Lost Property Office, Sebenico. NB: the article must be claimed in person, and a small fee will be charged."

Apart from this incident, there was nothing much else to report during these weeks: a drifting mine or two exploded by rifle fire; a few searches of coastal trabaccolos that seemed to be behaving suspiciously; and a number of reports from coastal stations of French submarines—invariably dolphins or floating wreckage. By the third week of May I began to detect the first signs that the men might be getting bored. After all, we were all volunteers and, whatever our tribulations with *U8,* we all had great faith in submarines as a potential weapon of war. It must sound crazy now, but there was a very real fear abroad among us that the war might end before we had been given a chance to show what we could do. The newspapers told us that our armies and the Germans were pushing the Russians out of

Poland while the Western Front was holding firm, so it seemed altogether likely that a peace might be concluded before the year was out; after which, presumably, it would be back to another half-century of polishing brightwork and watching the seniority lists. I sometimes fancied that I overheard post-war conversations in the Naval Casino:

"Who's that fellow at the table over there?"

"What, the grey-haired Linienschiffsleutnant? Oh, that's Prohaska, poor devil."

"What did he do in the war?"

"Not much really: he was in U-Boats."

"In what?"

"Submarines. Surely you remember—those silly little boats that kept breaking down and having to be towed back in."

"Oh yes—I'd almost forgotten. Crackpot idea. I always said they were a waste of money."

However, it seemed as though our prospects were looking up on the afternoon of 23 May. *U8* was in dock at Sebenico having the port engine repaired when a signal was hoisted for all captains to assemble aboard S.M.S. *Maria Theresa*. When we got to the Admiral's state room we found him in a sombre mood.

"Gentlemen, it is with great sorrow and disgust that I have to announce to you this afternoon that our one-time friend and ally, the Kingdom of Italy, has treacherously elected to join the ranks of our enemies. Accordingly, as from 4 p.m. today, Italy and the Dual Monarchy will be in a state of war. I think that I need not remind those present that our duty as officers of the Noble House of Austria is to exert ourselves to the utmost to punish Italy for her base and perfidious conduct. Now, gentlemen, detailed orders will be given to you shortly. In the mean time, let us raise three loud hurrahs for our Emperor and King Franz Josef the First!"

"Well my brave lads," I said to the crew of *U8* as I announced the news, "it looks as if we may see some action after all."

But I was mistaken: the next six weeks brought no variation in the usual business of patrolling the coast and islands. In vain might we scan the horizon for a sign of Italy's powerful fleet: they were in harbour, and clearly had every intention of staying there. Our only encounter with the Regia Marina came one hot afternoon in mid-June when we sighted a *PN*-class torpedo-boat about fifteen miles west of Premuda Island. The Italian was on a favourable bearing, so we submerged and began to manoeuvre for an attack. But the sea was mirror-calm: the very worst conditions for us since our periscope wave was visible for miles. In the event I think that we did quite well to get within two thousand metres of him before he spotted us and turned to run for home, firing a few retreating shots at our periscope. Disappointment set in once more and morale began to sag. Young and strong as we were, the hardships of U-Boat life—the constant patrols, the endless, wearying breakdowns and our more or less permanent state of petrol poisoning—were beginning to tell on us. A suspicion was gaining ground that the war had ended and they had forgotten to tell us, so that we would spend the rest of our lives buzzing around the Dalmatian islands until we came to pensionable age or *U8*'s bottom fell out. Also it was galling to us that we were apparently to have no opportunity of repaying the Italians for their treachery. This must sound idiotic to you now, in the last decades of the twentieth century when everyone expects governments to be liars and thieves or worse. But we were an innocent lot, we Europeans of 1915. Hundreds of thousands of your young men flocked to the recruiting stations because Germany had broken a solemn undertaking to respect the neutrality of Belgium; so perhaps, seventy years on, you will not deny their Austrian contemporaries a little idealism as well. The way you see things now may be right, but that was not how it seemed to us at the time.

5

FIRST BLOOD

IT LOOKED LIKE BEING YET ANOTHER FRUITLESS PATROL, that evening of 5 July as *U8* purred her way out of Sebenico harbour, past the fortress of San Antonio, out through the swept channel between the minefields and round the southern tip of Zlarin Island towards the open sea. Within an hour the peaks of the Dinara range were sinking out of sight astern, while to westward the great orange ball of the sun was already half-way below the horizon. We were outside the belt of islands now: ahead of us lay only the waves and the enemy—perhaps.

It had all begun that morning as *U8* lay alongside the harbour guardship *Maria Theresa,* recharging her batteries from the old cruiser's generators. I had been supervising on deck as the heavy cables were passed down through the torpedo-loading hatch in the foredeck. I was particularly concerned to see that the boat was properly ventilated: sailing aboard a petrol-driven submarine was dangerous enough without having to run the risk of hydrogen explosions as well. Suddenly a voice called from above:

"Schiffsleutnant Prohaska?" I looked up to see a messenger leaning over the rail.

"Herr Schiffsleutnant, the Sea Area Defence Commander presents his compliments and would like to see you in his cabin as soon as possible."

I scrambled up the ladder and made my way astern to the captain's state rooms, where I was received by the Sebenico regional defence commander, Kontreadmiral Hayek. He bade me sit down.

"Herr Schiffsleutnant, I have called you here as a matter of urgency because I have a special mission to entrust to you and your crew: a mission which may have a profound influence on the course of the Monarchy's war with Italy."

"I have the honour to report, Herr Admiral, that you may count upon us aboard *U8* to give of our utmost in the service of our Emperor and Fatherland."

"Splendid—I never doubted it for a moment. Now Prohaska, let's get down to business. Do you know the island of Prvastak?"

Yes, I did know Prvastak. My acquaintance with it was small, but then there was not a great deal to be acquainted with: just a tiny, arid, sun-bleached islet a couple of hundred metres across, jutting out of the sea about twenty miles south of Cape Planka and ten miles north-west of Lissa. Its only claims to attention were a lighthouse, extinguished for the duration, and a small fort used as a look-out post and telegraph station. We had sailed past it once or twice in the past few weeks and exchanged waves with its garrison: a half-company of Polish Landsturm reservists who divided their time between cursing every stone of their barren prison and thanking the blessed wartime fates that had sent them there, well out of reach of Serbs and Cossacks.

"Yes," I answered, "I know the island and landed there once when I was a cadet. We have been near it a couple of times lately but it's really no concern of ours: it's an Army garrison and they are supplied by a tender from Lissa. I can't say that I envy them, marooned out there."

"Indeed not, Prohaska, and you might have even less cause to envy them in a day or so's time. Now, I don't want to go too deeply into matters of espionage, but the fact is that our Intelligence Service has a first-class informant working in Italy, in the port of Ancona to be precise. And he has managed to provide us with advance warning that the Italians are preparing a coup de main against Prvastak. In fact, as we sit here now, an entire Alpini battalion is being embarked aboard an armed liner at Ancona in order to carry out a surprise attack on the island, either tonight or to-morrow night. Our agent's report is so detailed that it even describes the tactics to be employed. It appears that the Italians will take advantage of there being no moon by having the liner stand a mile or two out to sea and using its lifeboats to row their troops up to the island from all directions. The idea, presumably, is that the garrison will suddenly find themselves attacked on all sides by overwhelming numbers of men and will surrender without a fight."

"Yes, Herr Admiral. But permit me to ask why the Italians should wish to take Prvastak? The place is so tiny that I doubt whether a battalion of soldiers would find enough room to stand on it all at once."

"As you observe, Herr Schiffsleutnant, the island is insignificant in itself. But think of the propaganda value if the Monarchy wakes up tomorrow morning to find that one of its islands has been occupied by the enemy, at no cost to themselves. And there is also the fact that Prvastak is quite an important look-out post. If we lose it there will be a large gap in our defences between Lissa and the southern end of the Incoronata Islands. No, Prohaska: they must not succeed. But if you get there first with your submarine we may well be able to turn the tables on them and score a propaganda triumph of our own."

"I see—you wish *U8* to go there, lie in wait for the armed liner and sink it. Well, I see no problem there . . ."

"Yes, Herr Schiffsleutnant, but I fear that the task is not quite that simple. As I have said, we know what will happen in remarkable detail, but we are still not sure exactly *when* it will happen. And this is where the problem lies. Tell me now: how long can that little boat of yours lie submerged? I'm afraid that I grew up in the sailing navy and don't know a great deal about U-Boats."

"Hmmm, that depends," I replied. "We ourselves have never lain on the bottom for more than three or four hours at a time. But the captains of the other Holland-type boats think that it might be possible to stay down for about twelve hours before the air becomes too foul to breathe."

"Damn, that's far too short. You would have to stay down for sixteen hours at least: sunrise to sunset."

"Might I enquire, Herr Admiral, why *U8* can't cruise off Prvastak tonight and, if nothing happens, return here at daybreak, then go out again tomorrow night? After all, the distance is only thirty-five miles or so."

"No, Prohaska, no good I'm afraid. The garrison on Prvastak have reported seeing Italian aircraft—even an airship—overhead every couple of hours these past few days. If the Italians so much as suspected that a U-Boat was in the area they would simply call off the whole operation. No, if it isn't to be tonight you will have to submerge near the island and wait until tomorrow night. And just how you are to do that if, as you say . . ."

"Herr Admiral, I have an idea. Why could we not take some flasks of oxygen along with us? The last supply boat from Pola brought us something called an 'air-purifying cartridge' which is supposed to clean carbon dioxide out of the air. With that and extra oxygen we might manage to stay under from sunrise to sunset tomorrow. There is only one problem though."

"What is that, then?"

"To my certain knowledge the only compressed oxygen in Sebenico is that used for welding in the repair yard, which is not under the Navy's control. If we could requisition some . . ."

Hayek sat down at his desk and began to scribble furiously.

"Here, Prohaska, take this note with you to the repair-yard superintendent. Requisition as many flasks of oxygen as you need. Take it from him at rifle-point if you have to. But think of me and try to avoid shooting him if you can, even though he's only a louse-ridden civilian. I shall attend personally to the paperwork and the subsequent row. This is no time for bureaucratic hair-splitting: not when enemy troop-ships are out there just asking to be sunk."

So the oxygen flasks—eight in all—were duly requisitioned from the protesting repair-yard superintendent, who swore that we were no better than common looters who deserved to be court-martialled and hanged. Battery-charging was completed, petrol and lubricating oil were pumped aboard and *U8* was made ready to put to sea. The men knew that something was afoot, but seemed to expect little to come of it after the disappointments of the past few weeks. As for myself, for reasons of security I was determined to say nothing about the purpose of the operation until we were well on our way. But in my heart of hearts I too expected that we were merely in for another futile couple of days at sea, looking for an enemy who was not there.

We made our preparations, though: as conscientiously as if we expected something to come of them. The two torpedoes in the tubes were hauled back and the depth regulators were set for four metres. The wisdom in those days was that the deeper a torpedo exploded the more damage it would do, and I had ample reason to be sceptical of the destructive power of Austro-Hungarian torpedoes. There was nothing wrong with the design of the 45cm Whitehead torpedo itself—at least, it was no more mechanically unreliable than other torpedoes of its day. The trouble was rather that meagre naval budgets and our Austrian genius for half-solutions had equipped it with a warhead that was not quite large enough to be sure of sinking its target. The result was to be a long list of enemy vessels (including three of my own victims) hit but not sunk by Austrian torpedoes. Bear that in mind, and also the strong possibility that torpedoes might misfire or not hit at all, and you will understand why I had the depth regulators in the two reserve torpedoes set to four metres as well. This decision was to have serious consequences for me later on. By early evening *U8* was ready to put to sea. It remained only for our Diving Coxswain Steinhüber to embark rations for the patrol: three days' supply for nineteen men.

Like everything else aboard *U8,* messing arrangements were exceedingly primitive. We were better off than our sister boats in having a petrol stove built into the superstructure, but the rations themselves consisted largely of hard tack and canned meat. The hard tack—zwieback in its Austrian version—will surely need no introduction to anyone who has read anything at all of the literature of seafaring from about the time of the Phoenicians until the 1950s. It was a square, coarse-textured, greyish-brown slab of cement-like hardness and complete tastelessness, perforated with a pattern of sixty-four holes, so that (we said) dockyard workers would not be tempted to steal it for roofing their houses. In fact, the chief difference between zwieback and a roof-tile was that the latter would have about twice as much flavour. It seemed also that it was near-imperishable. At any rate, the previous month we had been issued with a bag stamped "1867," the year after Admiral Tegethoff had destroyed the Italian fleet off Lissa.

In all fairness though I must add that it was neither worse nor better than biscuit baked a few weeks previously.

Canned rations were a different matter, for here we had to reckon with the offerings of the Manfred Weiss AG of Budapest, by appointment Purveyors of Dead Dogs and Assorted Carrion to the Imperial, Royal and Catholic Sea Forces of His Apostolic Majesty. Everyone had his own favourite horror story about Manfred Weiss tinned food. One man would swear that his cousin in the k.u.k. Danube Flotilla had seen them stretching nets across the river during the spring floods in order to strain out carcasses for the factory's cauldrons. Then another would cap this by swearing that he had met a convalescent in Prague who had seen trainloads of dead horses trundling back towards Budapest from the Galician battlefields. But whatever the truth of these picturesque tales, there is no question that during the war Herr Weiss and his fellow-criminals did very well out of supplying us with food that was invariably rather nasty and frequently putrid.

However, it seemed that on this particular evening we were to enjoy two unexpected treats, for the Tauchführer and his assistants came down the gangway from the *Maria Theresa* bearing not only a sweet-smelling sack of freshly baked bread, still hot from the cruiser's ovens, but also two wooden cases of some sort of tinned stew in addition to the usual ration of Manfred Weiss canned meat. But there was no time to examine it closely: we would have to set sail in a few minutes if we wished to arrive at Prvastak just after sunset. Nor was I too bothered to observe the health regulation that freshly baked bread should be allowed to stand for a day before being served out. The air inside *U8* was humid in the extreme, and we knew only too well that fresh bread would soon go mouldy.

Our first night's patrol off Prvastak was certainly not encouraging. *U8* cruised at three knots on one engine from nightfall until dawn, but for all our staring into the darkness not a thing did we see: only heard a faint, distant buzzing at about 1 a.m. that might or might not have been a motor boat. By 3 a.m. I concluded that our search was futile. The Italian liner was certainly not going to show up now, with less than an hour to go before first light, so as officer of the watch I gave orders to get a hot meal ready for the crew. If we were going to be submerged for the whole of the coming day this was our last chance, especially as it might be too rough for cooking when we came up again. The cauldron was duly brought up and the petrol stove was lit inside its box in the fore part of the conning-tower base: a neat contrivance since the stove casing was completely light-tight, and therefore no danger to us on the surface at night. I ordered the duty cook, Elektromatrose Zaccarini, to open the cans of stew and save the Manfred Weiss canned meat for tomorrow, when we might not be able to cook.

As the packing cases were broken open, Béla Meszáros came up on deck for a smoke, complaining that it was too hot to sleep down below. We stood there together in a darkness illuminated only by the summer stars, which seemed to shine with double brilliance on these moonless nights.

"Well, Meszáros," I said, looking towards the eastern horizon, "not much time left now. It's going to start getting light before long. It appears that our Italian friends decided against visiting us tonight after all. I wonder whether we'll have better luck tomorrow night."

"I doubt it, Herr Kommandant," he said, puffing at his pipe. "When you get an intelligence report as detailed as the one from that bugger in Ancona, then it's a gulden to a copper farthing that he made it all up so that he could go on drawing his stipend to spend on champagne and trollops. In fact I wouldn't be a bit surprised if he was getting money from the Italians as well for feeding us drivel like that. I remember once . . ."

"Herr Kommandant, by your leave . . ." It was Zaccarini.

"Yes?"

"Obediently report, Herr Kommandant, that this stew, it is gone off." He held out the first of the opened tins for my inspection. It was impossible to see more than a dim shape in the darkness, but my nose told me that something was wrong: a powerful stench of decaying vegetable matter already pervaded the night air about us. I clambered down the conning-tower ladder into the brightly lit control room, carrying the tin. The label bore only the legend K.U.K. KONSERVENFABRIK NO. 109 HOF-MOKL UND SAWICKI. RZESZÓW, UL. JATKOWA. The tin contained an evil-smelling, brownish mass of shredded cabbage leaves. So, what we had here was tinned bigos. Those of you who have travelled in Central Europe will perhaps already be acquainted with this item of Polish cuisine: a sort of soup-stew made from sauerkraut, fresh cabbage, slices of sausage and diced meat. At its best, made with venison and mushrooms and red wine, it is a noble dish, traditionally served to hunters in the forest on New Year's Day. Even now its aroma brings back my youth and the smell of gunsmoke, the crunch of frozen pine-needles underfoot and the piercing blue of a Polish winter sky. At its more frequent worst, though, it is a sordid con-coction: the staple of shabby small-town cafés and institutional canteens, a sour, unwholesome slop compounded of the scrapings of last winter's cabbage barrel boiled up with all manner of dubious odds and ends of meat. It was clear that on this occasion we were faced with something closer to the latter version than to the former. Still, rations were rations, and if we didn't eat this it would be half a loaf of bread, then zwieback and Manfred Weiss tinned meat the next day. So I went back on deck to exercise positive leadership.

"Nonsense, Zaccarini; the stew is perfectly all right—just a bit too much pickled cabbage, that's all. Sauerkraut always smells like a country privy when you take the lid off the barrel. Just empty it into the cauldron and it'll be all right when you warm it up."

Despite the darkness I could sense that Zaccarini did not believe me. "For God's sake, man—if you don't eat this it's nothing warm for the next twenty-four hours at least. I quite appreciate that you southerners don't care overmuch for cabbage and knödeln, but you know that the boat's messing allowance won't run to pasta and risotto more than three days a week. So look lively there and get cooking—it'll be getting light soon."

Half an hour later all off-watch hands had been mustered on deck and served out with a steaming bowl of cabbage stew and half a loaf of bread. As I had predicted, the smell had largely dispersed during cooking, leaving something that, if not exactly appetising, was still quite edible. Only Béla Meszáros demurred, eating half a bowlful, then pausing.

"Holy Mother of God, what do they put in this Pole-fodder? I've eaten better horse-dung in my time," with which he discreetly emptied the remainder of his portion over the side. I was tempted to enquire in precisely what circumstances Fregattenleutnant Béla, Freiherr von Meszáros de Nagymeszárosháza had eaten horse manure, but there were other things to attend to. Dinner had to be taken to the on-watch hands, and then, once they had finished and were about to go off watch (it was nearly 4 a.m. now), half of their wine ration was served out to them. Because of the growing wartime shortages the daily half-litre wine tot had some months ago ceased to be issued in the surface fleet. But resourcefulness and my Second Officer's friendship with a merchant in Novigrad had served to keep it going aboard *U8*. So a quarter-litre of sweet Curzola wine was decanted into each man's tin mug, just as the first glimmer of grey appeared to eastward. Then it was diving stations in preparation for what had every prospect of being an exceedingly long and tiresome day on the bottom.

Diving was by now a precise and well-practised drill aboard *U8*, one in which—like all our evolutions—we prided ourselves on the quietness and calm with which orders were given and carried out, so unlike the raucous bellowing and crashing of gunnery drills aboard the battleships. First the ventilator cowls were unshipped from the conning tower and the air vents closed, then the surface motors were stopped and their exhaust valves were shut, after which all hatches but the one in the conning tower were closed and locked. As the electric fans were run to clear any remaining petrol vapour, the Detailführers reported back to me:

"Both surface engines shut down."

"Both E-motors ready."

"Battery state eighty-eight per cent charged; electrolyte level normal in all cells."

"All compressed-air flasks full."

"Diving tanks clear."

"Diving rudder clear."

Then at last the final report from the Tauchführer himself: "Clear to dive, Herr Kommandant."

I stood in the conning-tower hatchway and looked up at the stars fading in the sky above. As always, the thought crept into my mind: Will I ever see them again? And as always, it was promptly evicted by a swelling sense of the sheer adventure of it all. I pulled the hatch shut on top of me, locked it and applied the safety clips, then made my way down into the control room. I nodded to Steinhüber behind the diving-rudder wheel, then took up my position beside the periscope.

"Slow ahead, starboard E-motor." A soft, humming whine came from aft. "Flood main diving tank and forward trim tank A. Dive to forty metres at inclination five degrees."

The bottom here, two miles west of Prvastak, was marked as level sand at forty metres' depth. However, in those days before echo-sounders it was still wise to take things gently: the bottom might not be all sand and forty metres was not far short of *U8*'s maximum diving depth. The electric motor was duly stopped at thirty-five metres and the boat was left to sink slowly under her own weight. However, after a minute or so of watching the depth gauge and some pumping-out of water (the boat was by now compressing enough to lose displacement a little) we felt a gentle, grinding shudder as the boat's chin rubbed against sand or fine gravel. Having found bottom it was a matter of letting her swing round into the current, and then flooding the after trim tank to bring the stern of the boat down. At the end of the manoeuvre *U8* was sitting almost perfectly upright and with only three or so degrees of slope from bow to stern. The duty watch was stood down while I pencilled in the running log entry, made my rounds and handed over to Béla Meszáros. These duties completed, not having slept for the past twenty hours, I took my blanket and lay down thankfully to sleep on top of the small-arms locker. It was 4:33 a.m. on Tuesday 6 July.

For all my fagged-out state, I did not sleep soundly. I never suffered much from claustrophobia, even in the tightest corners of my submarining career, but soon I began to dream that I was being suffocated: buried alive under tons of blankets while my entrails were gnawed by rats. The lid of the small-arms locker seemed to have been replaced by a sheet of corrugated iron studded with hobnails. I half-slept, half-woke as hideous dreams tormented my brain: the set-to with the cannibals in New Guinea; the man I had seen quartered in China back in 1905 . . . At last I awoke to a full awareness of the dreadful things happening inside me. I pulled aside the blanket to look bleary-eyed at an abdomen so distended that my trouser-belt seemed in danger of cutting me in half. Damn it! I thought, it was that cursed bigos and the fresh bread. Zaccarini was right after all—we should have tipped the lot overboard. Then I looked about me, and saw that I was not the only member of the crew to be in a state of acute digestive upset. All around me men were groaning and holding their bellies while up in the fore-ends the off-watch who should have been sleeping soundly were tossing and turning and moaning softly to themselves.

Nor was it only the eye that took in this mournful scene: very soon the nose and the ear began to register the fact that our thirty-metre steel tube at the bottom of the sea now contained nineteen men suffering from severe flatulence. In fact, not to put too fine a point upon it, the air, already stale after three hours on the bottom, was rapidly becoming unbreathable. We were no shrinking violets, we U-Boat sailors. Foul air was part of our daily existence and anyway, most of us were already inured to dreadful smells by childhoods spent on farms in Slovakia or in the reeking alleyways of the Adriatic ports. But this stench was different both in kind and degree from anything that we had ever experienced before: a rank, vile, penetrating stink that could neither be ignored nor got used to. By 8 a.m. and the next watch it had made breathing a torture and exhalation a bliss—its joy tempered only by the knowledge that one would soon have to breathe in again.

My Second Officer took me aside for a whispered conference. He had eaten less of the stew than the rest of us, but he was still evidently in great discomfort.

"For God's sake, what are we going to do? Another hour of this and we'll all have suffocated. I just hope that I live to get my hands on those chiselling bastards of food contractors. Only save me a lid from a tin so that I can pursue Hofmokl and Sawicki to the ends of the Earth and cut their livers out with it. We've got to go up for air."

"Yes Meszáros, it's all very well for you to say that, but we're under strict orders to stay submerged for all of today. We both know that the Italians won't turn up, but if we break cover they'll blame us for scaring them away. I know those Army sons of bitches over there on the island, and believe me they'll telegraph back to Sebenico at once if we so much as show the tip of our periscope."

Meszáros thought for a few moments. "We could use the compressor to exchange the air in the boat for the compressed air in the flasks. That way we could change all the air in about a quarter of an hour."

So we did it, using up precious amperes to run the compressor and juggling the flask reduction valves to keep the pressure constant. In the end, though, the results were disappointing: our own generation of gas by now far outstripped the capacity of the compressor, the air filter and the oxygen flasks combined. Something would have to be done, and soon, for not only was there the danger of our simply suffocating; there was also the risk of our home-produced gases combining with the petrol vapour always present inside the boat to produce heaven alone knew what explosive mixtures, just waiting for an electrical spark to detonate them. It would be a fine joke, I thought, if we who were lying in wait to sink Italian liners merely succeeded in blowing ourselves to kingdom come. I looked at my wristwatch and groaned: thirteen more hours of this. No, let them court-martial me if they pleased: death itself was preferable to even another five minutes of inhaling this pestilential stink. Eighteen pairs of desperate eyes were looking at me, pleading silently. So far as I was concerned at that moment, the Emperor and the entire General Staff could be sitting up there watching and I still wouldn't care a fig.

"All hands to surfacing stations! We're going up for air."

The drill for surfacing was much the same as that for diving, only in reverse. First the fragile stern was lifted off the sea bed, one of the

E-motors was run just fast enough to give us steering way, then we began to nose our way towards the daylight. It was 8:27 a.m. In so far as I had a plan it was to get to the surface, open the hatches and run the ventilator fans as fast as possible to air the boat through, then dive again in the slender hope that we had not been observed. However, this was a war, flatulence or no flatulence, and a certain caution was necessary. So I took *U8* to periscope depth first for a quick look around before surfacing.

As I applied my eye to the rubber-cupped eyepiece of the Goertz periscope, my first thought was that the instrument had sprung a leak and flooded while we lay on the bottom. For instead of the expected circle of light, bisected by the dark blue sea horizon, there was only a blank disc of solid iron-grey, fogged by a swirling brownish cloud rather like sepia dribbled into a tumbler of water. Puzzled, I took my eye away, wiped the eyepiece with my cuff, then peered into it again. What I saw made me catch my breath in astonishment. The darkness was in fact a solid wall of grey, moving slowly from right to left across my field of vision: a wall perforated by portholes, then by the lower gun casemates of a warship, the gun muzzles pointing out over our heads.

"Quick, clear both torpedoes to fire!" I fumbled with the magnification switch on the periscope to change the view from x2 to normal. The ship in front of us still more than filled the periscope lens, but I could see enough of it now to—yes, there could be no doubt about it with those two widely spaced funnels and the single, heavy mast in between: it was an Italian armoured cruiser, *Giuseppe Garibaldi* class—eight thousand tonnes of her, steaming along at a stately four or five knots a mere 250 metres or so ahead of *U8*'s bows. I prepared to get the periscope down before they saw us. But as I did so the ship was blotted out in boiling clouds of orange flame, followed by that same swirling brownish fog that I had seen before. There was no noise of course, but the periscope still vibrated in my hands from the shock waves. The Italians were firing broadsides right over our heads, and it could only have been the smoke—and perhaps concentration on their gunnery—which had prevented their look-outs from spotting our periscope already.

I must say that the crew responded superbly, despite the foul atmosphere and their own state of digestive turmoil. The little vessel was a frenzy of ordered activity for thirty seconds or so as the torpedo-tube safety catches were unlocked and the bow cap was cranked open. Then the call, "Both torpedoes ready to fire," came to me from the fore-ends, where Torpedomeister Gorša crouched facing me between the tubes, one hand on each firing lever. An almost unbearable tension hung in the stinking air. I had already turned *U8* ninety degrees to port, to open the range a little and take us on a course parallel to our prey. Now I raised the attack periscope to take aim. My heart was pounding for fear that they would have seen us and veered away. But no—there she was, exactly where I had expected her to be: still steaming along at four knots and still magnificently unaware of our presence. I swung the periscope round for a quick tour d'horizon, and saw that two destroyers and a *Nino Bixio*-class scout cruiser were steaming on a parallel course, about six hundred metres eastward. All very professional, I thought to myself: that destroyer screen would have made it very difficult for us to get at the capital ship. What they had not taken into account though was the possibility that a U-Boat might simply bob up from the sea bed inside the screen. I also caught a glimpse of the reason for this force of ships, among which we had nearly surfaced. The lighthouse on Prvastak had already been reduced to rubble and smoke rose from the fort. As I watched they were blotted out by smoke and spray as another salvo of shells landed on the island.

But for the moment the fort could look after itself: there were more pressing matters at hand. My mind whirred with rapid calculations only practised before in mock attacks in the Fasana Channel. Say five knots: about 150 metres per minute. Torpedoes will take fifteen seconds to do three hundred metres—say twenty degrees deflection, with a five-second interval to space the torpedoes for maximum damage. It was almost too easy.

"Helmsman, turn seventy degrees starboard." The single electric motor was now pushing *U8* along just fast enough to give us steerage way. A last look through the periscope, and a sudden, split-second pang of regret at despatching death to this mighty vessel and six hundred men. The little red and white signal bat raised in my left hand. Then the order:

"Starboard torpedo, fire!" A hiss of compressed air from the fore-ends, a sudden pitch of the boat as the first trimming party rushed forward. A violent eruption of bubbles in front of the periscope, then the call back: "Starboard torpedo away!"

"Port torpedo, fire!" Another pitch of the boat and rush of boots on the deck. This time we were nearly unlucky: I suddenly saw a disc of bright blue sky as the bows pitched upwards, then, as they came down again, a glimpse of the torpedo's greasy brown back breaking surface before its regulator took it back to the preset depth. But somehow the boat stayed underwater, despite the loss of trim. We went down to ten metres and I took her back on to a parallel course. All that remained now was to hold our breath and count. You could have heard a feather fall to the deck in those interminable seconds. Ten, eleven, twelve—then the boat was shaken by two short, dull, heavy crashes, each rather as if some large piece of furniture had toppled over in the next room. A loud "Hurrah!" rang through the little boat's reeking atmosphere. So we had done it after all. Not five minutes before we had been a boat full of ailing wretches, forced to the surface half-way through a futile mission in circumstances which would make us a laughing-stock throughout the fleet. But now the fortunes of war had given us our chance and we had seized it. We steered parallel to our victim's last course at about one and a half knots while the crew sweated and cursed the two reserve torpedoes into the now empty tubes. That task completed, I turned *U8* in a tight half-circle to port to take us back on our tracks. It was now time for a look at our target, in case another torpedo should be needed to finish her off.

One look through the periscope was enough to tell me that no coup de grâce would be required. It was barely five minutes since our torpedoes had struck, but our victim was already well advanced in her death agony: still moving through the water, but by now heeled so far over to port that the waves were lapping over the edges of the decks. The heavy guns had been trained out to starboard in an effort to control the list, but to no avail. The water round about was already dotted with flotsam and the heads of swimming men, while the starboard rail, now high above the water, was clotted with a swarming mass of white-clad figures. As I watched, the list increased suddenly. The tip of the yardarm touched the water and fragments of the crowd at the rail broke away to skid helplessly across the decks into the sea. We heard it quite distinctly through the water: a long, dull rumble like distant thunder as the cruiser's bulkheads gave way and engines, boilers and hundreds of tonnes of bunker coal crashed from one side of the hull to the other. The ship hung there for a few seconds. A great blast of steam and soot erupted from the after funnel. Then she capsized: rolled clean over in less time than it takes me to tell you of it, and lay rocking from side to side as men scrambled across the dull red, weed-covered bottom. One of the two massive propellers was still turning as she sank. I watched with a sort of detached, horrified fascination as its blades smashed into a knot of swimmers struggling in the water, churning the sea to a pink-stained froth. There was a last glimpse of the rudder and of a man clinging to it, shaking his fist at our periscope. Then it was over: nothing left but boiling mounds of air bubbles, overturned boats, floating debris and the countless heads of swimmers like so many footballs bobbing on the surface beneath a thin haze of smoke and coal-dust. I glanced at my watch. It was 8:39 a.m.: not quite eight minutes since I had given the order to fire.

It had all happened too quickly for me to be left with anything but a curious, numb, hollow feeling inside, as if the terrible drama that I had just witnessed was really nothing to do with me. Fregattenleutnant Meszáros shook my hand and congratulated me on behalf of the crew, then I raised the periscope cautiously for one last look before we left the scene. The first thing that I saw was one of the Italian destroyers slowly edging its way in among the mass of swimming survivors, lowering its boats and throwing out scrambling nets as it did so. The thought of firing our two remaining torpedoes entered my mind, but was quickly dismissed. For one thing, sending a torpedo to explode among men struggling in the water was not my idea of waging war, even though the Italian ship was still in every way a legitimate target. For another, both torpedoes had been set to run at four metres, too deep to hit a shallow-draught vessel like a destroyer. No, I thought, let us now go and look for that scout cruiser if we want to spend the next quarter-hour as profitably as the last.

I swung the periscope around to bear ahead—and stood paralysed with horror. I can still see it now as if it were yesterday, every rust-streak etched permanently on some photographic plate of the mind: the lethal sharp stem and creaming bow wave of a destroyer, heading straight for us at full speed and already almost on top of us! My recollection of the next few seconds is fragmentary. I remember screaming, "Go deep!" and seeing the circle of light suddenly turn to bubble-streaked green as the periscope head dipped below the waves. Then came a fearful, booming concussion from above as the boat was knocked over to port and the periscope was whipped from my grasp and spun around so violently that one of the handles caught me a blow on the cheekbone which sent me flying across the control room to crash against a bulkhead. The electric lamps flickered and dimmed, then went out altogether as I lost consciousness.

6

AN AUSTRIAN TRIUMPH

I BELIEVE THAT I WAS UNCONSCIOUS for only a minute or so following our close scrape with the Italian destroyer. By the time I came round, though, things had settled down: the motors were humming steadily, the electric lamps were burning brightly once more and the crew, though tense and white-faced, were all at their posts as if nothing in particular had happened. Béla Meszáros was kneeling beside me, lifting me up and mopping blood from the cut on my cheekbone where the periscope handle had struck me. As I looked around I saw that the attack periscope had not only been knocked out of perpendicular but also driven downwards with such violence that the end was embedded a good twenty centimetres in the steel plates of the deck. I also saw that water was splashing down from the conning tower in a thin, ragged cascade, rather as if someone had left a bath running in the flat above.

"Are you all right?" Meszáros enquired.

"Yes, quite all right thank you—just a bit winded, and my head aches."

He looked up towards the conning-tower opening. "How are we up there, Maschinenmeister?"

Lehár's voice replied from above. "Not too bad, Herr Leutnant. A few seams have opened and the periscopes are done for, but the leaks aren't anything that the bilge pumps can't deal with."

So we had survived our little encounter, it seemed: battered but still afloat. However, we still had to evade our pursuers, no doubt thirsting for our blood after the sinking of their cruiser, then make our way back to harbour. This was not going to be an easy task, for we were now blind while submerged, and thus entirely dependent on a highly unreliable magnetic compass. The only course open to us was to run at about four knots on a south-easterly bearing at a depth of twenty metres. The idea was that this direction would lead us into deeper water—thus lessening our chances of running straight into a rock—while at the same time shaking off the Italian destroyers as they came within range of the fortress guns on Lissa. We heard the sound of propellers overhead several times during the next hour or so, and four or five small bombs exploded near by, but after a while the noises of pursuit died away.

We now began to feel a pressing need for fresh air. The excitements of the past couple of hours had distracted our thoughts from the fearful stench that had led us to surface in the first place, almost underneath the Italian armoured cruiser of recent memory. But now that the hue and cry was past, our sick condition and the foul atmosphere began to claim our attention once more. About 11 a.m. I gave the order to surface; my Second Officer perched inside the crumpled conning tower so that he could take a quick look around through the bull's eyes and tell us whether it was safe to come up. It was, but the conning-tower hatch had been jammed shut by the collision, so that we had to climb out through the engine-room hatch. Lord, did fresh sea air ever taste sweeter than it did that morning, after four or more hours spent marinading in sewer gases?

By the look of it though we had certainly had a close escape from drowning. The navigation periscope had been sheared clean off, the attack periscope was twisted over to one side like a bent pin stuck in a cork and the top of the conning tower was badly mangled, the streamlined outer casing deeply gashed on either side of the pressure-proof tower inside, which was itself crumpled and bent. It was only later that the significance of these two gashes became apparent: when I was rummaging around inside the ruined outer casing and found a lump of phosphor bronze, smoothly rounded on two sides and jagged on the third. This, I realised, was the tip of one of the destroyer's propeller blades, which had evidently come within millimetres of shearing the pressure hull open like a tin can and sending us all to the bottom. The conning tower's buckled plates were also streaked with red.

Meszáros scraped some of this off with his fingernail, sniffed it reflectively and remarked, "Well, I'll say this for the Italian Navy: their bottom paint is certainly a lot better than the rubbish that we have to use."

Damage aside, however, it became clear as we looked about us that the magnetic compass had let us down even more lamentably than usual. We had tried to steer due south-east to take us south of Lissa Island, but here we were now, well to the north of it. Also a breeze was beginning to blow up from the north-east: not a very welcome development for a damaged submarine whose only source of air for the engines was an open hatch about a metre above the water-line. It was this that decided me on heading north-east for Lesina rather than trying to go south for Lissa town. At least the long, mountainous bulk of Lesina Island to northward would give us some shelter from the weather. So the petrol engines were started up and we got under way, steering by shouting helm orders down through the engine-room hatch.

After about twenty minutes a cry went up: "Two-funnelled vessel—forty degrees starboard!" It turned out to be the old torpedo boat *Tb XIV,* commanded by a very young Linienschiffsleutnant who hailed us enthusiastically as they drew near.

"Ahoy there *U8* and congratulations—I take it that the Italian cruiser was your work!"

"Then you take it correctly. But how did you get to hear about it so soon?"

"The fort on Prvastak telegraphed Lissa. We were patrolling in the Neretva Channel when we got a wireless message to head for Prvastak to pick up wreckage before the wind blows it out to sea. But are you all right? You look pretty battered I must say. Do you need a tow into port?"

"An Italian destroyer rammed us just after the sinking, but it looks worse than it is. Don't trouble about the tow, though. We can get to Lesina under our own power, and anyway I want you to find out who that cruiser was. She was a *Garibaldi* class, but beyond that I didn't recognise her."

"Very good then, but permit us to use our wireless to let Lesina know that you're on your way."

We parted company with *Tb XIV* and resumed our journey. Before long though I began to wish that I had taken up the offer of a tow, as our port engine coughed and spluttered to a halt and refused all inducements to start again. The fuel line was disconnected, and when some petrol had been decanted into a jam jar it was found to be thick with flakes of the silvery-grey paint used to coat the inside of the fuel tanks. It seemed that the shock of the torpedo explosions had shaken it loose to clog up the fuel filters and the carburettor. So it was forward again on one engine. It was nearly 1 p.m. before we threaded our way between the easternmost of the San Clemente Islands and came within sight of our destination.

I had certainly been right about the shelter afforded by the mountains of Lesina. A blustery north-easter might be blowing out at sea, but here on the south side of the island hardly an olive leaf stirred. The white limestone town of Lesina lay ahead of us in the shimmering midday heat, dozing beneath the Venetian fortress squatting on the vine-clad mountain behind. It was all just as drowsily beautiful as I remembered it from my pre-war boating days, with the cicadas chirping among the cypress trees and the scent of lavender drifting down from the red-earthed fields terraced into the hillsides. Normally at this time of day scarcely a lizard would be stirring. But it looked as if today would be an exception.

"Well, Meszáros," I said, lowering my binoculars, "news certainly travels fast in these parts. It looks as if a reception committee has been formed already. Tell the men to get into their best whites. We'd better make a show of it from our side as well."

A guard of honour about eighty-strong could be seen forming up on the palm-shaded steamer quayside a mile or so ahead. The sun glittered on the instruments of a military band, and before long the familiar strains of the "Prinz Eugen March" came drifting out to us across the sapphire waves. Aboard *U8,* though, every minute that passed found us in a less and less fit condition for a triumphal entry, for it had become clear in the

past half-hour or so that the two villains Hofmokl and Sawicki had not finished with us yet: in addition to extreme flatulence their cabbage stew also
produced violent stomach pains and looseness of the bowels. Members
of the crew had been coming up on deck for some time past in acute distress, seeking privacy, and my own abdomen was beginning to churn most
unpleasantly as I struggled into my best white tunic down below. Still,
duty is duty, and the least ill-looking part of the crew were duly lined up
on deck as we neared the steamer quay, crawling along on the E-motors
since the starboard petrol engine had also died just as we entered the harbour. By this time the band was pounding through the "Radetzky March"
and we were close enough to examine the guard of honour. The men, I
could see, were middle-aged Landsturmers with ample paunches beneath
their old-fashioned blue tunics. At their head, sabre already drawn, was a
tall, burly-looking officer with a large moustache. By his side stood a bent,
much-bemedalled old creature wearing a general's white tunic and a
patent-leather shako of a type seldom seen since the turn of the century,
the kind that we used to call "the substitute brain." Near by stood a man
with a black cloth over his head, cranking the handle of a cine camera.

My own lads, I noted with pride, were managing to stand erect with
their heads up even if they were by now (like myself and Meszáros) grinding their teeth in an effort to contain themselves. The band struck up the
"Gott Erhalte" and Meszáros and I, on top of the battered conning tower,
stood to attention and saluted. Steinhüber was standing with his head out
of the engine-room hatchway, directing the helmsman and the engines as
we edged up to the quayside. The guard of honour had presented arms and
the flags had been dipped in honour of the Imperial anthem. We might just
do it, I thought . . . But then, disaster—the band launched into a second
verse of the "Gott Erhalte." We were in a desperate state by now, all of us.
My men hesitated, but in the end it was more than flesh, blood and writh-
ing intestines could bear. One man moved, then like a wall collapsing they
all sprang on to the quayside and rushed through the ranks of the guard
of honour into the *giardino publicco*: a narrow strip of shrubs and palm trees

between the quayside and the waterfront houses. I stood at the salute just long enough to observe the look of apoplectic horror on the face of the large officer on the quayside, then I too was obliged to leap across like a chamois, closely followed by my Second Officer, and rush into the bushes to join my crew. Meanwhile the band, splendid fellows, continued playing the Imperial anthem as if nothing had happened.

It was incumbent upon me of course as commander to button up my trousers first and emerge from the shrubbery as nonchalantly as I could to face the volcanic wrath of the officer commanding the guard of honour, a Colonel of the Fortress Artillery. So I marched up to him and saluted, dressed in my white tunic to be sure, but also sporting a day's growth of stubble, a good deal of general U-Boat grime, a black eye and a blood-stained pad of gauze stuck on to my face with adhesive plaster. The crowd of bystanders and the soldiers of the guard were perfectly silent, clearly relishing the imminent set-to between the land and naval forces of His Imperial Majesty. I noticed that the cameraman had tactfully ceased recording these scenes and had emerged from under his cloth to watch the fun. It was like the hush that must once have fallen over the Pola amphitheatre as the lion exchanged introductions with the criminal.

I imagine that the lion used to eye his meal up and down for a while much as the Herr Oberst and his aged companion eyed me. Then the silence was broken by a "Rührt euch!" which must have cracked windows on the other side of the harbour, followed by a loud clattering as the butts of eighty rifles grounded on the limestone pavement. The Oberst still had his sabre drawn, and for a moment I thought he was going to run me through with it. But he lowered it, clearly after an intense inward struggle, and I, still with my hand raised to my cap peak in salute, made my report:

"Herr Oberst, I have the honour to report the arrival of His Imperial Majesty's submarine *U8* after a victorious patrol. I present myself at your service as commanding officer of the vessel: k.u.k. Linienschiffsleutnant Otto Prohaska." He glared at me with a look of smouldering hatred, his neck bulging over the collar of his tunic. Meanwhile the aged General behind him mumbled something to himself in a rusty undertone amid which I could make out only comforting phrases like "court martial," "mutiny" and "firing squad."

The silence was broken at last by the Oberst. He sheathed his sabre and advanced upon me, thrusting his beefy red face down to mine since he was a good head taller than myself. His eyeballs were bloodshot with rage and bulged like those of an ox undergoing a heart attack.

"Herr Linienschiffsleutnant . . ."

"Herr Oberst?"

"Herr Linienschiffsleutnant," he repeated in the tone of a man struggling to hold himself in check, "I wish you to know that in all the thirty-four years in which I have served in the Imperial and Royal Army I have *never,* never do you hear me NEVER witnessed such a loathsome, swinish, despicable, utterly treasonable show of disrespect for the House of Austria and the banners of our Fatherland." He thrust his face even further into mine, so that I had to move back slightly. "I go further, Herr Linienschiffsleutnant: I will venture to say that if you were an officer of the k.u.k. Armee, and not of this rabble of pox-infested derelicts that calls itself a navy, you would even now be marching away in irons, in the middle of a prisoner's escort, on your way to court martial and execution for mutiny while your herd of swine of a crew would be heading for fifteen years' hard labour in the dampest, most tubercular prison-fortress in the whole of Austria." He paused; "Tell me, Herr Linienschiffsleutnant, what have I just said?"

"I obediently report that Herr Oberst was kind enough to remark that if I were an officer of the k.u.k. Armee I would now be marching off in irons towards a court martial and execution while my crew, whom the Herr Oberst was gracious enough to describe as a herd of swine, would be on their way to fifteen years' hard labour in the dampest and most tubercular prison-fortress in all Austria."

He nodded curtly: "Also gut! Anyway, Perkaska or whatever you call yourself, I am afraid that the *K.u.K. Dienstreglement* forbids me to deal with you and your gang of degenerates except through the proper service channels, which in this instance means the Naval District Commander at Sebenico. You may rest assured that he will receive a detailed report of this disgraceful incident by nightfall if I have to swim there with it myself, holding it between my teeth. But it appears that for the time being at any rate I shall be denied the pleasure of reading that you have been cashiered and shot for treason." He then turned to the old man behind him, snapped to attention and saluted:

"Herr General, would you care to add anything to what I have just said?"

I later learnt that this venerable figure was Infantry General Baron Svetozar von Martini, one of Austria's oldest surviving officers, who had served as a subaltern under Radetzky at Novara in 1849. He now lived in retirement on Lesina and had happened to be inspecting the local garrison when news had been received of our impending arrival. It appeared that his remarks on this occasion would be of a general nature:

"Atrocious," he creaked, "mutinous Italian dogs the sailors each and every one of them—Venetian scum—Radetzky should have strung the lot of them up in 1849; would have saved us no end of trouble. Should have left them to Haynau, I say. Sound sort of chap, old Haynau—knew only three words of Italian: 'hang,' 'shoot' and 'rabble.' Czechs aren't much better either if you ask me." He fell to muttering inaudibly once more, and the Oberst turned to me.

"Very good, Herr Linienschiffsleutnant, that will be all for now. Be so good as to collect your dirty rabble of dockside rats from the bushes where they have been skulking and wait here until such time as the Navy is able to send a prison ship to collect you all. If there is anything that you require in the mean time you have only to walk up there to the fortress, where there is a naval wireless post. I believe that they have a water tap, but I may be wrong about that. I bid you good-day." He bowed slightly, clicking his heels and tapping two fingers to the peak of his shako in ironic salute. "Servitore."

With that he turned and gave the order for the guard of honour and the band to form up and march back to their barracks. The crashing of their nailed boots soon died away in the stone-flagged streets, and we were left on the quayside, alone but for a motley crowd of idlers, children, black-clad fisherwomen and stray dogs. My crew were emerging sheepishly from the shrubs of the *giardino publicco* and endeavouring, as far as their condition would allow, to moor *U8* to the bollards of the steamer quay. Zaccarini came up to me, eyes downcast.

"Sorry, Herr Kommandant, but our stomachs . . . If we stay out there we fill our trousers for sure . . ."

"Don't worry, Zaccarini, I understand. Lot of blustering Army buffoons holed up here for the duration, well out of danger. You won't come to any harm, I promise you. Oh, and all of you—" The men paused in their work with the mooring warps and turned towards me "—all of you, thank you for what you did out there this morning. The Devil take spit and polish and stamping on parade grounds: that was real discipline, the way you all behaved. You were magnificent, every one of you."

They smiled, and resumed their work, but really they were too weak to do very much, and it was only with the help of some local fishermen and their wives that we finally got the boat tied up safely.

While I was lending a hand with these operations I heard a voice behind me.

"Linienschiffsleutnant Prohaska?"

I turned around: it was a young Army captain in the uniform of an Uhlan regiment. I saw that he carried his right arm awkwardly and that the hand was encased in a black leather glove. He extended his left hand for me to shake.

"Rudolf Straussler, 3rd Uhlan Regiment 'Erzherzog Karl.' I'm here on general duties for a while after getting part of my hand blown off in Galicia last autumn. I saw the set-to with our beloved garrison commander, so I've come to apologise on behalf of the k.u.k. Armee and offer our congratulations on your recent feat of arms."

"Thank you, but please don't apologise: I fully realise that we sailors are not too popular with some of the land forces especially when we save their garrisons from being blown to bits by Italian cruisers."

"Quite so. We call the old fool 'Mortadella,' you know half pig and half donkey. But you have to bear in mind that Herr Oberst von Friedauer is none too well disposed towards naval officers in the first place."

I stiffened at the mention of this name: "Oh, why ever not?"

"It's his wife, I believe. I've got a younger brother in the U-Boat Service up at Pola—Toni Straussler: I believe you know him—and he keeps me informed on all the local gossip. Old Friedauer's wife is quite a cracker—Hungarian I believe—and she certainly likes sailors. It seems she's been giving nocturnal riding lessons to half the naval officer corps during his absence."

I thought it wisest to keep quiet at this point, so I merely murmured in feigned surprise.

"Not that there's anything new in that though, by all accounts. They say that just before the war she nearly got one of your U-Boat fellows thrown out of the officer corps in disgrace."

"Really, how was that?"

"Oh, the usual: old Friedauer came home unexpectedly and the other chap left through the bedroom window minus his trousers."

"But surely, that's not a reason for cashiering people. If it was, then the entire k.u.k. officer corps would have been sacked years ago, except for the pederasts."

"No, but in this case the fellow was challenged to a duel by the Herr Oberst, then failed to turn up on the morning—another Hungarian I believe, called Meszakos or something. Anyway, there was all hell to pay after that: Court of Honour and the lot. He was sentenced to be publicly cashiered—epaulettes torn off and so forth. But he was lucky."

"In what way?"

The court met on Friday, but wasn't to confirm sentence until the following Monday. And the Sunday was the day our late Heir Apparent and his wife paid their visit to Sarajevo. They were short of experienced submarine officers at mobilisation, so the Emperor gave a special dispensation for him to stay on until the end of the war, on condition that he was broken down a rank and never allowed to rise above it."

So, I thought to myself, at last we had solved the mystery of why my Second Officer had that faint dark ring on the cuff of his jacket. I had heard nothing about all this of course, having been on my way to the China Station the previous June. Broken to Fregattenleutnant in disgrace though, and sentenced to be kept at that rank until the end of his career: no wonder he sometimes seemed a little bitter about things. Really the wonder was that he was such a competent and determined officer in spite of it all.

"Anyway," Straussler concluded, "it's good to have met you in person. My brother mentioned you in several of his letters and said that you were a pretty good sort. Now, as regards more practical matters, I myself will arrange medical attention and quarters for you and your men. I'm Adjutant at a hospital here and come under the Medical Corps for disciplinary purposes, so even though Friedauer is my nominal commanding officer there isn't a great deal that he can do to stop me offering hospitality. Expect a lorry here to pick you all up in about half an hour. And once again, my apologies for what happened."

We stayed at Lesina for the next two days, putting up at Straussler's hospital until a torpedo-boat arrived to tow *U8* back to Sebenico. Our triumphal entry there went a great deal better than the earlier disaster at Lesina. Bands played, bunting fluttered everywhere, and the crews of all the ships in the harbour lined the rails and the rigging to raise their caps in a "Dreimal Hoch!" which must have been heard in Pola itself. I had spent the stay at Lesina writing up my action report, which set out the circumstances of the sinking of the Italian cruiser in minute detail. I finished it just as we were about to enter Sebenico: ". . . I have the honour most obediently to submit the foregoing report, written by the undersigned k.u.k. Linienschiffsleutnant Prohaska, at sea between Lesina and Sebenico,

8 July 1915." This was handed to the local Sea Area Defence Commander on arrival so that copies could be sent to Pola and Vienna.

The next afternoon I was woken from a much-needed nap on my bunk aboard the *Maria Theresa* to be called to the Sea Defence Commander's office. Kontreadmiral Hayek was waiting for me, accompanied this time by a very suave-looking Naval Staff officer who was introduced to me as Vizeadmiral the Baron von Liebkowitz. It appeared that he had been flown down from Pola by seaplane that very day for the purpose of talking with me . . . Hayek started the interview.

"Well, Herr Schiffsleutnant, our warmest congratulations to you on your splendid feat of arms off Prvastak on the 6th. I am glad to see that my confidence in you and in your boat was so dramatically vindicated. It was a lesson that the Italians will not forget in a hurry. I think we can safely assume that, after this devastating blow, there will be no more such attempts at bombarding the coasts of the Fatherland."

"Thank you Herr Admiral, but really it was my crew who made it all possible: I merely aimed the torpedoes."

The Vizeadmiral entered the conversation at this point.

"Really, my dear Prohaska, your modesty is most becoming—as is the complete candour with which you have written up your action report." (He lifted the corner of a sheaf of typescript lying on the desk.) "The k.u.k. Kriegsmarine and our Imperial and Royal Monarchy have every reason to be proud of you, and I wholeheartedly endorse what the Kontreadmiral had to say concerning the effect of this sinking on the course of the war. In fact, Herr Schiffsleutnant," (he leant towards me) "in fact, we are putting you forward for the Maria Theresa."

Now, I was never a very keen medal-collector, but I don't mind admitting that my heart missed a beat or two at this piece of news. Decorations were decorations, but the Knight's Cross of the Military Order of Maria Theresa was something else altogether: the highest military honour that Old Austria had to bestow. Like your Victoria Cross, it was an insignificant-looking little thing. But unlike your Victoria Cross it was handed out in the tiniest numbers—no more than seventy or so in the entire World War, I believe. To become a Maria-Theresien Ritter was the ultimate, golden dream of every cadet at every military academy in the Danubian Monarchy, a distinction far more alluring than becoming a Field Marshal or Chief of the Naval Staff. I protested my unworthiness to receive such an honour, but weakly, since my breath had been taken clean away by the prospect. Liebkowitz waved my protests aside.

"However, Prohaska . . . However, there are certain points in your report of the action that require—how shall I say? some attention before the citation goes forward to the Imperial Chamberlain's Department . . ."

"And what are those, if I might enquire, Herr Vizeadmiral? Do you wish me to expand upon anything that I wrote?"

"No, no, not in the least, Prohaska my dear fellow. But you must appreciate that as a Staff officer I have to look at your report from a slightly different perspective than that of a fighting seaman. You see, I now have to prepare a recommendation for you to receive the highest military honour that our Emperor can bestow and, well . . . not to mince words . . . your report is—how can I put it?—well, rather inappropriate in certain respects."

"But Herr Vizeadmiral, I wrote only the truth about the circumstances of the action."

"Yes, yes, I'm sure that you did . . . but, well, this business of the tinned cabbage stew, and the—er—flatulence forcing you to the surface, then that stupid affair in Lesina. For God's sake man, try to see it from my point of view: Austria wants her heroes to be knights in shining armour, not grease-covered mechanics in a stinking tube who bob up from the bottom and assassinate passing ships. It simply isn't what Maria-Theresien Ritters are supposed to be!"

"I take your point, Herr Vizeadmiral, but we did sink the enemy cruiser after all, whatever the circumstances."

"Yes, I know you did. But look what you've written here: 'While preparing to surface, sighted the enemy cruiser about 200 metres ahead.' I mean, what sort of admission is that for me to release to the press? You seem to be saying that you let the Italian pass over you and that it was only by the merest luck that you sank him."

"With respect Herr Vizeadmiral, I would not say that it was pure luck, but luck played a large part in it as it does in all submarine actions. With a maximum underwater speed of eight knots, sustainable for about an hour, we can hardly go hunting our victims. We have to wait for them to come to us."

"So in other words it was pure chance."

"No, Herr Vizeadmiral: we are not a floating mine. But chance provided us with an opportunity, and the skill and excellent discipline of *U8*'s crew allowed us to take advantage of it."

The interview ended with my refusing, as politely as I could, to redraft my report in a more heroic vein. I was told in conclusion that I would be required to wait behind for an interview with a war correspondent, one Hauptmann Schlusser, who had travelled to Sebenico specially at the behest of the k.u.k. War Ministry.

Herr Schlusser (his military rank was evidently of very recent date) was a journalist attached to the War Ministry's propaganda department. His pre-war career had been that of a hack—albeit a highly paid one—kept on a secret government retainer to peddle the Foreign Ministry line in the *Reichspost* and the other august independent newspapers of Old Austria. It was clearly a trade admirably suited to his natural talents as a lickspittle, a bully and liar, and now the war had given him unbounded opportunities for furthering his career by manufacturing atrocity stories about the enemies of Austria and Germany. I have a vague recollection in fact that he might have been the original perpetrator of the horrid little couplet "Jeder Schuss ein Russ, jeder Stoss ein Franzos"—"A Russian for every shot, a Frenchman for every bayonet-thrust." He was a slim, neat, reptilian young man in his early thirties, with the restless eyes and the furtive, fake-genial manner of an inveterate schemer. All in all I think that I have rarely taken such an instant dislike to any creature as I did to Herr "Hauptmann" Schlusser, though I found it hard to say exactly why.

"Herr Schiffsleutnant," he began, "let me congratulate you on having struck such a devastating blow against the basest of the Monarchy's enemies." He addressed me with the familiar "du" customary amongst Austrian career officers, and this annoyed me considerably, coming from a mere pre-war Einjähriger, promoted no doubt for political services. I made a point of addressing him as "Sie" in reply.

"Thank you, but permit me to say —" He cut me off in mid-sentence:

"Not a bad morning's work anyway, Prohaska old man. You certainly sent a good few Italians to take an early-morning swim. I see here that we've just had a telegram from the Marine Oberkommando: it seems that the Italian minister in Zurich has been whining to our representative asking whether we picked up any survivors from their ship, which was the *Bartolomeo Colleoni:* 7,980 tonnes and about 730 crew, of whom fifty-three are still missing."

I brightened at hearing this. "Fifty-three men do you say? Thank God for that—I thought it would be far more."

I sensed immediately that I had said the wrong thing: Schlusser's smiling bonhomie remained, but had taken on a note of menace, like that of a police interrogator or a particularly nasty prosecuting counsel.

"Herr Schiffsleutnant, forgive me, but do I understand you as saying you are *glad* that only fifty-three Italians drowned? If you'll pardon my saying so, that seems an odd thing for an officer to be saying in the middle of a world war. Some might even consider it subversive of military morale and discipline."

I bristled at this: either this man was a blackguard, or more probably a Viennese coffee-house warrior who had never seen men die. But I tried to remain courteous.

"Quite the contrary, Herr Hauptmann: I think you misunderstand the rules of war and the code of the Imperial and Royal officer corps. We were attacking the ship, not the men inside her. When the ship was sunk her crew had lost any further capacity to harm us, so I was only too happy to see them being picked up. We would gladly have rescued survivors ourselves, but for the fact that our boat is too small and that there were other enemy warships in the area."

"So you have no personal hatred for the Italians, then?"

"None whatever. Why should I? We are pursuing a quarrel between governments, not a war of racial extermination, and as far as I am concerned the Italians are merely fellow-seafarers who happen to be acting on behalf of a government opposed to my own. They were Austria's allies this time last year, and for all I know they may be our allies again this time next year."

Schlusser gave me a meaningful look and scribbled something in his notepad.

"Yes, Herr Schiffsleutnant, I see we disagree on that point. But to get back to your report, it appears that panic broke out aboard the Italian ship as soon as your torpedoes struck, and that because of the vessel's shoddy construction it sank in less than five minutes . . ."

"I beg your pardon, but my report said no such thing. I saw the vessel some five minutes after the torpedoes had struck, and it is true that the crew were abandoning ship. But if I had been her captain I would certainly have ordered them to do so before that. The decks were already underwater and the ship was on the point of capsizing. As for construction, I do know a little about Italian warships, and I must point out that the *Garibaldi* class were always reckoned to be well designed and soundly constructed vessels."

"Oh, I see—so soundly constructed that it sank in five minutes."

"If you would trouble to read my report, *Herr* Schlusser, you would see that *U8*'s torpedoes struck at 8:31 a.m. and that the ship sank at 8:39, which I make to be eight minutes. As to the speed with which the *Bartolomeo Colleoni* sank, I can only say that warships built fifteen to twenty years ago are not nearly as well subdivided as those of today, while the destructive power of torpedoes has increased a great deal. Our German allies found that out last year when Weddigen sank three British armoured cruisers in an hour. And when Trapp sank the *Léon Gambetta* in April she went down in about nine minutes even though she was three times the displacement of the *Colleoni*."

I could see that Schlusser was in a spiteful mood by now. Geniality was cast aside as his voice reassumed its natural sneering tone.

"So, Herr Schiffsleutnant, I suppose you will tell me next that the Italian Navy are heroes and not a cowardly rabble of Latin degenerates?"

"Herr Schlusser," I replied, "that is a very interesting statement. You will doubtless be aware that His Imperial Majesty's armed forces contain a large number of ethnic Italians—including two of my own crew—who have fought these past ten months with impeccable gallantry. Do I understand you as saying then that all the Italians in the Kingdom of Italy are miserable cowards while ours are brave fellows? And if this is so, does an Italian change from a hero into a coward and vice versa when he crosses the border at Cividale? I ask these philosophical questions, Herr Schlusser, because I am only a simple sailor and look to educated literary gentlemen like yourself to provide me with guidance."

It was clear by now that the interview was over. We took our leave of one another as politely as we could and I made my way back to my cabin. Well, I thought to myself, there was a thing: the *Bartolomeo Colleoni*. My own feet had trodden her decks back in 1909 when we were visiting La Spezia, and now I had sent those spotless expanses of scrubbed teak and immaculate grey paintwork to be eaten by worms and pitted by rust on the floor of the Adriatic. Anyway, at least most of her crew had got clear. Somehow I wished that Herr Schlusser and his fellow hurrah patriots could have seen those poor devils being smashed to pulp by the propeller: perhaps it would make them think differently. But then again (I thought), perhaps not . . .

We spent another two days at Sebenico, until an order arrived for *U8* to proceed to Pola for repairs. The engines were in a bad state, so it was arranged that we would be towed by the battleship *Erzerhog Albrecht* on her way back from Cattaro. So there we were in the bright July sunshine, making our way up the Adriatic coast: ten thousand tonnes towing 240 tonnes, like a motor launch towing a wooden duck; the majestic, vastly expensive mountain of steel towing one of the ludicrous little vessels that were driving it and its kind from the seas. The battleship's officers were very courteous to Meszáros and myself of course, all the more so since I had served aboard her myself some years before and knew many of them. We were obliged to spend almost the entire voyage in the wardroom, being plied with drinks and made to tell and retell the story of our exploit. Beneath their hospitality and interest though I could detect a distinct note of envy. I well remember how the *Albrecht*'s officers used to lean on the stern rail watching our boat yawing to and fro at the end of the towing hawser, like some corpulent tunny mackerel on the end of a fisherman's line—and how the unvarying question was: "Do you mean to tell us you went out in that?"

We made yet another triumphal entry to Pola: more bands and bunting and cap-waving. Then *U8* was placed in the hands of the k.u.k. See Arsenal for repairs and a much-needed general overhaul while the crew were sent off on a month's leave. But not before we had all been decorated on the quarterdeck of the fleet flagship *Viribus Unitis*. The crew all received the bronze Gallantry Medal, with Lehár and Steinhüber getting the silver medal in recognition of their efforts. As for myself though, the previous day I had been called to see the U-Boat Station Commander, the Ritter von Thierry. He had been in a serious mood.

"Herr Schiffsleutnant, I am afraid that I have some bad news for you. Your recommendation for the Knight's Cross of the Order of Maria Theresa was turned down. You will be getting the Leopold Order instead."

"Might I enquire why, Herr Kommandant? I am not fighting for medals, so it doesn't matter a great deal to me one way or the other, but I would still like to know what happened."

"Well, Prohaska, it seems that in the first place it was because the Naval Commander-in-Chief set his face against it. Admiral Haus was very annoyed that you didn't go for the destroyers after you had sunk the Italian cruiser. He said that you had two torpedoes left, so why didn't you use them? I gather that 'back-garden hunter' was one of the more polite expressions used. Then there was that silly business at Lesina—though I must admit that it amused me a great deal to think of those pompous Army idiots fuming and spluttering—and the way that you refused to rewrite your action report. But what really clinched matters was your interview with that scab of a journalist."

"Why, was it published?"

"No, but only after strenuous efforts on the part of the Marine Ober-kommando. It seems that his article implied that sympathy for the Italians was widespread among officers from the non-German nationalities, and he had found out that your mother had an Italian name. Of course, that really put the cat among the pigeons with Haus. In future, my dear Prohaska, my advice to you is to be very, very careful what you say to bilge-rats like Herr Schlusser. Anyway, my condolences about the Maria Theresa."

"Herr Kommandant, it's nothing: it matters no more to me than a slice of cold boiled potato or a ten-Haller postage stamp."

Thierry smiled and walked across to me. He picked something up from his desk in passing, licked it and stuck it to the breast of my jacket. It was a ten-Haller postage stamp.

"Excellent fellow, Prohaska—that's the spirit I want in my officers. A true U-Boat man would exchange all the medals in Vienna for a dry pair of socks."

The evening after our decoration we were entertained to dinner aboard the fleet flagship, Béla Meszáros and I. As a creature officially devoid of honour, poor Béla had not received a medal, was not invited and was not supposed to have been there. But I got him in none the less, and a good time was had by all those present. It came to the drinking of toasts, and to our turn to propose one. I have never been much good at that sort of thing, and while I was thinking about it my Second Officer stood up, glass in hand. I had only to look at his smile to see that something dreadful was coming.

"Meine Herren, Kamaraden, I give you a toast—to the Italian armoured cruiser *Bartolomeo Colleoni* . . ." I winced inwardly: consternation was visible on the faces all about me "to the Italian cruiser *Bartolomeo Colleoni:* the only ship in history to have been sunk by flatulence!"

7

An Interlude
(which may be disregarded by those who wish to get on with the story)

THE TOWN WITHOUT A NAME

I SUSPECT THAT BY NOW, like my young friend Kevin Scully, many of you will be wondering how on earth it was that I, a Czech from the very centre of Central Europe, should have taken it into my head to make my career as a seafarer. So, by your leave, I shall now try to explain how this came about.

Despite the claims made by some of its natives when I was a boy, the small north Moravian town of Hirschendorf (pop. 9,000; district town on River Werba; ruins of 13th C. castle; inds.: brewing, sugar beet, sawmills; rly stn 2km; mkt day Weds; hotel ** Zum Weissen Löwe, 8 rms, restnt) was not the geographical dead centre of Europe. Numerous places used to lay claim to that distinction, and of course it all depends on how you define the extremities of the European continent. A couple of days ago, however, just for an experiment, I got Sister Elisabeth to procure me a school atlas, and found to my considerable surprise that if one takes Iceland as the westernmost point of Europe (which I suppose is just permissible) and Malta as its southernmost outpost, then the lines do in fact cross, if not at my birthplace, then not very far from it: about twenty kilometres to the north-east in what used to be Prussian Silesia.

In every other respect though, Hirschendorf in the last decade of the nineteenth century was the very image of provincial ordinariness: a small district town so exactly like hundreds of other small district towns scattered across that sprawling, decrepit, black-and-yellow Empire of ours that a traveller brought blindfolded to the town square would have needed to look twice before realising that he was in the Czech-speaking provinces and not in the South Tyrol or Croatia, or amid the rustling maize fields of the Banat. It was all there as per regulations: the ochre-painted, neo-Renaissance government offices on one side of the town square, looking at the nondescript little town hall on the other side across the Municipal Gardens, a railed-off rectangle of dusty shrubs surrounding a bandstand and a statue of Imperial General Prince Lazarus von Regnitz (1654–1731). On the lower side of the square, hiding behind a row of chestnut trees, was the two-storeyed hotel/restaurant/café with its miniature terrace, and on the upper side there was the local branch of the North Moravian Agricultural Credit Bank. In a street just off the square there loomed the great battleship-grey hulk of the parish church of St Johann Nepomuk, its twin copper onion-domes streaked pale green with generations of rain and pigeons, its interior a petrified riot of plaster saints gathering dust in a miasma of mouse-droppings and last week's incense. There were the usual shops: ironmongers, corn and seed merchants, chemists, drapers and so forth; and the usual public buildings: the barracks, the gendarmerie post, the Kronprinz Erzherzog Rudolphs Gymnasium and the Kaiserin Elisabeth Hospital. And there was the obligatory theatre on the Troppauergasse, where travelling repertory companies in moth-eaten costumes would put on the last season but two's offerings of the Viennese light operatic industry. At four hundred metres' radius from the town square the twin-storeyed stucco buildings gave way to one-storey houses of brick, while the streets turned from paving into cobbles. Four hundred metres further, and the dwellings had become wooden cottages, with sunflowers in the gardens and little orchards of whitewashed apple and plum trees. Then, quite suddenly, beyond the brewery and the sugar factory, the paved and gaslit streets of Austrian provincial civilisation petered out altogether amid the gently rolling, poppy-sprinkled fields of barley and rye, where larks twittered overhead and where the long, narrow Slav wagons lurched along rutted trackways towards the town on market-days.

An almost visible haze of respectable dowdiness hung over that little town in those far-off years of my childhood: the atmosphere of a place where nothing of any note had ever happened, or ever would happen until the Day of Judgement. Sometimes, even then, it seemed to me that our town square was nothing but an enlarged version of one of those German Renaissance clocks, where the chiming of the hours would bring out the local notables, wives on their arms, to raise their hats to other notables and their wives as they navigated their way among the heaps of horse-dung; where the stroke of midday would bring one of the town's two seedy fiacres clip-clopping up from the station to deposit a passenger at the hotel; and where each Sunday (April to October) would be marked by a military-band concert in the town square—clockwork musicians playing a music-box repertoire of marches and waltzes under the jerking baton of a moustachioed clockwork bandmaster.

Yet like so many appearances, this façade of immemorial peace was highly deceptive, because in the years of my childhood the town of Hirschendorf in fact harboured enough tensions and hatreds to devastate Europe a dozen times over and keep the world in wars to the end of time. Even without being blindfolded, many a traveller contrived to miss Hirschendorf altogether, because the odd fact is that for official purposes the place had no name. Its railway station was designated merely "Erzherzog Karls Nord-bahn, Oderberg Branch, Station No. 6," to the endless bewilderment and annoyance of the unwary.

This curious state of affairs arose not because Hirschendorf lacked a name, but rather because it had too many of them. As far as anyone could tell, the place had started life in the Middle Ages with the Czech name of Krnava, which German peasant settlers pronounced as "Kronau." So it had continued until the seventeenth century. But the Thirty Years War had almost wiped the town off the map, so when the local magnate, the Prince von Regnitz, rebuilt the place in the 1660s there was nothing to prevent him from renaming it "Hirschendorf," after the stag on his coat of arms, or from repopulating it with German craftsmen from Leipzig and Dresden. The local country people still called it Krnava, but who took any notice of them? German was the language of government and the liberal professions while Czech had sunk to the status of a peasant argot, barely capable of being written down. Thus the town continued unchallenged as Hirschendorf until the mid-nineteenth century: like all other towns in those parts, a German-speaking island set in a largely Czech-speaking country-side. But then came newspapers and schools and the railways. Coal-mines were sunk and steelworks were built in the Karvina Basin just over the hills. Czechs could read and write their own language now, and before long they had the vote as well. They wanted newspapers and schools and savings banks of their own, and seats on the town council, and jobs in government offices on an equal footing with German-speakers. Whatever its other faults, Old Austria was a fair-minded sort of state, so in the course of time most of these demands were granted. The result was that, while I was growing up, my home town was visibly ceasing to be the predominantly German town of Hirschendorf and was turning back into the largely Czech-speaking town of Krnava.

Human nature being what it is, this process was not at all welcome to the losing side. Every failed German stocking-knitter, driven out of business by the factories of Olmutz, tended to blame his misfortunes on the dirty, uncouth, prolific Slavs who were taking the town over before his eyes. Some even muttered that feeble old Austria was no longer firm enough to deal with its lower races, and began to look enviously over the border to Imperial Germany, where there was none of this spineless nonsense about equality of languages. Thus by the time that I appeared, things had come to such a pitch that every small-town issue, even the appointment of a lamp-lighter, was liable to be seen as part of an epic racial struggle between Germans and Slavs, and frequently ended up being debated in the Vienna Reichsrat. The government's chief concerns were public order and a quiet life, so Vienna's solution to such problems was usually to give in and appoint two lamp-lighters, one German and one Czech. The result was that by the late 1890s about a third of the town's population were public employees.

There was nothing particularly odd about this. The same play was being acted in dozens of towns and cities across the Danubian Monarchy in those last years of the nineteenth century—in every place where the old master races were being challenged by their former serfs. The script was the same, only the actors were different: Germans against Slovenes in Marburg; Poles against Ukrainians in Lemberg; Italians against Croats in Fiume. But what gave the national conflicts of Hirschendorf-Krnava-Kronau their peculiar, restless virulence was the presence of a joker in the pack in the shape of the local Polish community. Because as far as the latter were concerned, the town was neither Hirschendorf nor Krnava nor Kronau but a place called "Sadybsko."

I forget the exact grounds of the Polish territorial claim to my home town and its surrounding district. It was either that the area had once been held by the Cardinal Archbishop of Cracow as a fief of the King of Bohemia, or that the Bishop of Olmutz had once held it as a fief of the King of Poland. Anyway, it scarcely mattered: like most other such claims in Central Europe it could be argued either way, as best suited the arguer's purpose. The fact of the matter was that most of the town's Poles, though only about one in five of the population, regarded the place as Polish territory—that is to say, if and when a Polish state re-emerged. The Polish faction might be small, but what it lacked in numbers it made up for in noise. Without them, I suspect that the struggle between Germans and Czechs would eventually have been won by the latter. But every time it looked as if some quarrel had been settled—a public library, a street name, the appointment of a town clerk—the Poles could be relied upon to keep it going by siding with the losers. One might have thought that they would have made common cause with the Czechs, who were at least fellow-Slavs speaking a language closely related to their own. Not a bit of it: the Poles might have feared the Germans, but they despised the Czechs as peasant upstarts.

The railway had come to Hirschendorf about 1878, when a branch of the Erzherzog Karls Nordbahn was constructed between Oderberg and

Breslau, over the border in Germany. However, the town had to wait many years for a proper station because the railway company had gone bankrupt and been taken over by the government. In the end, though, when I was about eight years of age, the Imperial-Royal Railway Ministry in Vienna got around to replacing the wooden shed which had previously served as a station. A pattern-book Bahnhof, complete with glass canopies and a prefabricated Doric portico, was duly erected and got ready for its official opening by the Provincial Governor. My brother Anton and I were there in our sailor suits as the bands played and the red-and-white banners fluttered that hot summer's afternoon. Everything went beautifully until the Governor's wife cut the ribbon and the official party walked on to the platform, followed by the Mayor and the town council. I remember it well: even though I was a small child and could hardly see what was going on, I sensed that something awful had happened by the sudden silence of the crowd. There before us stood two freshly painted station-boards bearing the word HIRSCHENDORF. Mutterings were heard, then cries of "My Češi nechceme vaš 'Hirschendorf'!"—"We Czechs don't want your 'Hirschendorf'!" The upshot of it all was a walk-out by the Czech and Polish part of the town council, then a brawl in the station forecourt which ended with both German and Czech councillors being dragged off to continue their dispute from opposite cells in the gendarmerie station.

The next two years saw Vienna try every possible permutation of the names Hirschendorf and Krnava in an effort to soothe the feelings of its quarrelsome subjects: HIRSCHENDORF (KRNAVA); KRNAVA (HIRSCHENDORF); HIRSCHENDORF on the up-platform and KRNAVA on the down-platform; even the archaic KRONAU as a compromise. In the end, though, when some sort of grudging agreement had been secured for KRNAVA-HIRSCHENDORF on one platform and HIRSCHENDORF-KRNAVA on the other, the Poles announced that they would never accept anything less than SADYBSKO on *both* platforms. A demonstration was organised in front of the station one day in September 1896. The German and Czech factions turned up in force, and a riot developed which spread to the town square.

Soldiers from the barracks—Bosnian Muslims as it happened—were called in to restore order. A volley was fired over the heads of the brawling crowd, and an Italian waiter, who had been watching from an upstairs window of the hotel, fell dead on to the pavement. With this, Vienna gave up trying to name the station: from then until the end of the Monarchy both it and the town remained officially nameless.

So, you might ask, how did I fit into this dyspeptic little society? The answer to that, I fear, is that I fared rather worse than most, being the child of a Czech father and a Polish mother, but brought up to speak German.

My father, it must be said, was by today's standards a candidate for psychiatric treatment: a stiff, ill-tempered, pedantic, bullying martinet, liable to the most awe-inspiring rages about nothing much in particular. Yet the standards of today are not the standards of those days, and I must say that I remember him with a certain affection. Poor man: he had the misfortune to be endowed with great energy and powers of organisation in a country which had a deep distrust of both. For Old Austria was a state very much in the image of its aged ruler: tired, cautious, wearily pessimistic and convinced that change could only be for the worse. It followed naturally from this outlook that the people most dangerous to the state were those who wished to go about changing things: the class of person described disapprovingly as a "Frechdachs." My father fell squarely into this category, and really the only wonder is that he advanced as far as he did in the service of the Imperial-Royal Ministry of Posts and Telegraphs.

My father was born in 1854 in the village of Strchnice, near Kolin in eastern Bohemia, the son of a peasant family that was well enough off to send him to school. He became a telegraphic clerk in Troppau at fourteen, and by the time that I was born hard work and energy had raised him to the position of Deputy District Postmaster for the Hirschendorf region. I remember him as a stocky, square-set man with en-brosse hair and a heavy black moustache: a late-nineteenth-century Austrian provincial worthy in dress and deportment, but still very much a Czech peasant in appearance.

His manner can only be described as heavy: nothing made him laugh, and practically anything could drive him into a rage that would have caused a less sturdily built man to burst a blood vessel. Anton and I went in considerable fear of him. But I don't think, looking back on it, that we found this in any way odd. Fathers were supposed to be autocrats in those days, little replicas of the Emperor in the Hofburg, and I think we would have been embarrassed rather than anything else if he had romped with us on the hearthrug or tried to elicit confidences from us. Suffice it to say that, by his own lights and the standards of his day, he was a dutiful and conscientious father to us.

Not that he had a great deal to smile about, at least as far as his marriage was concerned. Even though it is speaking ill of the dead, I have to tell the truth about my mother, which is that she was one of the most vapid, ineffectual, utterly purposeless creatures that God ever permitted to use up oxygen.

Despite their name, my mother's family the Mazeottis were decayed Polish gentry from Cracow. The original Mazeotti had come from Italy sometime in the seventeenth century to build churches in southern Poland. He had married locally and stayed on to found a family; but apart from his name, he had bequeathed nothing to his descendants, who were Polish gentry-intelligentsia through and through: graceful enough in manner; good-looking in a pallid, fair-haired, blue-eyed sort of way; superficially cultivated; but otherwise about as devoid of energy, initiative or common sense as any family could be and still manage to perpetuate itself. The only member of my mother's family with any trace of the ability to get things done was my grandmother: Isabella Mazeotti From the House of the Krasnodębskis, as she used to style herself.

This fearful old harpy was the younger daughter of a Polish noble clan which had once oppressed its serfs over vast tracts of the Ukraine—that is, until the Polish gentry's abortive revolt against Austria in the summer of 1846, when her entire family had been butchered by their Ruthene peasants and their manor house (in fact a small palace, to judge from engravings) burnt down on top of them. Always quicker on the uptake than the rest of her relatives, Grandmother had shed her crinolines and escaped into the woods, where she would certainly have suffered a similar fate had she not been rescued by a Jewish tanner, who hid her beneath a heap of skins in his cart and smuggled her to the nearest town, where he kept her in his house until things had quietened down sufficiently for her to flee to Cracow. "Just imagine," she used to tell us as boys, her voice quivering with outrage, "just imagine it—a Polish noblewoman, bundled into a cart by a filthy Jew underneath a lot of stinking hides, then having to live in his house and even" (she shuddered) "even sit down to a meal with his awful wife in her wig and his vulgar, red-haired daughters. The wonder is that I stood it at all." I was once rash enough to observe that so far as I could see she had a great deal to thank the Jewish tanner for, since he had driven her a long way past armed gangs of Ukrainian peasants who would, I supposed, have had little more time for Jews than for Polish landlords. The words were hardly out of my mouth before a vicious box on the ear sent me flying across the room. "You miserable creature!" she shrieked, "son of that upstart Bohemian pig—you will never understand the personal honour of Polish gentlefolk as long as you live!"

However, the massacre of Grandmother's family had made her a very desirable heiress at the age of seventeen, and before many years were out she had been married off to my grandfather, Aleksander Mazeotti, philosopher and amateur poet of the city of Cracow.

My principal recollection of my grandfather is of a man who, through a lifetime of practice, had achieved an almost superhuman degree of indolence—idleness elevated to the level of a spiritual exercise. When my brother and I went to stay with our grandparents we would sit for hours, watching him for the smallest sign of life, even laying bets as to how long it would be before he blinked next. He was quite a handsome man, in a cloudy sort of way, and he was undoubtedly of good enough family for my grandmother's guardians to have accepted him as a husband for her. They married and five children followed at exceedingly long intervals—more

I suspect as a result of absent-mindedness and lack of initiative than of any deliberate policy of birth control. As for employment, my grandfather never had any after taking his degree in Law and Philosophy at the Jagiellon University. Commerce or industry were quite out of the question for a Polish gentleman in those days, while the Austrian Army or civil service were still not considered proper employment for a Polish patriot. So Grandfather devoted the rest of his futile existence to a little politico-artistic windbaggery in Cracow's coffee-houses and to the breeding of hobby-horses—or rather, of one particular hobby-horse.

Grandfather had once written a couple of articles for a Polish literary-patriotic journal, about 1860—his only paid employment, so far as I could make out—and one of these had subsequently been published by another journal without payment. This trifling matter had served to give Grandfather the one great passion of his life: the law of copyright. By the time I was a child this *idée fixe* had burgeoned into an overmastering obsession and had somehow become entangled in his mind with the cause of Polish independence. Within its first two minutes or so any conversation with Grandfather would swing round with all the inevitability of a compass needle to the subject of the law of copyright, and how the Polish state had fallen and been enslaved largely (it appeared) through its unwillingness to provide guaranteed payments for authors. One of my last meetings with my grandfather was in the year 1906, just after my return from nearly four years abroad, during which time I had travelled round the world, narrowly escaped being eaten by cannibals and become embroiled in the Russo-Japanese War. He gazed at me with his watery blue eyes as I outlined this catalogue of adventures, ruminated for a while, then said: "Japan now . . . curious . . . very curious . . . Tell me then, what sort of law of copyright do they have out there?"

My grandmother, as I have said, was a considerable heiress when she married. However, this fortune had been dissipated over the years in a series of ill-judged financial ventures, and by the time I was born the family estates had shrunk to a single manor house in the wide, marshy valley of the Vistula about sixty kilometres upstream from Cracow. The estate consisted of little but rough grazing and stunted pine forest, plus a single, wretched hamlet: ten or so dirty hovels and the obligatory vodka shop. This place—or rather, a railway siding in the woods behind it—was to acquire a considerable if temporary fame many years later as one of the world's busiest railway termini, where the trains always arrived full and left empty. I heard that my cousin Stefan, last survivor of my mother's family in Poland, went back there in 1946 to try to farm the few hectares left him after the Communists had broken up the landed estates. He found that the soil had changed colour during his absence, every handful turned grey by countless tiny, off-white fragments. He put half a hectare down to cabbages and was very pleased to see how well they did for the first few months. Then, one day, he saw to his horror that they had suddenly shot up to a prodigious height: two metres or more of spindly stalk surrounded at intervals by rings of leathery, completely inedible leaves. He crossed himself and returned to Cracow by the next train.

But forgive me: I am wandering away from my course again. Anyway, my mother was twenty-three in 1883 when my father—handsome, energetic and clearly destined for success—arrived in Cracow to take up his temporary posting with the local branch of the Ministry of Posts and Telegraphs. She was unquestionably pretty, to judge from photographs taken at that time; but it was becoming increasingly evident that something was badly amiss up top. Suitors had arrived, paid court for a month or so, then wandered away bewildered by a state of vapidity bordering on mental deficiency. The age of twenty-five loomed, and that awful condition of permanent spinsterhood, and my grandmother was desperate to get her youngest daughter off her hands even if it meant trundling her through the streets in a wheelbarrow with a FOR SALE notice around her neck. My father was, it was true, a Czech and therefore almost by definition of humble birth. But he was clearly well set-up in life, with good prospects, and anyway seemed not to be too bothered by my mother's yawn-inducing ambience when set against the prospect of marrying into a Polish noble family, even one as decrepit as the Mazeottis. Grandmother wrinkled her nose in disgust, but in the end she scraped together the remains of the family fortune to provide a dowry attractive enough to get my father to take her. This he did, promptly investing the dowry in German government bonds which were to provide us, if not with luxury, then at least with a standard of living well above what would have been possible on an Austrian official's salary.

The marriage was never a happy one, or even really a marriage except in the narrowest legal and physiological sense. After I was born my mother sank into a permanent state of terminal hypochondria and lived as a near-recluse, perhaps only seeing my brother and myself once or twice a week. She died—or rather, ceased to live—in 1902. I was at Capetown when the news reached me, hoisting in S.M.S. *Windischgrätz*'s boats preparatory to putting to sea. I stuffed the telegram into my pocket and carried on with my work, meaning to have a requiem mass said before we sailed. In the end though it was not until Table Mountain was already falling below the horizon that I remembered about it.

My father was far too busy with his official duties to see us more than once every three or four days; my mother was a bed-ridden recluse who might as well have lived in another country for all that we saw of her. What better recipe could there be, you might ask, for a miserable childhood and a warped maturity? Yet I remember my childhood largely as a happy one, and this is entirely due to the fact that our father could afford a nursemaid for us. Dear Hanuška: was there ever a more decent and capable soul in the whole world? She was a heavily built, middle-aged Czech country-woman with narrow, twinkling eyes; with her hair braided and coiled up into headphones and with a pendulous nose that gave her the look of a wise, kindly old elephant. She was the wife of old Josef, the head forester on the neighbouring Regnitz estates. Her four children had all grown up and left, so her little cottage was our real home throughout our childhood years, while she was for us both parents rolled into one: strict but kindly, simple but shrewd, devout without bigotry in a country where public devotion to the Catholic faith was usually no more than a display of loyalty to the Dynasty. How I look back with gratitude to those frozen winter afternoons and the stories that she used to tell us, sitting beside the tiled stove while the ginger cat Radetzky dozed in his basket. More than anyone else, it was thanks to Hanuška and her husband that I grew up with Czech as my mother tongue.

You will probably think that an odd thing to say, about Czech as my mother tongue. After all, was I not born and brought up in the Czech-speaking provinces of the old Empire, with a Czech father? Why on earth then should I have spoken anything else? True, my father was indeed born the son of Czech peasants in a village in eastern Bohemia. But like many able, energetic men, he seems, once he started to rise in the world, to have set out quite deliberately to sever the roots connecting him to his clod-hopping forebears.

I met my paternal grandfather only once, one autumn afternoon when I was about seven years of age. An old, white-moustached Bohemian villager, dressed in breeches and top-boots and an embroidered sheepskin jerkin, turned up at the door of our house on the Olmutzergasse, seeking my father in a dialect so clotted and archaic that even Hanuška had to ask him to repeat himself. Before he set off to look for my father at the District Postal and Telegraphic Offices he gazed wistfully at my brother and me (who had come to the door out of curiosity) with his slanting grey-blue eyes set in a face of finely wrinkled, polished leather. He uttered the words "Ano hezči kluci, hezči kluci"—"Yes, fine boys, fine boys," then wandered sadly away. We later learnt that since he could not write and distrusted trains, he had walked all the way from Kolin to tell my father that our grandmother was dead. Needless to say, my father was anything but pleased by this unexpected irruption of the rural past into the minutely ordered, wing-collared world of the Habsburg civil service. He came home that evening in an even viler temper than usual and was unapproachable for most of the next month.

Nevertheless, until I was about eight years of age my father remained at least nominally a Czech. Old Austria may have had many faults, but discrimination on grounds of nationality was not one of them: as far as Vienna was concerned, a man could be a Kanaka or a Mohawk Indian and he would still be acceptable for state employment, provided that he was loyal to the Dynasty and was able to speak passable Official German. However, in the year 1895 my father underwent a dramatic conversion: he became convinced that he was not a Czech but a German.

This volte-face, which would have been remarkable anywhere but Central Europe in the late nineteenth century, seems to have come about because my father was not only able and energetic but also remarkably far-seeing—even progressive—in his ideas. By the early 1890s that American invention, the telephone, had begun to appear in Austria. The Prince von Regnitz installed the first one in our area at the Schloss Regnitz about 1892, and before long the local mines and factories and government offices began to acquire telephones as well. Soon the question arose of an exchange. My father was already well briefed on telephones and had prepared plans for a network in the Hirschendorf district. But then he happened to read an article in a German newspaper describing how the Bell Telephone Company in America was encouraging subscribers (and thus revenue) by selling telephones at knock-down prices. This simple idea seized my father's imagination. Destiny seemed to be beckoning, and he sacrificed the entire fortnight of his annual leave preparing a closely argued memorandum to the effect that what Austria-Hungary needed was to encourage the widest possible use of telephones in order to reduce its costs per metre of line.

Now, short of Imperial China, it would be hard to conceive of a single country on earth where such a thesis would be less favourably received than in Old Austria, where the official view on telephones was probably that one apparatus per town was quite sufficient, and that installing any more was simply asking to have socialists and national agitators talking to one another. Likewise my father could scarcely have chosen a worse time to submit his memo. The post of k.k. District Postal and Telegraphic Commissioner had just fallen vacant, the incumbent having died from inhaling a cherry pip, and by all the rules of seniority my father should have got the job. But in the end he was passed over in favour of a much safer colleague, one Herr Strastil. This sort of thing was quite common in Old Austria, but my father chose to take it as evidence of a conspiracy against him, for Herr Strastil was not only a dullard but a Czech, as was the k.k. Minister of Posts and Telegraphs. His marriage to my mother was also in a bad way at the time, and everything seemed to conspire to turn my father's mind and fill him with a bilious loathing for all Slavs. Then he began to read the German nationalist pamphlets which were in such abundant supply in Hirschendorf in those days. He had probably been coming to the conclusion for many years past that our neighbour, Imperial Germany, was an incomparably more go-ahead and energetic sort of state than poor doddering Old Austria: the sort of place where prescient and well-argued memoranda on telephone networks would earn their author acclaim and promotion rather than a secret police dossier. Anyway, he now decided that Germany was the coming master of the world and German the language of the future.

Once decided upon, my father's change of national allegiance was carried through with his customary thoroughness and energy. Within months, Czech and Polish were forbidden in our household. Old Hanuška would have ceased to be our foster-mother, except that no German woman would have taken the job at the rate offered. So she was permitted to go on looking after us on condition that we spoke German all the time. In her usual way, Hanuška treated this as a huge joke and we were soon engaged in an elaborate Czech-speaking conspiracy to thwart my father's wishes. Unknown to our father, Hanuška had been in service before her marriage and had lived with families across most of northern Germany. So it was a simple matter for her to tutor Anton and myself in all the most obscure and frightful German dialects, then sit back and watch the fun at Sunday dinner when my brother and I would suddenly start talking in Hamburg or Berlin accents, or perhaps in thick Frieslander.

Old Austria did not discriminate on grounds of nationality, but it had a powerful mistrust of nationalism, the German variety as much as any other. Before long, Father's new-found enthusiasm for all things German (or "Prussian," as they were described in Austria) started to lead him into trouble with his superiors. Matters came to a head in 1896, during the railway station troubles, when Father took it into his head to enforce use of the name "Hirschendorf" by administrative means: that is to say, by simply instructing the sorting office to return any letters with "Krnava" or "Sadybsko" or even "Kronau" on the envelope. An official reprimand followed: Father would keep his job and his present rank, for the sake of peace with the local German faction, but he was given to understand that he would never be promoted or moved to another district.

You will perhaps have concluded from the foregoing that neither Hirschendorf in the 1890s nor a household like ours was the healthiest place in the world for two boys to grow up in. Yet most of this passed over our heads while we were children: it was only as our ages began to enter double figures that the awfulness of our surroundings began to dawn upon us. The loss of innocence in my case came with the year 1896, when I entered the Kronprinz Erzherzog Rudolfs Gymnasium: a dismal, square building of stuccoed brick built like a prison around a cobbled central courtyard (kept permanently locked) which looked as if it ought to have had a gallows in the middle. I recall without any affection its cheerless corridors and the dingy buff paint on their walls, shaded about a metre and a half above floor level with a band of grime left by the rubbing of countless shoulders passing from one dreary lesson to the next; and the echoing stairwells, their clammy wooden banisters sticky with generations of adolescent hand-grease. The education that I received there was unquestionably thorough in conception. But it was heavily classical—lots of Latin and Greek, which I detested even though I was always good at languages—and was taught with insane rigidity by bored schoolmasters serving out life sentences. In winter the classrooms were cold and dark as prison cells; in summer the windows (which were never opened) were covered with white paper to stop us from gazing up at the swallows wheeling in the sky above.

Still, this was nothing out of the ordinary. Schools have always been rather nasty places, and at least I was far better off there than in one of those extraordinary jails that would have been my lot had I been born in England. No, the trouble with the Erzherzog Rudolfs Gymnasium was rather that the tensions of the town outside were seeping into the life of its pupils. Boys who would have been bullies became German Nationalist bullies (the children of Czech nationalists went to the new Palácky Gymnasium on the other side of town), while sneaks and informers became nationalist sneaks and informers. With our Czech surname and appearance my brother and I were natural targets, but we were sturdy boys and could look after ourselves. The chief sufferers were the Poles, who were outnumbered, and of course the Jews, who committed the additional sin of being cleverer than the rest.

I forget when it was that the idea first began to occur to me of swimming clear of this stagnant little puddle of hatreds. All I know is that as the years went by the stifling, land-locked atmosphere of the place became increasingly oppressive to me. Looking back on it, I think that it must have had a lot to do with the boys' adventure stories that were coming into vogue at this time: Rider Haggard, Ballantyne and G. A. Henty in translation (all of which I read avidly) and the German writer Karl May. From about the age of eleven I was an insatiable reader of tales about Darkest Africa and South America and the great seas of the world. I soon had a globe in my room, and charts on the wall, and every book on seafaring that my pocket money and our friendly Jewish bookseller Herr Zinower could procure for me. I started trying to teach myself navigation, and was officially cautioned for taking midday observations with a home-made sextant on top of Castle Hill by a gendarme who thought that I must be a spy. The smell of the ocean seemed to come drifting to my nostrils from hundreds of kilometres away across the pine forests and potato fields of Central Europe.

Then came the summer of 1897. My father had made some money on the Berlin Stock Exchange, so a family holiday was decreed and the fashionable Adriatic resort of Abbazia was the place chosen. I shall never forget it, leaning out of the railway-carriage window as we rattled down towards Fiume: the sudden flat blue expanse ahead of us, then—indescribable moment—the rush across the promenade in front of our hotel to dip my hand for the first time ever into this new element, in all probability the first Procházka to see or taste salt water since the end of the Ice Age. After that consummation there was never any further question about my future career.

The practicalities of going to sea began to press upon me with increasing urgency as I neared the age of thirteen. I considered running away to Hamburg to enlist as a cabin boy, but the details of this were so imprecisely described in the stories I read that I gave the idea up as impracticable. No, I would have to seek a seafaring career in a proper, above-board manner. But how? Clearly the matter would have to be raised with my father at Sunday dinner, when he would perhaps be in that rare condition which (for him) approximated to a good humour.

It was the usual Sunday dinner, after mass and the band concert. Anton and I sat there, rigidly to attention in our Sunday best. Our mother had been suffering from the vapours and had retired to her room. My father sat at the head of the table, like a minor but still active volcano, in a frock coat and a wing collar of such merciless stiffness as to resemble more a surgical appliance than an item of dress. The usual respectful silence was observed by the rest of those present as Father held forth upon the latest advances in postal organisation in the German Empire. He paused to pick at his food—roast pork with caraway seeds and sauerkraut—and I seized my opportunity to present my petition to our domestic autocrat.

"Father, by your leave . . ."

He looked up and fixed me with one heavy-lidded eye, as was his manner. "Speak."

"Father, I want to go to sea."

"You what?"

"I wish to go to sea—to be a sailor."

The effect was rather like that of a heavy shell hitting a warship: the same awful split-second pause between penetration and the internal explosion which sets the paintwork on fire and makes the steel underneath glow a horrible, dull red. My father's eyes bulged. He dropped his fork on to his plate. He gurgled and choked slightly, so that he was obliged to take a gulp of beer. I sat shrinking into my chair, waiting for the fiery whirlwind of wrath to blast me. But nothing happened; my father only excused himself weakly, got up from the table and left without another word. He was not seen for the rest of the day, until at 8 p.m. I was called to his presence.

"Did I hear you correctly as saying that you wished to become a sailor?"

"By your leave, Father, you heard correctly." I winced again, expecting the blast of anger that had failed to materialise at dinner. But again, nothing, only: "Very good then. That is all: you may leave."

It was at this point that I began to realise what was happening: my father was simply unable to take in the information being presented to him. It was as if I had announced my intention of becoming a manufacturer of square circles. For you must bear in mind that, of all the Great Powers of those days, Austria-Hungary was by far the least sea-minded. Most people were vaguely aware that the Dual Monarchy had a navy, and also a sizeable merchant fleet, but hardly anyone had ever seen it, or knew what it did with itself, or knew anyone who had served in it. If I had announced that I wished to become a circus tightrope artist or a mandolin player my father would have worked up an impressive rage, because he had been to a circus (just the once) and detested the sound of mandolins. As it was, though, he had neither the remotest conception of seafaring nor any idea of how one took it up as a career. However, my father was nothing if not a conscientious man, so he sought advice the next day from the only source at hand: a half-pay Major called Kropotschek with whom he played billiards once a week. Herr Major Kropotschek had once served in Trieste, but his opinions of the Imperial Navy were highly unflattering: it was manned (he said) by a gang of treacherous Italians—probably practitioners of unnatural vice—and by uncouth Slav tribesmen from Dalmatia who lived on a diet of sardines and polenta. The result was a series of volcanic rows in which my father said that he would rather see me hanged in Olmutz jail than join the Navy.

That appeared to settle the matter for the time being. But then my father read an article in the violently pan-German magazine *Das Volk*. It was by a Professor von Tretschow, an expert on Weltpolitik and the racial issues of contemporary Europe. This article stated quite categorically that the great historic foe of the Germanic peoples was England: that archipelago populated by renegade Nordic tribes and lying athwart Germany's access to the world's oceans. According to the learned Herr Professor, France and Russia were but tools in the hands of the English and their mighty fleet, so that when The Day came, Germany would have to have her own, even mightier fleet ready to eliminate these pirates and race-traitors once and for all. This article set my father's mind working: perhaps there was a place for me after all as a sea-borne soldier of Greater Germany. But not in Austria's ludicrous fleet: only the Navy of the German Empire would do. So in November 1898 my father set off for Berlin in the hope of persuading the Navy Minister to let me study at the Imperial German Naval College at Murwik.

He returned a few days later in a sulphurous bad temper, and all mention of the Berlin visit was henceforth *verboten* on pain of death. It was not until many years later that I got some idea of what had happened—when I met a German Naval Staff officer at Cattaro who had been a young Leutnant in the Reichsmarineamt on that fateful day.

"Prohaska?" he had said. "Funny thing, but I remember a chap of that name coming for an interview with old Alvensleben when I was on his staff. Odd sort of fellow—an Austrian postman or something, with a thick Czech accent. Wanted us to let his son into the Naval Academy. He blustered and spluttered, but of course we had to show him the door. No offence meant to yourself, Prohaska, but the minister had to tell him that the German Navy was for Germans, not for just anybody. We had enough problems holding down our own Poles, so why should we want to take more Slavs into the Navy?"

So, the ultra-German-by-adoption had found himself snubbed and humiliated by the Germans for being a Slav. In the end, however, this worked to my advantage. Like a bull with its head down to charge, my father was capable of looking out of only one eye at a time, and instead of making him reconsider the idea of a seafaring career for his son, his rebuff merely made him more stubbornly determined than ever. I could not join the Imperial German Navy? Very well then: the Austro-Hungarian Fleet would have to do instead. Application was duly made to the War Ministry's marine section in Vienna, and to the k.u.k. Marine Akademie in the Adriatic port of Fiume. The latter replied that if I was able to pass the rigorous entrance examinations for the year 1900 I would be admitted to the Academy as a Cadet for a course lasting four years, at the end of which I might apply to enter the k.u.k. Kriegsmarine. The War Ministry for its part was prepared to award me a scholarship, provided that I undertook to join the Navy on completion of my studies.

The entrance exams for the old k.u.k. Marine Akademie were reputed to be tough; not surprisingly, since each year's intake consisted of a mere thirty or so Cadets. There were examinations in mathematics, physics, chemistry, geography, German and one other of the Monarchy's languages. None of these was likely to present me with too much trouble, given a little extra tuition here and there. The one subject that did cause my father and me to worry though was English, a compulsory subject of the first importance in those days when Britannia not only ruled the waves but also produced most of the world's charts and pilotage guides. English was nominally taught at the Erzherzog Rudolfs Gymnasium; but the truth is rather that English appeared on the timetable, because our classes in that language happened to be conducted by a master of quite outstanding incompetence: one Herr Goltz.

Herr Goltz was a large, shambling, unmade bed of a man in his late thirties: a breathless, wild-haired creature who seemed always to have lost something or just missed a train. Not only was he incapable of keeping order in the classroom; he was one of those unfortunate individuals whose mere presence seems to provoke riot and hilarity among even normally well-behaved pupils. Also his grasp of the English language was patently not up to the standard even of northern Moravia in the late 1890s. The only item of his English tuition that sticks in my mind is that he once rendered the phrase "On Sunday I shall write to my sister" as "An Suntag, I ham go riding mei schwister." Indeed, I think it possible in retrospect that Herr Goltz might have been a complete impostor. Certainly the sounds that issued from his lips—that is, on the rare occasions when anything could be heard above the din—might as well have been Mongolian for all the sense that they made. One term we had a boy in the class who had spent several years in Chicago, living with an aunt and uncle who had emigrated there. His considered opinion was that the wretched Herr Goltz was no more than a common cheat.

This would all have been rather amusing, I suppose, if it had not been for the fact that under Herr Goltz's tuition I would most assuredly plough the entrance examinations for the k.u.k. Marine Akademie, which included not only two written papers in English but also a gruelling hour-long oral interrogation. Something had to be done, and fast. Luckily for me, that something eventually assumed the formidable shape of Miss Kathleen Docherty LRAM.

Miss Docherty moved into our house in the autumn of 1899 in the office of governess with special responsibility for teaching English. My father, realising that my English was in a bad way and that time was pressing, had tackled the problem with his usual energy, placing newspaper advertisements for a resident tutor as far away as Prague and Brünn. He had also shown a good deal of his native peasant shrewdness in realising that nine months of live-in tuition was likely to be a worthwhile investment for my brother as well, who was inclining towards an Army career and might get a Staff post or even become a military attaché if he knew languages. So much for the plan, but how to realise it? In the end, the acute shortage of native speakers of English in a provincial hole like Hirschendorf meant that my father was not able to be too exact in enquiring into the character and antecedents of the one person who answered his advertisements. For the truth is—although I did not quite understand it at the time—that Miss Docherty was what used to be called "a fallen woman," though others in Hirschendorf were less oblique and referred to her simply as "that Irish whore." Also the question of her nationality was not examined too closely. She spoke English and was a subject of Queen Victoria, so that (as far as my father was concerned) was that. Marvellously ignorant of the world outside Austria, he assumed that anyone who came from Ireland but spoke English must be English, much as a German-speaker from Hungary would consider himself a German and not a Hungarian. "If she were Irisch," my father had pronounced confidently, "she would speak Irisch. As it is she speaks Englisch; therefore she must be Englisch."

But whatever else she was, Miss Kathleen Docherty was certainly not English. About thirty-five years old when she came to us, she was a native of Mallow in County Cork and had studied music in Dublin, then at the Royal Academy of Music in London. She had later travelled to Leipzig, where she had studied under Brahms—quite literally, if rumour was to be believed—before becoming the mistress of the composer Waldstein, then of a whole string of Central European composers of the day, and finally mistress of the Prince von Regnitz. Looking at her one could understand why, for, though handsome rather than beautiful, she was certainly a woman of striking looks, with strongly chiselled, sharp features, thick raven-black hair (now beginning to grey a little) and a disturbing stare which with her aquiline nose and hooked chin made her uncomfortably reminiscent of a bird of prey beginning to think about its next meal. She had lasted about two years with the prince; mostly in Biarritz and Locarno, but latterly at the Schloss Regnitz, where a final, tumultuous quarrel had ended with her being evicted to earn her living by giving piano lessons.

The wonder is really that the prince managed to put up with her for two years, because my brother and I soon came to the conclusion that Miss Docherty was more than a little insane. She was unquestionably a woman of great intelligence, strong personality and considerable musical talent. She had even written a three-hour patriotic opera entitled *Finn McCool,* which had been performed—only once, and to a rapidly emptying house—in Dresden some years previously. But like my Polish grand-mother, she was liable to fly into the most murderous rages; the difference in my grandmother's case being that with her, at least the barometer glass fell for some hours beforehand, while with Miss Docherty the tornadoes invariably came shrieking out of a tranquil blue sky. Her language was unrestrained, and she also smoked cigarettes and drank spirits.

For all these shortcomings, Miss Docherty gave us excellent value over the next nine months. Her method of teaching English was simple: she simply refused to speak with us in any other language, even though her German was excellent and her Czech tolerable. I suspect that with any other teacher such a policy would have reduced us to glum silence. But Miss Docherty was like no other adult that we had ever met in that dull little town of bores and monomaniacs: a gorgeous, extravagant, outrageous walking circus of jokes and mimicry and impromptu rhymes, endowed with a highly gratifying talent for using her razor-silken tongue to slit open the sawdust-filled little colossi who bestrode our childhood world. By the end of the nine months I was fluent enough in English to pass my Marine Akademie entrance examinations with distinction. The only drawback was that it gave my English (I was told) a distinct Irish flavour which it took many years to lose.

Thus the last days of August 1900 found me making my final preparations for leaving Hirschendorf/Krnava/Kronau/Sadybsko. Not that the town seemed unduly concerned at my imminent departure: there was yet another row going on among the nationalities—this time over the appointment of a municipal dog-catcher—and the place was in an uneasy mood. Every wall was covered with posters, all leave had been cancelled up at the barracks and gendarmes were patrolling the streets, rifles slung over their shoulders. However, my trunks were packed, my railway ticket to Fiume was booked and the town tailor had made me my Marine Akademie Cadet's uniform—from a book of patterns, since he had never seen one before. As for myself, I was in a fever of excitement, sad only at the prospect of leaving my brother, who was staying on at school until seventeen to enter the Army as an Aspirant. Miss Docherty's appointment was at an end, of course, but my father had allowed her to stay in our house until she had made arrangements to move to Prague, which was her next port of call.

I was duly delivered about 6 a.m. one Friday to the nameless railway station in order to catch the train for Oderberg, whence I would travel to Brünn, then to Vienna and Fiume. My trunks had been taken to the station the evening before in a carrier's cart, so it was only myself and my family that set out in the two fiacres from the house on the Olmutzergasse. My father was in the leading cab, bullying the driver as usual for going too fast or too slowly. My mother was beside me, dabbing her eyes, and Anton (who was travelling with me as far as Oderberg) sat opposite. Hanuška, Josef and Miss Docherty followed in the second fiacre. We rattled across the town square, watched only by a bored gendarme and by a waiter who rested briefly from his early-morning sweeping-up of nationalist leaflets and broken glass from the terrace of the Café Zum Weissen Löwe. Then it was over the bridge and along the poplar-lined road to the station, where we all debouched on to the up-platform. My father cleared his throat to make a speech, but we were late and the train was already in sight, snorting up the line from Oppeln in a bother of steam and coal-smoke. My mother kissed me goodbye with all the passion of someone posting a letter; Hanuška kissed me and wept profusely and pressed a medallion of Our Lady of Kutna Hora into my hand (I wear it still, polished almost perfectly smooth with the years). Old Josef also wept profusely and nearly stripped the skin off my face with his hard, bristly chin in kissing me goodbye. As for Miss Docherty, she kissed me a great deal more effusively than would have been thought proper at the time, and asked me to remember her when I was with the girls on shore-leave. Then Anton and I climbed up into the carriage and waved our farewells out of the window as the station master in his red-topped shako rang his little silver-plated bell. Soon they were all falling behind us in the distance, then disappeared altogether as the train entered the cutting.

Thus the small district town of Hirschendorf (or Krnava, or Sadybsko, or Kronau) dropped out of my life. Oh, I went back there from time to time of course, but less and less frequently as the years passed and the people of my childhood either moved away or died. The last time (I think) was for my father's funeral in 1919. And the town itself? You will look for it in vain in your atlas. It became part of the new Czechoslovak Republic in 1918, when the old Monarchy collapsed, and was promptly occupied— first by the Poles, then by the German Freikorps, then by the Czechs once more. They kept it until the Munich crisis in 1938, when it was seized by the Poles again and held for eleven months, until Poland in its turn was crushed by Nazi Germany. Hirschendorf was then incorporated into the Greater German Reich. In April 1945 it became part of "Festung Nordmähren" and was the scene of a week-long defence by a division of the Waffen SS against the advancing Russians, a defence so effective that by the end of it scarcely one brick was left standing on another. Then, a few days after the German surrender, what little was left of the town was blown sky-high by the explosion of a huge ammunition dump in the vaults beneath the castle. This proved to be the long sought-after final solution to the Hirschendorf question, for in 1947 the new Czechoslovak government simply bulldozed the remains of the town into the huge crater left by the explosion, concreted over the top of it and built a factory estate called Slanskov, later changed to Novotnin when Slansky was hanged. About three years ago, in Ealing, a young Polish engineer visiting an aged relative told me that he had been there the previous summer. Nothing at all remained of the town in which I was born, he reported; not so much as a lamp-post or a horse-trough. It seems that the only pre-1945 building left anywhere in the vicinity was the little railway station, with its Doric portico and its two glass canopies over the platforms.

8

THE OCARINA BOATS

NYWAY, THAT IS QUITE ENOUGH about my childhood, and let us get back to the World War. Let me see now, where did we leave off? Ah yes, it was July 1915 I think: the month in which we sank an Italian armoured cruiser. I narrowly missed being awarded the Knight's Cross of the Order of Maria Theresa, Austria's highest military decoration, but even so I found that I had become a national celebrity, unable to travel by train or to appear on the streets of small provincial towns without people coming up to me, asking to shake my hand or requesting my autograph. As for my gallant crew, they had been sent off on a month's much-needed leave while *U8*, badly damaged during the engagement, underwent repairs in the Pola naval dockyard. I spent my month's leave in the city of Budapest as a guest of the family of my Second Officer Béla Meszáros. It was there that I was introduced to a second cousin of his, the Countess Elisabeth de Bratianu. She will figure quite large at a later stage in this narrative, if I live that long, but not just yet.

There will be yet another delay here in resuming the war though, because the day after I returned to Pola, while inspecting the repairs to my boat, I slipped in a puddle of oil at the bottom of floating dock H and fell with my foot jammed between two baulks of timber. The resulting sprain was so bad that I was declared unfit for service until mid-September at the earliest. Meanwhile *U8* completed her repairs, and was placed in the hands of Fregattenleutnant Meszáros for diving trials. It was while surfacing from one of these dives, off Fort Peneda, that she was run down by a light cruiser. Fortunately the submarine's bow reared up in the air for a few minutes before she sank, so everyone managed to scramble out through the torpedo-loading hatch, and the subsequent court of enquiry decided that the collision was entirely the fault of the cruiser, which had wandered into the U-Boat practice area by mistake. As for our boat though, she lay on the bottom for a week before divers could raise her and bring her back to the repair yard which she had left only a few days before. It would take at least six months to get the boat back into commission, so once my ankle was better I would be in the invidious position of being a submarine commander without a submarine. Here the k.u.k. Marine Oberkommando intervened and announced that my crew, Meszáros and I were to be assigned to one of the new German-supplied BI-class coastal U-Boats currently being assembled at Pola.

Those BI boats were a remarkable testimony to that frightening German capacity for getting things done. I believe that it had taken less than a hundred days from the designer reaching for his pencil to the first boat being launched at the Weser Yard in Bremen. The idea had been to mass-produce small, simple, cheap submarines that could be carried in sections by rail for use against the British from the German-occupied ports in Flanders. But then it was realised that these little vessels could also be carried through the Alpine tunnels to the Adriatic. There was no prospect of our own shipyards being able to provide us with new submarines much before 1916: shipwrights were in short supply and the Austrian bureaucracy still proceeded at its stately pre-war pace. So in the end the Imperial German government consented to sell Austria six BI boats—at full cost price, naturally. These were duly delivered to Pola in the summer months of 1915 and work was set in hand assembling them for use, with teams of Weser Yard riveters working around the clock. The arrangement was that the first batch of these boats would be manned by Germans for two months or so, until Austro-Hungarian crews were ready to take them over.

I first set eyes on one of these peculiar little vessels in floating dock T at Pola in about the middle of September 1915. It was plain at first glance how the BI boats had acquired their universal nickname "the Ocarinas." Indeed, I think that in all my naval career I never saw a less warlike-

looking warship: so much like a child's toy in fact that I half expected to
see a huge key lying near by for winding it up. Take a twenty-metre length
of steel drainpipe, about three metres in diameter. Fix crudely sharpened
bow and stern sections on to the two ends and solder a large oil drum to
the middle for a conning tower. Then drill a hole in the back end for a single
propeller, and two larger holes in the front end for a pair of 45cm torpedo
tubes. Equip this contraption with a 60hp Körting diesel engine (originally
designed for Norwegian fishing boats) and a Siemens electric motor of
the kind used in Munich trams. Fill it with pumps, diving tanks, batteries,
fuel tanks and all the other things necessary to a submarine. Then squeeze
fifteen human beings into the spaces not already occupied, and hey presto!
you will have a 1915 BI series U-Boat.

But while there is no denying that the Ocarinas lacked elegance, and
were also very cramped and uncomfortable to live aboard, they certainly
had their merits as fighting vessels. True, they were miserably slow on the
surface: a bare six knots, which would soon fall to three knots or even
less with a headwind; they had only one periscope; and their single engine
made battery-charging a nerve-racking business, the boat lying stopped
with the deck just awash while the diesel throbbed away below and the
look-outs gazed their eyeballs raw, scanning the surrounding sea for the
tell-tale plume of a periscope. On the credit side though the Ocarina boats
were very sturdy: rated safe to fifty metres, but capable of going down to
sixty or even seventy in an emergency. They could dive in twenty seconds,
and they handled well underwater, remaining stable even when both torpedoes were fired at once. The little four-cylinder diesel—generally known as
"the sewing machine"—was robust and easy to repair. There was a Lorenz
wireless installation, and even a proper gyro compass at last. As for accommodation, even if the BI boats were more cramped than *U8* of blessed
memory we did at least have proper folding bunks for the first time: eight
of them for the fifteen crewmen sleeping watch-on, watch-off. Above all,
they ran on diesel oil, which was safe and gave off no intoxicating fumes.

However, before the k.u.k. Kriegsmarine took delivery of its new
U-Boats our German allies insisted in that plodding, pedantic way of theirs

that the officers assigned to command them should undergo a month's training, so it was agreed that all prospective Captains, Second Officers and Chief Engineers would be sent on BI boat courses in Germany. I was due to go on one myself, early in October 1915. But then fate intervened: the Second Officer of one of the German Ocarina boats fitting out at Pola fell sick. No replacement could be brought from Germany in time since the boat, *UB4,* was due to sail for Cattaro the next day. So an urgent request was made to the k.u.k. Marine Oberkommando, and thus it came to pass that I was temporarily seconded to the Imperial German Navy, receiving my month's training aboard *UB4* while earning my keep as Second Officer to her commander, Kapitänleutnant Erich Fürstner. I was also to be responsible for local pilotage: a very sensible idea since we had to negotiate three hundred miles or so of treacherous, rock-studded coastline on our way down to Cattaro without benefit of lights or navigation buoys.

I have not said much so far about our Imperial German allies, largely because we saw so little of them in that first year of the war. The Mediterranean was not an area of great concern to Berlin, once Berlin had realised that its Austrian and Turkish allies were liabilities rather than assets. But early in 1915 the Germans found that their large, seaworthy U-Boats could reach the Mediterranean without too much difficulty by way of Gibraltar, then use Austrian ports to go marauding against that great highway of the British Empire, the steamer route from Suez. Once that discovery had been made we began to make the acquaintance of the Kaiserliche Deutsche U-Bootsflotille on a large scale. Feelings were mixed on both sides.

I suppose that Kapitänleutnant Fürstner was not too bad a fellow in his way: younger than myself in years and much younger in appearance, with his butter-blond hair and smooth, pink face and cornflower-blue eyes. But his manner was stiff, and it rapidly became apparent that he had no sense of humour whatsoever—certainly not the smallest trace of our weary Austrian irony, surprised by nothing and expecting nothing. He was undeniably a highly competent officer, superbly trained and far less lax in his ways than his k.u.k. counterparts. But like most young German officers trained up in Kaiser Wilhelm's battle fleet, his experience of the world was sadly lacking: limited, it seemed, to endless gunnery exercises in the Baltic shallows and the dreary estuaries of the North Sea coast. Until he came to Pola the furthest that he had ever sailed was Portsmouth, for the 1911 Coronation Naval Review. I never felt at ease with him or with his crew, who were three-quarters of them conscripts. Somehow they always seemed to me to smell of the Potsdam parade ground rather than the free, salt air of the oceans. They wore sailor's hats and not spiked helmets, but the contents of the cranium beneath seemed to be much the same in both cases.

UB4 set sail for Cattaro on 14 September. Things went well for the first two days: despite our ant-like five knots we reached Zara on the evening of the 15th, then set out again the following morning for our next port of call, the town of Lissa. By midday, though, the barometer was falling rapidly. The air felt turbid while a thin, brown-tinged haze veiled the sun and hung over the surface of the sea. It was evident that we were in for a spell of the sirocco, the powerful south-easterly wind that sometimes blows across from the Sahara during the Adriatic autumn. We reached Lissa without difficulty, but by dawn the wind was blowing so strongly that I advised Fürstner against putting to sea. But he was adamant: our orders were to sail from Lissa on the morning of the 17th to reach the Gulf of Cattaro by nightfall, so sail we would, even though a hurricane should be blowing. After all, he said, this was the twentieth century. Nature was there to be defeated by technology, and he saw no reason whatever for us to waste a day skulking in harbour at Lissa. Besides, he added, what was there to worry about? Anyone could see that the sun was shining almost as brightly as ever.

By midday however the Kapitänleutnant was repenting of his rashness as *UB4* endeavoured to claw her way south-eastwards through the Lagosto Channel in the teeth of a Force 8 gale and waves ten or fifteen metres high. In its way it was all astoundingly beautiful: each wave a shimmering mountain of tarnished silver in the hazy sunshine, with streaks of spray like diamond dust being stripped from the crests by the screaming wind. It was a highly dangerous beauty though, and most certainly not one to be admired from the conning tower of a BI U-Boat. For the truth is that whatever their considerable merits as fighting submarines, the Ocarinas were just about the worst sea-boats that I ever had the misfortune to ship aboard. Despite being fitted with a heavy ballast keel, the little boat's cylindrical hull rolled with a particularly vicious, unpredictable motion: over to starboard until it seemed that she would roll right over, then back a few degrees, then slam! over to starboard again, then suddenly right over to port to lean on her other ear. And not only that: the shortness of her corpulent hull and the lack of buoyancy at the two ends caused her to pitch and stamp most alarmingly, yawing up and down with a crazy, anarchic violence as she tried to aim her torpedoes at the sun, then changed her mind and attempted to stand on her head like a duck in a farm pond.

A few hours of this would have reduced Odysseus to seasickness. Fürstner and I clung to the periscope standard like two drunkards to a lamp-post, soaked through despite our oilskins and feeling very wretched. The Kapitänleutnant was most unwell, while as for myself—who had been twice around Cape Horn—even I must admit that I felt distinctly queasy. Fürstner shouted into my ear above the howling of the wind.

"I have never before encountered anything like this. How is it that the sun still shines while it's blowing a full gale?"

The roar of the wind left little room for subtle nuances of expression, but the Kapitänleutnant's tone of voice left me in little doubt that he considered this state of affairs to be at the very least highly irregular, and probably my own personal fault. I cupped my hands to reply.

"I dare say you haven't seen anything like this up in the North Sea. But this is the Adriatic, and the sirocco can blow even worse than this when it wants to."

"How long do you think it will last?"

"It should blow itself out by evening. Permit me to observe though that we are making no headway whatever."

This was in fact a considerable understatement: not only was *UB4* not making any headway into the wind and sea; she was being driven back towards Lissa at a good two or three knots, as could readily be observed by noting the position of shore marks glimpsed briefly from the crest of each wave. The diesel had been rattling its gallant heart out at full speed for the past three hours, but its efforts were patently getting us nowhere—hardly surprising in view of the fact that each wave lifted the propeller out of the water for five seconds or so, to spin helplessly in the air before being plunged back in again.

"What do you advise then?" Fürstner yelled. His face was the colour of lettuce and his oilskins adorned with a delicate tracery of vomit.

"My advice is to go about, then take the boat round the western tip of Curzola and through the Drace Channel towards Gravosa."

"But that's well out of our way—we have to make the Gulf of Cattaro by nightfall."

"I know. But we'll make better progress in the lee of Curzola, and also the current through the Drace Channel reverses direction after the sirocco has been blowing a couple of days. That will work in our favour."

He looked at me suspiciously. "How do you know that? There's nothing about it in the pilotage directions."

"I know there isn't, but it still happens. Believe me—I've been sailing these waters for fifteen years now and I know my way around."

Fürstner bit his lip. I could see that he was inclined to keep on battering into the wind regardless. But at this point old Neptune intervened by sending a wave to break clean over the conning tower. Fürstner and I only narrowly escaped being swept away as a huge, solid lump of sea water fell through the open hatch into the control room below. There was a mighty crashing of crockery and loose gear, followed by some of the foulest language ever to pass the lips of seafaring men. The matter, I sensed, had been resolved in my favour.

"Very good then, prepare to go about!"

"No!" I yelled, "not on the surface. The waves will roll us over if they take us broadside on. Better go down to ten metres and then go about!"

So *UB4* dived below the waves, then turned north-westwards. It is a commonly held fallacy that the sea is always calm underwater, even if a gale is blowing on the surface. Even at fifteen metres *UB4* was rolling heavily. But at least we were out of the wind, and within the hour we had rounded the western end of Curzola and surfaced in the calmer waters to leeward of the island. The passage through the Drace narrows near Curzola town was rough, but the current was in our favour as I had predicted, and by evening our little submarine was waddling towards Gravosa, the port of the ancient city of Ragusa, or Dubrovnik as they call it nowadays. We were bone-weary and caked with dried salt; also the diesel was running noisily after its immense exertions earlier in the day. But we were nearing our destination. Midday on 18 September found us exchanging recognition signals with the fort at Punto d'Ostro, the entrance to the Gulf of Cattaro, which was destined to be my home port for most of the next three years.

I insist that if ever you get the chance you should visit the Bocche di Cattaro. I think that there can be nothing like it in the whole of Europe: as if one of the most splendid Norwegian fjords had been sawn off and towed south to the latitudes of cactus and lemon trees and bougainvillea, where pine-clad mountains of limestone plunge down sheer into the indigo waters of the three bays and where the walled city of Cattaro lies in the shadow of Mount Lovćen, so that even at noon on the hottest summer day the streets are cool and dark. In those days the Bocche was very nearly the southernmost tip of the Habsburg Empire; but Austria was Austria, and, as one might have expected with such a superb natural harbour located at the very mouth of the Adriatic, next to nothing had been done in the years before 1914 to turn it into a naval base. After all, the civil servants in Vienna had argued, Italy was our ally, while our meagre naval budgets barely provided enough money for new ships, let alone bases. Communications with the rest of the Monarchy consisted of a single-track narrow-gauge railway line running down from Mostar. This had been half worn out even in 1914, so heavy stores like torpedoes and diesel oil had to be brought down from Pola by coastal steamer. But even so the railway line was outrageously overloaded, so that a sailor with a ten-day leave pass to go home to Pilsen could easily spend four days of his precious freedom in travelling. For all its outstanding scenery and sub-tropical climate the Bocche was never a popular posting.

The results of this negligence were all too plain to see that afternoon as we tied up to the jetty at Porto Rosé, the makeshift submarine base on the southern shore of Topla Bay. A few wooden barrack huts littered the shore, while the old battleship *Erzherzog Rudolf* and a requisitioned merchant steamer had been moored offshore to provide accommodation and workshop space. For the rest, a pervasive air of Schlamperei hung about the place—Austria at its worst: a slovenly, hapless chaos where stores and spare parts lay about everywhere, heaped into untidy tarpaulin-covered pyramids or simply left exposed to the weather. *UB4* had not been at Rosé more than a few hours before Fürstner and his Chief Engineer were complaining to me in the bitterest tones about the unhelpful attitude of the U-Station Commander and his officials. It seemed that not only were there no spare parts to repair our exhaust manifold, which had blown on the way down from Gravosa, but even workshop space and dockyard hands were out of the question. As for bunks on shore and a bath, were we quite out of our minds? The forms for such things had to be filled in weeks in advance. In the end we did the work ourselves, tired out as we were after our four-day voyage, and slept aboard when we could work no longer. I lent as much of a hand as I could—partly from the universal solidarity of seafarers in the face of dockyard officials and partly from sheer embarrassment at my own countrymen.

Things were to get even worse though. I think I mentioned that during our attempted passage of the Lagosto Channel I had seen Kapitänleutnant Fürstner's normally rosy complexion turn a delicate green? Well, on the third day of our sojourn at Rosé I was treated to yet another variation of colour: this time the livid white of a man struggling with an overpowering urge to homicide. I was standing on the jetty, filthy with oil and grime and taking a breather from the engine repairs. Fürstner had been called away to the telegraph office on shore. Now he had come back with a telegram in his hand and the look of a man tried beyond endurance.

"Herr Leutnant," he said in a strangled voice, "I would like to speak with you for a moment, if you please." We walked away from the jetty, out of earshot of the crew, and he told me of the contents of the telegram, which he would not show me since it was marked TOP SECRET. It appeared that from 14 September until further notice *UB4* and her crew would officially be transferred to the Imperial and Royal Austro-Hungarian Navy, to operate henceforth under the red-white-red banner as His Imperial Majesty's Submarine *U9*.

The reason for this order, so distressing and humiliating to Kapitän-leutnant Fürstner and his crew, lay in the rarefied upper atmosphere of European diplomacy, far above the heads of us simple seamen. In brief, the position in September 1915 was that while Italy was at war with Austria-Hungary, she was still not formally at war with Germany. This anomalous state of affairs presented great difficulties for the growing number of German submarines operating from Austrian ports. What were they to do if they were attacked by Italian vessels? And what was going to happen if they encountered, say, Italian and French ships together in a convoy? They could hardly expect an Italian destroyer captain to knock politely on the conning-tower hatch before attacking and enquire whether the men inside were Austrians or Germans. Likewise, if a German U-Boat attacked an Italian ship and was subsequently sunk, the Italians would be quite within their rights under international law if they hanged the survivors for piracy on the high seas. The obvious course would have been for Germany to tidy matters up by declaring war on Italy. But I suppose that the Germans felt they had enough enemies to be going on with, so a more underhand solution was adopted: henceforth, German U-Boats sailing from Austrian bases would be re-designated as Austrian vessels, complete with fictitious Austrian numbers, and would operate under the Austrian flag whenever necessary. For all practical purposes however they remained German U-Boats, taking their orders from Berlin while their crews retained their German uniforms and were paid and supplied by the German Navy. The only practical difference was the injury to German professional pride in being obliged to fly the flag of Austria-Hungary, "the Corpse-Empire," as our allies were wont to refer to us among themselves.

Thus it came about, on the morning of 22 September, that we hauled down the German naval ensign and ran up the flag of Austria prior to departing on *UB4,* alias *U9*'s, first combat patrol. Our task was to sail down the coast as far as Corfu, there to seek out and attack vessels carrying supplies and reinforcements to the Italian armies in Albania.

It certainly seemed for the first three days as if we were going to find precious little to attack. The seas off northern Albania were clear of ships, apart from a British *Weymouth*-class cruiser sighted off Durazzo on the second day out, too far away for an attack. Really there was not a great deal for me to do; only stand watch and generally make myself useful as *UB4*'s titular Second Officer. The Germans were well trained and smart about their duties, but I could still detect a strong resentment on their part at having to take orders from an Austro-Czech officer. German racial arrogance was well developed even before 1914, and it was plain that they felt there was something vaguely wrong in German sailors being ordered about by a Slav officer from an inferior fleet; much (I suppose) as British ratings of the period would have felt about taking orders from a half-caste officer of the Royal Indian Marine. I often heard my accent being mimicked; and there was also the problem of language. Both navies were German-speaking, but I soon discovered that Austrian German was not quite the same thing as German German. I well remember the looks of bewilderment that greeted my order "Sood lenzen" when I wanted the engine-room bilge pumped out. The correct order, I was informed, was "Bilge ausleeren."

But there: my business was not to like the Germans but to learn how to operate one of their U-Boats, and in this I was lucky to be sailing with their senior Warrant Officer Lehmann, a native of Emden. He was quite an agreeable sort as north Germans go, and he certainly taught me a great deal about handling Ocarina boats underwater, where their single diving rudder and fixed bow planes made them tricky at low speeds. I was pretty well acquainted with the boat after two days at sea. The only question now was how *UB4* would behave when attacking. Or being attacked.

That question was answered just after 9 a.m. on 25 September, about ten miles off the western tip of Corfu and six miles south of the mountainous island of Fáno. I was up on the conning tower smoking a cigar, having come off watch an hour before. The look-out reported smoke to north-westward. Fürstner studied it for a while through his binoculars, then handed them to me, remarking that "they," whoever they were, were heading in our direction. I opined that it was perhaps three or four vessels, moving slowly, and that they were heading for Santi Quaranta on the Albanian coast.

"Good then," said Fürstner. "We shall dive and wait for them."

We submerged in a leisurely manner and set course to intercept the convoy. After about twenty minutes Fürstner ordered the periscope to be raised. The electric winch whined as it reeled in the wire rope and the shining bronze shaft slid noiselessly up from its well in the deck. Fürstner applied his eye to the viewfinder and scanned the horizon with an air of magisterial self-confidence.

"Aha," he said, "just as I expected: a two-funnelled liner and two smaller steamers, escorted by a destroyer."

"Any idea of their nationality?" I enquired.

"It scarcely matters: in these waters they can only be enemy, and if they are neutrals they have no business to be here. I propose to attack. Anyway, have a look for yourself." I stepped over to the periscope and peered into it. Yes, it was an Italian warship all right: a *Sparviero*-class torpedo-boat to be precise. As for the two-funnelled ship, I was fairly sure that I recognised the French Algerian mail packet *Ganymède*. The other two vessels were a small cargo steamer and a green-painted steam coaster of about two hundred tonnes. Only the torpedo-boat was flying a flag. They were coming towards us at an unhurried six knots.

Orders were barked—the Germans always seemed to make a virtue of barking orders—and within a few seconds the crew were at attack stations. The red-painted safety covers were removed from the torpedo-firing buttons on the control room bulkhead. Fürstner stood behind the periscope and manoeuvred the boat with impressive calm, lining up for the attack.

"Very good," he observed. "I think that we shall go for the destroyer. Both tubes, stand by to fire!" There was an aching silence for a minute or so, then the order:

"Port torpedo, fire!" There was a roar of compressed air. *UB4* pitched slightly as the torpedo was blasted out of its tube. Then, "Gottverdammt—Go deep!" A few seconds later there was the unmistakable whirring of propellers above our heads, then the sharp concussions of two or three bombs exploding near by. It transpired that our torpedo had run straight towards its target for the first five seconds or so, then sunk. The Italian had seen the torpedo track and had turned to run along it in the hope of being able to ram us before we could dive. He missed us, but the attack forced us to stay at twenty metres for the next half-hour or so, during which time the torpedo-boat and the two-funnelled steamer had vanished entirely from the scene of action. When *UB4* came back to periscope depth there was nothing to be seen but the two smaller ships, which had evidently turned around after the flight of their escorts and were now steaming at full speed back towards Italy. The larger of the two steamers was in the lead, bustling along at about eight knots with thick smoke pouring from its funnel and towing a lifeboat. As for the small coaster, she was a good mile astern, obviously unable to keep up.

Strictly speaking, as laid down by international law, we ought to have surfaced and seized the two steamers as prizes after first making appropriate arrangements for the safety of their crews and passengers. Fürstner would have none of this however, arguing that it was perfectly legal to sink merchant vessels without warning if they were part of an escorted convoy, and that the fact that the escort had now vanished was neither here nor there. The starboard torpedo was fired at the larger steamer at about four hundred metres' range, and twenty seconds later we were rewarded with the dull boom of an explosion. A well disciplined cheer went up. Fürstner peered intently through the periscope for a minute or so, then stepped back looking very pleased with himself.

"Cowardly rabble, those Italians," he observed. "You should have seen them scramble into that boat they were towing. They had cut the rope and were rowing away almost before our torpedo struck. Shockingly slovenly seamanship as well, towing a boat like that: it makes me wonder . . ."

He never finished the sentence. Or if he did I failed to hear it, for everything dissolved in a shower of stars as I was lifted off my feet and hurled across the control room. It was the most colossal explosion that I have ever experienced: a brutal concussion like two planets colliding. I had endured 30cm battleship broadsides and I would be depth-charged a hundred times afterwards, but all those appalling noises were no more than the bursting of so many paper bags when compared with the fearful hammer-blow that smote *UB4*. The explosion of Krakatoa must have sounded very similar. The breath was knocked out of our chests, our ear-drums caved in, our brains shuddered like jellyfish and spun helplessly within our skulls as we were flung about inside the rolling, pitching boat. Gear crashed from the bulkheads, men cried out in terror as the lights failed. Then there was a dreadful, sinister hush as the little boat regained her equilibrium: an ink-black silence broken only by groans and the vivid blue flashes of electrical short circuits. Water was hissing and trickling as air howled from ruptured high-pressure lines. Only our courageous little electric motor was still humming to itself as if nothing had happened.

Dazed and battered, I staggered to my feet with sea water and lubricating oil pouring over me. Then a pocket torch clicked on somewhere up in the fore-ends. It revealed a scene of utter devastation. Everywhere, jets of salt water were hissing from a thousand racked seams and sprung rivets.

The deck was awash and already a sinister taint of chlorine hung in the air as sea water slopped into the battery cells. As for the crew, they lay about everywhere, buried beneath loose gear or struggling to get back on to their feet. *UB4* had only minutes to live.

"Where's the Captain?" I shouted.

"Over here, Herr Leutnant!" came the reply. Bleeding profusely from a head-wound, Fürstner was being dragged out from under a pile of oxygen flasks which had fallen on him from their racks beneath the deckhead.

"Quick!" I shouted, "prepare to abandon ship—we haven't got long!" Then I turned to Lehmann, who was climbing back into the diving helmsman's chair. "Lehmann, steer for the surface. I'm going to blow all tanks—we're losing a lot of air, but we might still have enough buoyancy to get us there. You two men there—up into the conning tower and open the hatch when I shout up to you. Then scramble out as fast as you can and pull the others out as they come up—we'll only have a minute or so before the boat sinks and I don't want anyone getting stuck in the hatchway!"

"The boat's not answering, Herr Leutnant. The diving-rudder linkages must have been broken!"

I fought my way across the debris to the valve panel and opened all the blowing valves. The air lines were so badly ruptured that very little air was finding its way into the tanks, but somehow the boat began to rise. The depth gauge was smashed of course, but as I kicked off my seaboots ready for swimming I saw that the water outside the bull's eyes in the conning tower was getting lighter. The men were struggling out of their overalls and assembling in the control room, ready to rush up the ladder when we broke surface and the hatch was opened. They were obviously frightened and some were injured, but their discipline was still most impressive. I glanced up at the bull's eyes again: nearly there now.

"Stand by to open the hatch, you men up there!"

Then I stared in disbelief as the whole conning tower suddenly crumpled like a cardboard tube. There was a hideous tearing, shuddering crash as the boat was forced back down into the water. The two men crushed inside the tower screamed, then were silent. The conning tower was torn bodily from the pressure hull as the keel of whatever had rammed us scraped overhead, then as the boat bobbed back up again a solid cascade of green water came rushing through the hand-wide gap which had opened at the rear of the tower. Water was foaming about our knees almost before we realised what had happened, and a vicious crackling and a volley of blue flashes from aft announced that the electric motor had finally given up the struggle.

"Lehmann!" I yelled above the roaring of the water. "The engine-room hatch—for God's sake, open the engine-room hatch!"

Two men struggled with the locking wheel, and the hatch was flung open. Water came pouring in, but also daylight. We were on the surface. But certainly not for long.

"Quick—everybody out!"

The crew needed no second bidding: they scrambled up the engine-room ladder as if all the devils in hell had been in pursuit, dragging Fürstner and the other injured men with them. Within a few seconds only Lehmann and I were left, the water by now up to our waists.

"Is everybody out?"

"I think so, Herr Leutnant."

"Come on then Lehmann, let's not hang around here. After you."

He rushed up the ladder and out through the hatch. I prepared to follow him, but as I did so something made me pause and shine my battery lamp down into the engine room. Its beam revealed a young stoker, paralysed with fright, clutching a handrail as water surged around his chest. I churned my way back towards him and seized him by the collar.

"Come on you stupid bastard, do you hear me? Come on!"

In the end I had to prise his hands loose from the rail and drag him to the engine-room ladder like a sack of meal. As we reached it though the stern of the boat suddenly began to sink. I struggled up the ladder, hauling the young German after me, but as we neared the hatchway the hatch cover (which opened forward) suddenly fell shut. I wrestled with the locking wheel with my free hand. It was no good: everything was slippery with oil, and the interior of the boat was now in total darkness. I put my shoulders under the hatch cover and heaved, but to no purpose: the boat was sinking and the water pressure was holding the hatch closed. Within a few seconds the foaming water was up to my neck. It was like being tumbled in a butter churn half filled with sea water and diesel oil and chlorine: impossible to see, impossible to breathe, impossible to think. They say that a drowning man's whole life passes before him, but I can only record that for me it was not like that: just a wild confusion and roaring of water, and at the centre of the chaos a still, quiet place and a firm but kindly voice, remarkably like that of my old nursemaid Hanuška:

"Well, young Master Ottokár, you wanted a life of adventure and you have had one. I am afraid that this is where the bills fall due for payment."

I tried to remember the Act of Contrition, without much success, then grew impatient for it all to be over and done with. I was gulping sea water and oil now as the last air bubbled out of my lungs. Then my fingers lost their grip on the rung of the ladder, and everything went black.

9

A SHORE OUTING

MY FIRST THOUGHT, I REMEMBER, was that if this was the next world, then they might at least have had the courtesy to pump me out at reception. To be sure, it conformed in certain respects to the advance billing offered to me many years before at catechism classes in the parish church of St Johann Nepomuk: I was floating without weight while above me there soared a vault of purest azure, dotted here and there with those little puffs of high, white cloud that we used to call "cherub's farts" during my sailing ship days. Gradually, though, as I spat out sea water and wiped the stinging diesel fuel from my eyes, it dawned upon me that the interview with my maker had been postponed until another day; and, to be more precise, that I was treading water in the middle of a spreading pool of oil and wreckage on the calm blue surface of the Ionian Sea. As I cleared my waterlogged lungs and nasal passages I became aware that other heads were bobbing around me; also that my left arm was still clasped around the chest of the young engine-room rating whom I had just rescued from the sinking *UB4*. He was alive, but still rigid with fright. Thinking about it afterwards, I suppose that as the stern of the sinking U-Boat dropped downwards the remaining air in the after-ends must have rushed upwards as one great bubble, blown open the engine-room hatch and carried us with it to the surface.

But whatever the exact mechanism of our escape, it was evident that our reprieve from drowning might be very brief. Merlera Island was about four miles to the north, while the coast of Corfu must have been at least seven miles to south-westward, I thought. As for the ship that had rammed us as we surfaced, she was a good mile off now, steaming away from us with one of her lifeboats hanging upside-down from its davits and trailing in the water.

The first oil-covered head that I recognised near by belonged to Lehmann. He swam over to me.

"All right, Herr Leutnant?"

"Not too bad, thank you," I replied, expectorating a large quantity of diesel fuel. "How many of us got clear?"

"Six men over here, counting yourself and the stoker. And there are some more over there. Can't make out what the silly buggers are up to though—they seem to be fighting over something."

There was indeed a group of men in the water about a hundred metres away, shouting at each other and flailing their arms as they milled around a long piece of floating wreckage. I prepared to swim across to them; at least the wreckage might serve to keep us afloat for a while. I let go of the young stoker, but this brought him out of his trance. He clutched at me in panic.

"Please, Herr Leutnant, please, I can't swim!"

I looked around me. A few metres away one of the U-Boat's kapok-filled seat cushions was bobbing on the water. I seized it and thrust it under the young sailor's armpits. Then I began to swim across to the other group of men.

It was painful work. I had imbibed too much chlorine and diesel for my own good, and also my right side was beginning to hurt from violent contact with a valve wheel when the explosion flung me across the control room. As I swam I noticed that the water was tinged a dirty ochre colour and covered with debris, most of it finely splintered wood and altogether far too much to have come from *UB4* alone. Here and there dead fish floated serenely, silver bellies upwards.

I arrived at last among the quarrelling knot of men, and saw that they were fighting over a ship's boat, full of water to the gunwales but still right way up. I also saw that most of them were not survivors of *UB4,* in fact not Germans at all, with their dark complexions and black, curly hair.

Blows were being exchanged in an ineffectual sort of way, rather as one would expect when the two factions are simultaneously trying to hang on to a swamped boat, and insults were being traded in German and in what I recognised as Sicilian dialect.

"You men here—what the Devil do you think you're doing? What's going on?"

A sailor turned to me. "It's these Italian pigs, Herr Leutnant. They're trying to stop us hanging on to their boat."

I swam up to the other end of the boat and hailed the men in Italian. It was even money whether they would understand my Venetian brand of Austro-Italian, but it seemed worth trying.

"Good morning my friends. I am an Austrian Naval Lieutenant. What seems to be the trouble here?"

There was a brief, surprised pause, then I was engulfed in a torrent of passionate and barely intelligible Italian. Once they had calmed down a little, though, the story of the past half-hour began to emerge. It appeared that they—twelve of them, all from the same family—were the crew of the ship that *UB4* had recently sunk, the *Giuseppina Bianca* of Palermo. Their vessel had been on charter to the Italian Army to convey a cargo of pioneer's stores from Bari to Albania where they were to be used by sappers building roads in the mountains. Just before the ship sailed, they said, the authorities had made them load a deck cargo consisting of eighty tonnes of time-expired gelignite, which was to be used for blasting. They had not been at all happy about this; particularly since the explosive was old and dangerous. So they had resolved to tow their boat astern, and to jump into it and row for dear life at the first sign of trouble. They had abandoned ship as soon as *UB4*'s torpedo had struck. But just as the sinking steamer's mastheads disappeared beneath the waves, they said, BOOM!—a mountain of water had been thrown a hundred metres into the air, swamping their boat and pitching them into the sea. The green-painted coaster coming up astern had swerved to avoid them and had run down the stricken ruin of the "sottomarino austriacco" as it tried to surface. I asked why the coaster had not stopped to pick them up.

"No, no," they said. "They all went crazy and tried to lower their boat, only it tipped up and they fell into the sea and drowned."

So that was the curious end of *UB4:* the unsuspecting predator blown up by her late victim. It was a singular history, but one which was unlikely to be recorded unless we did something pretty soon to get ourselves ashore. The swamped boat was a heavy, half-rotten old tub about seven metres long, but it was our only hope of reaching land. It occurred to me even now that we ought to try and make for Corfu in the hope of being interned by the Greek authorities. I knew that for some months past the Italians had been offering rewards for a German submarine crew captured alive, and I was anxious that it should not be us.

I was never cut out for the diplomatic service, but even so I think I did a neat job of international negotiation there in the water off Corfu, swimming from one end of the boat to the other. With the Germans of course it was easy: they were by no means happy at the idea of collaborating with their enemies of a few minutes before, but it would never have occurred to them to refuse an order from an officer, even when that officer was just another half-drowned wretch like themselves. The Italians were a tougher proposition. We had sunk their ship beneath them, and they had just had a narrow escape from being blown to atoms, so it took a good deal of argument and appeals to common sense before I managed to persuade them that we would all drown together if they didn't lend a hand to bale out the boat. A measure of common purpose was thus established, and we set to work taking turns with a leaky enamel bucket discovered in the boat's bilges. It was hard work, but after about forty minutes we had the boat clear and afloat. The only means of propulsion was a single oar found floating near by. I arranged this over the stern with a rope lashing and we started to scull our way along, picking up the rest of the survivors as we went. It was a tight fit: twelve Italians and a total of eleven men from *UB4.* Two of her crew were known to be dead, crushed in the conning tower, and two were missing, but this figure fell to one when we came across our Petty Officer telegraphist, Sulzbach. He was still dressed in his leather U-Boat overalls and floating face-downwards.

"What shall we do with him, Herr Leutnant?" asked Lehmann. "Somehow it doesn't seem right to leave him here."

I considered for a moment. "No Lehmann, we've hardly got enough room for the living. Better let him lie where he is." I was soon to regret this decision.

In the end we managed to rig up a crude sail, using the oar and a tarpaulin found in the boat's bow locker. A north-westerly breeze had sprung up, and it was about 3 p.m. that our boat ground on to the shingle of a small, wooded bay on the northern coast of Corfu. We staggered ashore, a sorry-looking company. Our Italian companions set off along a pathway leading into the pine wood, hoping to find a village, but for my part I was less keen to go looking for help. Corfu was Greek territory, but it was already reported to have French and Italian troops garrisoned on it, and I had no wish to meet either. In any case we were not prepared for long walks: Fürstner had a fractured skull; several other members of the crew were suffering from broken bones; and we were all barefoot, having got rid of our seaboots as we prepared to abandon ship. No, far better to wait here and destroy the evidence of our identity, after which Lehmann and I would set out to make contact with the Greek authorities.

Luckily for us someone had a watertight tin of matches tucked into the top of his seaboot stocking, so we lit a fire of driftwood and gorse while the men turned out their pockets. Then the evidence was consigned to the flames: pay books, identity papers, cap ribbons, letters and paper money. Coins and identity discs were flung into the sea. But as I examined their remaining clothes my heart sank: every single item seemed to be stamped MARINE BEKLEIDUNGSAMT KIEL. But even if we had burnt all our clothes the case would have been no better, for as the men removed their singlets I saw that many chests and arms were decorated with large tattoos of an aggressively patriotic nature: German naval ensigns; Prussian eagles; portraits of Kaiser Wilhelm; and Gothic-script mottoes like PREUSSENS GLORIA, GOTT STRAFF ENGLAND and DEUTSCHLAND ÜBER ALLES. Short of skinning them alive I could think of no way in which I could plausibly maintain that we were really Austrians.

It was Lehmann who roused me from these gloomy reflections. "Look, Herr Leutnant—out there, it looks like the Italian torpedo-boat that we missed this morning." He pointed out to seaward. It was indeed a *Sparviero*-class torpedo-boat, heading in our direction from the place where *UB4* had sunk. I ordered the fire to be put out, but it seemed that he had not seen us after all, because he soon turned away to southward and was lost to sight behind the headland.

"Well," I said, "it looks as if they aren't going to bother us just yet. Come on, Lehmann, let's go and explore a little inland. There must be a village near here, and if we could steal a fishing boat we might manage to get home. Spending the rest of the war in a Greek internment camp doesn't appeal to me."

"Nor me," said Lehmann. I had not yet said anything about the possibility of our falling into the hands of the Italians, but I sensed from his manner that he had realised that for him, capture might entail far more unpleasant consequences than an indefinite spell in jail. We did what we could to make the injured men comfortable, then the two of us set off.

We were soon clear of the woods, and found ourselves climbing the scrub-covered ridge separating the bay in which we had landed from the one next to it. Inland, a rough trackway ran parallel to the coast while olive groves and fields were visible in the distance. As we breasted the top of the ridge, though, we caught our breath and stared in disbelief. Down there, in the little rock-bound cove, her bows just resting on the beach, was the same green-painted steam coaster that had run down *UB4* a couple of hours previously. A thin wisp of smoke still drifted from her funnel, but otherwise there was no sign of life whatever, and her boat still hung forlornly from its davits, half-in, half-out of the water.

"Well, I'll be damned," said Lehmann. "There's a stroke of luck if ever I saw one. Do you reckon we could get her afloat, Herr Leutnant? She certainly doesn't look to be stuck fast, and the tide's rising now. It's only about half a metre around here, but it might be enough . . ."

"Let's go and see."

We scrambled down into the cove, as fast as our bare, bleeding feet would allow, then splashed through the water up to the ship's bows. Her stem was battered from the collision with *UB4,* but the damage appeared not to be too great, and the vessel was certainly not fast aground. We clambered aboard and began a hurried tour of inspection. The boiler fire was still glowing weakly, but there was not enough steam pressure left to turn the single propeller. We concluded that after her crew had abandoned her in panic the ship must have gone on steaming in a huge circle to starboard until she had grounded in the cove on her last few puffs of steam. She had taken in a few tonnes of water from the leaks caused by the collision, but otherwise she seemed quite seaworthy. All we had to do was get our companions aboard, stoke up the boiler fire to raise steam, run the engine full astern to pull her off the beach and then head for home, pumping for all we were worth. It might not work, I thought, but at least drowning was preferable to seeing my German comrades hang for piracy. Whatever we did, though, we would have to do it fast: it was well over an hour since the Italians had left us, and they would certainly have raised the alarm by now.

We tumbled over the side and waded back to the shore. Then we set off at a run back towards our companions. As we got into the pine wood though, Lehmann suddenly stopped, crouched down and motioned me to be quiet. Someone was walking down the path towards the bay from the other direction. We crept through the undergrowth for a better look. It was a portly man in a rather shabby black uniform, with a rifle and a bandolier slung over his shoulder. The same thought seemed to occur to us simultaneously. We let him amble past us, then crept along behind him, silent in our bare feet, and sprang upon him together. There was a brief scuffle, and a good deal of what must have been very bad language if we could have understood it. At the end of it, when the dust had settled, the stranger was lying on the ground face-downward with me sitting on his shoulders while Lehmann covered him with the rifle. He was winded, and evidently much put out by our ruffianly assault upon him, but he seemed little disposed to offer violence in return when I let him get up. Why should he? He was merely a Greek rural gendarme sent to investigate the shipwreck survivors down on the beach.

We led him down to the bay where our companions were waiting. Questioning the man was not easy, but one of *UB4*'s crew had once worked in Piraeus and knew a little Greek, while the policeman knew some Italian. It emerged that he was from the fishing village of Antikoraxion, about three kilometres down the coast. A group of Italian seamen had arrived a while before, reporting that they had been sunk by a U-Boat whose survivors were now marooned on the beach. Just as he was about to set out, he said, he had received a telephone call from the gendarmerie headquarters at Paleokastritsa. An Italian torpedo-boat had just arrived there bearing the corpse of a German U-Boat Petty Officer. The dead man's comrades were believed to have landed on the coast and the Italian garrison commander was very anxious to interview them in connection with recent attacks on Italian ships. Troops were being despatched to arrest them, but in the mean time would he go down to investigate on behalf of the Greek government?

So there we were: the Italians knew who we were, and more or less where we were. We had not got long, perhaps only half an hour, before the soldiers arrived to take us prisoner. I still had my Austro-Hungarian identity tag, but the Germans were, to put it mildly, in a tight corner. I explained the position as succinctly as I could to the crew of *UB4*. To my surprise, though, they showed little enthusiasm for escape.

"Germany and Italy are both signatories of the Hague Convention on the treatment of prisoners of war," said Fürstner in that irritating, solemn tone of his, "and the Italians will be obliged to treat us as proper military captives. Why," (looking around him at our dishevelled, near-naked condition) "they are even obliged to provide us with proper clothing." Given our desperate situation, this complacent little speech irritated me more than I can tell you: in fact annoyed me so much that I quite forgot myself.

"You thick-headed Prussian dimwit!" I said. "The only clothing they'll give us will be tight hemp collars fitted early one morning. For God's sake, you imbecile, wake up—Germany and Italy aren't at war and they have every right to try the lot of you for piracy on the high seas!"

This outburst seemed to snap the men out of their lethargy: there was aghast silence for a few moments, then a low murmur of assent. Five minutes later we were all hurrying up the path towards the cove, half-carrying Fürstner and the other casualties and dragging the Greek policeman along behind us. I had considered letting him go, but Lehmann had pointed out that we would need every able-bodied man we could get to work the coaster's pump. As we began to climb the ridge we heard the distant sound of a motor vehicle. I looked back and saw a ball of dust coming along the track towards us, about two kilometres away. It was a motor lorry.

"Lehmann," I said, "it looks as though the Italians are after us. Get everyone aboard the steamer and work for all you're worth to raise steam."

"What about you, Herr Leutnant?"

I looked about me, and suddenly an idea struck me. "Quick—give me the rifle and the bandolier. I can get up on the top of that ridge and hold them off for a while. If there's only one lorryload there can't be more than about ten of them. I think I can hold them up for about half an hour with any luck."

"And what then?"

"Never you mind about that: I've still got my Austrian identity tag, so they'll take me as a prisoner of war. Don't worry."

I must say that I was a good deal less confident on this score than I sounded. But I took the rifle and ammunition and shook hands with Lehmann, then scrambled up through the scrub as he and the rest of the crew hurried down into the cove, which was invisible from the track. Breathless, I reached the top of the ridge and lay down among a cluster of boulders and sage bushes. It was excellent cover, and better still, it gave a superb field of fire over the approaches to the cove. There was not long to go now: the lorry was bumping and lurching up the track below me. As I laid the policeman's rifle in a crevice between two boulders I noticed with some amusement that it was an Austrian Mannlicher, 1888 pattern, identical to the one I had spent so many boring hours carrying around the parade ground at the k.u.k. Marine Akademie. It was dirty and pitted with rust, but the bolt still worked, and I had twenty-five rounds of ammunition. I settled down and waited.

Yes, they were certainly Italians in those grey-green uniforms: nine of them, jumping down from the lorry and running up from the track towards the cove. I thought it likely that my ultimate fate would depend on how many I had killed or wounded, so the first shot would be a warning. I took careful aim above the head of the first of them, then squeezed the trigger. The weapon jolted against my shoulder and kicked up a small flurry of dust in front of my hiding-place. There was no smoke though, thank heaven: the old Mannlichers used to fire black powder cartridges, but evidently this one had more modern ammunition. The soldiers hesitated and looked around them, then began to run forward again. Well, I thought, if you will not heed reasonable warning, so be it . . . I pushed another cartridge into the breech, took aim and fired again. The leader staggered and clutched his shoulder. His men halted and stared at him, then dived for cover amongst the heather. A spatter of shots cracked like dry sticks in the warm afternoon air. A few bullets whined over my head, but they had no real idea of where I was and seemed not to be disposed to come looking for me. The wounded man scrambled back down towards the lorry and the others lay where they were. It looked as if it would be stalemate until reinforcements came up and they had enough men to storm the ridge top. They contented themselves with firing the odd shot towards me every now and then, while all that I had to do was to fire a shot every time anyone lifted his head out of the scrub, which was not often. There was no way of telling how long this would last, but the Italians had no idea of what was going on in the cove, and every minute was a minute longer for the Germans to raise steam and drag the coaster clear of the beach.

It was curiously peaceful, lying there in the afternoon sun while the lizards scurried around me, quite unaware of the drama being acted out above them. These were perhaps my last minutes on earth, for I supposed that the Italians would not be too scrupulous about giving quarter if they had to storm the ridge to get me. But strangely enough this did not bother me a great deal. Since my narrow escape from drowning a few hours before, death seemed to have lost any of its residual terrors.

After a while though, reality began to obtrude once more: two clouds of dust were coming up the trackway towards me. I loaded another round, waited until the first lorry came within range and pulled the trigger. Clack!—nothing happened. I jerked back the straight-pull bolt to eject the cartridge, reloaded and fired again. Damn and blast!—still nothing. I opened the breech once more and peered inside. The firing pin had snapped from years of neglect. So there was nothing to be done now but wait for them and lay about me with the rifle butt. It must be about half an hour, I thought: surely they would be getting the ship off the beach by now.

Suddenly I heard a rustling in the scrub behind me. I turned around, intending to give my assailant a piece of rifle butt to chew upon. But just in time I saw that it was a German: the young stoker whom I had rescued that morning.

"Please Herr Leutnant—the ship is afloat now and about to leave. I've come to collect you."

"What do you mean, collect me, you silly idiot? There are three lorry-loads of Italians down there—we'll be riddled like colanders before we've gone two metres."

"No, please Herr Leutnant, I came here specially—we can still make it!"

Well, I thought to myself, I might as well be killed there as here. So off we went, dodging and ducking along the ridge top as the bullets whizzed and spacked around us. Then, just as we reached the end above the cove, the air was torn to tatters above our heads as a machine gun came into action. Somehow though we managed to tumble unhurt down the slope to the beach. The ship was afloat now, and sounded her whistle as we ran across the beach towards the boat. We tumbled into it and began to paddle like maniacs as the first Italians reached the lip of the cove. Bullets plopped in the water around us as we neared the ship, and the gunwale exploded into splinters just where my hand had been a second before. But I suppose that the Italians were too breathless from running to take accurate aim. The boat bumped against the ship's side, and I managed to pull myself up a rope and over the bulwark as bullets spanged off the steel plates, spattering us with molten lead. I fell on to the deck, then turned to pull my German companion over the rail. He got half-way over, then stopped with a preoccupied expression on his face, rather as if he had just remembered leaving the gas on at home.

"Come on!" I shouted, and reached out to haul him aboard. He coughed, then shuddered slightly and let go of the rope. I leant over the rail and saw my rescuer sinking towards the bottom of the cove, pumping blood into the water as he sank. I suppose that his bones lie there still. I never did know his name.

We made it out of that cove, somehow or other. Bullets whined around us and rattled on the ship's sides as Lehmann and I steered, lying on the deck beneath the wheel. It was lucky for us that we did so, because just as we cleared the cove a well aimed burst of machine-gun fire smashed both wheel-house and wheel to matchsticks, obliging us to steer thereafter by means of a large adjustable spanner clamped on to the wheel spindle. But after twenty minutes or so the shots became thinner as we steamed out of rifle range. The coaster's funnel and upperworks were riddled with bullet-holes and the vessel was taking in water from the sprung seams in her bows, but for the time being the pump seemed capable of dealing with it, provided that two men worked at it all the time. Evening was approaching now, so at least we would have the cover of darkness to make our way up the Albanian coast.

Dawn the next day found us south of Durazzo, still in the combat zone and now with no coal left, so that we were obliged to rip up the deck planks to feed the boiler furnace. About 6:30 a.m. a cry went up from the look-out:

"Four-funnelled vessel, fifteen degrees starboard!"

We waited, holding our breath as the stranger closed with us. It would be a wretched finale to our daring escape if we were taken prisoners on the last lap. Then relief—it was an Austrian destroyer, in fact none other than S.M.S. *Kaiserjäger,* commanded by my old Marine Akademie friend Korvettenkapitän the Ritter von Ubaldini. He stood on the bridge and hailed us through a speaking trumpet as they drew near.

"Ahoy there! What ship?"

"Italian coastal steamer, name unknown," I replied through cupped hands, "on passage from Corfu to the Bocche and manned by thirteen survivors from the Imperial German submarine *UB4,* plus an Austrian naval lieutenant and a Greek policeman."

It was most satisfying to see the way old Ubaldini's monocle dropped out of his eye when I stood before him on the deck of the *Kaiserjäger—* a ragged, unshaven, oil-saturated vagrant dressed only in a torn singlet and trousers and covered in coal-dust from a long spell down in the stokehold.

"Du lieber Gott, Prohaska, is that really you under there?" was the best that he could manage.

The *Kaiserjäger* towed us back to a hero's welcome at Cattaro. Fürstner was taken aboard a hospital ship for an operation to repair his skull, and made a good recovery. He later returned to Germany, was given a much larger U-Boat to command, and failed to return from a patrol west of Ireland in 1917. As for myself, I was given the German Iron Cross First Class and more important to me personally—had my papers stamped as being competent to command a BI-class U-Boat.

The only residual problem was the Greek policeman, who was being held in custody at Cattaro while the authorities decided what to do about him. The story was being put about in the Allied and neutral press that we had cut his throat and dumped him overboard. A protest note had been lodged by the Greek Minister in Vienna while the pro-Allied faction in the Greek government was demanding the severance of diplomatic relations with Germany and Austria. The problem was finally solved by my old comrade the Ritter von Trapp of *U14*. He arranged to take the man south with him on his next voyage, and land him on the coast of Corfu near Antikoraxion under cover of darkness. The policeman was in fact none too anxious to return home to his wife and seven children, but in the end Trapp contrived to mollify him a little by presenting him with a knapsack full of cigars, chocolate, brandy and other treasures captured by *U14* on her last patrol.

"After all," Trapp had said to me before leaving, "if one is going to return from the dead, then the only way to travel is first-class."

10

LUCKY THIRTEEN

I WAS GIVEN A MONTH'S LEAVE after the sinking of *UB4,* partly to recuperate and partly because my own promised Ocarina boat was still not ready. The month's leave was spent in Vienna, staying with my mother's widowed elder sister Aleksandra at her flat on the Josefsgasse in the 8th District.

To all appearances, fifteen months of world war had not made any great mark upon the daily life of our windswept imperial city not-quite-on the Danube. Men in field grey and invalid blue were everywhere; and women in black. Posters exhorted contributions to the Red Cross and subscriptions to the War Loan. But otherwise the whirlwind set in motion on the Ballhausplatz that afternoon the previous July seemed now to have passed the city by. The shop-windows on the Graben still looked prosperous enough, and the coffee-houses still flourished as ever, even if they now dispensed a nauseous infusion of burnt barley and acorns. It took a discerning eye to notice that many of the goods offered for sale in the shops now carried the sinister qualifications "ersatz" or "surrogat," harbingers of the miseries to come; or that the bread contained a growing proportion of potato and maize meal; or that every single scrap of copper and brass had disappeared as if by the wave of a magician's wand. The civil populace still looked adequately fed, though tired from long working hours and queuing; the prostitutes still plied their trade on the Kärntnerstrasse, catering now for a largely uniformed clientele; while as for the theatres, they did business as never before, every third-rate operetta or cabaret filling the house to standing room.

I must confess however that all this made little enough impression on me, because on the third day of my leave I visited the Imperial Parliament building on the Ringstrasse. A strange place for me to be going, you may well say. But of course the Reichsrat was no more: that futile assembly had been dissolved for the duration of the war and the building, with its great white statue of Pallas Athene leaning on her spear, was now a hospital for wounded officers. It was here, visiting a comrade of my late brother Anton, that I ran into a distant acquaintance: Nursing Sister the Countess Elisabeth de Bratianu, to whom I had first been introduced the previous summer in Budapest. Now, this encounter would have been a delight however fleeting it had turned out to be, because Elisabeth was not only outstandingly pretty, with a delicate oval face and black hair and deep, dark green eyes, but also amusing and vivacious and blessed with a disarming directness of manner that made anyone to whom she spoke feel they were the most important person on earth. She struck me even at this brief meeting as being about twice as alive as anyone else that I had ever met. But this encounter was destined not to be our last. I asked her out to the theatre that evening, without any real hope of being taken up on the offer, but to my astonishment she smiled graciously and accepted the invitation. I think that it was Nedbal's *Polenblut* at the Karltheater, but I cannot really remember: it might just as well have been the Cardinal Archbishop of Vienna walking the tightrope, for my thoughts were quite elsewhere throughout the performance. To cut a long story short, by the time that my leave ended we were engaged to be married.

It seems strange to think of it now, but though barely twenty-one years of age Elisabeth was a widow, one of the many thousands of young women in those years who were fated to become widows without ever having really been wives. She was the daughter of a Magyar-Romanian landowning family from near Klausenburg in Transylvania, though she had spent most of her childhood in Bucharest and travelling with her parents in France and Italy. Her mother had died of diphtheria when Elisabeth was ten, then her father had been killed in a motoring accident when she was twelve, leaving her and her younger brother to be brought up by kinsfolk: the Kelésvay family of Schloss Kelésvár, deep in the forests of the Transylvanian Alps. In those days and among the nobility of that region, girls were destined for only one thing: to marry and to perpetuate the noble Magyar nation. Thus Elisabeth was betrothed at the age of fifteen to Prince Jeno Erlendy. This was by any standards a grand match: the foster-daughter of hard-up Transylvanian backwoods nobility marrying into one of the wealthiest and most powerful families of old Hungary, with estates covering most of Debrecen county and interests in everything from coal to sugar beet. Also the prince himself (to judge from photographs) was by no means a bad catch even for a girl as pretty as Elisabeth: an almost indecently handsome young Magyar blood decked out in the gorgeous uniform of the 12th Royal Honvéd Hussar Regiment "Graf Kálnoky," in which he was a Captain.

But Elisabeth had no wish for the marriage: she found Magyar noble society unspeakably dull and regarded her future husband, quite frankly, as a moronic lout: "So stupid" (she used to say) "that if he'd been any more stupid his heart would have stopped beating." She had managed to postpone the wedding for several years on one pretext or another, even feigning tuberculosis in order to get herself sent to a sanatorium in Switzerland. But then came July 1914 and the general mobilisation. Both families intervened, Elisabeth was bundled on to a train at Zurich and the wedding was hurriedly celebrated in the Votivekirche on 1 August. The mobilisation was by now in chaos, so the honeymoon came to an abrupt end the next morning as the prince leapt into his motor car and sped away to Györ, where his regiment was entraining for the Polish front a week ahead of schedule.

The prince's squadron began the war for the Austrian side just after dawn on 6 August at the Russian frontier just south of Kraśnik, charging down a straight, sunken road beyond the customs post to attack a pair of Russian horse-drawn ambulances. And for them the war ended there, for the "ambulance carts" were recognised, too late to turn back, as the tatchanki of a Russian machine-gun section. There followed a brief but dramatic demonstration of the utter helplessness of cavalry in the face of automatic weapons. A single survivor limped back on to Austrian territory later that day, carrying his saddle over his shoulder and with his fur-trimmed dolman jacket torn and blood-stained.

Elisabeth was still in Vienna when she was informed of her widow-hood. Her relatives would have come to drag her back to Hungary, but with her usual quick-wittedness she forestalled them by volunteering as a nursing sister. Many noblewomen volunteered as nurses in those early days of the war, then drifted away as the months dragged by and the smell of blood and gangrene became too much for them. But Elisabeth was made of sterner stuff: she stuck at it, and after a year transferred to a spe-cial facial injuries unit run by Professor Kirschbaum of the University of Vienna's Medical Faculty. Perhaps war in the trenches led to a dispropor-tionate number of head-wounds; or perhaps advances in antisepsis meant that many a man who would once have died could now survive to look forward to perhaps half a century of life with his entire face and lower jaw missing from the eyes downwards, able to take nourishment only through a tube. Anyway, whatever the reasons, by the summer of 1915 there was no shortage of patients for the professor and his assistants, grafting flesh and bone in an attempt to reconstruct the devastated faces that streamed in from the base hospitals of Austria and Germany.

It was hard work for all those involved; most of all for the ward staff, who had to be nurses and faith healers rolled into one to keep up the spirits of some poor young wretch who faced perhaps two years of painful opera-tions, quite possibly with nothing to show for it at the end. But Elisabeth excelled at this sort of work. Not only was she a very intelligent, methodical nurse and a good linguist: she was also a natural uplifter of the disheart-ened, someone who, however tired she might be, could always find time to sit and talk with her hideously maimed patients, quite irrespective of whether they were a "Von und Zu" prince or a Silesian coal-miner. I asked her once whether she was not worried that her patients would all fall in love with her. She sighed, and lowered her eyes: "Yes, I know that they do. And I know it's a rotten confidence trick. But it seems to help them get better, so what am I to do about it? The professor says that all medical staff are members of the acting profession, whether they like it or not."

The world war came as a calamity for tens of millions; but for more than a few I suspect that it was a liberation, an unlooked-for opportunity that allowed (for example) this daughter of the most bigoted, most igno-rant, most utterly benighted nobility in Europe to break free from her pre-destined world and discover a new life. When she was a girl (she told me) the Kelésvay family had been shocked when they had learnt that she knew how to read and write. Why should a Magyar noblewoman need to read, they had asked, when she had inherited all she would ever need to know along with her blood and her coat of arms? And now here was this impos-sible, magnificent young woman making serious plans to study medicine once the war was over.

To this day I cannot imagine what should have attracted this glorious creature to a workaday career naval officer descended from Czech peas-ants on one side and from decayed Polish gentry on the other. But there: ever since the world began Cupid's choice of targets has been a source of disquiet to all orderly and right-thinking people. I was certainly not disposed to question her choice, and all I know is that from then on we were never happier than in one another's company. Oh, I was no trembling seventeen-year-old virgin I can assure you: I had served as a naval officer for upwards of fifteen years now, and had led an active social life ashore, taking full advantage of the opportunities offered to a vigorous, reasonably good-looking young man with no ties, a smart uniform and a salary too miserable to allow him to think of marrying. My private life had not been one long debauch, ending with an artificial nose; but I had loved if not hun-dreds, then at least a good few tens of women over the years, some mere passing fancies, others much longer-lasting passions. Over the years I had come to value women as much for their delicacy and grace as for anything else that they might have to offer: for their gentleness and their profound common sense and their freedom from the idiotic blustering and turkey-cock posturings of the male sex. But something had changed now: as if all the women up until now had been practice for this one woman. Perhaps my recent escape from drowning had changed me more than I knew. I was just as ready as ever to give my life for Emperor and Fatherland, but now I began to realise for the first time that life would not go on for ever: that even if I did retire with the rank of Kontreadmiral in 1956, without a wife and children I would leave nothing behind me but a yellowing folder in the War Ministry archives and a gravestone in the Pola Naval Cemetery. I began to suspect that there might be a life beyond the Imperial and Royal Fleet, and that love might mean something more permanent than going to bed with corn merchants' wives and actresses from provincial theatres.

My leave over, I kissed Elisabeth goodbye at the Südbahnhof and set out once more for Pola. When I arrived I found that my brand-new BI-type U-Boat was ready at last in the drydock on the Oliveninsel, just about to be launched. I also found to my dismay that, thanks to a truly epic succession of misunderstandings between Berlin and Vienna, the only number now available for the new submarine was *U13*. Now, I am not and never have been a superstitious man, but there was no question that in the Mediterranean most seafarers were. It was not long before rumours began to reach my ears that in the dockside cafés of Pola bets were already being laid as to the life-expectancy of the new submarine and her crew.

These prognoses were very nearly fulfilled one November night off Budua. The moon was bright and a chill breeze was blowing down from the mountains of Montenegro, already capped with the first of the winter snow, as we lay about a mile out to sea, charging our batteries. Now, as I think I have mentioned, battery-charging was a hazardous business for a single-engined Ocarina boat. In theory it should have been possible to apply a running charge, clutching the diesel to the propeller shaft through the E-motor so as to generate a current while moving the boat through the water. But in practice our puny 60hp engine made this a futile exercise, and we soon found that the lesser evil was to lie stopped, decks awash, for sometimes a couple of hours at a stretch while the diesel rattled away at full speed, stuffing amperes into the battery cells for all it was worth.

I had taken the precaution of having *U13*'s conning tower painted with a pattern of wavy horizontal stripes to break up its outline, but even so I would be extremely glad when the ammeter needles reached "Vollgeladen" and we could get moving again. My earnest hope was that we were hidden within the moon-shadow cast by the high cliffs behind Budua . . . Suddenly there was a flurry among the waves about five hundred metres to starboard. Dolphin, I thought to myself—then froze in horror: a ruler-straight line of phosphorescence was streaking through the water towards me. There was no time to shout a warning, nor any point, since it would have taken at least half a minute to clutch in the propeller and get moving. All that I could do was shut my eyes tight and wait to be blown to bits. But there was no explosion: only a dull, booming impact and cries of alarm from down below, then a grating noise as the torpedo scraped beneath our keel to leap out of the water on the other side, hissing like a thousand serpents before it plunged back to continue its headlong rush into the darkness. I climbed down the conning-tower ladder, legs like sticks of gelatine, to find that, apart from a large dent in her pressure hull and a few sprung rivets, *U13* had suffered no damage. An Army patrol found the torpedo next morning embedded in the beach near Cape Platamone. It bore the stamp of the Toulon Naval Arsenal and was found to have a defective nose pistol, which had fired but failed to detonate the main charge. After that there was no more talk of bad luck: in fact as the months passed our boat became known as "der glückliche Dreizehner"—"Lucky Thirteen."

And not only lucky: the cup of *U13*'s offensive capability was soon filled to overflowing by the addition of real artillery to supplement our 8mm Schwarzlose machine gun. This was a 4.7cm gun salvaged from an old battleship. It was mounted on a pedestal on the foredeck and served by two men standing on a flimsy folding platform made out of two hinged steel plates. The gun's value seemed largely symbolic at the time, since its shell weighed barely a kilogram, but it was to come in useful on a number of occasions over the next few months.

The winter of 1915–16 brought a good deal of work for us along the coasts of Montenegro and Albania. Serbia had been overrun by the Central Powers, and the Serbian Army, along with many civilians, had set off on what was to become one of the most dreadful episodes of even that murderous war: a mass retreat on foot through the Balkans in the middle of winter. Perhaps three hundred thousand people set out; a mere fifty thousand reached the coast of Albania two months later. Starvation, cold, typhus and exhaustion had done for the rest, so that for years afterwards the terrible crags of the Drina Pass were littered with the skulls and bones of the fallen. What was left of the Serbian Army was by now such an emaciated wreck that our Fleet Commander Admiral Haus gave an order that we were not to attack the ships carrying its remains to Corfu. I would not have done so anyway. The Serbs had dragged thousands of Austrian prisoners along with them, and I still cherished some faint hope that my brother Anton, missing in Serbia since August 1914, might be among the survivors.

The annihilation of Serbia seemed to open up many new opportunities for Austria in the Balkans. The mountain kingdom of Montenegro was now suing for an armistice, so Vienna's thoughts began to turn towards Albania, which might perhaps be annexed along with Montenegro once the war ended. Poor old Austria: even in these twilight years she still cherished the habits that had once made her great, always seeking to purloin a kingdom here or a province there while the other Powers had their backs turned. Looking back on it now, it was all very ridiculous and rather unedifying; as if an aged pickpocket on his deathbed should have attempted to steal the priest's watch while being administered the last rites. But the Monarchy's sudden interest in Albania meant that we were now to become exceedingly familiar with the coastline of that wild and primitive land.

"Kreuzung vor Albanien . . .": how that laconic log entry brings it all back to me. I can still recite the landmarks of that desolate coast, a litany intoned against the steady chugging of a four-cylinder diesel: San Giovanni, the Drina Estuary, Cape Rodoni, Cape Pali, Durazzo, Cape Laghi, the Skumbini Estuary, Karavasta Bay, the Semani Estuary, Saseno and Cape Linguetta. I still smell the rotting-swamp odour borne out to us on the wind; hear the screaming of the wildfowl that would rise in vast clouds from the marshes at every gunshot; still see, always, the eroded grey-brown mountains looming in the distance like a row of decayed teeth.

We soon formed the opinion that if Vienna or Rome or anyone else coveted this poverty-stricken country then they were more than welcome to it. The only settlements of any note were Durazzo in the north and Valona in the south. I never saw Valona; but if Durazzo was anything to go by I can scarcely think I missed very much. For far from being a town, Durazzo was nothing more than a run-down fishing village of old Venetian houses crumbling away beneath the overgrown ramparts of a Turkish fortress. As for the few other coastal settlements, they were no more than clusters of mud hovels inhabited by perhaps a few dozen malaria-ridden fishermen who might have been degenerate Italians or degenerate Greeks, but were certainly degenerates of some kind. One such hamlet, I remember, was populated by Negroes: inbred descendants of the survivors from an eighteenth-century slave-ship.

But why should it have been otherwise? Albania had no industries other than brigandage, no roads, and a total of one kilometre of railway line, which an Italian company had built for loading bauxite at Valona. One of our duties in those last months of 1915 was to stop and search trading vessels along the Albanian coast, since the political situation was confused in the extreme, with some parts of the country under Allied occupation while others were under the nominal suzerainty of pro-Austrian bandit chieftains. In practice though we found the distinction between allied and enemy shipping was not an easy one to draw, for once we had stopped them with a shot across the bows most turned out to be decrepit sailing trabaccolos of no more than a few tonnes' displacement, without flags, without papers and without any discernible idea of whose side they were on—or indeed of who the sides were. They were usually laden with cargoes that would have been familiar to Homer: a few dozen stinking cheeses, resin, dried fish, empty sacks, olives or poisonous local wine which on one occasion (I swear to it on my honour) was being carried in earthenware amphorae. We usually let them go their way unmolested: the k.u.k. Kriegsmarine might have been the smallest Great Power navy, but we were still a reputable firm and not in business to oppress the poor. The only favour that we asked of these vessels in return was to let *U13* lie alongside for a while, using them as cover while we charged our batteries.

A frequent task for us during those months was the transport of secret agents along the Albanian coast—spies, couriers, saboteurs and emissaries to the warring factions inland. Naturally, it was no business of ours to enquire into the affairs of these eminences, some of whom were Albanian political émigrés who could not talk with us, others Austrian intelligence officers who would not. Our job was just to embark them in the Bocche and run them south to the appointed place, where they would be rowed ashore in our tiny collapsible dinghy. However, we were able to surmise that the local population was perhaps not quite as pro-Austrian as Vienna had hoped, because it was very rarely that one of these mysterious personages ever returned for us to pick them up again. Most were shadowy figures, but one of them does stand out in my recollection: Professor Arpád, Count Gyöngyös de Rácspolata und Nagyfutak.

We first made his acquaintance one drizzly December afternoon on the jetty at Gjenović in the Gulf of Cattaro. *U13* was taking on fuel and stores for a five-day patrol down to the Skumbini Estuary. However, our orders had just been changed: we were now to deliver a very important political emissary and his bodyguard to a point on the north side of Cape Laghi, then loiter offshore before re-embarking our passengers at the same spot three nights later.

I was given no idea as to the identity of these two people, so it was a considerable surprise to me, supervising the pumping of diesel oil in my wet, dirty overalls, when a Staff car drew up on the quayside and disgorged two creatures who might have just stepped off the stage at the Theater an der Wien. The effect on my crew was much the same: every last one of them had dropped what he was doing and was staring open-mouthed at this bizarre apparition.

One of them—clearly the more important of the two was a man of small stature with a slim, almost girlish figure, dark brown eyes, a flashing smile beneath a curled moustache and a mass of black ringlets. His costume simply beggared description, a style that blended Viennese operetta with all the illustrations to all the travel books I had ever read: a fawn sheepskin hat with a cockade of pheasant's feathers, a high-collared green cloak, a cummerbund stuffed with daggers and pistols, blue-striped breeches and red morocco top-boots. Behind him though, in case anyone should have been disposed to laugh, there lumbered a creature who made even our ex-circus strong man Grigorović look like an underdeveloped youth: a great, shambling, hirsute monster dressed in a goatskin jerkin—about four or five goats' worth by the looks of it—a white skull-cap and baggy greyish pantaloons over leather slippers. He too carried a small armoury stuck into his cummerbund; but I got the impression that in this case the weapons were more for use than for decoration. His face was more disturbing than any amount of weaponry though: something hacked from an oakroot with a blunt hatchet, with two glowering coal-black eyes set one on either side of an enormous eagle's beak of a nose, so huge that he seemed unable to see ahead with both eyes at once. These two picturesque figures were accompanied at some distance behind by an embarrassed-looking young Staff officer.

My crew remembered themselves at last, sprang to attention and saluted. Then introductions were exchanged—rather hurriedly, since I divined that the Staff officer was deeply anxious to be rid of his charges.

"Herr Graf Professor, allow me to introduce Linienschiffsleutnant Otto Prohaska, the Captain of *U13*. Herr Schiffsleutnant, may I introduce Herr Graf Professor Gyöngyös and his manservant Achmed."

Without further ado, before I knew what was happening, the Graf Professor stepped forward with a radiant smile, flung wide his ringed hands and embraced me warmly, planting a kiss on my horrified cheek as he did so. I noticed that he smelt strongly of scent. The men gazed in awe.

"Ah, my dear Herr Leutnant, what a pleasure to meet you and your brave sailors. I trust that we shall all enjoy our voyage . . . However," (turning towards *U13* at the quayside) "I must say that your boat looks a good deal smaller than I had been led to believe. But then, Napoleon travelled from Corsica in a rowing boat, did he not?"

I was unable to answer him on this last point, only to make a feeble attempt at welcoming him aboard, and stare in horrified fascination at the Minotaur looming behind him. The Graf Professor sensed this and beamed once more.

"Ah yes, this is my bodyguard Achmed, who will accompany me on this momentous journey of ours."

"Good day Achmed," I ventured, not sure in what language (if any) I should address this brute, "I trust that we shall have a good voyage if the weather sets fair." He glared at me without the slightest flicker of expression, then turned and spat into the water beside the jetty, kicking up a splash like that of a rifle bullet.

"Oh, please excuse him," the count warbled. "He's a Mohammedan and has to clean his mouth out after talking with infidels."

"But he didn't say anything . . ."

"I know; he had his tongue cut out some years ago."

Perhaps in retribution for my making small talk about the weather with a follower of Islam, the two-day voyage to Cape Laghi was one of the most exquisitely miserable of my entire life. A vicious north-westerly gale sprang up out of nowhere as we passed Durazzo. There was no chance of landing our passengers in such weather, nor was *U13* much good at riding out storms; so in the end we dived to fifteen metres to try to escape the worst of the short, heavy seas and the driving rain. But even at this depth our little boat rolled and pitched in a most alarming manner. Everything was wet through, it was cold and nothing could be cooked; but after a few hours of this none of us wanted to eat anyway, as one by one we fell into the grip of acute seasickness. Before long an evil-smelling enamel bucket was being passed around like some obscene communion chalice—not always in time, either.

This was all wretched enough no doubt, but such things were the common lot of submariners in those days. No, what made it all utterly unbearable was the presence of our two passengers. Achmed seemed unaffected by the queasy rolling of the boat, content merely to sit motionless, almost filling one bench in the tiny officers' quarters, glaring straight ahead of him as the hideous reek of his damp goatskin jerkin provided a sort of basso continuo to the symphony of stenches that pervaded our ship of miseries. The count, however, was anything but silent. Seemingly immune to seasickness and entirely indifferent to the sufferings of those around him, he chattered endlessly, tirelessly, manically about his own remarkable person, character, connections and accomplishments; all in a lisping, sing-song Magyar German which was all the more hateful to me, I must confess, because I could hear in it a faint echo of my beloved Elisabeth's accent. At least while I was on watch in the control room I had some respite—though he did make his way there at one point to offer some helpful hints on submarine navigation. But then it came to Béla Meszáros's turn to stand watch, and I think that in all my career as a naval officer I never saw a man smarter about reporting for duty as he emerged, grey-faced and trembling, at the end of a four-hour stint with the count and his manservant. As he squeezed past me in the narrow passageway he struck his forehead expressively with the flat of his hand, rolled up his eyes and uttered the words, "Kristus Mária!" It was now my turn to face the heavy artillery as I sat down, sick and bone-weary, on the bench opposite the count and Achmed.

It appeared that Professor the Count Gyöngyös was a world-renowned ethnographer, explorer and archaeologist now engaged, with Vienna's blessing, in no less an enterprise than that of claiming the throne of Albania, a position for which he was uniquely qualified (he said) by his intimate knowledge of that unhappy land, his unparalleled gift for winning the trust of savage peoples and his complete fluency in colloquial and literary Albanian (one of the twenty-seven languages of which he claimed total command). He was in short a man who had been everywhere, who had done everything and who was on terms of intimacy (as he had remarked to the King of Denmark only last month) with absolutely everybody who counted for anything in the world. It also transpired that he was a writer of great note: author, about 1910, of a seminal work which proved conclusively that the Magyars were not a minor Turkic tribe who had somehow wandered into Central Europe but the founders of all the world's great civilisations, including those of Latin America. All in all, it was one of the great living nightmares of my life, like being locked in a railway compartment with a lunatic. A lunatic, moreover, who had a disturbing habit of punctuating his endless discourse by leaning across and placing his hand on my upper thigh . . . The minutes ticked by like weeks, broken only by spasms of retching on my part as the boat's motion grew crazier and the waves of stench from Achmed's goatskins hit me with renewed force. The count seemed quite oblivious to my sufferings, only pausing once to remark helpfully, as I tried to bring up my liver, that this was only to be expected if one tried to make sailors out of a land-locked people like the Czechs. At long last, after four hours, I was able to make my excuses and prepare to go back on watch, just as the count set about demonstrating to me that "Aristotle" was in fact a corruption of the Magyar "Háry Stotul."

"Rather trying, isn't he?" Fregattenleutnant Meszáros remarked pleasantly as I crawled back into the control room. I groaned.

"For God's sake Meszáros, you deal with him. He's one of your demented tribe. Why should I be Head Keeper in a floating asylum for escaped Hungarians?"

"Don't worry—I can manage him. It's easy if you know how."

With that the Fregattenleutnant made his way back to the officers' compartment and resumed his place on the bunk opposite our two passengers. It gave me considerable satisfaction to observe how, about five minutes later, without the slightest warning, Achmed suddenly leant over and vomited copiously into his lap.

The gale abated at last and we were able to come up again to land the count and Achmed at the appointed place, our intense pleasure at being rid of them alloyed only by the knowledge that we would have to come back for them three nights later. The count kissed me once more as he stepped into the dinghy, assuring me that he would shortly call for me to make me Grand Admiral of the Albanian Navy. Then he and Achmed disappeared into the darkness, leaving me to soothe an indignant young engine-room rating whose backside the count had fondled while making his way to the conning-tower ladder.

There were no lights on the shore when we came back to collect them three nights later. I was nervous of hanging around for long in the darkness, so I called for a volunteer to go ashore and see whether they were waiting for us. Of course, Grigorović had offered himself for the job before anyone else could open his mouth: our big Montenegrin was always ready for any desperate adventure. He thumbed the edge of his knife, thrust the weapon back into its sheath with a theatrical flourish, then clambered down into the dinghy, filling it like a bullock in a washtub. The machine gun was set up on its tripod atop the conning tower and the searchlight was made ready, just in case, but after an anxious ten minutes or so we heard the faint splash of oars in the darkness, then the soft bump as the little canvas boat came up against *U13*'s side. Grigorović scrambled on to the deck, saluted and whispered hoarsely, "Obediently report, Herr Kommandant, that I find nothing, only this on a stone."

He handed me something wrapped in a damp sheet of paper. I took it down into the control room and opened it. As I did so two fleshy objects fell out on to the chart table. They looked at first like lamb's kidneys, but were rather lighter in colour. The bloodstained paper that had wrapped them bore a crudely scrawled message in blue crayon:

AUꙄTRIA ꙄWINEꙄ

IF YOU WANTꙄ THE REꙄT OF YOUR "KING," COME AND GET HIM!

Such little failures aside though, we had every reason to feel pleased with ourselves as 1916 began; for on the third day of the new year, off Valona, a French destroyer had been unlucky enough to wander across our bows.

We were on the second day of a patrol down the Albanian coast with instructions to interfere with the troop convoys ferrying men across from

Italy. By early afternoon we were about eight miles offshore, north-west of the twin-humped island of Saseno and the approaches to Valona. The sun was shining weakly and there was only a light swell running, but a cold wind was blowing down from the mountains and drifting occasional thin curtains of sleet across the face of the sea. About 2:30 p.m. the look-outs sighted a smoke-cloud to westwards, and within a few minutes the tops of their masts were visible: at least five ships, steaming straight towards us. I rang the alarm bells for diving, and within five minutes I was examining them through the periscope. There was a grey-painted, twin-funnelled liner of about eight thousand tonnes followed by no less than four cargo steamers and escorted by two destroyers. As they drew nearer I was able to get a better look at the two warships. One was Italian, *Nembo* class. The other vessel was unmistakably French, with its two pairs of thin, tall funnels, one pair at each end.

The torpedo-tube bow caps were opened and the portable firing buttons were hooked on to the front side of the periscope. These were an idea of my own, and made at my own expense: a pair of buttons with a trailing wire lead so that I could aim and fire the torpedoes myself instead of losing that vital split-second while the order was being transmitted.

I raised the periscope for a quick look around. We were now some five hundred metres off the liner's port bow. She was steaming at about twelve knots, to judge by the position of the stern-wave, and she was evidently a troop-ship, her rails packed with a solid mass of grey-clad Italian infantry. I hauled down the periscope and turned the boat twenty-five degrees port to give us our deflection. We had now closed to four hundred metres from our prey. I raised the periscope again to take aim, and pressed the starboard firing button when I judged the angle to be right. Air bubbles boiled up in front of the periscope. I counted up to five—important not to get the torpedoes too close together—but just as I was about to fire the port torpedo, the sea was suddenly lashed into a fury of spray. The Italians had spotted our periscope and were blazing away at it with their rifles. I hauled it down again smartly: it was only the thickness of a broomstick and the range was three hundred metres, but with a thousand men emptying their rifles at it the statistical probability of a hit was very high. *U13* had only the one periscope; if we lost it we were blind.

We counted and waited, but there was no explosion: the torpedo had missed. I took the boat down to fifteen metres under the track of the convoy and bobbed up again a couple of minutes later on the other side. It certainly looked as if the moral effect had been nearly as devastating as a hit: the convoy was scattering in all directions, and two of the cargo steamers had collided in their haste to escape. They were now waltzing around, locked together like a pair of mating scorpions. I was deciding whether to give them our port torpedo when a much more tempting target hove into view from behind them: the French destroyer, clipping along at a good twenty knots with smoke streaming from her spindly funnels. I cannot really say what instinct made me do it; certainly there was no time for any rational calculation of range, speed or angle on the bow. I just pressed the firing button, saw the torpedo begin its run and then went deep without waiting for further particulars. Quite frankly it was—how do you say?—a pot-shot, so no one was more surprised than I when after ten seconds or so the boat shuddered to the noise of an exploding torpedo. The men cheered, and I stepped from behind the periscope, smiling modestly and trying to look as if I had planned it all in advance. After two minutes or so we came back up for a look, just long enough for me to catch a glimpse of the Frenchman, stopped in the water amid a haze of smoke and steam and already well down by the stern. Then it was back to twenty metres—and not a moment too soon, since propellers rushed overhead a few seconds later and a bomb exploded close enough to break two light bulbs and put the gyro compass out of action. The crew spent the next five minutes draining the starboard tube and loading our single reserve torpedo, but by the time we were able to rejoin battle the ships of the convoy had become mere smudges on the darkening horizon, leaving nothing behind them but a quantity of wooden wreckage, a few coal sacks and a life-jacket. The sleet flurries were thickening now as the daylight faded, so we broke off the action and turned towards home.

We reached the Bocche about midday the following day, to be told on arrival that one of our seaplanes had watched the French destroyer sink just before nightfall as they tried to tow her back to Brindisi. I never did learn her name while the war was on, and in the years after 1918 I had more important things on my mind. But a few weeks ago my young friend Kevin Scully went to the reference library in Swansea and took some notes from a book about French warships. It seems that the destroyer *Turco,* 530 tonnes, was sunk by a U-Boat in the Southern Adriatic on 3 January 1916. So I suppose that must have been me.

We were all paraded on board the divisional flagship when we got back to Cattaro and congratulated on our victory by the Archduke Ferdinand Salvator, C.-in-C. of the Balkan Army Group, who happened to be visiting the Bocche.

"Ah, Prohaska," he had said, "I understand that you are a Czech?"

I considered for a moment: true, I had been born a Czech, but for fifteen years I had been an Austrian officer, and therefore without nationality. However, the Archduke was clearly taking an interest in the nationalities question; and anyway, one could not contradict members of the Imperial House.

"Yes Your Imperial Highness, I have the honour to report that I am a Czech, but an officer of the House of Austria."

It appeared that this mildly non-standard reply caused two wires to touch momentarily in the archducal small-talk circuits. Consternation flickered across his features. But only for an instant.

"Ah yes, I see . . . splendid . . . er, excellent. And tell me now, how long have you been a Czech?"

"Well Your Imperial Highness . . . really since birth I suppose . . ."

"Since birth you say? Amazing, quite extraordinary. And tell me, when did you decide to become one?"

By now I too was beginning to lose my bearings in this conversation.

"Um . . . I . . . well, the matter was really decided for me by my parents, Your Imperial Highness."

"By your parents?—excellent, capital. And how are they?"

"I have the honour to report that my father is in very good health, but that my mother has been dead since 1902."

"Since 1902, you say? Splendid, delighted to hear it! Well Pokorny, convey my regards to her and tell her that I wish her a speedy recovery!"

The Archduke and his ADC, General Hermann Stolp von Klobuczar, came for a dive with us later aboard *U13*. The Archduke was greatly impressed, the General less so. He took me aside later, flicking the skirts of his greatcoat with his riding crop in annoyance.

"Herr Leutnant," he rumbled, "I note with the gravest displeasure that it is the custom aboard this boat of yours for enlisted men to reply to orders without the regulation 'I most obediently report' and without standing at the salute three paces in front of their superior until receipt of the order has been acknowledged."

"But Herr General, this is scarcely practicable when diving . . ."

"Silence!" he growled. "The day that rankers are treated as sentient creatures with minds of their own Old Austria will perish."

And after all this I was obliged to put on my best uniform and pose for a photograph. This was later turned into a postcard, No. 27 in a series entitled "War-Heroes of the Dual Monarchy." I also began to receive a growing volume of letters from young females proposing marriage. I sat one morning aboard the depot ship at Gjenović, opening yet another batch of mail. I read the first, and groaned loudly.

"Oh God no, Meszáros, not another delegation of patriotic Viennese schoolgirls. This lot are from the Lyceum for the Daughters of the Nobility; they're on their way here to meet me in person the day after tomorrow and present *U13* with an embroidered tablecloth." The Fregattenleutnant sucked at his pipe reflectively.

"Permit me to observe that it would be nice if *U13* had a table to put it on."

"Help me, Meszáros, I'm a sailor, not a matinée idol, and this is the fifth patriotic delegation this month."

He thought for a while, then brightened. "I'll tell you what, Herr Kommandant. I'm due for three days' leave from tomorrow morning and I was going up to see a lady friend in Sarajevo. Let's send them a telegram that I'll travel up to meet them there. I can collect their damned tablecloth on your behalf and save you the trouble of receiving them."

"Good man, Meszáros. I shall be eternally grateful to you."

He returned three days later. I was sitting at breakfast in the wardroom as he tottered in and slumped down at the table, pale and hollow-eyed. There was real coffee going, requisitioned from a captured Italian steamer, so I poured him out a cup of this almost forgotten luxury. He stared at it dully, then spoke in a listless voice.

"Little bitches—what's the world coming to?"

"What happened Meszáros? Speak to me, man."

"They arranged to meet me in the Hotel Slavija: three of them with their stringy old duck of a schoolmistress. Then the schoolmistress was suddenly taken ill, just before I got there, and the girls arranged to meet me in a private suite—'to make the presentation away from the hustle and bustle' they said. Not bad-looking girls either, all about sixteen, I'd say. Well, they got me in there, and the girl in charge gave me a funny look. Then I heard the door lock behind me, and things went on from there. The little whores wouldn't let me go until that evening, taking turns with me— kept threatening they'd call the manager and have me arrested for rape if I didn't do what they wanted, then sobbing and saying that I was a callous brute who had no pity for poor girls who'd lost their sweethearts in the war and were all going to be old maids for the rest of their lives. I tell you, by the time they let me go I could hardly remember my own name."

"Meszáros, you idiot—you could be had up for sexual assault on minors if this got out. The penalty for . . ."

"Don't you worry about that; they don't know who I was."

"However not?"

"I told them I was you."

"You . . . what?"

"Oh, the eldest one gave me a funny sort of look and said that I hadn't got a moustache and that I looked shorter than in the photographs. But I explained it away—said that I'd shaved it off to avoid being assassinated by Allied agents. Anyway, they pretended to believe me." He paused to take a gulp of coffee. "Oh, by the way, I forgot the tablecloth."

11

SILVER TO THE SAHARA

I T WAS LATE IN FEBRUARY 1916. *U13* had been drydocked for
repairs at Gjenović and her crew had departed on a fortnight's leave;
that is, except for Maschinenmeister Lehár and myself, who had delayed our departure by a day to assist the naval repair-yard men. There had
been trouble with the diving rudder, and I wanted to make sure that it was
put right. After that we would be off on leave like the rest: Lehár to visit his
ironmonger's widow in Pola, I to meet my fiancée Elisabeth in Agram.

There we were in our overalls, scrambling about under the dripping,
weed-hung stern of our boat, when suddenly a voice called down from the
side of the floating dock:

"Hey, you down there, damn you!" I crawled out, straightened my back
and looked upwards. A Seekadett, barely eighteen years old by the look of
him, was calling down to me from the railing around the edge of the dock.
"You there, you insolent pig—stand to attention when you speak to an
officer or I'll have you put under arrest. Where's the Captain of this boat?"
Of course, I had no cuff-rings on my overalls, so I reached as casually as
possible for my cap and placed it on my head.

"I have the honour to report, High-Born One, that I am the Captain
of this boat. Might I enquire by whom I have the honour to be called a
pig and threatened with arrest, and in what I might perhaps be of service
to Your Excellency?"

He turned a rich plum colour, saluted, and glared at me with barely
concealed loathing.

"Herr Schiffsleutnant Prohaska of *U13* is requested to report immediately to the Flag Officer of the 5th Heavy Division. The Admiral's launch
is waiting alongside."

"But I must wash and change out of my overalls first."

"I obediently report that the Admiral's instructions were that you should report at once: the matter is very urgent."

So there I was, still dressed in my overalls, with only my second-best peaked cap as a concession to naval etiquette, whisked away in the Admiral's gleaming motor launch. It gave me intense pleasure to see the agony on my young companion's face as I sat down on the spotless white bench-cushions—prior to giving him my views on respectful treatment of subordinates.

I cannot pretend though that I felt anywhere near as confident as I appeared that sunlit morning as the motor launch purred across the smooth waters of Teodo Bay, bearing me towards my interview with the Admiral, for a recent incident was preying on my mind.

It had all happened one morning about three weeks before. The k.u.k. Armee had just occupied the port of Durazzo, and *U13* had received a wireless message telling us to assist the land forces by bombarding enemy positions at a place called Kephali, about twenty kilometres down the coast towards Cape Laghi. The enemy was not specified, and when we consulted the charts for the area, which were very poor, we could find no such place. In the end we stopped a passing trabaccolo and asked for directions. "No, no," they said, "no such place as Kephali; you must want Kephrati." Well, Kephrati seemed at least to be in the right place, more or less. So about 9 a.m., just as the early mists were clearing, *U13* surfaced and commenced bombardment from a range of five thousand metres.

"Bombardment" is a grand-sounding word for what actually took place: we fired off thirty or so shells from our ludicrous 4.7cm popgun, to no apparent effect other than knocking a corner off one hovel, setting fire to the thatch of a second and demolishing a rowing boat pulled up on the beach. The grey-uniformed defenders replied with a spatter of rifle fire which, at that range, was entirely ineffectual. Still, it made a change from the monotony of patrolling: the crew had great fun treating our silly little gun like the main armament of a battleship, with a train of layers, loaders and ammunition-handlers to serve a weapon which a ten-year-old could have loaded with one hand and fired with the other. Béla Meszáros assumed the role of Gunnery Officer, perched on top of the mine-deflector wire supports like a tubby sea-gull and observing the fall of shot through his binoculars. Suddenly he lowered his glasses, swallowed hard and peered through them again intently, then yelled:

"Quick—cease fire!"

"What's the matter?" I called up to him.

"Those fellows over there—I think they're ours!" I clambered up on to the conning tower, snatched the binoculars from him and stared hard at the cluster of huts on the distant shore. A light breeze had sprung up and a flag that had hung limply from a pole over one dwelling began to flutter in the wind. It was red, white and red with a black-patch—perhaps the Austrian eagle—in the middle. I also saw that the soldiers were wheeling up a field gun! There was nothing to do but snatch down our Austrian ensign, turn the boat bows-on and withdraw from the scene as discreetly as possible. The first shell screamed overhead as I closed the conning-tower hatch.

On our return to the Bocche I had written out my combat report—how shall I say?—tactfully, and had submitted it in the hope that everything would blow over. It had seemed at first as if this idiotic incident had escaped notice. But then, that very same morning in the wardroom at Gjenović, I had happened to pick up a copy of the *Armee Zeitung*. My eye was drawn to a report near the bottom of the first page:

HEROIC DEEDS OF OUR U-BOATS

Pola, 28 January

It was reported here today by the k.u.k. Marineoberkommando that on the 26th of this month one of our U-Boats—*U13,* commanded by Lschlt Otto Prohaska—carried out a daring raid of the Albanian port of Kephali. Taking advantage of early-morning mist, *U13* shelled the harbour for over an hour, causing severe damage to military installations, setting warehouses alight and sinking a cargo steamer moored alongside a wharf.

The defenders are reported to have fled in panic and disorder, making hardly any attempt at resistance and allowing our U-Boat to withdraw unharmed once her work had been done.

Lschlt Prohaska is one the Monarchy's most skilful U-Boat captains, having already sunk the Italian cruiser *Colleoni* off Lissa last year and a French destroyer near Valona earlier this month.

This was bad enough, I thought: certainly my report had omitted to mention some particulars, but at least everything that it had contained had been the truth. But then I turned the page, and felt a peculiarly unpleasant sensation as my eye fell on the first column:

HEROIC DEFENCE AGAINST ENEMY SUBMARINE

Mostar, 29 January

It was reported here today in a communiqué from Armeeoberkommando Bosnien that on the 26th of January the Albanian coastal village of Kephrati was successfully defended by our troops against an attack from a large enemy submarine.

The enemy vessel surfaced just after dawn and commenced shelling the positions of k.k. land troops from its two heavy guns. Despite intense bombardment the 14th Company of Landwehr Infantry regiment No. 32, commanded by Oberleutnant Dornberger, made a heroic resistance and returned the fire so effectively that their cowardly assailant was forced to stay too far out to sea for his fire to be effective. The fighting spirit of our men was so splendid that they were seen to stand up in their trenches, shaking their fists at the enemy vessel and shouting, "Long live our Emperor and Fatherland!" and "To the gallows with Asquith and Poincaré!" In the end, fire was opened from the guns of a near by heavy howitzer battery. The submarine was seen to have been hit several times and is believed to have sunk.

Then came the item that sent iced water trickling down my spine:

Throughout the action the enemy vessel was observed to be treacherously flying the red-white-red ensign of the k.u.k. Kriegsmarine.

You can perhaps imagine, then, that I was doing some hard thinking as the motor launch came alongside the division flagship, the old battleship

Monarch. How far could I plead the vagueness of my orders and the inadequacy of the coastal charts? And if the worst came to the worst, to what extent would a sunken French destroyer offset the shelling of our own troops?

The flagship's pale grey paintwork was spotless and its brass gangway railings blazed like gold as the young Seekadett came aboard with his grubby and dishevelled charge in tow. We were piped aboard at the head of the gangway by the sentries in their blue jerseys and immaculate striped vests. I heard the thin whistling falter slightly as they caught sight of me. I was ushered below, and before long I was standing in front of the panelled mahogany door leading into the Admiral's cabin. Somehow I wished that I were more suitably dressed for what might be a hearing preliminary to a court martial.

Kontreadmiral Alexander Hansa was a large, bearded man of about sixty with an air of permanent dyspepsia. His companion, I noted with some relief, was in civilian dress; I could not make out who he might be, but at least he was not the half-expected Oberstauditor of the Navy's legal branch. He was a smallish, rather sallow man in his mid-fifties with a sharp, intelligent, not particularly benevolent face and a neat pointed beard, and he wore a black frock coat which, though worn about the cuffs, was superlatively well cut. The Admiral introduced him to me as Baron von Horvath, of the Imperial and Royal Foreign Ministry's Levant Section. He studied me intently, and if the vagabond-cum-engine-driver figure in front of him was not what he had expected, his training as a diplomat prevented him from betraying it. None the less I felt that some apology was called for.

"Gentlemen," I said, "you must excuse my appearance, but I was called here as a matter of urgency and had no time to wash or to change out of my overalls."

Baron Horvath looked me up and down with his bright, boot-button eyes. "Curious, Herr Schiffsleutnant; very singular. Do you often have to carry out repair work on your ship then?"

"Yes, Herr Baron: I'm afraid U-Boats are packed solid with machinery.

and their crews are very small. Obviously, I don't know as much about the boat's engines as my Chief Engineer, but I still have to know nearly as much, and be prepared to get my hands dirty when necessary."

This seemed to displease the Admiral. He snorted like an aged bison and shook his head.

"New-fangled nonsense . . . Not a bit like when I was young. In those days the officers were for fighting the ship and the mechanics were for working the engines. Mark my words, no good's going to come of mixing the two." He thought for a moment, then turned to me again. "Anyway, Prohaska, I have called you here to meet Baron von Horvath because we wish to entrust to you a particularly delicate and hazardous mission . . ."

"A mission," Horvath added smoothly, as if on cue, "which requires an exceptionally capable officer to lead it and upon the success of which . . ." (a dramatic pause) "may depend a great deal of Austria's foreign policy in the years after this war."

"Now," said the Admiral, "if you will be so good as to sit down, the baron will outline the operation to you. I need hardly stress that you are to maintain the strictest secrecy as to what is said at this meeting."

"You may depend upon me for that, Herr Admiral."

"Excellent. Now, Herr Baron, if you would be so kind . . ."

Horvath laid a thick leather portfolio of documents on the long, highly polished conference table, put on a gold pince-nez, then began.

"Herr Schiffsleutnant, I take it that you are aware of the struggle currently being waged by the Senussi Brethren against the British and the Italians on the borders of Libya and Egypt?"

I was not too well up on this, I must admit, but I tried to look as if this uprising of Saharan tribesmen was a matter particularly close to my heart.

"Yes, Herr Baron, I have heard a good deal about it recently while talking to German U-Boat officers here in Cattaro. I understand that a number of them have made voyages running arms and ammunition to the North African coast."

"Perfectly correct, Herr Schiffsleutnant: our German allies have been doing a great deal in recent months to arm the Senussi against our enemies. And that is why the k.u.k. Foreign Ministry is deeply concerned to take part as well." He pressed his fingertips together and paused, leaning back in his chair to regard me with his bird's eyes. "You see, my dear Prohaska, we are concerned that when this war ends in victory for the Central Powers, as it certainly will before very long, the Mediterranean should not be monopolised by Britain and Germany to the exclusion of Austria-Hungary. The Italians of course are a negligible quantity and will be disposed of without difficulty at the peace negotiations. Likewise the French presence in the region will be drastically reduced. But it is clear that, for the foreseeable future, Britain will maintain a strong Mediterranean fleet while Germany will gain a foothold by perhaps annexing Morocco or Tunisia from the French. What we are really concerned to do at this stage is to prevent Germany from gaining an unhealthy predominance in North Africa, while at the same time preparing the foundations for Austria's emergence as a major Mediterranean power in the 1930s and 40s." He paused to draw a sheet of paper out of the portfolio, then passed it across the table to me. "Here, Herr Schiffsleutnant, tell me what you think of this."

It was a sheet of squared paper bearing three rising lines, one in red ink, one in blue and one in brown. The brown line started well below the other two, but rose rapidly to cross first the blue line, then the red one. I looked at it, mildly puzzled. Horvath smiled.

"The chart represents the growth of the British, French and Austro-Hungarian Mediterranean battle fleets from 1910 to 1970, based on 1914 rates of construction. As you will see, the brown line, which represents us, is set to cross the blue line, which represents France, about 1938, and the red one, which represents Britain, about 1963. The reason for our rapid rise in relation to the other two navies is of course that Britain and France will still have heavy naval commitments elsewhere, while the Dual Monarchy, being purely a Mediterranean power, will be able to keep every dreadnought she builds stationed at Pola."

"Extremely impressive," I remarked. "But please tell me, Herr Baron, how does this fit in with the Senussi revolt?"

"The link is this. As you see, our rivalry with the British will become acute some time in the late 1950s. Now, we at the Foreign Ministry are concerned to see that before that happens, the Imperial and Royal Monarchy should have built up its position in the lands around the southern and eastern shores of the Mediterranean. You are surely aware that one of our beloved Emperor's titles is 'King of Jerusalem'? Well, we intend to make that into a reality."

I whistled inwardly, awed by this serene self-assurance.

"Permit me to observe, Herr Baron, that you diplomats amaze me. Here am I, a U-Boat officer, never sure that he will live to see the next sunrise, and yet you plan for decades ahead."

He smiled a smooth, cat-like smile. "Ah, my dear Prohaska, such is the art of diplomacy. Let me assure you that it is not for nothing that for the past half-millennium the Noble House of Austria has been the principal earthly guardian of the Catholic Church. Like Rome, Vienna has learnt to think in centuries rather than in years."

"So," I ventured, "I take it that you wish me to lead an Austrian gun-running expedition to the Senussi? Well, Herr Baron, as I need hardly tell you, I am your man for any such venture. But permit me to observe that the task will not be an easy one. The Allies keep a close watch on the Otranto Straits, while as for rifles, I must say that I can't think where we are going to obtain them when we can hardly arm our own troops —" Horvath halted me in mid-sentence with an angry flash of his eyes.

"Really Prohaska—be so good as to answer questions when you are asked them, not before. And as for your views on the capabilities of the Monarchy's armaments industry, they are quite uncalled-for." His beard twitched, and his voice settled back into its habitual smoothness. "Now, if you will perhaps allow me to continue. I would like to point out, since you seem not to have noticed it yourself, that I said nothing about shipping arms to the Senussi—at least, not arms as you would probably understand the term." He paused, and rummaged in his trouser pocket like someone digging out a biscuit for a particularly tiresome dog.

"Here, Herr Schiffsleutnant, tell me if you recognise this . . ."

He rolled a large silver coin towards me across the table. It trundled round and round a few times, then lay still. I picked it up and examined it.

I once knew—but have long since forgotten—exactly how it was that Austrian silver dollars of the reign of the Empress Maria Theresa came to be accepted as legal tender throughout almost the whole of the Middle East from the Yemen to Morocco. I think it was something to do with a failed Austrian Levant company in the 1780s, but I forget the details. However, such was and (I believe) still is the case. Certainly the coin I held there that morning was an impressive-looking thing: a good five centimetres across, of thick, heavy silver, embossed with the double eagle of Austria on one side and the heavy-bosomed profile of our late Empress on the other. As I looked at it realisation began to dawn upon me.

"I think I see," I said. "You intend subsidising the Senussi with money instead of rifles."

"Precisely. The supply of coins has been cut off for two years now and demand is intense. Whoever controls this source of money will count for a great deal in the politics of the Levant—far more so in the long run than any mere supplier of Mauser rifles. But the Senussi will not be the end-recipients of most of this consignment: the bulk of it will make its way overland to the Emperor of Abyssinia."

I blinked slightly at this. Horvath smiled indulgently. "Ah, my dear Prohaska, there is more afoot than you fighting men dream of. I don't intend going too far into details, but I am sure you will be aware not only that Abyssinia has a long-standing quarrel with the Italians, but also that it is a Christian country and the last unclaimed territory in Africa. Personally I always considered it a great mistake that the Dual Monarchy never interested itself in colonies . . . But there, this does not concern us now: our immediate problem is that of getting the coins to the Saharan coast—one hundred thousand dollars in this consignment, which makes . . . let me see . . . just over three tonnes inclusive of boxes."

"Well," I said, "that shouldn't pose any particular problems. A fishing cutter could carry that much and we might manage to slip through the straits in a night—" Horvath drummed his fingers on the table.

"Herr Schiffsleutnant! You really must try to listen to what I have to say to you and refrain from offering your own opinions until asked! I said nothing about a surface vessel: as you yourself have observed, the Allies guard the Otranto Straits far too closely to make such a proposition worthwhile. And in any case, Herr Schiffsleutnant, do you think that if we intended using a surface vessel I would have wasted my valuable time travelling all the way down here to interview a U-Boat captain?"

"But, Herr Baron," I protested, "there is only one Austrian U-Boat at present which is sufficiently large and seaworthy to get to North Africa: Trapp's *U14,* and she is currently in the middle of a six-month refit at Pola."

Horvath snorted softly, and when he finally spoke, did so with the air of one reasoning with a child of limited intelligence.

"Exactly, Herr Schiffsleutnant: you have got it at last. We want you to make the voyage in your own *U13.*"

I sat back in my chair, speechless with sheer amazement . . . Surely, not even these civilian idiots could seriously . . .

"Well, Prohaska, what do you think of the idea?"

I swallowed hard and tried to keep calm. I noticed that the Admiral (who had said nothing throughout Horvath's lecture) was intent on studying a fly on the deckhead at the other side of the cabin. I did my best to make my reply sound calm and considered.

"Herr Baron, you know that I will give of my utmost in the service of our Emperor and Fatherland. Also I flatter myself that my record as a U-Boat commander speaks for itself. But I have to tell you here and now that *U13* is a small, coastal submarine quite unsuited to long voyages on the open sea. I doubt whether the boat could even reach North Africa, let alone get back again."

Horvath merely remarked "Hmmmph!" gave me a dismissive glance over the top of his pince-nez and looked down at his papers. "Forgive me, my dear Herr Schiffsleutnant, but I took the trouble to obtain information from the Marine Section of the War Ministry before I set out for Cattaro, and they tell me that your BI-type U-Boats have a range of 1,200 nautical miles on the surface, or 1,500 if extra tanks are filled with oil. Now, I have measured the distance from Cattaro to—let us say—Derna on the map, and I make it just under 1,300 miles there and back: less if you came back to Durazzo. Now, please tell me, what objection can you possibly have?"

"Yes, Herr Baron," I replied. "But with respect, your measurement is 1,300 centimetres over smooth paper, not 1,300 miles over the high seas. Give us a head wind both ways and *U13* would barely make nine hundred miles. The BI-type are extremely bad sea-boats, and your calculations make no allowance for battery-charging, which uses up diesel oil for no distance covered. Also you omit the problems of food and water for perhaps a two-week voyage, not to speak of the difficulty of stowing three tonnes of coins aboard a boat where there is barely room to lie down."

Horvath drummed his fingers on the table with exasperation. "Really Prohaska, from the reports that I had been given of you before I came here I would have expected better. But there it is—the mission must be undertaken: Vienna and Budapest are in complete agreement as to that. The coins are to be delivered by mid-April at the latest, so you are to work out a plan for this operation and submit it to the Admiral within twenty-four hours. Now, if you will excuse me, I must begin my journey back to Vienna. I have to travel by boat across to Zelenika and then spend a day on your villainous narrow-gauge railway before I reach civilisation. I bid you adieu."

He collected up his papers, stood up, shook hands with Kontreadmiral Hansa and me, and was then ushered out to the gangway and the waiting motor launch. After the door had closed behind him the Admiral turned to me. He avoided meeting my eyes.

"Sorry, Prohaska—sorry. I never did care for the diplomats: even less than the politicians in fact. We sailormen just can't talk them down." He sighed. "They've given us a job and a half here, I must say."

"Herr Admiral, you know that I will do my best to carry out my orders."

"Yes, yes, I know that. But you shouldn't have to. Damn it man—I did my best to talk the idiots out of it, and I know that Haus did his best with them up in Pola. Losing a U-Boat and one of our best crews for nothing, we said. But I'm afraid it didn't do any good: Vienna and Budapest are dead set on the plan, just as that louse Horvath said. You know why, I suppose?"

"It never crossed my mind to ask, Herr Admiral."

"No. Well, it's the Magyar scum behind it all. They're scared stiff in Budapest that when we win this war Austria will have to annex territory: perhaps Serbia, perhaps Poland, but certainly somewhere that will bring a great many more Slavs into the Monarchy. And if that happens, then one day the Slavs might gang up with the Germans to force them to treat their serfs better. So that's why the Hungarian government is so interested in colonies: anything to stop Vienna getting more territory in Europe. Anyway, Prohaska, I'm afraid that the Navy is locked into this crazy scheme, so just tell me what you think you will require and I shall do my best to see that you get it."

My plan, such as it was, was ready by the next afternoon. *U13*'s existing tanks were to be filled to capacity with diesel oil: 5,200 litres, giving a theoretical range of 1,500 nautical miles plus a further five hundred miles' safety margin. Two extra tanks to be installed beneath the deck casing to allow the amount of lubricating oil carried to be doubled from eight hundred to 1,600 litres. All three torpedoes plus the gun and its ammunition would be landed, and the crew would be reduced from sixteen to eight, the bare minimum necessary for standing watches. The displacement thus saved would be devoted to three tonnes of coins, packed in wooden boxes to form a false floor on the deck, and in canvas bags for stowage inside the torpedo tubes. Food and drinking water would be fitted in wherever possible. Finally *U13* would be towed as far as possible south of Cattaro on the outward voyage, and met as far south as possible on the homeward trip.

I must confess that I smiled as I wrote the words "on the homeward trip." From what I had seen of the Ocarina boats and their seakeeping abilities I doubted whether we would make it even one way, let alone back again. It would only take one decent gale or—more likely—the breakdown of the single engine and we would drift helplessly until a sea broached us and rolled us over. The best that we could hope for, so far as I could see, was to be picked up by an Allied ship and then spend God alone knew how long in a prisoner-of-war camp. But orders were orders, and if it was the Imperial and Royal Monarchy's pleasure to sacrifice one of its few effective submarines in a crazy prestige display—which would doubtless turn out to be the very opposite—then who was I to protest, who had sworn many years before to give of my utmost in the service of the Noble House of Austria ". . . on land and water, in the air and under the water." Poor Elisabeth though: a widow once already, and her fiancé now being sent off in all probability to an unknown grave somewhere west of Crete. Not for the first time it occurred to me that women are war's real heroes.

My recommendations were accepted, so it only remained for me now to give up my two weeks' leave so that I could put the arrangements in hand with the U-Station workshops at Gjenović: chiefly a matter of manufacturing and installing the necessary extra tanks. The days passed quickly: soon the crew would be back from their leave and I would be faced with the task—to which I did not in the least look forward—of selecting the seven lucky men who would have the privilege of accompanying me on this voyage to nowhere. Perhaps mercifully, I was so busy that there was little time to think about the possibility that I would never see Elisabeth again.

Until very early one morning, about ten days later, an orderly woke me in my room in the wooden hut that served as sleeping-quarters for U-Boat captains on shore.

"Obediently report, Herr Schiffsleutnant, that there's a young lady waiting to see you at the main gate: a Countess Erlendy-Bratianu." Hardly able to believe my ears, I leapt out of bed, dressed hurriedly and rushed over to the orderly room at the gate. There she stood, tired and travel-stained, but still as luminously beautiful as ever.

"Otto, my dearest love. It seems that you didn't get my telegram after all? Well, never mind; I'm here."

"But . . . How did you . . . This is a war zone . . . Civilians aren't supposed to . . . ?"

"Two days on the footplate of a locomotive: the driver and fireman were very sweet about it. Anyway, I'd better tidy myself up before we go to breakfast. I'm dying to meet your brother officers: they sound great fun, going by your letters." She thanked the guard detail, leaving them bemused in the middle of an almost visible golden haze: even Provost Petty Officer Krawczyk, who was seen—for the only time in recorded history—to undergo a sort of momentary facial spasm that might have been a smile. Then we made our way across to the mess; the stones of the barrack square turned to air-cushions beneath my feet as she walked beside me, her arm tucked under mine.

The next four days passed in a dreamlike state of happiness. Most of the work in preparation for the voyage was now well in hand, so I could take some time off to wander with her through the olive groves on the hillsides above the Bay of Teodo, or sit perched among the limestone screes above the tree-line and look down at the warships moored like wooden toys on the ultramarine waters below. Love is a strange thing. There we were, about to be parted perhaps for ever, and yet I remember it as one of the happiest times of my life; the joy of her nearness somehow all the more poignant for the knowledge that these might be our last days together.

She left, and the men returned from their leave; I was faced with the onerous duty of selecting my crew for the voyage. It proved to be a difficult task, but not quite in the way I had anticipated: for the truth is that every single non-commissioned member of the crew volunteered to go, even married men with children like Warrant Officer Steinhüber. I had made it clear that our mission would be a dangerous one and the chances of success not high, but go they all would, and in the end we had to draw lots. I asked Steinhüber why everyone was so anxious to come along. He thought a little and sucked his teeth.

"Well, Herr Kommandant, we all volunteered for U-Boats, and most of us volunteered for the Navy, and I suppose we want to have some yarns to tell our grandchildren when we're old."

"But how do you know that you're going to get back to have grandchildren?"

"That's true; but for one thing I might stay behind and still get run over by a tram in Pola, and for another, wanting grandchildren to tell about it will make us a lot more careful to see that we all get home."

In the end I selected a crew. It comprised Lehár, Maschinenquartiermeister Kucharek and Elektromatrose Zaccarini to manage the engines and electrical systems; myself, Béla Meszáros, Steinhüber, Grigorović and Telegraphist Stonawski as the seaman branch responsible for navigation, weapons, wireless and everything else. It was a meagre complement even for so small a vessel as *U13,* but it was the largest we could carry, given the extremely limited space available for rations and drinking water once our cargo had been stowed aboard.

The cargo gave us more trouble than anything else in those last days of March 1916. The boxes and bags of silver dollars were brought by rail to Zelenika, under heavy guard and in conditions of secrecy so elaborate that before long the whole military and civil population of the Bocche was talking of nothing else. Then it was loaded on to motor lorries and brought to the quayside at Gjenović with an armed escort that most people would have considered excessive had the boxes contained the Imperial crown jewels, the national gold reserves and half the Holy Relics of Europe. And the paperwork—my god, the paperwork! Nothing in my career, even in the bureaucracy-ridden armed forces of the Dual Monarchy, had prepared me for the exhausting paper-chase that filled the next eight or nine days. A small army of auditors, clerks and chair-polishers of every description had descended on U-Station Cattaro-Gjenović, which had been cleared of all unnecessary personnel as if the smallpox had broken out. Each box of coins was carried from one shed to the next in the midst of a platoon of armed sailors, then the triple seals were broken open in the presence of myself and three auditors and the dollars were solemnly counted out, one by one. Then the boxes were resealed, and everyone present had their pockets searched by another detail of auditors. I would sign my way through a sheaf of papers until my wrist ached. Official stamps— Treasury stamps, War Ministry stamps, Marineoberkommando stamps, 5th Division stamps—would pound between ink-pads and papers like horse's hooves on the Schmelz during the spring parade. Then the box would be carried out again amid an armed guard and up the gangplank on to *U13*'s deck, where it would be passed down the hatch and solemnly stowed below while I and the auditors went through yet another round of signing, stamping and having our pockets searched. All in all, I think that it was about the most exquisitely exhausting, time-consuming, utterly pointless ritual that I ever saw or took part in: pointless, because it seemed never to have occurred to the swarming Treasury officials that once *U13* was at sea all we would need to do, had we been so inclined, would be to run her ashore in some secluded bay on the coast of Corfu, bury the silver, have ourselves interned for the duration and then come back to dig it up once the war was over. Still, somehow we got it all done. The last boxes of rations were stowed below decks, the last checks made and the last letters were written home. Before long we were ready to set sail.

The day before our departure there was a surprise for us: it was suddenly announced that we would be carrying a passenger with us. He turned out to be a Fregattenkapitän Richard Friedenthal of the Marine Evidenzbureau, the Austrian naval intelligence service. He was a tall, lean, grey-haired, taciturn man in his late forties, an eminent Arabist and an explorer of some note. He was to travel only one way with us, going inland to visit the Grand Master of the Senussi before travelling south across the Sahara en route for the Sudan and Abyssinia, where he was to conduct secret negotiations on Vienna's behalf. That was as much as I was able to gather, since he spoke very little to us. His presence was not altogether welcome, being an extra mouth to feed. But at least he was a naval officer and would thus help lighten the burden of watch-keeping aboard an undermanned, grossly overloaded submarine.

The morning of 30 March dawned cloudy and wet as *U13* cast off her moorings and edged away from the jetty at Gjenović. A thin drizzle was falling, and rags of low cloud drifted through the stunted pine trees on the mountainsides above the Kumbor Narrows as our little vessel waddled out on to the waters of Topla Bay. There we carried out a brief dive to adjust our underwater trim, then set off again. Once we had cleared the outer minefields around the entrance to the Bocche, off Punto d'Arza, we fell in with the destroyer S.M.S. *Honvéd,* which was to tow us the eighty-odd miles down the Albanian coast to the Semani Estuary, the southerly limit for Austrian surface vessels in daylight.

Even this first leg of our journey proceeded at the pace of a floating funeral cortège, for *U13* was so low in the water that if the destroyer tried to tow us at much above eight knots our diving planes would keep digging into our bow-wave and trying to trip us up. Dusk was already falling as we reached our point of departure. *Honvéd* stopped her engines and we slipped the steel towing hawser. Then the destroyer made a wide turn and came past us, heading for home. As she passed by a voice boomed out through a speaking trumpet.

"Addio, *U13*. We don't know where you're off to, but may you break your neck and your legs anyway!"

"Thank you *Honvéd,*" I shouted back. "We can't tell you where we're going, but when we get back from China we'll bring you a bird's nest."

Honvéd's stern slipped past us and began to disappear into the evening murk. Many times before then and since I have felt the loneliness of command. But never as acutely, I think, as that drizzling evening off the coastal swamps of Albania, standing there in dripping oilskins on the conning tower of that tiny submarine, so overloaded that the oily swell slopped and gurgled in the flooding vents along the lower edge of the deck casing. Somewhere in the back of my head there echoed the tap-tap of a mason's hammer, cutting a marble tablet for the Marinekirche in Pola: TO THE MEMORY OF THE OFFICERS AND MEN OF S.M.U. 13, LAST SPOKEN OFF THE COAST OF ALBANIA 30 MARCH 1916—MIT GOTT FÜR KAISER UND VATERLAND.

But there; "The task of an officer of the Habsburgs" (they used to tell us at the Marine Akademie) "is to lead his men forward fearlessly and resolutely to win ever greater victories for the Noble House of Austria: yes, even though he should have filled his trousers with fright a minute before." And anyway (I thought to myself) if you were so scared of drowning you could have stayed in Hirschendorf and become a pharmacist or a schoolmaster—in which case you would also have become a reserve Army officer and the crows would long since have picked your bones in some field in Serbia or Poland. So it was with a resolute hand that I reached out and pulled the handle of the engine-room telegraph back to "Start Engines." There was a pause, then a hiss of compressed air from below decks, then a sudden snort of dark grey smoke as the Körting diesel rumbled into life. I let it run for a minute or so to warm up, then pointed the signal lamp in the direction of *Honvéd*—by now a faint, dark smudge to northwards—and blinked out the message "Everything in order." A light winked back, then the destroyer vanished into the drizzle. I turned to Grigorović, standing ready behind the surface steering wheel at the front of the conning tower.

"Prepare to steer compass course 120 degrees."

"Compass course 120 degrees, Herr Kommandant." Then I slid the telegraph handle to "Half-Speed Ahead." Down below Maschinenmeister Lehár let in the clutch, and a wave began to surge along the sides of the deck casing. We were on our way.

12

TO THE SHORES OF AFRICA

ESPITE MY FOREBODINGS, our passage through the Allies' "Otranto Anti-Submarine Barrage" proved to be remarkably easy. But that was always the way with the Otranto Straits: one never knew quite what to expect. I made the passage twenty-eight times in all between 1916 and the end of 1918. Sometimes we would be harried without respite from the Semani to Fáno Island—chased by destroyers, harassed by armed trawlers, depth-charged while submerged and machine-gunned by aircraft and motor boats when we attempted to surface. At other times though, even in the last months of the war, we were able to make the entire fifty-mile passage on the surface in broad daylight with no one apparently taking the slightest notice. But I suppose that this was only to be expected. The Otranto Straits are forty miles wide and eight hundred metres deep in the middle: far too deep for the minefields which made life so hazardous for our German comrades trying to run through the Dover Straits. Nor can it have been easy to maintain a submarine-tight barrier with three navies—British, French and Italian—who were barely on speaking terms for most of the war.

U13 ran the first twenty miles or so on the surface, relying on darkness and the thick weather for protection. Despite possible minefields, I chose to keep in close to the Albanian shore rather than trying our luck out in the middle: the British had recently brought a hundred or so Scottish fishing boats here to patrol the Straits, and reports from our German allies indicated that they were becoming a considerable nuisance. However, nothing much happened until we reached Saseno Island, where a powerful searchlight beam sweeping the sea a mile or so ahead of us persuaded me that it was time to dive. Once we were running safely underwater I ended my watch and handed over to Béla Meszáros—but as I did so our hearts were suddenly clutched by fingers of ice: something metallic was scraping along the hull. It passed though, whatever it was, and we all resumed breathing. Shortly after this I turned in for a few hours' sleep, still dressed in my oilskins. I was woken by the noise of a distant explosion, about 2 a.m., but it seemed not to concern us so I went back to sleep.

The cloud and rain of the previous day had cleared by the time we surfaced a few miles south of Fáno, and as the first rays of the sun streamed over the snow-capped mountains of Albania they disclosed *U13* wallowing in a slight swell, charging her batteries on a sea that was otherwise empty except for the red sails of a few fishing boats away to eastward under the hills of Corfu. We were not far from where I had nearly drowned aboard *UB4* the previous autumn. Her wreck was down there somewhere, rusting on the bottom as the fish picked the bones of . . . But no, it was not profitable to let such thoughts steal into my head, neither for me nor for the eight men whose lives depended on me. My immediate concern was to charge the batteries and get under way instead of sitting here on the surface in broad daylight. So as soon as the meter needles touched "Fully Charged" we were off again, on our way south towards Africa.

The next week passed uneventfully enough. The weather was remarkably good. The seas were light and no head winds held us back; in fact the breezes that blew were all steady westerlies, so that for much of the time we could hoist the triangular auxiliary sail carried by all Austro-Hungarian submarines. It gave some assistance to the engine and saved a few litres of our precious diesel oil. Life aboard *U13* soon resolved itself into a routine more appropriate to passage-making in peacetime than to a fighting vessel in a war zone: largely a matter of standing watch, maintaining our course and marking in the boat's position every hour, and taking turns off-watch to sit out on the narrow deck (sea permitting) in our two folding chairs.

That and caring for the diesel engine on which all our lives depended. Indeed, I think that no new-born infant was ever cosseted as anxiously, no tribal god ever served as diligently as that shuddering four-cylinder machine whose grumbling rattle formed the background to our lives for nearly seven days and nights: endlessly lubricated and cleaned; its temperature monitored for the slightest overheating; its pulse constantly felt for the faintest irregularity; its consumption of diesel fuel and lubricating oil measured down to the last gram and chalked on the engine-room blackboard to be compared in endless, anxious pencilled calculations with measured propeller-shaft revolutions and our estimated position. Yet the Körting "sewing machine" never missed a stitch. Instead a purposeful seam of pencilled crosses crept down the chart: past Corfu and Paxos, past Cephalonia and Zanté and the looming headlands of the Peloponnese, past Cerigo and Cerigotto and round the western tip of Crete into the deep, indigo waters of the central Mediterranean.

Of course, we sighted other vessels during those seven days, especially when we crossed the steamer lanes near Cerigo and (a few days later) the Malta-Suez route. I had resolved however not to dive for merchant ships unless they altered course towards us. Few merchant steamers carried wireless in 1916, and with those that did it was nothing but a clumsy spark-transmitter rasping out a slow message into the crowded long-wave band. Warships were a different matter though: they were fast, had efficient wireless transmitters and kept sharp look-outs. But we only sighted warships once during our outward voyage: a French *Bretagne*-class battleship and her escorts about six miles away—too far for an attack even if we had been carrying torpedoes.

By mid-afternoon on the seventh day out—my thirtieth birthday as it happened—*U13* had almost reached her destination. The breeze had veered southerly and bore a curious dry, musty smell, rather like that of an old leather suitcase, which I recognised as the smell of the great desert. The sea turned a paler blue, then a few birds were seen. Finally, just after 6 p.m., the look-out sighted land to southward: a low, pale brown streak which I calculated to be the top of the Cyrenaican plateau just south of Derna. It had been arranged that our rendezvous with the Senussi would be a point on the coast about midway between Derna and the small town of Tobruk, just south of Cape Ras-el-Tin. This stretch of coast was in the hands of the Senussi; or, to be more accurate, not in the hands of anyone else. The Italians, who had seized Libya from the Turks only in 1912, had withdrawn most of their scanty garrison the previous year. That left only a small British land force across the desert frontier in Egypt, and two Royal Navy gunboats patrolling the coast. It was because of these gunboats that my orders instructed me to arrive off the coast under cover of darkness and to wait for the appearance of three signal bonfires near our landmark, a ruined watch-tower. However, no instructions had been given as to how long we were to wait if no fires appeared.

We made our landfall off the ruined tower just before darkness fell, and a long period of waiting ensued. The stars shone above as the waves lapped invisibly on the distant beach. But no lights glimmered on the faint, dark shoreline.

"Damn them," I remarked to Friedenthal, standing beside me on the conning tower, "where are they? We've arrived on the very day appointed and still they haven't come to meet us."

Friedenthal had changed into full explorer's rig: corduroy jacket, breeches, top-boots and slouch hat complete with knapsack, pistol and water bottle.

"Don't fret, Prohaska," he replied, "the Bedouin are reliable enough fellows in my experience; it's just that they lack precision as to time and place."

But by the time the sky began to lighten in the east there was still no sign of our hosts. I waited as long as I could, then settled the boat on to the sandy bottom fifteen metres down. The day dragged by interminably. The boat became stuffy—we were carrying no reserve oxygen—and also hellishly hot because of the warm surrounding sea. We could not sleep, no cooking was possible and drinking water was short. Everyone was pre-occupied with the unspoken question: What if we have come all this way for nothing? Friedenthal—never the most agreeable of companions, I suspected—was irritable, several times ordering the men to be quiet if they ventured to talk or even to play cards. I brought the boat to the surface around midday, to get some fresh air, but the air sucked in by the ventilator fans now seemed even hotter than that inside. At last the clock ticked towards 8 p.m. It would soon be dark enough for us to surface and resume our vigil. Already my mind was being gnawed by the question: At what point do we give up and turn for home? After all, our food and water were limited, and there was clearly no prospect whatever of obtaining supplies on this barren coast. My main problem was Friedenthal: he was my passenger and I was commander of *U13*, but he was my superior by two ranks, and by the looks of him he would cheerfully see us drinking sea water and eating the leather of our boots before he gave up waiting. Once again we waited . . . and waited. Our hearts sank as the night hours ticked by. Then, around midnight, as the watches were changing, a call went up from the look-out:

"Light on shore—ten degrees port!"

We all rushed to look. Yes, a tiny, flickering light had sprung up among the coastal sand dunes. We waited for the second and third fires, but nothing happened. At last I seized the signal lamp and flashed it at the shore three times, as arranged. Still nothing.

"Well?" I asked Friedenthal. "What do you think, Herr Fregatten-kapitän? It might only be a Bedouin campfire."

He thought for a few moments. "I'll go and see for myself. Have one of your men row me ashore."

Kucharek was detailed as oarsman, and the two men splashed away into the darkness with the machine gun and two rifles covering them. The shore must have been about a kilometre distant. At any rate, about twenty minutes later I saw through my binoculars that figures were moving around the fire, then other glimmers of light appeared as if from electric torches. Ten minutes later Kucharek reappeared out of the gloom.

"Obediently report that the Herr Fregattenkapitän says that everything is all right, and that you must join him in your best uniform at once, Herr

Kommandant." I groaned inside: so he had been serious about the best uniform after all. Friedenthal had ordered me to bring it, despite the lack of space aboard, but I had secretly nursed a hope that he might have forgotten about it. So I went below and changed quickly from my sweat-soaked working rig into my full gala uniform. As I did so Friedenthal's words to me at Cattaro rang in my ears:

"It is most important, Herr Schiffsleutnant, to impress these Arabs. I shall be dressed for travel but you, as commander of the vessel, will be an ambassador from His Imperial Majesty in the eyes of these simple fellows. You have travelled in Arabia yourself and you must be aware how much importance they attach to pomp and ceremony."

So it was that I emerged ten minutes later in the archaic full dress of a Naval Lieutenant of the Emperor Franz Josef, a costume that would not have looked out of place a century before, with its gilt-buttoned frock coat, its fore-and-aft cocked hat, its heavy gold-fringed epaulettes and its black-and-yellow sword belt. My main concessions to modernity were a 9mm Steyr pistol tucked into the belt of my white duck trousers and a pair of stout leather seaboots, worn in the certainty that I would have to wade ashore from the dinghy. Before long, feeling indescribably foolish, I was sitting in the stern of the little boat with my sword between my knees as Kucharek rowed me ashore. Fortunately there was not much of a sea running, so I managed to reach dry land with my trousers soaked only to knee-level and with my dignity still reasonably intact. I strode up the sand towards the signal fire, feeling the butt of my pistol beneath my coat and wondering what exactly I was walking into. Shadowy figures moved about the fire which burnt in a small hollow of the dunes and Friedenthal's voice greeted me out of the darkness.

"Ah, Herr Kommandant, welcome to the soil of Africa. The Followers of the Prophet wait to greet you as representative of His Imperial, Royal and Apostolic Majesty the Emperor of Austria and King of Hungary." He was accompanied by five or six white-robed figures, faces indistinct, but evidently well armed. Mules wheezed somewhere in the darkness near by. Friedenthal salaamed deeply towards the waiting figures and I, having a little experience of the Arab world, removed my hat and did likewise. Friedenthal then launched into a long and evidently very elaborate oration in Arabic, of which I understood barely a word. I nodded and smiled gravely whenever he seemed to be indicating me. He finished at last, and I stood waiting for an equally long-winded reply, so you may imagine my surprise when one of the men—their leader by the looks of it—came up to me and addressed me in faultless German with a strong Bavarian accent! The firelight revealed him as a small, grey-bearded man with a sharp, secretive face.

"My dearest Captain von Prohaska, what a pleasure for me to be able to welcome you to our shores after you have travelled so far in your most excellent submarine. But allow me to introduce myself—Mohammed Amin Wazir KCMG, Chief Minister to our leader Sayid Ahmed, Master of the Senussi Brethren and Captain of the Hosts of the Faithful. But you may call me Vizier." He nudged me in the ribs and wheezed a gale of evil-smelling breath over me. "Heh! Do you like the 'KCMG,' Herr Kapitän? The damned fool British King gave it to me last year through his blockhead of a Viceroy in Cairo—'Throw a few pretty medals to these simple Arab johnnies, don't you know? Keep the silly beggars quiet, what!' You know what 'KCMG' stands for? 'Kindly Call Me God'!" He turned without waiting for an answer and looked out to sea.

"Anyway, Herr Leutnant, I believe that your esteemed Emperor has sent us a quantity of silver dollars with which to buy ourselves one or two useful items. But one thing worries me." He turned back to face me. "That little boat of yours cannot be carrying very much: in fact I would say that one of the German submarines could have brought us far more. They are certainly much bigger."

The cunning old devil! I thought to myself, he's been watching us all day from the dunes. But the prestige of the Monarchy had to be maintained at all costs.

"Ah, esteemed and most wise Vizier," I replied, "that is because our

Austrian submarines are not to be compared with those of Germany as regards design. Ours leave only a very little showing above the water. What is below the water is much larger." I considered this to be rather a neat lie, but a slight snort from the Vizier convinced me that I was mistaken.

"Yes, yes Captain: no doubt Allah the All-Seeing will bear witness to the truth of what you say. But come, there is little time. It will be daylight in a few short hours and we have far to travel."

I thought at first that by "we" the Vizier meant himself, his entourage and Friedenthal. But gradually it dawned upon me that I would also be required to make a journey of indeterminate length into the Cyrenaican hinterland.

"Damn it all," I whispered to Friedenthal when the Vizier seemed out of earshot, "I can't leave the boat to go trudging off on official visits into the desert, and certainly not in this pantomime get-up."

"No help for it, Prohaska," Friedenthal hissed in return. "Sayid Ahmed himself has commanded that you should attend an audience with him. Things haven't been going too well for our Senussi friends lately, by the looks of it, and he has important personal despatches to send to Vienna."

"But how far is it?"

"Only about fifteen kilometres inland I think, just up on the edge of the escarpment. You can easily get there and back in a day, and anyway, your crew aren't going to be able to land all the silver tonight. Send back a message to your Second Officer and tell him to wait until dawn the day after tomorrow."

So off I went into the Sahara Desert, jogging along in acute and growing discomfort on a mount provided for me by the Senussi, in the midst of a band of about thirty armed horsemen. Like most sailors, I was not a good rider, and would gladly never have thrown a leg across another horse's back after completing my compulsory riding course at the k.u.k. Marine Akademie. Even so, this journey was even worse than I expected.

The saddle was hard and high, in the Arab style, and my mount had a lofty trotting step which undoubtedly looked splendid but which was most uncomfortable. Neither was there much in the way of scenery to distract my attention from my aches and pains, for when the dawn came up it revealed nothing but a vast expanse of reddish stones broken here and there by tufts of scrub and an occasional outcrop of boulders. The desert rose in a series of steps from the coast to a low plateau, on top of which we were now riding.

At long last, about 7 a.m., just as I was beginning to suspect that I had died in the night and been sent to suffer a novel form of eternal torment, our column entered a wadi, a shallow, winding defile cut into the surface of a low swell in the plateau. Then, relief: a rifle shot rang out, and white-robed figures appeared as if from the stony soil at the sides of the gulley. We dismounted—myself rather in the manner of a prisoner of the Inquisition being taken down from the rack—and proceeded up the wadi on foot, leading our horses by their reins. Half dead with weariness and pain (I had not slept and hardly eaten for nearly two days), I saw that we were entering an encampment, cunningly sited in a shallow dish-shaped hollow in the summit of the rise. It was only a few metres deep and perhaps two hundred across, but it held about thirty low Bedouin tents in complete invisibility except from above.

Our hosts seemed short of food: their horses were thin and the men looked gaunt and hungry. But they were evidently not short of weapons, for nearly every man carried a German Mauser rifle with bandoliers of ammunition. Three or four light field guns were parked about, while up on the lip of the depression, hidden among the rocks, I could see several Maxim machine guns. Friedenthal informed me later that the Senussi had recently suffered a severe thrashing at the hands of the British, when their main host had been shot to tatters by the Duke of Westminster's armoured-car squadrons at Sollum, just over the border in Egypt. The survivors had retreated to this secret camp to reorganise themselves.

After a pause for a meagre breakfast of sandy dates and tepid, brackish water—no cooking fires could be lit during the day, of course—I was ushered into the presence of the Grand Master of the Senussi Brethren, Sayid Ahmed. The audience was quite short. The Master, an imposing old man in his elaborate robes, restricted himself to a few formal compliments, translated into German for me by the Vizier, then presented a series of pleas for assistance from Austria and Germany. He thanked me for the delivery of the silver dollars, gave me a sealed box of despatches to the Austro-Hungarian High Command, and announced by way of conclusion that I was to convey a special, personal gift to my Emperor. I was motioned to get up from the cushions where I sat cross-legged and to accompany the Vizier and Friedenthal outside the Master's tent. There I was confronted with a young, milk-white camel, about the size of a horse's colt. As the appalling implications of this present dawned upon my fatigue-heavy brain Friedenthal, sensing my thoughts, whispered to me:

"No good I'm afraid—you'll have to take it with you. The worst insult that you can offer an Arab is to refuse a gift." So I smiled as complacently as I was able and thanked the Vizier for the Master's gracious present. The Vizier smiled in return—rather maliciously I thought.

"The Master of the Senussi Brethren is pleased to present this fine pedigree racing camel to your Emperor and King. Camel-racing is a fine sport for a monarch, and even one in such robust health as your venerable Emperor Franz Josef cannot but have his years prolonged beyond measure and his vigour maintained by its practice." Dismal though my situation was, I could not help but smile inwardly at the sudden, delicious mental picture of our aged monarch enjoying an early-morning canter on camel-back beneath the chestnut trees of the Prater Hauptallee. Never mind, Ottokár, I thought to myself, you can always lose the beast on your way back to the coast.

The rest of my day in the Senussi encampment dragged by wearily. I tried to sleep, but even this early in the year the stagnant heat of our shallow hole in the ground was most oppressive. Swarms of flies buzzed everywhere as I wandered restlessly between the tents. I managed to talk a little with Friedenthal, who seemed slightly more affable since we had disembarked from *U13*. I also made the acquaintance of some of my fellow-inmates of this torrid dust-bath. The tent next to mine was the domicile of Yussuf Akhbar Mullah, the itinerant imam who accompanied our particular band of Senussi as a sort of chaplain to the Grand Master. He was a mild, benevolent-looking old gentleman with a long, grey beard and steel-rimmed spectacles and a mouthful of gold teeth, the very picture of a spiritual guide and pastor of souls—had it not been for the long-barrelled revolver which appeared to be as permanently fixed in his right hand as the fly-whisk in his left. This weapon was not for ornament: he had an unnerving habit of firing it, playfully and quite without warning, at any object that caught his fancy—a pebble, a scorpion, a piece of camel-dung—so that the stillness of the camp was punctured every few minutes by the crack of a shot, as little regarded as a sneeze or a cough. Fortunately the mullah was a good marksman, otherwise death and injury would have been very frequent among the unwary.

I also discovered that the ranks of the Senussi contained quite a number of Turks, some of them leftovers from the war with Italy a few years before, others supplied since then by courtesy of the German Navy. One of these was a Berlin-trained doctor called Beshti Fuad, an ugly, pock-marked fellow, but quite intelligent and no great admirer of the Senussi Brethren. He would kiss hands and exchange salaams with Sayid Ahmed and the rest, but when he got back to the tent he would spit on the ground and denounce them as a bloodthirsty gang of savages.

The desire for a cigar came upon me very strongly as the day wore on. I was by no means a nicotine addict, but it was a good three days since I had tasted tobacco and the box of cigars in my waistcoat pocket was declaring its hard shape more eloquently with every hour that passed. So I left the tent, retired to the edge of the encampment and lit up. I drew in the first few blissful mouthfuls of smoke, exhaled, then replaced the cigar between my lips. But just as I did so, paff! it was blown to fragments. I do not know whether you have ever had a revolver bullet pass within an inch of your nose, but the sensation is rather like a heavy slap in the face. I staggered back, dazed and half blinded.

"Himmelherrgottsakra! . . . was bedeutet . . . ?" Then as my eyes began to work once more I saw the old mullah seated at his tent flap about twenty metres behind me, the revolver smoking in his hand. He smiled at me indulgently with his gold teeth and wagged his finger in reproach. I retreated to my tent in high disgust and reported the matter to Friedenthal. Beshti Fuad laughed grimly:

"Ah, my dear Herr Leutnant, you got off lightly because you are a guest and the Austrian Emperor's emissary. The Senussi abhor alcohol and tobacco. The punishment for drinking is a thousand lashes, and for smoking, amputation of the hand—under proper medical supervision of course. My God, you should have seen the last one they caught drinking—half a bottle of wine looted from an Italian lorry. I had to be there as medical supervisor, but there was little point: his backbone and ribs were gleaming white after two hundred lashes and I think he died somewhere about the four hundredth, but they still went on to the full thousand. I tell you, these brutes are crazy. I've had to amputate three hands of smokers since I came here last year."

"But what about your Hippocratic Oath . . . ?"

"Bah! Hippocratic Oath be damned—they told me that if I didn't do it they would cut my hand off, tchump! under my own medical supervision."

Some time after this Friedenthal and Beshti Fuad went out carrying a box between them, along with a spade and a coil of wire. They gave no explanation of their errand, but when they returned Friedenthal reported:

"I think that we may be in for trouble soon, Prohaska. Our scouts have spotted an Italian native levy force moving this way. There will probably be an attack this evening, so you had better be ready to leave as soon as darkness falls. I've arranged two guides to get you back to the coast."

The remainder of the day wore by, broken only by a meal of boiled rice, without salt, but well speckled with dark bits that might have been raisins and might have been dead flies. I prepared for my departure, checking my pistol and filling a large aluminium water bottle procured for me by Friedenthal. As the short desert twilight began to descend, a distant, dry crackling of rifle fire broke the silence. Armed men started to run hither and thither among the tents, clambering up on to the lip of the depression.

"Here they come," said Friedenthal. "This will probably be nothing but their scouts, but be prepared to clear off as soon as this attack finishes, because their main body will be here soon. In the mean time though you might as well come and watch the fun."

I drew my Steyr pistol—quite useless in the circumstances I am sure— and followed Friedenthal up to a group of boulders some way out from the rim of the depression. I noticed that a faint trackway ran past the boulders. Beshti Fuad was already crouched among the rocks, a small tin box balanced on his knees. We got down beside him just as the first wave of white-clad horsemen came pounding across the desert towards us in the dim light. A machine gun rattled among the rocks near by, then another. The horsemen wheeled and broke formation about a hundred metres ahead of us, then vanished like smoke, leaving a few hummocks lying on the ground. But then a regular, solid cloud of dust came roaring towards us across the arid waste, spitting fire as it neared us. It was an armoured car, racing along the trackway and spraying bullets over our heads as it came. The distance narrowed to three hundred metres, then two hundred. We ducked among the rocks as bullets whined around us—except for Beshti Fuad, who sat calmly, measuring the range. Then he pressed two contacts together. The ground erupted beneath the front axle of the oncoming vehicle. A wheel detached itself and went spinning down the trackway. The armoured car hurtled along for a couple of seconds, kept upright by its own momentum, then ran off the trackway and crashed into a large rock, where it toppled over and burst into flames. We ran across to try and extricate the survivors, if there were any, but there was little point since we were greeted by a vicious rattle of ammunition going off inside the crew compartment. As we left the scene I noticed that the armoured car's radiator bore the Lancia emblem, and also that a body lay near by, dreadfully still and unmarked except for a twisted neck. He was a European, dressed in khaki; an upturned pith helmet lay beside him. But as we made our way back into the hollow a renewed din of musketry and machine-gun fire broke out in the darkness. Clearly the second attack was beginning rather earlier than scheduled. For my part I was neither suitably dressed nor equipped for infantry warfare in the African desert. Also my ship and seven of her crew were at the coast waiting for me to take them back home. No, I thought, now is the time to be leaving. I found my two Bedouin guides waiting with my horse, said a few hasty farewells, then climbed into the saddle.

Soon the three of us were making our way down the wadi. Things were really getting hot now: the clatter of machine-gun and rifle fire filled the air and rocket flares lit up the sky above the camp. Then suddenly the wadi in front of us was filled with horsemen. All I can remember is spurring my horse forward and drawing my sword: a puny ceremonial thing, about as much use as a paper-knife. Two mounted figures wheeled to block my way. There were shots. I lunged instinctively with the sword as I closed with one of my assailants, heard a gasp and felt the weapon enter something solid. Then the sword snapped off in my hand as I passed my victim, leaving me holding the hilt and a few centimetres of blade. Someone slashed at me in the darkness, catching my hat with the edge of his sabre, but somehow I managed to break away from them. Bullets whined about my shoulders as I galloped on down the wadi. It seemed that my two guides had not been so lucky. I was free to go on my way—but alone.

It sounds an unenviable predicament: to be on my own at night, in the Sahara Desert, with enemies all around me, with no map, no compass and only a litre or so of water. But in fact it was not so bad: I was away from the encampment, where battle was still raging as I drew out of earshot, and all I had to do now to find my way to the coast was to navigate by the stars and go down the successive slopes of the escarpment. Above all, I was away from the racing camel, in circumstances such that no one would be able to accuse me of having refused a gift. As dawn began to lighten the sky the dark plain of the Mediterranean lay before me in the distance. All I had to do now was to pick up the coastal road—the Grand Khedival Highway—and make my way along it until I sighted the ruined watch-tower near which *U13* would be lying submerged. The road was all mine to travel.

I found the watch-tower after riding about twelve kilometres along the coastal road. I dismounted, weary and unspeakably stiff, then slapped the horse hard on the haunches to send it neighing away into the dunes. The only question now was how to make contact with *U13,* which was presumably still lying offshore on the bottom after landing the remainder of the silver the previous night. I was just beginning to exercise my fatigue-numbed brain upon this problem when a familiar voice spoke in German from just behind me.

"Good morning, Herr Kommandant. And how does this morning find you?" It was the Vizier, smiling that close, malicious smile of his and rubbing his hands. He was accompanied by two attendants holding the party's horses.

"I trust that your journey here was not too awful, Herr Leutnant. As for myself, I had the good fortune to leave the encampment yesterday evening just before the trouble started. I reasoned that you might have difficulty getting her here, so I took the trouble of bringing her myself."

I saw to my horror that the "her" referred to was the young racing camel, being led towards us by one of the servants and evidently in an evil temper even this early in the day.

I tried to make contact with *U13* by wading out into the sea up to my waist and banging my aluminium water bottle repeatedly with the butt of my pistol, hoping that the sound would be sharp enough to carry through the water. I must have beaten out the morse message "*U13*—SURFACE" a score of times, and was rapidly giving up hope, when there was a sudden disturbance about eight hundred metres offshore. To my unbounded joy the little submarine rose from the waves like some ungainly Aphrodite. The dinghy was launched, and within a few minutes I was shaking hands with Béla Meszáros. They had not heard my signals, but had been making hourly sweeps with the periscope since dawn.

Farewells were said as hurriedly as possible, for I had no wish to keep my boat lying offshore in broad daylight. But a difficult matter remained to be broached. The Vizier was European-educated—a diploma in Electrical Engineering from the Munich Technical University according to Friedenthal—so perhaps he would be amenable to reason.

"Honoured Vizier," I began, "while I am sure that our Emperor would be most grateful for the gift of this splendid beast, I fear that a submarine is not the most suitable of vessels for conveying live animals."

"And why should that be, Excellency?"

"Because of the lack of room below . . ." I bit my tongue, but too late. The Vizier smiled sweetly.

"Ah, but did not the Herr Leutnant tell me the night before last that, unlike the vessels of the German Kaiser, the submarines of Austria are much larger beneath the water than they appear to be on the surface? Surely, such a vessel will have room enough to stable whole troops of camels. Or did the Herr Leutnant not tell me the entire truth . . . ?"

I was beaten, and I knew it: the Vizier and his men left us as we tried to truss up the biting, struggling, retching, swearing animal for loading into the dinghy. I shall never know how we got the creature through the torpedo-loading hatch and safely tethered below decks; it was a nightmare lasting nearly an hour, with half the crew on deck trying to push the wretched beast through the aperture and the other half inside pulling at a bowline around its neck. By the time the camel and its bales of fodder were installed between the torpedo tubes in the fore-ends, four of the crew had received bites while Maschinenmeister Lehár had taken a hoof in the groin.

Fregattenleutnant Meszáros gave me his report on the previous thirty-six hours. The money had been delivered safely to the shore and handed over, all except one box, which had been dropped while it was being hauled up the conning-tower ladder and had burst, spilling its contents into every crevice and corner of the control room. But far worse, just before the boat submerged at the end of the first night's unloading, it was noticed that a large oil slick was spreading across the surface of the sea. A valve joint in one of the reserve lubricating-oil tanks had opened—perhaps from the constant vibration of the diesel—and three hundred litres of oil had been lost. What remained was about two hundred miles too little to see us back to Durazzo. The next nearest friendly port was Smyrna, on the Aegean coast of Turkey. Our oil should just about suffice to get us there, and we also had the wireless recognition codes for that part of the Mediterranean. So I decided that we would head for Smyrna by way of Crete, calling at that island (which was Greek territory) for the twenty-four hours allowed under neutrality rules. Who could tell? We might be able to obtain lubricating oil there. And we would certainly be able to rid ourselves of our unwelcome passenger—one way or another.

I have lived now for over a century, yet I can still say with complete confidence that no one can claim to have plumbed the depths of human misery who has not shared the fore-ends of a submarine with a camel. I was already acquainted with these beasts from that time, at the end of 1914, when I had travelled up the Arabian Peninsula on my way home from China. However, it was not an acquaintance that I would have wished to extend. Their wayward, unpredictable habits and their vile manners were not new to me, but I must say that this beast of ours—perhaps more highly bred than its workaday Arabian cousins—surpassed the lot of them in arrogant baseness. True, the creature had a good deal to be peevish about, tethered fast between the torpedo tubes at the end of a stuffy, hot, evil-smelling tunnel with the floor constantly swaying and rolling beneath its hooves. But even so its ingratitude was without measure. It had straw to lie on and water to drink—water taken, needless to say, from our own dwindling ration. The Vizier's servants had provided it with hay and two bags of corn for sustenance during the journey. Its dung was cleared up twice daily, and in the mean time it was permitted to urinate copiously all over the deck, causing electrical short circuits and generating a smell which, before long, far outdid the monkey cage in the Schönbrunn zoological gardens on the hottest day in August. We felt for its dumb unhappiness and would have commiserated with the creature if it had let us. But no: it bit whenever we untied its muzzle to let it eat; it kicked viciously and with great accuracy whenever anyone came within range; and when these means failed it the brute spat gobbets of loathsome green cud again, with frightening accuracy—or simply blasted us with its noisome breath. And all the time, day and night, it would practise an extensive repertoire of belches, gurgles, snorts and hiccups which deprived us of any hope of sleep. The ratings would have mutinied if they had been forced to share quarters with the animal, so Meszáros and I moved into the fore-ends. The second night out it managed to work its muzzle binding loose and bite the Fregattenleutnant in the calf, causing him to wake with a howl as from a whole tribe of Red Indians. As I applied iodine and bandages I could offer comfort only by telling him that I had read somewhere that camel bites almost always turned septic.

All in all, I think it reflected great credit on us that we did not simply shoot the beast and tip it overboard once we were out of sight of land. I must admit that I considered it, but I was restrained by the certain knowledge that a report would get back to the Senussi via the Turkish ambassador in Vienna if *U13* arrived home minus the camel. After all that we had been through these past ten days I had no wish to be blamed for having wrecked Austrian policy in North Africa single-handed. No, we would just have to grit our teeth and comfort ourselves with the knowledge that Crete was only three or four days away.

The camel was not the only problem on this first leg of our journey back from the shores of Libya. We had just landed over three tonnes of silver, lost a passenger and used up about half of our fuel, so even with every trimming and compensator tank flooded the boat was still running light and bobbing about among the waves like an empty oil drum. Also the previously fair weather began to worsen as the African coast disappeared astern. A strong, hot, dust-laden southerly breeze blew up out of the desert, pushing up a nasty following swell that kept trying to get under *U13*'s stern and throw her off course. But we persevered, and early on our third day out we sighted the summit of Mount Ida on the horizon to northward. A few hours more, and the whole mountainous spine of Crete was visible in the distance.

U13 arrived off the harbour entrance at Ierapetra about midday on 12 April and dropped anchor among the brightly painted fishing caiques. Small boats soon surrounded us, and before long a rowing cutter came out towards us, propelled by two red-shirted fishermen and with an important-looking figure in mock-naval uniform sitting in the stern sheets. It turned out that this was the chief customs official and Harbour Master. He addressed us first in Greek, then in bad Italian, informing us that under neutrality rules we were entitled to remain in Greek waters for only twenty-four hours and to purchase stores only of a non-military nature. I replied that all we desired was to obtain lubricating oil, to take on food and drinking water and to land a certain article after making contact (if His Excellency would permit) with the Austro-Hungarian Consul in Kandia. The Harbour Master sucked his teeth and thought for a few minutes: evidently he was not used to dealing with such exalted matters as consuls and visits by belligerent warships.

"No, Capitano, it will not be possible to obtain engine oil: that is a military store and in any case, we have none in the town."

"But surely, Harbour Master, you have fishing boats, and there must be a garage in Ierapetra."

He laughed sardonically. "Hah! As you see," (waving his arm with a dramatic sweep) "all the fishing boats here are sailing vessels, and as for a garage, it is months since the town saw a motor car. No, you will not find a drop of motor oil within fifty kilometres. But the item that you wish to land—is that perhaps also an article of a military nature?"

"No," I replied, "it is a young racing camel: a present to the Austrian Emperor from the Master of the Senussi Brethren."

I imagine that some of the fishermen knew a little Italian, because a roar of laughter went up as this remark was passed from one to the other. The Harbour Master swelled up with injured dignity, but in the end contented himself with muttering something about quarantine regulations. Then he turned to his rowers and ordered them to head for the quayside below the ruins of the castle, indicating that we should follow. Within half an hour we were warping our boat into the quayside under the gaze of several hundred of the town's inhabitants. They had even more cause to stare a few minutes later as the torpedo-loading hatch opened and *U13* gave birth to a struggling, hissing, belching, swearing camel, dragged out front-hooves-first by Kucharek and Zaccarini while Lehár and Stonawski pushed from below, being rewarded for their trouble with a torrent of urine. I got the impression that Greek fishermen were not the sort of people who were easily surprised, but even so I detected a certain wonderment and even admiration among the rows of impassive mahogany faces gazing at us from the harbour wall. At any rate, when the creature was finally landed to stand unsteady and blinking on the quayside, a round of applause broke out.

I sent Béla Meszáros and Stonawski to look for provisions and water, and Lehár and Kucharek to see what could be found in the way of lubricating oil. Then I set off, accompanied by Grigorović and followed by a large crowd, to try to make contact with the Consul in Kandia. I knew that Austria had a representative on Crete because back in the late 1890s we had landed a sizeable force to intervene in a local civil war, and had kept an interest on the island ever since. How to contact him, though—that was the problem. The local post office was closed for some saint's day, so in the end I was forced to call at the gendarmerie headquarters. The gendarmes had what I wanted: a telephone. The line was atrocious, and I had no idea of the name of the person with whom I wished to speak. Somehow though, after an hour of bellowing into the receiver in bad French, the Austro-Hungarian Consul on Crete was procured for me: one Herr Hödler. He sounded as if he had just been dragged out of bed and was far from willing to help us. But after I had dropped the name of Baron Horvath of the k.u.k. Foreign Ministry and threatened to have him sacked for negligence he consented to hire a taxi and travel the fifty or so kilometres to Ierapetra.

I thanked the gendarmerie captain as best I could and returned to the harbour, followed by the same wondering crowd as before. I was pleased and surprised to find that Béla Meszáros had enjoyed some success in persuading the local victuallers to part with their wares in exchange for promissory notes written out on behalf of the Austrian Consul. The provisions did not look particularly appetising however—flat Greek bread, a jar of olives, some rancorous cheese and a sack of even worse-smelling salt cod—but we were not in a position to be finicky, now that our own tinned rations and hard tack were running low. More important, a water cart was brought up and several hundred litres of water were hosed into *U13*'s tanks.

Maschinenmeister Lehár had also been lucky in his search. "Obediently report that it was no good, Herr Kommandant. The Harbour Master was telling the truth: there's not a drop of engine oil in the place. In fact I doubt whether they even know what it is. But we found this." He handed me a glass jamjar. It contained olive oil: thick, dark, strong-smelling stuff which seemed however, when I rubbed some between finger and thumb, to be about the same viscosity as our own lubricating oil.

"We could try mixing the two," Lehár suggested. "If we try not to run the engine too hard and filter the waste oil for re-use we might make Durazzo."

"How much of it is there?"

"About two hundred litres back at the shop. The merchant is a Hungarian Jew—speaks a little German, and told us that we could have it because it's end-of-season stuff and going rancid anyway. He won't accept anything but hard cash though: we tried him with promissory notes but he wouldn't budge."

"But how the Devil are we going to . . . ?"

The same thought seemed to strike Meszáros and me simultaneously:

"Of course—the silver dollars, the ones from the burst box! Leave him to me." With that my Second Officer strode off along the quayside.

As might have been expected, on being shown several of the silver dollars and having bitten one or two of them experimentally our merchant suddenly became passionately attached to his olive oil, swearing that diamonds and rubies would not induce him to part with it. But in the end Meszáros talked him round. After all, what is a Magyar but a Levantine bazaar-trader dressed up as a German? Two hours and a great deal of haggling later the oil was being pumped into the tanks after I had endangered my career by disbursing about twenty times what it was worth in silver. We were still a long way off and this was worth a try, rather than having to run twice through the heavily patrolled and thickly mined approaches to Smyrna.

We began to stow our provisions below decks, then cooked our midday meal. Shortly after 4 p.m. there was a commotion among the crowd of onlookers, then the distant, impatient honking of a motor-car horn. The noise heralded the arrival of Herr Hödler: dust-coated, weary and jarred in every bone after a three-hour drive from Kandia along execrable mountain roads. He climbed down from the vehicle and pushed his way through the crowd towards us.

"My dear Herr Kommandant, what a pleasure it is for me to greet you in my capacity as Consul for the Imperial and Royal Monarchy. And in what may I perhaps be of assistance to you and your gallant crew during your brief stay on this island?" (He laid some emphasis on the word "brief," I noticed.)

"Herr Konsul," I replied, "I hope that you will be so good, in your official capacity, as to take charge of a gift presented to our Emperor by a foreign potentate." I saw that he brightened perceptibly at this, perhaps already imagining himself signing his name "Baron Hödler."

"Why yes of course, Herr Kommandant. It will be a great honour for me to discharge this . . ." His voice trailed away as Zaccarini came into view, dragging the camel by a halter. He stared at the beast, goggle-eyed with disbelief. Beads of sweat began to ooze through the caked white dust on his forehead.

"But surely . . . you cannot possibly mean . . ."

"I'm afraid that I do, Herr Konsul. It is a personal present from the

Grand Master of the Senussi Brethren to our Emperor. I am entrusting the beast to your care until such time as conditions permit you to arrange for its transport to Austria."

"But I cannot . . . I live in a flat . . . I have no means of . . ."

"Ah, Herr Konsul, I believe that you are paid a stipend by the Imperial and Royal Government to deal with exigencies such as this. Now, if you would be so kind as to sign this receipt for the animal. There are also one or two items of stores for which your payment would be appreciated."

The last I saw of the camel, Herr Hödler and the driver were trying to manhandle the creature into the back of the taxi under the gaze of a wondering crowd. I never did learn what became of it.

We sailed from Ierapetra just before sunset, waved on our way by several hundred Cretan fisherfolk for whom we had provided a rare day's entertainment. In the event our homeward voyage along the south coast of Crete did not work out too badly. The wind was favourable, and if *U13* was scarcely in the ocean greyhound class she still performed quite creditably, wallowing along with all the grace of a cow in a farmyard pond and leaving a blue haze of burning olive oil behind her.

We made it through the Otranto Straits on the night of 20 April, running submerged on the E-motor until the batteries were nearly exhausted. Morning found us a few miles north of the straits, drifting helplessly on the surface and trying to start the diesel, which was by now hopelessly clogged and coked up with its unusual lubricant. All that we could do was to tap out urgent wireless calls for assistance as the sun came up over the mountains to eastward. Luckily for us, the naval base at Durazzo was quick to respond: we were given air cover before the hour was out, then a torpedo-boat to tow us to safety.

There was no hero's welcome when we arrived back at the Bocche. Our departure had been secret, so our arrival had to be secret as well. No recognition could be given of course, other than an "Expression of the All-Highest's Satisfaction" for myself and my crew in discharging a difficult and highly dangerous mission. I received this by the same post (so to speak) as a letter from the k.u.k. Ministry of Finances. It demanded that I should account for the sum of 183 silver dollars disbursed by myself without permission or delegated powers of expenditure and for which I might in consequence be held personally liable if official investigations etc., etc.

Was it worth it? I cannot say. The Maria Theresa silver dollars—the only consignment as it turned out—sank like water into the sands of the desert. The Senussi continued their struggle against the infidel without Austria's assistance, and after the war they remained outside Vienna's sphere of influence, for better or for worse. And Friedenthal? He was never heard of again: vanished without trace, perhaps killed in the battle at the encampment, perhaps murdered afterwards by the Senussi or their German and Turkish advisers. But it was not for me to ask whether it was worth it or not. We had orders to carry out and in the end, after more than three weeks, we had carried them out—and returned to tell the tale.

13

LOVE AND DUTY

FTER OUR RETURN FROM AFRICA I was given a month's leave while the boat was overhauled at Pola. There was no question about how the leave was to be spent: I made straight for Vienna and Elisabeth. We were to be married in mid-July, and there were numerous arrangements to make before the wedding. Not least among these was a pro forma visit to Elisabeth's foster-parents at their Schloss in the wilds of Transylvania. Count Kelésvay and his wife had been violently opposed to the marriage at first, but realising in the end that there was little they could do to prevent it under Austrian law, they had grudgingly come around to accept its distasteful inevitability. The count had spent several days poring over the *Almanach de Gotha* and was eventually able to console himself a little with the discovery that the Czech peasant blood on my father's side was counteracted in some degree by that of my Polish great-grandparents the Krasnodębskis, whose coat of arms had more quarterings than the Kelésvays' and the de Bratianus' put together. In the end, it seemed that the best was to be made of a bad job: Elisabeth would have me and could not be brought to her senses by threats of being disinherited. Well, it could have been worse: the son of a Finanzbaron or—God forbid—a Jewish lawyer. Elisabeth warned me that it would be a grim visit, the barest acknowledgement of my existence, but that we had to go through with it.

I spent ten days in Vienna waiting for Elisabeth to get leave from the hospital. However, the time was relieved to some extent by the company of Béla Meszáros and of Elisabeth's younger brother, Ferenc, who was just nineteen and resembled his sister in liveliness and general enthusiasm for everything. He was a sailor as well, just coming up for his commission examinations as a wartime Seeaspirant. His ambition above all others was to become a U-Boat officer, so in his eyes Meszáros and I were objects of veneration, constantly badgered to recount our experiences to him. At last the day came for Elisabeth to start her week's leave. We boarded our train at the Staatsbahnhof, seen off by Ferenc. His last words to me as the train drew away from the platform were, "Auf wiedersehen, Herr Schiffsleutnant. I shall see you in Pola when you get back!"

It is a strange thing, but although I had already sailed around the world and visited every continent I had never travelled a great deal within the Monarchy. I had grown up in the bourgeois civilisation of northern Moravia, so it was something of a shock to me that the Habsburg domains should be so vast and so variegated. I knew in theory how large the black-and-yellow empire was: like every other school in Austria, mine had had its map of the Danubian Monarchy pinned up on the classroom wall beneath the portrait of the Emperor in his white tunic. But nothing had prepared me for the reality of the Hungarian Plain, shimmering in the early-summer heat as the arms of the balance-wells nodded listlessly in the distance and the train crawled caterpillar-like across its dreary vastness, stopping every couple of kilometres to let a troop-train pass by. For nearly thirty-six hours we trundled across its interminable, aching flatness, from Budapest to Kecskemet and from Kecskemet to Szeged and from Szeged into the valley of the Maros and the foothills of the Transylvanian Alps.

I was even less prepared for what awaited me at the other end. Certainly Hermannstadt was a civilised enough place; in fact it might well have passed for a small town in the Rhineland, had it not been for the gypsies, Turkish pedlars and sheepskin-clad herdsmen who jostled with the black-coated burghers on its pavements. But once we had boarded the narrow-gauge railway and were puffing our way up into the mountains it soon became apparent that if Austria-Hungary touched Switzerland at one end, this was most decidedly the other. As we climbed up into the hills the landscape became dramatically wild and unkempt: the valleys clothed in oak and beech forest on their lower slopes, then the bare rock of the mountainsides towering above. Likewise the villages underwent an amazing transformation within a few kilometres, from neatly kept little German Dorfs to ragged clusters of huts, then to single hovels so crude that a Hottentot would have scorned to live in them.

There was no station where our train stopped, only a forest track crossing the railway line. Elisabeth and I climbed down with our luggage. Then the engine tooted its whistle and wheezed away uphill into the forest, leaving us coughing in a haze of lignite smoke. We were alone.

"Oh the idiots!" said Elisabeth, "what on earth are they thinking about? I wrote to them telling them exactly which day we would arrive, and there's only one train a day, yet still they manage to miss us. Honestly, they haven't the sense to come in out of the rain."

This closing remark turned out to be remarkably apt, for about ten minutes later a black thunderstorm caught up with us. I rigged up a shelter with a groundsheet, so we only got moderately wet. But once the rain had stopped there was still no sign of the carriage that was to have met us. Midday passed.

"How far is it to the Schloss?" I enquired of Elisabeth.

"About twelve kilometres up the valley I think, but the road's bad and there are wolves and bears in the woods."

I had my pistol with me, but somehow bear-hunting appealed to me even less than twelve-kilometre walks encumbered with luggage. So we sat and waited until about three in the afternoon, by which time I was seriously debating in my mind whether it would be better to light a fire here and camp out overnight until the next train arrived, or to abandon our luggage and set off back down the line towards Hermannstadt. Then we heard a curious dunking noise in the distance, accompanied by a thin, undulating, high-pitched wail like that of a Chinese professional mourner. A few minutes later an ox-cart came into sight lumbering up the track towards us. I stepped out into the road and hailed the driver in German. As soon as he set eyes on me though he howled in terror and leapt from the seat to disappear into the undergrowth, from which he was only coaxed out some time later by Elisabeth calling to him in Romanian. In the end the peasant, a half-starved, wild-looking creature dressed in skins and with his feet bound in rags, consented to carry us and our baggage to the Schloss Kelésvár in return for five Kreuzers, which he clearly regarded as a fortune.

I cannot recommend Transylvanian ox-carts as a means of transport for anyone not performing a Lenten penance. Not only was the cart spring-less and the road extremely bad, but also the ungreased wooden axle kept up a constant, piercing screech which Elisabeth told me was supposed to keep away the spirits of the unquiet dead. By the time we drew near to the Schloss, about three hours later, we were bruised and stiff in every limb from the lurching of the cart while our ears ached with the noise of the axle. Yet the view was magnificent, with the rocky peaks of the Făgăras range crowding the horizon above the head of the densely wooded valley. As for Schloss Kelésvár itself, it was a great surprise. I had expected that Elisabeth's childhood home would be a neat eighteenth-century house painted Schönbrunner yellow, like most of the other Schlosses that I had encountered across the Dual Monarchy; at any rate, nothing like the build-ing which suddenly loomed ahead of us, perched on a rocky spur above the trees—a very real, unadorned and decidedly menacing medieval fortress, with a battlemented tower at each corner and a gate-house in the middle of the wall facing us.

Our ox-cart squealed its laborious way up the ramp towards the gate-way just in time to meet an antiquated, very shabby four-horse carriage coming the other way. This was the family coach, which was just setting off to meet us from the train. Both vehicles were forced to halt and the next quarter-hour was spent in deadlock as the terrified cart-driver tried to back his protesting oxen down the slope. In the end both vehicles had to be uncoupled and trundled backwards by teams of labourers, who then carried our baggage up to the castle courtyard for us. A closer view revealed that the Schloss Kelésvár was badly in need of repair: the windows were dirty and broken, sections of roof evidently collapsed and large areas of stucco crumbled away to reveal the masonry beneath. As we walked up towards the gateway a section of plaster detached itself from a wall near by and fell with a crash and a cloud of dust into the nettle-clogged moat. Nobody remarked on this or even seemed to notice it.

We entered the castle courtyard through a crowd of evil-smelling and ragged servants to find a small man dressed in plus-fours, a Norfolk jacket and a wing-collar, swinging a golf club at a ball balanced on a tee stuck between the paving stones. He looked at us and adjusted his monocle. Elisabeth rushed up to him and greeted him in a flood of Magyar, of which I understood very little. Then she turned towards me and spoke in German.

"Uncle Sandor, permit me to introduce my fiancé, Linienschiffs-leutnant Otto Prohaska."

He adjusted his monocle and surveyed me coldly from head to toe. I proffered a hand, but he refused to take it, only remarking in heavily accented German, "Herr Leutnant, we are honoured that you should visit us."

Then he turned back to Elisabeth and resumed the conversation. Soon he was joined by a tall, heavily built, rather greasy-looking man in his late twenties who regarded me with even more evident dislike than the count. This, I learnt, was Miklos, the count's eldest son. While this was going on a servant brought my bags up from the cart and placed them beside me. I thanked him in the few words of Magyar at my command and tried to slip a few Kreuzers into his hand by way of a tip. He stared at me as if I were a cannibal and scuttled away in terror. The count noticed this and surveyed me icily.

"Herr Leutnant, you must remember never to show these animals any kindness or gratitude such as you would offer to a human being. They neither understand it nor appreciate it."

With that he swung back his club and let drive at the ball. Glass tinkled somewhere on the other side of the courtyard.

Having thus been welcomed by my hosts, I was shown to my room: a dark, damp chamber in a corner tower with bats nesting in the cobweb-hung corners and a huge oaken four-poster bed hung with crumbling brocade curtains. The only other furniture was a stool, a wash-stand and a chest which seemed to have been constructed from railway sleepers. The only light came from a single glazed arrow-slit high up in one wall. Everything stank of mildew. But once I had had the opportunity to inspect the rest of the Schloss, I found that I had not been discriminated against: the other rooms were every bit as bad, if not worse. In fact it seemed that whenever a section of roof fell in the family simply abandoned the rooms and moved elsewhere. The household servants were very numerous, but as far as I could make out they slept in corners or under tables in the great cavernous kitchen, black with the soot and grease of generations but equipped with a modern cast-iron kitchen range bearing the embossed legend WM. LAIDLAW & CO. KILMARNOCK.

Dinner that evening allowed me to examine the Kelésvay clan at close quarters. The countess—Aunt Sári—was unquestionably a very fine-looking woman in the Magyar fashion: not tall, but erect, with a haughty manner and a gimlet stare. It only took about five minutes, though, to discern that this impressive façade concealed the mind of a near-imbecile. She spoke only Magyar, which I understood hardly at all, but even so her stupidity was of an order that transcended the barrier of language. Things were not much better with the rest of the family: two sons, one daughter, one foster-daughter and a retinue about fifteen-strong of cousins, nephews, nieces and hangers-on of indeterminate status. My own mother's Polish gentry relatives had always struck me as some of the most futile creatures that ever walked the earth, but they were intellectual Titans compared with these Magyar provincial nobility. At least they could boast some superficial acquaintance with the arts and with literature, had travelled, and could speak several languages even if they could say nothing sensible in any of them. But as for Elisabeth's foster-family, it was hard to say whether they impressed me more by their bovine lack of curiosity or by their almost Ottoman indolence. None except the count and Miklos (who were parliamentary deputies) had ever been beyond Hermannstadt or spoke any language other than Magyar, except for a little Romanian for cursing their peasants, nor had they the remotest idea of the world outside Hungary. Indeed, they seemed to have very few ideas about anything except heraldry and genealogy, or any opinions beyond a well-rehearsed litany of Magyar noble grievances against Vienna, the Jews, the great magnates and the Romanians. The only time the count took any notice of me was to complain to me in bad German that Vienna proposed forcing a number of iniquitous laws on Hungary, one of which would prevent landlords from using corporal punishment on their labourers "in such a manner as to cause a wound that does not heal after eight days," another of which would forbid the shooting (or "elimination," as the count called it) of suspected poachers. As for the war, it might not have existed. Miklos and his brother were of military age, but their father had used his position as local magistrate to get them exempted. Otherwise the family's war work so far had been limited to rounding up all the local undesirables—teachers, trade unionists, Jews and so forth—and carting them, bound hand and foot, to the recruiting depot in Kronstadt.

It was a long evening, redeemed only by the presence of Elisabeth and by the food, which was excellent. When it was over Elisabeth kissed me good-night and told me to be ready to get up early next morning. Then she entrusted me to the care of the family's head retainer, Jonel, a wrinkled, yellow-toothed old rogue dressed in a pewter-buttoned blue tail-coat of a cut that would have been fashionable in Vienna about 1840. He escorted me to my chamber with a smoking mutton-fat candle. He was a Siebenburger Saxon, speaking a medieval German dialect that was barely intelligible to me. The old man wheezed out of the room with much bowing and scraping to "der gute Herr Leutnant" and closed the massive oak door behind him. I washed as well as I could, until I found a dead bat lying at the bottom of the wash-bowl, then undressed and climbed into the damp-smelling bed. I smoked a cigar, then blew out the candle and lay down to sleep.

I was tired out from a two-day journey followed by hours of dinner-table conversation in a language of which I understood next to nothing.

So I fell asleep quite quickly despite the fact that the bed's mattress seemed to have been packed with half-bricks. I cannot say how long I slept; perhaps an hour or so, but I was soon woken by the creak of the door opening slowly. Command of a U-Boat had made me a light sleeper, so I was awake within a few seconds. Now, I am not a superstitious man, but the ambience of the castle was far from friendly, and it was not pleasant to sense that someone, or something, was in the room with me. Then the thought flashed through my mind that perhaps Elisabeth's foster-family had decided to resolve the fiancé problem by drastic and direct means . . . I slipped my pistol out from beneath the bolster, then reached to the bedside table for the matches. Taking the pistol in my right hand, I reached behind me with my left, and suddenly scraped the match along the wall. Imagine my surprise, then, when the flaring light revealed a thick-set country girl of about seventeen or eighteen, standing stark naked in front of the closed door, hands folded awkwardly and looking down at the floor with a face absolutely devoid of any expression. She was by no means a bad-looking girl I suppose: heavy-breasted and broad-hipped, with a luxuriant growth of pubic hair to match her thickly coiled, dark brown braids. But there was something so wretched about her pale, already rather pudgy flesh and her air of cow-like resignation that I was overwhelmed by a mixture of embarrassment and pity. I lit the candle, leapt out of bed and rushed over to open the door and bundle her out into the passageway, trying to apologise as I did so. She was quite unresisting as I pushed her out into the corridor. But then I saw a light outside: it was old Jonel, who tried to push the girl back in again.

"What? Do our village maidens not appeal to the Herr Leutnant? See what fine breasts the trollop has—still a virgin, and guaranteed free from infection by none other than the bailiff himself. Perhaps the fine lord will reconsider . . . ?"

"Damn and blast you and your village maidens, you old whore-monger!"

"Aha, but perhaps the fine lord's preferences are otherwise? I have heard that it is often so with the Herren Offiziere. Perhaps a village youth would be more . . ."

"Get out, you poisonous old rascal and take your village maidens and village youths with you before I wring your filthy greasy old neck!"

I landed Jonel quite a respectable kick in the backside as I jostled him and his protégée down the passageway. Then I went back to bed, too angry to be able to get back to sleep much before dawn.

As I lay half dozing, and the black Transylvanian night turned to grey in the arrow-slit up in the wall, there was a gentle tap on the door, then another. I got up, cursing devoutly, and made my way across to the door, half expecting that Jonel would be waiting outside with a troop of naked gypsy girls.

"Who the Devil is it?"

A familiar, musical laugh sounded from the other side. "The Devil it's me, Elisabeth."

"Heilige Gottesmutter, Liserl—what on earth do you want at this hour?"

"Let me in, we can't talk like this."

I put my dressing-gown on, then opened the door as softly as I could. There she stood, smiling and as fresh as the morning dew, dressed in a very smart green loden jacket, a heavy tweed skirt, a felt hat with a feather in the band and a pair of walking boots. Despite the awfulness of the hour I could hardly deny that she looked extremely pretty. She entered and I shut the door behind her.

"Liserl, is this some kind of elaborate practical joke on your part? Please tell me, because I've just had a very bad night and I fear that my sense of fun may be impaired."

She placed a canvas haversack on the table. "Come on, Otto my love, get dressed. We're going for a walk."

"A walk—are you mad? What time is it, in God's name?"

"It's 4:30 and we're going mountaineering." She smiled, and her dark green eyes sparkled. "Really, Herr Kommandant, I would hardly have thought that a distinguished Imperial and Royal U-Boat captain and officially certified war hero would have made such a fuss about being woken up just before dawn."

"But mountain-walking, at this hour . . ."

"My darling, it's either that or spend the rest of the day with my relatives. Now tell me truthfully, which would you prefer?"

I agreed that I would prefer walking up mountains, barefoot if necessary. So I sent her out, washed and shaved as well as I could and dressed, putting on my hobnailed service boots. She handed me a hunting rifle "in case we meet a bear," and we set out through the gateway just as the servants were rising bleary-eyed to begin their day's toil about the Schloss.

We must have cut a strange figure as we climbed up the mountain pathway through the forest: a slim, pretty young woman who, but for her Magyar-Latin looks, might have been an English governess on holiday in Switzerland, accompanied by a Naval Lieutenant in a bow-tie and starched shirt. But before long there was no one to remark on our appearance. The path climbed steeply up the mountainside and before an hour was out we were sitting just below the tree-line, eating a breakfast of bread and salami and brewing coffee in an Army mess-tin over a fire of twigs. I put my arm about her waist as we sat in the first rays of the morning sun, watching the ragged net-curtains of mist disperse from the hillsides below us. The Schloss Kelésvár lay far below, perched on its spur of rock.

"Awful, aren't they?" she said after a while.

"To whom do you refer, my love?"

"The Kelésvays, silly. Who did you think I meant?"

"I'm sorry: I hardly wished to agree to the proposition that my bride-to-be's foster-family are awful; even if it is true."

"Very diplomatically put. Yes, to be fair, they took Ferenc and me in when Papa was killed, and they did their best for us in their way. And I suppose that I love them in my way—at least, Aunt Sári and Uncle Sandor. But I still thank God every night that I grew up abroad and managed to escape to Vienna when the war came, because if I'd spent all my life here I would have been as dreadful as they are." She turned towards me suddenly. Her luminous eyes gazed searchingly into mine.

"Tell me. Did they send a girl to you last night?"

"Why . . . yes, there was such an incident."

"And . . . did you?"

"Good God no! What do you take me for? I bundled the poor creature out of the room and threatened your father's butler with a broken neck. But please tell me: is it the custom for guests at the Schloss Kelésvár to have naked peasant girls introduced into their rooms at dead of night?"

She sighed. "Yes, I'm afraid it is. And not only the guests either: that oaf Miklos calls it 'using the village women.'"

"I see. And what view do the village men take of all this? I suppose that these wenches have fathers and brothers and sweethearts."

"There isn't a great deal they can do about it. Or at least, there wasn't, but I think that things are changing now. Did you know that Miklos had an elder brother?"

"No. What became of him?"

"It was about four years ago. He used one of the village girls and her betrothed lay in wait for Laszlo one night with a spade. He crept up behind him and split his head down to the chin."

"Excellent: pity he didn't do Miklos as well while he was about it. Did they catch him?"

"No, he got away. So the gendarmes took his brother instead and hanged him in Kronstadt jail, after a ten-minute trial in Magyar without an interpreter. Uncle Sandor and the other magistrates said that even if he hadn't done it he certainly would have, given half the chance—which I have no doubt is true."

"Delightful—I can quite see why you want to be away from here."

We put out the fire and continued our climb up through the forest, Elisabeth striding ahead with that graceful, hip-swinging walk of hers, myself following with the rifle and the haversack. We climbed upwards until the oak and beech forest gave way to pine and birch. Then, quite suddenly, we found ourselves on the edge of a great expanse of mountain meadow on top of a ridge, about two thousand metres up I should think.

"Glorious, isn't it?" said Elisabeth, panting a little in the thin air. "Ferenc and I often used to come up here when we were children, to get away from the Schloss. Come on, let's rest a while. It's getting warm."

It was indeed surprisingly hot in the sunshine. She took off her jacket, and I took off mine for her to rest upon. She lay back and closed her eyes, luxuriating in the sun's warmth. I lay beside her, propped up on one elbow, admiring the serene perfection of her face: so delicate, yet without any hint of fragility. She opened one eye and smiled at me.

"Say something to me then. I so like it when you talk to me." She took my hand and placed it on her breast, small and firm beneath her blouse. These were strait-laced days and this was the furthest that we had so far gone in physical intimacy.

"Oh Otto, why can't it always be like this? No war, no U-Boats, no wounds to dress; only us like this for always."

"Yes. But I don't suppose it's a wish that will ever be granted. Somehow there always seems to be enough pain in the world to go round; and we've both got to go back to it all the day after tomorrow."

She was silent for a while, then she said suddenly, "Tell me Otto—why do you have to go back?"

The question was so directly put that it took some time to sink in.

"What do you mean, why go back? Damn it all, woman, if I don't go back I'll be arrested as a common deserter, even though I'm an officer, and probably get shot for it. Even getting back a day late without reasonable excuse would get me court-martialled."

She looked at me, her eyes shrewd and searching beneath their strong, black brows. "Very good then: become a deserter if that's what you want to call it; you'll certainly not be the only one. I was talking with Dr Navratil back at the hospital just before I left, and he said that the forests in Bohemia are thick with them. If they're going to shoot you for not fighting their rotten war for them then I don't think they deserve you anyway."

I was speechless for a while, so outrageous—almost blasphemous—was this talk to someone who had spent his entire adult life as an officer of the House of Austria. Finally my voice returned.

"Elisabeth, have you gone completely mad? I'm an Imperial and Royal naval officer with twelve years' seniority, not some half-witted Ruthene ploughboy making a dash for the Russian lines . . ."

"Yes, and I'm the woman who loves you and I don't give a copper farthing any longer for Austria or the Navy or the war after what I've seen. Listen, there's a shepherd's hut not far from here, over in that next valley. He owes me a good turn from when I was a girl and brought him some medicine when his wife had fever. I got a message to him before we came here and he says that he'll gladly hide you. They'll never find you up here, or not until the war's long over, and I can always spin them some tale about you falling over a cliff. If the soldiers can walk out on the war, then why not the officers as well?"

"But Elisabeth—be reasonable for God's sake: I'm a U-Boat commander fighting the enemies of the Father—"

"—and before long you'll be a dead U-Boat commander rotting away in your horrible boat at the bottom of the sea while all the counts and princes have wangled their miserable sons nice safe little jobs in the munitions factories . . ." Tears began to well in her deep green eyes. ". . . and the Princess Erlendy-Bratianu or whatever I'm called will be a war widow for the second time, only this time without even having been married first." She pulled me towards her and clasped me in her arms, surprisingly strong for such a slim young woman.

"Oh Otto, you dismal plodding Czech, can't you see? You're one of the best submarine captains they've got, and they'll just keep on sending you out, voyage after voyage, until one day you don't come back . . . No dearest, you're the only man I'll ever love and I'm not going to let them take you from me."

We began to kiss: not with the decorum hitherto thought proper to our betrothed state but wild, intoxicating kisses. She pulled me on to her lithe body, and began to fumble with my clothes.

"Otto, make love to me here . . . don't go away from me."

"Liserl, are you crazy? We're due to be married in July . . ."

"Yes, and by July the fish may be picking your bones. Something awful is going to happen—I know it . . . I don't want to be left an old maid."

"Old maid? But you're a widow . . . ?"

"On paper, yes. But the wedding night was inconclusive: the prince was too drunk for anything much, and anyway, the man was a raging pervert: I had more idea than he did." She kissed me again. "Come on then, aren't you going to show me how it's done. You've spent the past fifteen years fornicating your way around the world, so surely one little nursing sister isn't going to make much odds."

Well, here was a curious turn of events and no mistake: the seducer of many years' standing, practised in all the arts of getting women into the horizontal, now faced here with this delectable young woman importuning him to render his services—yet unaccountably reluctant to pay the tribute demanded of him. But please understand that whatever our own feelings in the matter, there were other considerations. Old Austria was a curious society, very prim in some respects and extremely licentious in others, but with very strict unwritten rules of behaviour. And while it was only expected that an unmarried officer should expend his vigour quite freely among actresses and shop-girls or even the daughters of the liberal intelligentsia, pre-marital relations with a noblewoman to whom one was betrothed were a slightly different matter. Quite apart from the lady's own honour, there was that of her family to be considered—that is, unless one wished to risk ending up like my old friend Max Gauss, whom I had last seen very early one morning in a Viennese park, slumped in a gardener's wheelbarrow and dribbling a thin trail of blood across the grass as they wheeled him towards the undertaker's van. I may sound like a cold-blooded calculating brute, but I knew that the Kelésvays would dearly like me out of the way; also that Miklos was reputed to be an excellent shot . . .

But in the end these hesitations were pushed aside like so many sheets of wet paper by the rising flood of our passion, that morning in the high, flower-sprinkled mountain meadow as the eagles wheeled in the sky above us. I had been loved by many women before then—and sadly, would be loved by a good few afterwards—but never as she loved me there that day. When it was over she lay beside me, my arm around her and her beautiful face, smiling but sad, resting on my shoulder. Yet even as I gazed at her there I could not quite silence her words running through my head: ". . . sure that something dreadful will happen . . . sure that something dreadful . . ."

We returned to the Schloss that evening, where I was ignored as usual. The next day it poured with rain. With so many servants about there was no opportunity for further amorous adventures, so we sought refuge in the library, the one room (we guessed correctly) where none of the Kelésvay family was likely to disturb us. It contained nothing worth reading, only worm-eaten and disintegrating tomes on heraldry and mildewed theological works. Like Béla Meszáros and many of the Magyar gentry, the Kelésvays were Debrecen Calvinists. Not that one would have noticed however: the doctrine of Election through Grace seemed to have done little for them other than reinforce their disdainful arrogance towards their peasants, who were of course Orthodox and therefore conveniently damned in this world and the next. There we sat together as the rain cascaded outside, gurgling and splashing from the castle's ruinous gutters. We longed for each other, but somehow the longing now seemed more endurable than mere bodily lust. After all, for those who are really in love, what is love-making but a means to union? Her embraces had been sweet; and they promised to be even sweeter in the future, so for the time being it was quite enough that we should be together, basking in the warmth of one another's nearness.

We set off next morning in the coach, bidden a frosty farewell by the Kelésvay family. As the Budapest train steamed out of Hermannstadt station Elisabeth looked back up the valley of the Maros. She was silent for a while, then spoke.

"I'm never going back there—never."

We arrived in Vienna late on the evening of the next day. As the train rattled across the flat fields of the Burgenland towards the capital, Elisabeth spoke to me.

"Otto."

"My love?"

"Otto, have you thought about what I said to you up there on the mountainside, about . . . about resigning from the war?"

We were both silent for a while: a delicate matter had been broached.

"Yes Liserl, I have thought about it, and I'm sorry for being such a dolt. I can quite see your point of view: but for God's sake try to see mine. I've got eighteen men and their families dependent on me, not just you. With me in command and with a good helping of luck they might just live to see the end of this war; but if I walked out on them there's no telling what sort of half-wit they'd have put in charge of them. No darling one, it just won't do I'm afraid: like it or not, we're in it together to the end."

She sighed. "Same here: I can't walk out on my patients. One way and another it looks as if this rotten war has got us both by the scruff of the neck."

Our first combat patrol after *U13*'s refit began on 5 June. We were based at Brioni now, and our area of operation was to be the Italian coast just south of Ancona. We were to loiter there, lying submerged during the day, and come up at dusk to molest coastal shipping. We surfaced about 8:30 p.m. on the 6th, ventilated the boat and then set off on a leisurely progress down the coast, about five miles out to sea. It was the ideal U-Boat time: still light enough for us to see them, but too dark for them to see us. The sun was sinking below the land horizon and a faint smell of hay was blown out to us from the meadows along the low-lying coast. Before long a smoke cloud was sighted to southwards: large, and coming towards us at some speed. We waited, and before long the ships began to materialise over the horizon: two large vessels, in line ahead and escorted by three or four torpedo-boats. We set course to get out to seaward of them, so that they would be silhouetted against the sun's afterglow, then we submerged. It was two liners, one of them a Puglia Line mail packet. Both were steaming northwards at about fifteen knots. It was not going to be easy at that speed, but the prize was worth the effort. *U13* closed with the convoy, diving almost beneath the bow of the leading torpedo-boat before swinging hard starboard to fire both torpedoes at the leading liner. Then we turned about and raced away, almost being run down by the following torpedo-boat. Bombs showered about us, but our work was done: after thirty seconds or so there was a loud bang as one of our torpedoes found its target, then a series of confused, rumbling explosions which I suppose must have been the boilers bursting as the sea poured in. *U13* was obliged to dive and weave and turn for the next twenty minutes or so to evade the searching torpedo-boats, but it was getting dark, so we shook them off without too much difficulty. When the danger was past I called Steinhüber to the control room and congratulated him. The electric firing system had short-circuited just before the attack and he had been sent up forward to fire the torpedoes by means of the hand levers. It had been a tricky task, requiring split-second timing, but he had done his duty admirably.

About 10 p.m. we surfaced and crept quietly back to the scene of the action. The escorting warships were gone, but lights flashed here and there in the darkness and the sound of voices came to us faintly across the water. Wreckage lay all around us—and several bodies, floating backsides-upwards in the ungainly posture of drowned men. We could not turn on the searchlight to investigate so we contented ourselves with fishing out a few items of flotsam to confirm our victory: a soldier's paybook, belonging to one Corporal Antonio Batistella of the 12th Bersaglieri Regiment, and a lifebelt marked CITTÁ DI TARANTO.

We arrived back at Brioni early on the morning of 9 June, having sighted nothing worthy of our remaining torpedo. Once the boat was tied up the crew were sent off to the Hotel Neptune for a much-needed bath and shave. For my part, though, I sat down in my office to draft our report of the voyage. I always detested paperwork and preferred to get it out of the way as soon as possible. About mid-morning, as the report was being typed out, I was suddenly summoned to see the U-Boat Station Commandant, the Ritter von Thierry. He welcomed me into his office, cordial and kindly as ever.

"Well Prohaska, 'der Glückliche Dreizehner' has lived up to her name once more: only it appears that she was not so lucky for the Italians. You sank a troopship on the 6th: the *Cittá di Taranto* as you surmised. She was carrying an entire Bersaglieri regiment up from Albania as reinforcements for the Asiago front." He paused, shuffling uncomfortably and avoiding my eyes. "The ship sank in about three minutes, following boiler explosions or perhaps ammunition going off. It appears anyway that there was heavy loss of life."

My mouth had suddenly gone dry. "Might I enquire how heavy, Herr Kommandant?"

"About two thousand we think, going by intercepted telegrams. One of our agents has reported numerous bodies being washed up on shore."

"But why? The water was warm and there wasn't much of a sea running, and anyway it was only a few miles offshore. Why didn't the escorts do anything?"

"We don't know. As I have said, the liner sank very quickly. Also it was getting dark, and they were busy trying to sink you as well as escorting the other ship clear. We just don't know." He got up from his desk and walked round to where I was sitting. "I know how you feel, Prohaska: we were trained as fighting seamen, not as butchers. But bear in mind that what you did was quite right and proper under all the accepted rules and customs of war. It was a military convoy, under naval escort, and the *Cittá di Taranto* herself was an armed merchant cruiser. Also the men who drowned were all armed . . ." (Armed, I thought to myself: a great comfort to have a rifle to defend yourself against a U-Boat) ". . . and you weren't to know how many men were on board. It could just as well have been a cargo steamer laden with empty sacks." (. . . Or a refugee ship packed with women and children, I thought.)

"And in any case, you only did to them what they would certainly have done to you if the positions had been reversed. For God's sake, Prohaska, is it any worse to kill a thousand men than to kill one? If those fellows had got to the trenches they could all have been blown to shreds in a morning's artillery barrage and nobody would have noticed. All you did was to compress a few hours of what I believe the generals call 'routine wastage' into five minutes."

"Yes, yes, Herr Kommandant, you must excuse me. It's just that I find it difficult to get used to the idea of having killed two thousand men."

"I know: it doesn't seem right somehow. Wretched business, this modern war; give me cutlasses and muzzle-loaders any day. Heaven alone knows what devilry they'll have invented by the time you come up for retirement."

"Herr Kommandant?"

"Yes, Prohaska?"

"Might I make one request—that the number of dead should be kept a secret? I think it would have a bad effect on the men's morale if it became known."

Thierry considered for a moment. "Very well: it will be kept in strictest confidence. In any case, the only people who know about it here at Brioni are you, myself and the duty Signals Officer. The message came by telephone from Pola, so no one here saw any telegrams."

So next morning the crew of *U13* were paraded on the deck of S.M.S. *Pelikan* and congratulated on having sunk the Italian armed merchant cruiser *Città di Taranto,* 6,230 tonnes. There was the customary "Dreimal Hoch!" then the men were sent about their duties for the day. Only Steinhüber remained behind, staring over the rail into the water. He seemed very quiet, so I walked up to him.

"Hello Tauchführer, you don't seem too cheerful this morning. What's the matter?"

He turned round smartly and saluted. "Obediently report that not in the least, Herr Kommandant."

"Come on Steinhüber, we've shipped together too long for me to believe that. What's the trouble?" He hesitated for a while, examining the deck planks, then spoke.

"I know about it, Herr Kommandant. I was manning the switchboard when the message came through, standing in for the operator while he fell out for a smoke. I overheard what they said—about the Italian ship, and all those men who went down with her."

"I see. Well, Steinhüber, only the two of us and the U-Station Commander know about it. I admit that it doesn't exactly leave me with a warm inner glow of pride and satisfaction from a job well done, but there we are: wars kill people, and what's done is done. Anyway, not a word about this to the others, do you understand?"

"Very good, Herr Kommandant."

Steinhüber was as good as his word. But from that day on he was a changed man: solitary, silent, gazing into nowhere, spending most of his free moments studying the little Bible that he carried around in his kitbag. He was as dependable and competent as ever, but inside the hard carapace of discipline, training and duty he was going to pieces with alarming rapidity. I hoped that he would get over it with time, but instead he merely got worse, to a point where I was considering an interview with the station Medical Officer.

It was a fine Sunday morning about two weeks after this. We had all been to Sunday Divisions and mass at the little church behind the Hotel Neptune—all, that is, except for Béla Meszáros and Steinhüber, who were Protestants and therefore excused church parades. We were a profane lot, we submariners, and the mass was not treated with any great solemnity. However, I was rather more thoughtful than usual as the host was placed on my tongue by the Naval Chaplain. The *Città di Taranto* was still weighing on my mind more than I cared to admit, even to myself. But anyway, mass was over, and I was taking a stroll along the quayside in the June sunshine. The lemon trees spread their scent, the naval orchestra was giving a Sunday concert in front of the hotel and the war might have been on another planet. And

I had a letter in my pocket from Elisabeth, full of the most intimate endearments. I passed Workshop No. 6, a wooden shed on the quayside used by the electricians for maintaining battery cells. The door was ajar and banging in the warm midday breeze. I walked over to close it—the electricians were at dinner—but something made me look into the hut first. A curiously unpleasant, sour, burning smell filled the air. I peered down the long, bench-lined interior and noticed smoke and steam rising from behind some shelves. Suspecting a fire, I ran down the hut to look. Then I saw a figure crouching behind a bench. It was Steinhüber, naked to the waist and apparently fishing for something inside a porcelain battery cell. He seemed not to see me. I sensed something wrong and strode towards him—then recoiled in horror.

"Steinhüber—what the Devil . . . ?"

The battery cell was steaming and bubbling like a witch's cauldron. A foul brown scum was already slopping over the edges and dribbling across the floor, causing the boards to smoulder as it did so.

"Quick! Guards! For God's sake come quick—bring the Medical Officer!"

Steinhüber seemed to remember himself and stood up, staring blankly, his face contorted almost out of recognition. He tried to salute, and nausea overcame me as I saw the ghastly thing that had been his right hand: now little more than a dissolving stump of bone, dribbling blood and froth. For some seconds the sheer awfulness of the sight deprived me of the will to do anything. Then I came to my senses: I seized Steinhüber by the arm and dragged him, sheep-like and unresisting, across the hut to plunge the stump of his hand into a bucket of lime-water kept for acid spillages. He mumbled disjointedly as I did so, as if none of this were really any concern of his.

"Obediently report that he is accursed who raises his hand against his brother . . . 'If thy right hand offend, cut it off' . . . This was the hand that fired the torpedoes you know, Herr Kommandant . . . Well, it won't be doing much more of that, now will it . . . ?"

Two sentries were running into the hut, carrying rifles with fixed bayonets. Dr Jedlička came bustling along after them, carrying his black bag and grumbling bitterly at being called away from his dinner to attend silly fools who . . . He blenched as he saw the dreadful stump. One of the young sailors turned aside and retched violently. As for myself, once the Medical Officer and a couple of sick-bay attendants had set about applying a tourniquet to Steinhüber's wrist, I tottered weakly out into the fresh air, trembling at the knees and shivering from a deathly chill inside me. The midday sun blazed down as the waltz "Lippe Schweigen" drifted from beneath the lemon trees.

There was a fearful row of course. The Naval Prosecutor's Department was all for having Steinhüber charged with wilful self-wounding in an attempt to evade military service, an offence which, in wartime, carried the death penalty, and which would certainly earn him the living death of twenty-five years' hard labour in a prison-fortress. In the end though, after much reference to Steinhüber's impeccable service record, Thierry and I managed to get the charge dropped and have him declared mad instead. We argued in particular that if a man merely wished to get out of the war he would chop a couple of fingers off, rather than deliberately filling a battery cell with concentrated sulphuric acid and then holding his hand in it for fifteen minutes or so, oblivious to the pain, until it had almost dissolved away. But there, even being declared insane was an unenviable fate in the Austria of 1916. The poor wretch was committed for life to a military lunatic asylum in Brünn, far away from his wife and little ones. Lehár and I managed to visit him some months later, after dispensing numerous bribes, but he recognised neither of us. In the end he died of despair on Christmas Eve 1917. May the God of Protestants grant him rest.

14

THE MAKING OF A HERO

A S YOU MIGHT IMAGINE, this dreadful incident cast a black shadow over us. I said as little as possible, and all other witnesses were sworn to secrecy for fear of the damage to morale, but still the word soon got around Pola that the chief Warrant Officer of *U13* had gone mad and mutilated himself in some spectacularly gruesome manner: self-castration with a pair of bolt-cutters, according to one version; gouging his own eyes out according to other well informed sources. A sense of unease hung over the boat as we loaded fuel and torpedoes for our next foray against the Italian coast, scheduled for 27 June but delayed for two days until I had managed to borrow a new Tauchführer from one of the other Ocarina boats. He was a fellow called Spengler—in his late twenties, but said to be very experienced and reliable. It was not that the patrol looked like being particularly hazardous in itself though: just the usual four- or five-day trip across to harass coastal shipping, this time in the shallow waters off the Po delta, from the latitude of Ravenna up to Chioggia and the southerly entrance to the Venetian lagoons. We had strict instructions, however, not to sail north of the latitude of Chioggia—for our own safety, since a German mine-laying U-Boat would be at work between Venice and the shoals known as the Cortellazzo Bank.

I had paid a visit to this minelayer a few days before in Pola at the invitation of her commander, Kapitänleutnant Breishaupt. *UC8* was a half-sister of my own *U13,* the only difference being that, instead of torpedoes, she carried twelve mines inside six vertical chutes forward of the conning tower. The mines would be dropped out of the bottom of the chutes, each dragged down by the weight of its concrete sinker block. Once the mine had reached the bottom of the sea a soluble plug would dissolve and release it to rush back towards the surface until its mooring cable snubbed it short like a toy balloon on a string. That at any rate was the theory, but according to Breishaupt the practice did not always work out so smoothly: sometimes the soluble plug would dissolve too quickly, allowing the mine to bob up underneath the U-Boat, and sometimes the mines would explode inside the tubes—especially the last one or two, when the boat would be light and rolling about. All in all, I gathered that mine-laying aboard a *UC*-type boat was a hazardous trade, and also—judging by the hapless Breishaupt—a duty to which the Imperial German Navy did not commonly assign the best or the brightest of its officers.

We set sail from Brioni and made landfall near the southernmost arm of the Po on the evening of the same day. We lay on the surface all night—there was little danger from patrol craft off this coastline of swamps and mudbanks—then set off northwards just before dawn. A thick, white, early-morning mist lay over the surface of the sea, oozing out from the marshes of the delta. Yet this mist was only about four or five metres deep, so that a look-out perched on top of the mine-deflector wire supports could gaze out across a sunlit sea of milky white. About 6 a.m. there was a call from the look-out: "Sail in sight—fifteen degrees starboard!" About eight hundred metres away the masts and sails of a small brigantine protruded from the level, cotton-wool carpet of mist, hanging limp in the still early-morning air. We closed with the vessel in silence, using our E-motor at "Slow Ahead," and as we crept in under the ship's bow I hopped across into the bowsprit rigging, followed by two armed ratings. Seconds later, pistol in hand, I was jumping down from the bulwark on to the vessel's deck, just in time to meet her skipper and crew emerging bleary-eyed and bewildered from the fo'c'sle hatch. I bid them *buon giorno,* introduced myself as Linienschiffsleutnant Prohaska of the Imperial and Royal Austro-Hungarian Navy, and asked to inspect the ship's papers while my men searched the hold.

The vessel was the *Salvatore* of Pescara, 158 tonnes with a crew of ten, laden with a cargo of horse-beans and general wares en route from Rimini to Venice. The Captain and Mate argued vociferously with me, calling upon the entire calendar of saints to support their contention that they were mere innocent civilians (which was true); that the war was no business of theirs (which, sadly, was also true); and that they were long-standing admirers of the Imperatore Francisco Giuseppe (which was certainly a lie). But there: they knew as well as I did that the Laws of Prize applied in their case. I apologised, but informed them that they had ten minutes in which to gather their personal effects and get into their boat. The sun was well up now and the mist was clearing fast.

It was the usual treatment for small wooden sailing ships. They were not worth a torpedo, of course, and I did not like sinking them with the gun, which took ages and might set the ship on fire, warning other potential victims to steer away and perhaps attracting a destroyer towards the smoke cloud. No, we used a ten-kilogram charge of TNT slung beneath the keel amidships. We lit the fuse and scrambled over the side on to the deck of *U13,* which promptly withdrew to a safe distance. It was always sad for us seamen to witness the death of a sailing ship. There was a dull "crump," and the sea boiled up white beneath the brigantine's topsides. She arched up slightly amidships as her back broke. Then she settled and began to sag in the middle. Timbers squealed and groaned, rigging snapped and spars crashed down as the fore and main masts leaned towards one another. The ship hesitated for a few seconds, as if reluctant to bid goodbye to the sunlight, then she sank in a tangle of ropes and canvas. Her skipper and crew stood silent in their boat, watching glumly as their home and livelihood disappeared beneath the waves. Then they looked apprehensively at us. I called out to them to throw us their painter, and we gave them a tow for a few miles towards the coast. By the time we cast them off their spirits had revived to the extent that they were able to revile us as *porci, ladroni, canaglia* and other choice epithets, all reinforced by a great deal of spitting and indecent gestures. Poor devils: I would have felt just the same myself.

It was now time for us to go down for another hot, stuffy, tedious day on the sea bed, marked here, about five miles east of Chioggia, as "Level Mud —30 metres." So the diving tanks were flooded and down we went. Just before closing the conning-tower hatch, now that the mist had cleared, I used the sextant to take a quick position fix from the campanile of Chioggia church and the light-towers at Rosalina and Pellestrina. I would use it to write up the running log, then turn in for a few hours.

Sleep, when it came, was far from easy because *U13* had taken the ground with a ten-degree slope down by the bow. This meant that for all of us, "rest" was a vexing business of continually sliding downhill and having to haul ourselves up again. By the time I awoke at midday to take the next watch everyone was peevish. The new men moved to their posts as the old watch stood down. Then, quite suddenly, the boat gave a slight lurch to starboard and began to move, slowly but quite perceptibly, before coming to a stop about four metres deeper than before. We must have been balanced on the edge of some sort of shallow depression in the sea bottom, so that a few men changing places had caused *U13* to slide forward before coming to a halt in the ooze. I was not too bothered about this, but life on the slope was getting tiresome and I was keen to move the boat a little to settle us on a level patch of mud. I ordered the men to surfacing stations, then blew the main diving tanks to lift us clear of the bottom before starting the E-motor. Nothing happened; we were stuck.

Becoming *eingeschlammt* was by no means an unusual occurrence for submarines operating at the head of the Adriatic, where the Po and its tributaries bring down vast quantities of silt each spring from the Alpine valleys and the plains of Lombardy. The ground in these parts was generally soft. It was certainly no cause for alarm though: all we had to do was to work the boat backwards and forwards for a while, rocking her from side to side, and soon she would break free of the bottom.

The next eight hours were among the most bitterly frustrating of my life: eight hours of sixteen men, stripped to the waist and streaming with sweat, rushing first starboard, then port, then starboard, then port again as the little electric motor whined full ahead and full astern until its armature windings glowed red-hot. Yet each time the boat would do nothing more than lean slowly a few degrees to one side or the other, rather as if she were embedded in putty. Every tank had been fully blown, the batteries had been run down to a point where I had extinguished all lights except one in each compartment, the temperature was in the mid-forties and the air was so thick as to be scarcely breathable. Gradually it dawned upon us that, if anything, our efforts were merely swaddling the boat down into the mud more firmly than ever.

"Well, Meszáros," I said, "it looks as if we're well and truly stuck this time. We've blown every tank that can be blown, so what now?"

"What if we fired off the torpedoes? That would lighten us by nearly two tonnes if we shut off the compensator tanks and blew the water out of the tubes afterwards."

So we tried to open first one then the other of the torpedo-tube bow caps. Our hearts sank: both refused to open, confirming my suspicion that the boat's bows were half buried in the slime. We went back to another hour of to-and-fro to try to dislodge the boat, again with no effect other than to use up more electric current and more oxygen. The crew were by now visibly depressed: apathetic and listless. Finally, some time after 9 p.m., Maschinengast Souvlička spoke out.

"Let's face it, Herr Kommandant: we're stuck fast, aren't we?"

I paused for a moment, wondering whether to place him on a charge for insubordination, but decided in the end that this was neither the time nor the place for a display of Old Austrian discipline.

"Yes Souvlička, we're stuck." I could see that everyone was looking at me, waiting for me to think of something. Their faith in my ability to work miracles was heart-breaking. But in the end I had little comfort to offer.

"Very well men, the position is this. We have enough oxygen to keep us alive for perhaps another twenty-four hours. The batteries are nearly flat, and about half of our compressed air has gone. The only thing that we can jettison now is diesel oil, of which we have about a tonne and a half. I'm going to release the telephone buoy now, then pump out most of the diesel tomorrow morning in the hope that someone will see the oil slick. We're only five miles off shore after all. If they see it, and manage to send a salvage vessel out before it's too late, we'll all spend the rest of the war in a prison camp. If they don't, then we shall be dead of suffocation by midnight tomorrow."

U13 had no form of escape apparatus—not even life-jackets—so we released the telephone buoy, and waited. Oxygen was bled into the atmosphere until the flasks were nearly empty. Then, just after dawn the next morning, we began pumping out the diesel oil after coupling the fuel feed-line to the bilge pump. In the end, after four hours, we had pumped out 1,500 litres without any appreciable effect on the boat, which seemed to be set in concrete. I kept 150 litres of oil as a reserve: it would be a poor joke if by some miracle we got to the surface, only to find ourselves drifting helpless in a gale.

It is best to say as little as possible about the rest of that awful day as we lay there, motionless in the failing light, using up as little oxygen as possible and trying in our various ways to face our imminent end. Some huddled together; others made feeble efforts at writing last letters. But only one seemed to break down: the new Tauchführer, Spengler, who muttered and cursed "the stupid bastard officers who got us into this mess" until the rest told him to shut up and he crawled away into the engine room to sit alone. It was not a nice way to die, though, having so much leisure to think about it. Death was a constant presence in those years, and we used to refer to the boat half-jokingly as "der Eiserne Sarg"—"the Iron Coffin." But somehow we had never given it much thought, always imagining that it would never be us; or that if it was, our end would come in a split second: the brutal crash of a torpedo or a mine, a rushing wall of water, then oblivion almost before we knew what had happened.

My own thoughts were far from pleasant. It looked as if Elisabeth's womanly intuition had been right after all. I reached down and felt her letter in my pocket, also the reply that would never reach her now. She would probably never know what had become of me. We would die here, then after a week or so, once the bilge pump had stopped, the seepage of water would fill up the hull. Our corpses would swell and bob up to the deckhead, then sink again over the months as we rotted and fell to pieces. And the Po and the Adige would bring down their silt every spring as the snow melted, piling up the mud year by year, century by century, until the rusty barnacle-covered tip of the periscope disappeared at last and His Imperial and Royal Majesty's Submarine *U13* and the bones of her crew passed from history into geology. Already in my mind I seemed to see rank upon rank of faceless, grey-clad figures waiting to speak with me as I arrived in the place to which I had so recently despatched them. "Lucky 13" had waited a long time to avenge her number.

By 8 p.m. the last of the air was almost used up. Our chests heaved and laboured as our lungs struggled to extract the last few atoms of oxygen from the dead, steam-bath atmosphere. The batteries were flat by now, so I switched on the emergency lamps. Why not? At least we would not die in the dark. Men took their last farewells of one another while they still had the strength. Then a rating crawled up to me in the control room and gasped out a strange request.

"Herr Kommandant . . . Can you . . . can you hear confessions and . . . give absolution?"

I thought for a few moments. "Yes, of course . . . Ship's captains . . . have always had the power to . . . to conclude marriages and burials . . . so it follows that they can . . . administer the other sacraments."

It was a shameless lie: an outrageous fraud practised on a dying man. But it seemed to give him courage—and not only him, but a long string of other penitents over the next half-hour, all of whom were absolved *in nomine patri et filii et spiritus sancti* with as much Latin as I could remember. It was the usual catalogue of fornications, petty theft, missing mass and so forth. Somehow, it seemed to give them courage.

Only one man—Matrose Tomić, who was only nineteen—seemed unable to face the end. He clung to my arm and refused to let go.

"I don't want to die, Herr Kommandant . . . I don't want to die like this . . . not like this . . ."

"Ah, Tomić," I said, gasping for breath, "I don't want to either . . .

But we all die one day, sooner or later . . . It doesn't make much difference when . . . Anyway, would you rather die like my father? Spinal cancer . . . eight months of agony before it killed him." (This was another black lie: my father was alive and in sturdy good health.) "No, lad . . . it could be worse . . . Anyway, sit here by me if you want . . ."

I was growing sleepy now, finding it difficult to keep my thoughts on course. Soon I would fall into a spell of drowsiness from which I would not emerge, like a swimmer going down for the last time . . . Suddenly I was aware of Lehár by me, whispering something. My oxygen-starved brain struggled to grasp what he was saying.

"Herr Kommandant . . . The torpedo equalisation tank . . . we forgot about the torpedo equalisation tank."

This was a small sea-water tank right up in the bows. It had been installed by *U13*'s German builders to compensate for the fact that Austrian torpedoes were each about thirty kilograms lighter than their German equivalents, but might one day be made heavier. We generally disregarded this tank, which contained only about sixty litres, and kept it flooded all the time at sea. It might be worth a try: at any rate it was better than sitting here waiting for the end . . . Lehár and I slid down the deck on our backsides, too feeble to stand, until we arrived in the torpedo compartment. There I struggled to my feet, and after infinite exertion managed to let some compressed air from the torpedo-firing reservoir into the equalisation tank. Nothing happened, except that the boat shuddered faintly.

"Well Lehár," I said, "no use . . . Still, it was a good idea . . . Anyway, shall we stay here . . . or try to go back to the others?" We thought for a while, wondering whether to lie where we were. But some instinct drew us to die in company, so we set off back up the sloping deck like two mountaineers struggling up Everest. It was indeed fortunate that we did so, because the weight of our two bodies moving aft must have been the last hair that tipped the scale. I was just staggering towards the torpedo-compartment bulkhead when it happened. It seemed for a moment as if the deck had leapt up and tried to hit me on the back of the head, like a garden rake. Then I was sliding helplessly aft towards the engine room amid a howling mass of bodies.

It is one of the great regrets of my life that I was not on the surface that night to witness the arrival of *U13,* because it must have been a most singular spectacle. I cannot say whether or not the little boat leapt clean out of the sea, like a fat dolphin, but it certainly felt like it to judge by the shuddering slam as she fell back into the water. There was an eerie silence as the boat rocked placidly from side to side. Then bodies started to disentangle themselves from the confusion of limbs and loose gear lying in the engine room.

I shall never know how Grigorović managed to open the conning-tower hatch. When he did though the locking wheel was snatched from his hands with a loud bang as the hatch blew open. Our ear-drums cracked agonisingly, and suddenly the vessel was filled with a dense yellow fog as the drop in pressure caused the moisture in the saturated air to condense. Then a blessed freshness came rushing into the boat, like the breath of God into Adam's nostrils. Grigorović dragged himself out through the hatchway, and suddenly I saw it above me: a disc of indigo, sprinkled with the bright summer stars that I had never thought to see again. I hauled myself up, hand over hand, until Grigorović reached down and dragged me up by the collar like a kitten. Then we lay there in the moonlight, gasping like two expiring fish. The sudden surfeit of oxygen was too much for me, and before long I had to drag myself to the edge of the conning tower to vomit violently into the darkness. Once we had recovered our strength a little the two of us set about getting the others up from below. In the end I had to tie a bowline and go below, loop it under the arms of each of them in turn and then shout to Grigorović to haul them up into the air. It was slow work, but as men recovered they were able to help, and within half an hour we had everyone back on their feet.

The next thing was to trim the boat down, since with all her tanks blown she was bobbing about like an empty barrel. Then we started the diesel to get some power into the batteries and to refill our compressed-air flasks. I was uneasy though: the water was calm and the moon was nearly full, turning the sea into a plate of silver on which we must have been visible for miles around. About 12:30 Béla Meszáros suddenly caught my arm.

"Listen—what's that?" It was not easy to make out any sound above the rumbling of our own diesel, but soon I became aware of a deep, heavy, throbbing noise in the night air.

"Look—there it is!" Meszáros pointed to northward, in the direction of Venice. About eight kilometres distant an airship was moving over the sea. It could only be an Italian semi-rigid, the kind they used for submarine-spotting. I had the boat trimmed down as much as possible and ordered the machine gun to be set up on its tripod. We could move under diesel power, but we still had too little battery charge or compressed air to be able to dive. For a while it seemed as if the airship had missed us. Then, about ten minutes later, the thing reappeared, gleaming silver in the moonlight. It was heading straight for us! A belt of ammunition was snapped into the breech of the Schwarzlose, and Torpedomeister Gorša took up his position in the conning-tower hatchway, waiting. Suddenly we were blinded by a great glare of white light. Bullets began to shower around the boat and rattle on the plating. The airship had a searchlight! Our machine gun clattered and shuddered as cartridge cases tinkled down into the control room. But it was hopeless: the airship was only about two hundred metres up now, but the dazzle of light defeated any attempt at taking aim. It passed dead overhead. The air was filled with screaming, then a wild chaos of noise and water as a cluster of bombs exploded in the sea around us, missing the boat but drenching us to the skin. Gorša swung round to fire at the airship as it passed over us. Its searchlight beam lost us, so we could see its great dark bulk above us now, blotting out the moon: less than half the size of a German Zeppelin, I should think, but still filling us with the sort of feeling that a mouse must have under the shadow of a hawk. Bullets whined around us once more as the machine gunner in the stern gondola opened up at us. Gorša fired again, then suddenly slumped back. There was a hole in his forehead, and blood pouring profusely from the back of his skull.

They got him below as I took his place. I took aim at the great bulk overhead and squeezed the thumb-trigger again. The gun jolted and clattered, but it was not a lot of use without a proper anti-aircraft sight. Then it stopped as the belt reached an end. I snapped the hot breech open.

"More ammunition, for God's sake!" The airship would soon turn and come back for another bombing pass, perhaps with better luck this time. Hands held up a belt to me. I locked it into the breech, then fired again. To my astonishment, a curving arc of golden fire leapt up towards the dark shape in the sky. But there was no time to wonder, only to concentrate the fiery stream on the airship's tail as it moved away from us. I fired, paused, then fired another long burst until that belt too came to an end.

"More ammunition!"

"There is none, Herr Kommandant!"

It happened slowly at first, like that dull glow in the end of a cigar just as one lights up. The incandescence became brighter, like a paper lantern, then a sudden blaze of white flame erupted under the airship's tail, pausing a second or so before racing along its belly and sending fingers of fire clawing up its sides. We all gazed upwards, silent and open-mouthed as the terrible white light engulfed us. The airship's nose tilted up into the sky as a vast column of smoke and sparks rose up to blot out the moon. Fragments of burning fabric detached themselves and floated lazily down into the sea. Soon only the screaming engines were keeping the great blazing ruin up in the sky. We watched as one of the engine gondolas fell off to plummet into the sea, the wooden propeller on fire but still turning as the waves swallowed it. Béla Meszáros swore afterwards that he saw a man, clothes on fire, leaping from the forward gondola. Then it was all over: the flaring mass sank slowly towards the water, and within moments it was gone, leaving nothing more than a few patches of burning oil on the waves. Altogether I suppose that this entire ghastly spectacle could not have lasted more than two minutes. We still stood there, silent until Meszáros spoke.

"Holy Mother of God—what a sight. They must have seen the blaze back in Pola."

"Meszáros," I enquired, "those incendiary bullets—where did we get them? U-Boats are only issued with standard ammunition. I thought that only the naval flying service got phosphorous ammunition because of the expense."

"Ah yes, Herr Kommandant . . . It's like this. While you were on leave and I was still in Cattaro I went for a walk on Obostnik one afternoon when one of the flying boats got his navigation wrong and flew into the mountainside. I got to the wreck before the crash teams from Kumbor. I found that belt in the wreckage and I thought it might come in useful."

"And what about the pilot and observer—what did they have to say about it?"

He avoided my eyes. "They were not in a condition to argue, Herr Kommandant." I saw that he had a hand in his jacket pocket, trying to hide a splendid Swiss wristwatch which he had been sporting for the past couple of months.

"I see. Well, Meszáros, I don't know that I regard picking around the dead in crashed aircraft as a suitable occupation for an officer of the Habsburgs, but it saved our necks this time."

"Glad to have done it."

By about 2 a.m. our batteries and compressed-air flasks were in a fit state for us to think of making for home. Just as we were about to get moving there was a call from Grigorović:

"Vessel in sight—forty-five degrees starboard!"

I snatched up the night glasses. Yes, there was something about four thousand metres distant, heading towards us. As it came closer I saw that it was another submarine, travelling at about ten knots and apparently unaware of our presence. The torpedo tubes were made ready to fire as I waited and watched. The German minelayer boat would not be this far south and anyway, it was a day too late for her. No, it must be an Italian boat coming out from Venice to see what had happened to their airship.

The mysterious vessel was about a thousand metres away now, and had turned to run at right angles across our bows. I could see that, whatever she was, she was certainly not German or Austrian. All submarines look much alike at a distance and at night, but this one had a long, low, flush deck with a small, squarish conning tower. As the submarine passed broadside on to us her navigation lights flashed on and off, twice. Well, that decided the matter: this was no recognition signal known to us.

"Both torpedo tubes—stand by to fire," I called softly down the voice pipe, as if the Italians would hear me. Then the enemy submarine began to turn away from us. The range was extreme, so I took a quick decision.

"Both torpedoes—fire!"

There was a sudden, angry snort of foam in front of our bows as the torpedoes were blown from their tubes. I saw the two trails of phosphorescence streaking away from us, then lost sight of the target. Damn them, had they seen us and dived? I waited, counting the seconds. There was a distant spout of spray and a shock came to us through the water, followed by the sound of an explosion. We let in the clutch of the diesel and moved forward to look for survivors. All we found was a patch of oil, some splintered wooden wreckage and a reek of petrol and TNT fumes in the air. The smell of petrol clinched the matter as far as I was concerned: no German U-Boat and no seagoing Austrian boat now had petrol engines, so it could only have been an Italian.

"Well," I said, "we've had quite enough excitement for one night: in fact more than most people manage in a lifetime. Perhaps we ought to be heading for home."

U13 arrived at Parenzo the next morning with barely a cupful of diesel oil left in the tanks. I went ashore at the mole and made my way to the naval signal station, from where I telephoned the news of our double success to Brioni. It seemed that the glow of the dying airship had been seen there, a good hundred kilometres away across the Gulf of Venice. I returned to the boat, and, after a hurried breakfast of zwieback and coffee, took her out again for the journey down to Brioni. Down below, Torpedomeister Gorša lay stretched out on a bunk, wrapped in a blanket. He had died in the small hours without regaining consciousness.

As we neared Brioni that afternoon a message winked out from Fort Tegetthoff: "*U13* to proceed at once to Kriegshafen Pola. Crew to wear best clothes." Tired out after the night's excitements and two escapes from death, we nevertheless struggled into our best whites and shaved with the last of the fresh water. Then we lined the narrow deck in parade order as we made our way across Pola harbour, between the moored lines of battleships as the flags fluttered and the bands played and the crews manned the rails. There was something faintly ludicrous about it all, I thought: our preposterous little boat, which the morning before last had been sinking a scruffy coastal brigantine laden with horse-beans and galvanised buckets, now returning to a hero's welcome with a dead man stretched out stiff and pale down below.

But then Old Austria was sorely in need of heroes, that summer of 1916. The great spring offensive against Italy had achieved nothing. Then in June, on the Eastern Front, Pfanzer-Balttin's 4th Army had been swept away by a new Russian offensive under General Brusilov. Austria had lost half a million men in a single week, most of them taken prisoner without firing a shot. Once again, only the intervention of our German allies saved the k.u.k. Armee from total disaster. Things were in a sorry state for the House of Austria, so it was scarcely surprising that a few circuses should have been arranged to divert the public—especially now that bread was running short.

It was in these circumstances that I was transformed from Otto Prohaska, a successful if rather pedestrian submarine commander, into Ottokár, Ritter von Prohaska: superman; Knight of the Military Order of Maria Theresa; incarnation of all the military virtues; fiancé of a beautiful Hungarian countess; *chevalier pur et sans reproches*. I have it here in my hand as I speak to you now: a ribbon of age-brittled silk, printed with a crude likeness of myself, and of an airship being shot down and a submarine being sunk simultaneously. It bears the legend VIVAT—DOPELLSCHUSS, 3 JULI 1916, and then underneath my portrait: PROHASKA—DER HELDENMUTIGE

KOMMANDANT VON *U13*. Many of these "Vivat ribbons" were printed in Austria during the war to be sold in aid of the Red Cross and other such causes. Mine was only on sale for three weeks or so, however, before being abruptly withdrawn from sale in circumstances which, by your leave, I shall now relate.

It had all begun at Pola the day after our triumphal entry. I was suddenly summoned to the Marineoberkommando building on the Riva to meet the Naval Commander-in-Chief himself, Admiral Haus. He was a rather peppery man with hooded, hawk-like eyes—"der Alte Nasowas" we used to call him, from his habit of stroking his pointed beard and pronouncing the phrase "na so was"—"well I never." He was in poor health when I saw him, already dying from some awful lung condition, but he seemed cordial enough and had evidently forgotten how, a year before, he had blocked my citation for the Maria Theresa. In fact he told me that I was now to be awarded that much-coveted honour.

"Not bad eh, Prohaska? Four Maria Theresas for the Navy already and three of them to the U-Boat Service. The Promotion will be in Vienna on the 19th."

"But Herr Admiral, I am due to be married on the 19th . . ."

"Well I never. Excellent—double the show for the public then. Better have the wedding postponed to the following Saturday."

I made my way back to Brioni to pack my belongings for the train journey to Vienna. As I was packing there was a knock on the door of my room. It was my old acquaintance Toni Straussler, now a Linienschiffsleutnant and waiting at Brioni for a berth aboard a U-Boat.

"Hello, Prohaska. Sorry to disturb you. Do you mind if I come in?"

"No Straussler, not at all. Always glad to see you. What's the news?"

"Not a great deal, except that *UC8* is overdue."

"What, the German minelayer boat? That chap . . . er . . . Breishaupt wasn't it?"

"Yes, that's the one. They were due back four days ago. Did you see anything of them?"

"Not a thing I'm afraid. But four days overdue: that's a long time if it's just an engine breakdown. I suppose they've been blown to bits by one of their own mines."

"Prohaska, I'm afraid that I have bad news for you: your future brother-in-law was aboard *UC8*." I was silent for a while, too shaken to speak.

"Fregattenleutnant Graf Ferenc de Bratianu. He arrived here the day after you sailed and managed to talk Breishaupt into letting him come along as Second Officer." He paused. "Don't worry Prohaska old man—we don't know what's happened. It might be an engine breakdown after all, or perhaps they went aground off the Lido and the Italians took them prisoner."

The journey to Vienna was overshadowed by this news. Elisabeth took it quite well I suppose, buoyed up by my assurances (of which I was far from confident) that her brother had probably been taken prisoner. In the circumstances I thought it best not to let her know that she had nearly lost her fiancé as well in the same waters. We had little enough time to be together though over the next ten days. The wedding was duly postponed to 21 July, to make way for my decoration at Schönbrunn by the Emperor himself. Otherwise it was an unending, exhausting round of interviews with journalists—German, Swiss, Turkish, even American—and sessions with photographers, tailors and portrait artists. As the days wore by I began to feel less and less like myself and increasingly like a tailor's dummy for the now moth-eaten vestments of Habsburg Imperial favour. Not the least of my problems was what I should call myself once I had received the Maria Theresa. Knights of the Order were supposed to be elevated immediately to the Freiherrstand. But then there was the problem of where I was to be Freiherr of. In the end I elected to become Freiherr von Strachnitz, the German version of my ancestral village of Strchnice. But the Chancellery of the Order would only give me the title provisionally because they thought that there might be a Freiherr von Strachnitz already; so I remained a Ritter while the Chancellery and the Imperial Chamberlain's department argued it out between them. I understand that the matter was still unresolved in 1918 when the Monarchy collapsed.

I was duly decorated in front of the palace at Schönbrunn on the morning of 19 July, before a large crowd of cheering, flag-waving Viennese schoolchildren and a guard of honour drawn from the Navy and the Deutschmeister Regiment. It was a beautiful day, a last, defiant display of pre-war colour and festivity amid the encroaching, hungry drabness of the war. Our ancient Emperor fixed the little white-enamelled cross to my coat, his knobbly arthritic old fingers fumbling to get the pin into the heavy blue serge. Suddenly I felt a sharp stab of pain: he had stuck the pin through coat and shirt-front into the skin of my chest. I managed not to wince, but then his burly oaf of a Flügeladjutant, seeing His Imperial Majesty in difficulties, came to his aid and skewered the pin a good two centimetres into the flesh! Still I could show no sign of distress, but had to stand there smiling as the Emperor told me that it had been very pleasant; he had enjoyed himself very much. Yet despite the pain, I could not help but feel a deep pity for this desiccated old creature—like a worn-out old clockwork monkey in a pale blue tunic, still jerking through the motions of nearly seventy years as the rusty spring unwound its last few turns. "Old Prohaska," they used to call him in Vienna, since mine is one of the commonest of Czech surnames. His eyes were still bright blue, but watery now, and filmed like those of a dead fish. And as for the famous side-whiskers (which I must say had always put me in mind of a baboon), they obviously owed a great deal to barber's glue. There we stood in the sunshine as the blood soaked into my shirt: Emperor and war hero; ruler and subject; both of us now little more than sandwich-board men for the Propaganda Ministry. As the Emperor and his entourage left, and I wondered when I could decently pluck the pin out of my chest, I noticed that two Imperial German Naval ADCs at the rear of the procession had stopped to regard me with no obvious favour. One narrowed his eyes and said to the other, "Yes, that's the fellow . . ." Then they passed on.

I had returned to the War Ministry after the ceremony, and was sitting there as a sick-bay attendant dabbed iodine onto the puncture in my chest. An orderly entered.

"Herr Schiffsleutnant the Ritter von Prohaska is requested to report at once to the office of the Assistant Chief of Naval Staff."

I dressed hastily and followed the orderly through the labyrinth of brown corridors and staircases to the third floor. I was ushered into a conference room, and found myself facing Vizeadmiral the Baron von Liebkowitz, three or four other senior naval officers—and an Oberst-auditor from the Navy's legal department. I had no idea what was the purpose of the meeting, but submarine commander's instinct told me that it boded no good. I was invited to sit down, with an oily smoothness that was the very opposite of reassuring. The Admiral began.

"Herr Schiffsleutnant, you will doubtless wonder why you have been called here in such haste so soon after being decorated with our Monarchy's highest military honour. Now, you are not to regard this as a formal court of enquiry, but the fact is that during the past two days certain discoveries have been made relating to your double victory in the Gulf of Venice on the night of the 2nd to the 3rd of July: discoveries which I am afraid may have a grave effect on the Monarchy's relationship with the German Empire."

I listened in a daze, too bewildered even to think. But the Oberst-auditor soon brought me back to my senses.

"We would like you to answer a few questions, Herr Schiffsleutnant, concerning your sinking of an unidentified submarine east of Chioggia in the early hours of 3 July. I have your combat report here, but I would like you to fill in a few small details for us."

"Please ask me whatever you wish."

"Thank you. Our first question concerns your exact position at the time of the sinking. Now, you have given it here . . ." (adjusting his pince-nez) "as 45° 9′ North by 12° 31′ East. Tell me now, how did you come by that position?"

"By shore bearings, Herr Oberstauditor."

"Aha, by shore bearings. And when precisely did you make these observations? I understand that you had recently surfaced in darkness after nearly thirty-six hours on the bottom and near-death from suffocation; also that less than two hours before you had been bombed by an Italian airship, which you subsequently shot down. It seems to me that you would not have had a great deal of opportunity for navigation."

"You are quite correct. The bearings were taken from Chioggia church-tower and from the light-towers at the mouth of the Adige and the entrance to the lagoon just before we submerged on 1 July. Obviously, we surfaced at the same spot, and we moved very little from it over the next few hours because, as Herr Oberstauditor observes, we were too busy recharging our batteries and then fighting off air attacks."

"And there is no current there?"

"Very little. But please, Herr Oberstauditor, might I ask where all this is leading? Have I been called here to be accused of negligent log-keeping or is there some more serious purpose behind all this?"

The Admiral intervened. "Yes, Prohaska, I think that it is only fair to tell you what has happened and why you are here. You are aware, I take it, that the Imperial German minelayer submarine *UC8* has now been posted missing?"

"I was not, Herr Vizeadmiral, but before I left Pola I heard that she was overdue."

"Well, the fact of the matter is that the Germans now have strong reasons for suspecting that you sank their boat by mistake on 3 July. Not to put too fine a point upon it, Prohaska, they are demanding your head: asking what sort of allies we are to go around giving our highest military honours to fellows who sink their U-Boats."

"But Herr Vizeadmiral," I protested, "this cannot be possible. The vessel that we torpedoed was an Italian, probably *Foca*-class, and certainly not a German boat. The air reeked of petrol when we reached the place, and anyway it was well south-east of *UC8*'s zone of operations."

"Yes Herr Schiffsleutnant, I take these points. But I am sorry to say that the Germans now have some damning evidence that makes it very difficult for us to tell them they are wrong." He whispered to an orderly, and a folder containing three or four photographs was brought to me. They depicted some splintered boards stencilled MARINE VERSORGUNG-SABTEILUNG 30, WILHELMSHAVEN, a water-crinkled paybook made out in the name of one Bootsmann Peter Gantz, and a silk cap ribbon embroidered with the words UNTERSEEBOOTS FLOTILLE in Gothic letters. "These were picked up three days ago by *UC15* very near to the position that you gave for the sinking. It also appears that a lot of oil was coming up to the surface. Gantz, it seems, was *UC8*'s leading mine-hand."

"Herr Vizeadmiral, permit me to observe that this is not conclusive evidence. The *UC*-type boats are always being blown up on their own mines, and the current could quite easily have drifted these items from where the boat sank."

"But you said that there was no current," said the Oberstauditor.

"Enough to drift light objects a few miles a day."

The Admiral rejoined the attack. "Herr Schiffsleutnant, did anyone but yourself see the submarine broadside-on?"

"Yes, my Quartermaster was on the conning tower with me. You may take a sworn statement from him if you wish. The submarine was a long, low vessel and it winked its navigation lights at us."

"But did the possibility that it might be a German U-Boat cross your mind? By your own admission you had not slept for nearly thirty hours, and you were in a poor state after your sojourn on the bottom and the excitements of your battle with the airship. I put it to you also that the petrol you thought you smelt immediately after the sinking was in fact fumes from the wreck of the airship, which had come down not far away."

"Of course I considered the possibility, Herr Vizeadmiral, but I dismissed it because, firstly, the submarine was patently not German in appearance; secondly, because we were well outside *UC8*'s zone; and thirdly—well—because winking navigation lights was such an idiotically un-German thing to do."

Liebkowitz cupped his chin in his hands. "You put me in a very difficult position, Prohaska. On the one hand we have great faith in your considerable experience and proven judgement as a U-Boat commander. But on the other our German allies have lost one of their submarines and are quite convinced that you did it. They have been alleging for nearly two years now that Austrian signals procedure is slovenly and that our naval officers are not nearly as well trained as theirs. Now it seems that they have some hard evidence of this, and they are going to use it. The fact of your Maria Theresa merely seems to have increased their desire for your blood. And frankly, after this summer's performance by the k.u.k. Armee we are hardly in a position to refuse them anything."

At this point I began to rebel. "Might I then respectfully enquire of the members of this panel exactly what it is proposed to do with me? Am I to be court-martialled? Because if not, then I demand a court martial to allow me to clear my name."

Liebkowitz answered. "Good God man—you must be mad! Fine fools we would look, giving you the Maria Theresa one day and court-martialling you the next. No Prohaska: I'm afraid that for the greater good of the Dual Monarchy and its alliances you will have to be . . . removed from the scene somehow. Now, if you would care to wait in the corridor outside. I am afraid that we must discuss this in privacy."

As I paced the corridor outside the conference room visions poured through my mind: visions of an ante-room with a small table bearing a bottle of schnapps and a pistol. No, I thought, the Devil take the lot of them—let them put me in jail, or do their own dirty work if they want me dead. What right had they to require an innocent man to take his own life just to mollify the Germans? I would still give my life a hundred times for the House of Austria, facing the enemy, but self-murder to save national face was another matter . . . Just as I was rehearsing my defiant speech to the unofficial court martial I was astonished to see Elisabeth's foster-brother Miklos shambling along the corridor in his untidy, rather unsavoury way. I knew that he was in Vienna as part of the Hungarian parliamentary delegation, but I had no idea what brought him here. He stopped and regarded me as if I were a heap of filth on the parquet floor.

"So, Herr Schiffsleutnant," he sneered, "getting your just deserts after all, I hear. I always said that it was impermissible for a Magyar noblewoman to mingle her blood with that of a common Czech swineherd like yourself. Now that you have murdered her brother perhaps she will believe me."

"How did you get to hear . . . ?"

He smiled. "Let us say that Budapest likes to maintain its own discreet channels of contact with Berlin. Anyway, you may consider the marriage to be cancelled, and if I see you near the Princess Erlendy-Bratianu again I shall take the greatest delight in shooting you dead. I bid you good-day."

"Why you dirty Magyar louse, I'll . . ." The door opened.

"Herr Schiffsleutnant the Ritter von Prohaska is requested to enter the conference chamber."

I entered, and found myself facing the panel of enquiry. Liebkowitz stood up to deliver its verdict.

"Herr Linienschiffsleutnant, this unofficial board finds the case against you . . . not proven. However, it is my regrettable duty, in the face of overwhelming and irresistible pressure from our German allies, to inform you that you are to be removed from command of the submarine *U13*. As to the question of your . . . doing the honourable thing, we have decided that the interests of the Monarchy would not best be served by the suicide of a man awarded the Knight's Cross of the Military Order of Maria Theresa only the day before. Therefore we have decided on the next best thing: from tomorrow you will be transferred as an observer to the Imperial and Royal Flying Service on the Isonzo Front."

I left the building as grimly determined as ever I was in my life: I would see Elisabeth before I left for Italy or die in the attempt. Not a thousand Kelésvays armed with 30cm howitzers would have stopped me as I rattled along in a fiacre towards the Reichsrat Building where she worked as a nurse. I had my sword with me, and I was determined to run Miklos through with it if he tried to stop me. Passers-by had jostled to see me as I left the Marine Section building; schoolchildren had begged for my autograph; pretty girls had seemed to faint with delight at the sight of the little white cross pinned to my coat. How could they know, poor deluded fools? Tomorrow the Vivat ribbons would suddenly and mysteriously vanish from sale, and another war hero would be manufactured for them. Then a couple of weeks hence the newspapers would carry a brief report of my gallant death in aerial combat over the Alps ". . . having volunteered specially for flying duties as the only way left to demonstrate yet again his matchless heroism in the service of Emperor and Fatherland."

But what did I care, as I ran up the steps of the Parliament-building-turned-hospital? I reached the entrance hall, expecting a scene if I was refused permission to see her, and prepared to flash my decoration on all sides to get on to her ward. But there she was, standing at the foot of the main staircase, pale and tired-looking and red-eyed, but still beautiful even in her shapeless nurse's overall. She smiled as if she had been expecting me.

"Darling—how good to see you. Aren't you going to kiss me then?"

"I've come to say goodbye."

She seemed curiously unperturbed. "Why goodbye?"

"Haven't they told you?"

"Yes, they told me. I had that buffoon Miklos in here after I came back from Schönbrunn this morning, babbling some nonsense that you had killed Ferenc and that the wedding was off."

"What did you say?" She laughed. "I told him to go to the Devil—but not quite as politely as that: that I'm an independent woman now and I shall marry whomsoever I please."

"And Ferenc . . . ?"

Her eyes misted. "I don't believe that you had anything to do with it. And anyway, even if you had I still think he would have wanted me to marry you. This is a world war, not a game, and people get killed by accident all the time."

"But they'll disinherit you, disown you. . ."

She took me aside, behind a pillar, and held me in her arms, gazing into my eyes. "Otto, you're too decent a man for your own good. Can't you see? Old Austria's dying around us, bleeding to death amid the mud and the barbed wire. I don't know what's going to come after it, but somehow I don't think that titles and run-down estates in Transylvania will be much use to anyone. All I want is to spend my life with you: the rest doesn't matter a fig."

"Are you sure of that, still?"

She smiled, and squeezed my hand. "Yes, I'm sure. And I'm sure of something else too, now. I'm two months pregnant with your child."

We married on 21 July as planned, but in a registrar's office in the 8th District, with Dr Navratil and Béla Meszáros as witnesses. There was a small church wedding, mainly to please my aunt, then a brief honeymoon in a Gasthaus before I departed next morning, en route for the Isonzo Front. But that is another story.

Even so, through all the years that followed, a ghostly doubt lingered in my mind about the sinking of *UC8* and the death of my brother-in-law. Had the Germans been right? Had I perhaps seen what I wanted to see, fuddled with carbon dioxide and fatigue? Then about two weeks ago, one sunny afternoon, I was sitting out in the garden. Suddenly the sound of footsteps made me turn around. It was Kevin, accompanied by a sturdy-looking, dark-haired man in jeans and a singlet. He was introduced to me as one Ken Williams, late Petty Officer Diver in the Royal Navy and an old shipmate of Kevin's, now running a civilian diving business undertaking all manner of salvage and construction jobs. We were introduced, and chatted pleasantly for some time. Then he remarked:

"Kevin here tells me you were a submarine captain in the Adriatic back in 1916, near to Venice?"

"Yes, that's correct. When I was Captain of the Austro-Hungarian *U13* we carried out a number of patrols in those waters. I have bored Kevin with my adventures these past few weeks, but he is a polite boy and pretends to believe me."

"Funny that, because I was working there myself the year before last, clearing the ground for the new oil terminal off Malamocco. I took some photos that I think might interest you."

He reached into his back pocket and produced a cardboard wallet of photographs. I put on my reading glasses and examined them. It was difficult to make out at first exactly what they represented: various views of a rusty, tangled, weed-festooned heap of wreckage lying on a dockside beneath a gigantic floating crane. Then I saw what it was: the wreck of a small submarine, either UB or UC type. The conning-tower casing and the deck had succumbed to the years, but the hull shape was unmistakable. The wreck appeared to have been cut in half for ease of lifting. The after part was reasonably intact, but the bow section was a barely recognisable chaos of twisted plates.

"This is very interesting," I said at last, "I myself commanded a very similar vessel in 1916. And you say that this one was salvaged just south of Venice?"

"Yes, about four miles out, just in the way of the new tanker channel they were dredging. The local fishermen reckoned their nets had been snagging on something for years, but it wasn't until we went down that anyone knew what it was. Well stuck she was too. Had to weld on ringbolts and cut her in pieces to pull her out, we did."

"Tell me, did you have any idea as to this boat's identity?"

"Not really; we're divers, not archaeologists, and we were being paid by results. But when we got the wreck up the Italian Navy sent some people along to clear it out. Lots of rubbish inside—and bones too. We helped the Italians sort them out into lefts and rights on a tarpaulin: brought out eight skeletons in the end we did, plus some odd bits. A couple of West German War Graves blokes came along and packed them into boxes to take back for burial. I got talking with one of them before they left—spoke really good English he did—and he said it was a German minelayer sub: blown up with one of her own mines. Here," (he pointed with a nicotine-yellowed finger) "see the way those plates are blown out? Whatever did that was inside, not out, he said: a torpedo would have blown the plates inwards."

Before he left he showed me some souvenirs from the wreck: a rusted iron cross dated 1914, a German Imperial Navy button—and something else.

"Here, I don't know what this is. The German War Graves man didn't know either: said he'd never seen one like it."

It was a curious feeling to hold it in the palm of my hand: a simple white metal badge consisting of an anchor entwined with the letters UB. We Austrian submariners used to wear them on the left breast of our jackets, as proudly as Ferenc must have worn this one, brand-new that morning as he set out on his first and last voyage. I slept soundly that night. Seventy years on, at least one ghost had been laid to rest.

15

THE NOOSE AND THE RAZOR

IF YOU HAVE MANAGED TO STAY WITH ME THIS FAR, you may recall that in July 1916 I was awarded Austria's highest military honour, the Knight's Cross of the Order of Maria Theresa, then stood before an unofficial court martial, accused of having mistakenly sunk a German U-Boat with all hands. For the sake of relations with our German allies I was relieved of my command. I was also informed that my forthcoming marriage to the Countess Elisabeth de Bratianu, pregnant with my child, had been cancelled. Even so, we married a few days later. Our child would at least be born legitimate; but it also seemed likely that it would be born fatherless, since I had just been seconded to the Imperial and Royal Flying Service on the Italian Front. It was a posting that was likely to be of short duration—perhaps no longer than a single flight, in fact.

I have seen though that in this world things rarely turn out quite as we expect, either for good or for bad. I survived five months of the k.u.k. Fliegertruppe, despite a couple of very close calls, including a crash-landing on a glacier—long enough at any rate for new evidence to come to light concerning the loss of the German U-Boat. The War Ministry in Vienna hated changing its mind about anything, but in the end protests from my former brother officers of the U-Boat Service caused it to revoke its verdict and reinstate me as a submarine commander.

It also happened that about this time, in the closing months of the year 1916, my old crew from *U13* found themselves suddenly unemployed after their new Captain, a Linienschiffsleutnant Galgotzy, had mistakenly pushed the engine-room telegraph to "Full Ahead" while approaching the quayside at Gjenović. The results had undeniably been interesting, to judge by the photographs, but they had done little for the submarine's diving capabilities. A long spell in drydock was called for, and the crew had been assigned to general duties at Pola pending completion of one of the new BII-class U-Boats. It was at this point, as I came back into the underwater warfare trade, that the Marineoberkommando had one of its rare strokes of imagination. I was reunited with my old crew just before Christmas 1916 as we took over a brand new submarine: *U26*.

The BII-class boats were certainly a vast improvement both on the museum pieces with which we had begun the war and on the sturdy but wretchedly slow little Ocarina boats. Though German-designed, the nine boats had all been built in Austria-Hungary this time. Four of them were the work of the Ganz-Danubius yard at Fiume; but owing to the acute shortage of skilled labour the remaining five boats—including our own *U26*—had the odd distinction of being constructed on the banks of the Danube, at the Imperial-Royal Steam Navigation Yard in Budapest, then dismantled and brought several hundred kilometres by rail to Pola for completion. We were not too happy at first, putting to sea in a submarine built by a freshwater yard, but in the end the five Budapest boats turned out to be the most reliable of the lot.

The shortage of workers meant that both the Pola Naval Arsenal and Ganz-Danubius were now having to employ large numbers of prisoners of war. Bear in mind also that a high proportion of their civilian employees were ethnic Italians, and you will see why we were very nervous about the possibility of sabotage. *U26* got off lightly: nothing but a piece of wood jammed suspiciously in a flooding valve during our first trial dive. But others were not so lucky. We passed Fritz Fähndrich's *U30* as they were leaving the Bocche on their first patrol, and I had my men line the deck and give them three cheers. We must have been the last to see them, for they disappeared without trace. The official version was that they had probably been mined in the Otranto Straits, but few of us believed it. Rumours abounded, including one that an Italian agent had been arrested at the Danubius yard and had boasted of blocking the manometer of *U30*'s depth gauge so that it bottomed at twenty-five metres, leaving the boat to go on diving until the pressure crushed it like a tin can under the wheel of a cart.

For all that, the BII boats were at least submarines worthy of the name, so sound a design in fact that twenty years later, when the Nazi Kriegsmarine began building U-Boats, all it had to do was to blow the dust off the plans and build a modernised version. Ten metres longer than the Ocarina boats and twice the displacement, they were still coastal submarines, but coastal submarines which at last had enough range and just enough living space to allow the Austro-Hungarian U-Boat Service to extend its operations into the Mediterranean. They were not comfortable even by Second World War standards, but they could undertake two-week voyages without the crew falling over with fatigue. They were not fast—a mere nine knots on the surface—but they were good sea-boats, and had two diesels so that they could cruise on one while charging the batteries with the other. They had a second periscope, a proper Siemens-Halske wireless set and a decent gun: a specially designed 7.5cm Skoda cannon. They even had a tiny galley and a captain's cabin: a sort of curtained-off coffin in a corner of the control room with a bunk and a folding desk. They were not bad-looking vessels either, with their smart, pale blue-grey topsides and their dark blue decks—quite the popular conception of a U-Boat in fact. As we put our new boat through her paces in the Quarnero Gulf there was no doubt in our minds that we would soon be able to show our disdainful German allies what the Imperial and Royal U-Boat arm was really made of.

In those early weeks of 1917 it certainly seemed that we would soon be required to do our utmost for Emperor and Fatherland, for it was during that winter of 1916–17 that the war turned serious for us subjects of the House of Austria. Or perhaps it was rather that we woke up belatedly to its seriousness. Before then the conflict had really seemed little different, except in scale, from any of Austria's previous wars. True, the casualties had been enormous; but the fighting fronts were far away in Russia and the Alps, and if a fortress were lost there and a town recaptured here it made little difference to people's daily lives. There were shortages and grow-ing hardship, but in the end (everyone was sure) it would end like all the previous campaigns of the House of Habsburg. A province or two might be amputated if we lost; a province or two might be annexed if we won. But at the end of it the Emperor would still reign and Austria—thousand-year Austria—would emerge from the peace conference much as before.

That winter changed everything. Food and raw materials had been growing scarce for a year past as the British blockade took effect. First coffee had vanished, then rubber and copper. Soon milk and meat were scarce, and butter only a distant memory. Bread was replaced with gritty Kriegsbrot, in which the proportions of flour grew smaller and sawdust greater with every week that passed. Before long even potatoes were hard to come by. Then, disaster: the harvest of 1916 failed throughout Germany and Austria. Hunger and wretchedness began to stalk the two empires. The overloaded railways could no longer carry even the little coal left over from the insatiable blast furnaces and munitions factories, so there was neither electricity nor gas. That winter of 1916 was bitterly cold: a winter spent trudging to and from work in leaking shoes and shabby pre-war clothes, when people shivered in bed at three in the afternoon in unlit, unheated rooms, and when all that stood between the populace and starvation was a meagre ration of turnips—turnip stew, turnip paste, dehydrated turnip, turnip jam, even turnip sausage.

This was all miserable enough. But as that awful winter began our old Emperor had died after a reign of sixty-eight years. It may not sound much now: a worn-out old man turning up his heels in the middle of a war in which young lives had been squandered by the million. Think what it meant to us though, when only the very old could remember any other ruler. It was like the cough that starts an avalanche: centimetre by centimetre at first, then the whole mountainside moving and gathering speed until it sweeps forests and villages before it. Somehow, without quite knowing why, we sensed that something had broken; at any rate, even in the first months of his reign I remember hearing people refer to our new Emperor as "Karl the Last." The gentle, easygoing world of Imperial Austria—old Auntie Austria, so dowdy, so unenterprising and so comfortingly safe—

was passing like a dream as we were bundled harshly into the new era of barbed wire and poison gas. This was no dynastic war now; the Allies and the Central Powers were locked together in a fight to the death: the one pulling a noose tight about his opponent's neck, the other trying to get at his enemy's throat with a razor.

But these grim thoughts were far from me in those first hours of the year 1917 as I lay in bed with Elisabeth, now seven months pregnant, in my aunt's flat in Vienna. Millions were perishing on the battlefields; great empires crumbled about our heads. But as we lay there in the quiet of the small hours, feeling the new life stirring inside her, none of it seemed to matter any more than the fluttering of snowflakes on the window pane.

"What do you want it to be?" she asked, laughing, "a boy, to grow up to be another Radetzky or Schwarzenberg or Prinz Eugen, bringing glory to the Monarchy and new lustre to the name of Prohaska? Surely a Maria-Theresien Ritter would be content with nothing less?"

"No," I replied, "I want a girl as clever and as beautiful as her mother, who will grow up to be a socialist minister, and devote her life to knocking some sense into the heads of all the fools who cheer as their children go off to the slaughterhouse."

I think that the vehemence of this reply—not far short of treasonable from an officer of the Habsburgs—surprised me even more than Elisabeth. Perhaps the war was beginning to disturb me more than I had realised. But we had just come back from a New Year's party where I had met a fellow Maria-Theresien Ritter, Oberleutnant Oskar Friml, hero of a hundred exploits with dagger, grenade and spiked club in the trenches of the Isonzo Front. He had saved my life some months before after a forced landing in no man's land. But now he was a pitiful spectacle: shifty-eyed, laughing nervously, hands trembling, starting at the slightest noise. As we parted I had noticed a dark, spreading patch at the crotch of his breeches. He was killed a few weeks later I believe.

Next morning it was back to Pola for me, to rejoin *U26* and complete her acceptance trials. Before I left I took Elisabeth to the station to catch a train for Cracow. She was off to stay with my cousin Izabella and her husband near Myślenice. Vienna was no place for an expectant mother now. Iza and her husband Andrzej, an electrical engineer, were very decent, sensible people—the only ones among my Polish cousins for whom I had much time—and I was confident that they would look after her and the child. They had a sizeable estate and anyway, the food situation was not quite so bad out in the country.

The crew of *U26* was scarcely changed from that which had sailed with me aboard *U8* and *U13,* except that it now consisted of nineteen men instead of fifteen. The BII boats were rather bigger than their predecessors, and this meant that we could carry a larger crew to lighten the burden of work on long patrols. In particular, we could now ship a Third Officer, thus allowing us to work a three-watch system instead of the exhausting watch-on, watch-off aboard the Ocarina boats. The Marineoberkommando's choice for us was a nineteen-year-old Viennese aristocrat fresh from a wartime Seekadett's training course. His name was Fregattenleutnant Franz Xavier Baudrin de la Rivière, Graf d'Ermenonville. You will doubt-less be expecting me to tell you that with his background and his exiguous sea-training he was a great pain in the neck: at best a feather-brained grinning incompetent; at worst an arrogant, snobbish incompetent. But nothing could be further from the truth. He was a delightful boy: good-humoured, always courteous and tactful, popular with the men and already a capable seaman as a result of numerous pre-war yachting expeditions. He knew when to speak and when to keep silence, was unfailingly conscientious, and, in a word, showed every sign of making a very good U-Boat officer. His family were French nobility who had emigrated and entered the Austrian service in the 1790s, so despite his sonorous name they were really pretty middling people by the standards of the Schwarzenbergs or the Esterhazys.

This is something, by the way, that I find people in England quite fail to understand: that Central Europe in those days swarmed with petty nobility who possessed little more than their titles, which passed to all their children and were almost impossible to lose. Old Austria was a snobbish society I suppose, but its snobbery was of a gentle, old-fashioned kind, quite unlike the raging social insecurity of more energetic countries. I well remember how shocked I was, in about 1906 on my first visit to Berlin, to see little notices in a park, NUR FÜR HERRSCHAFTEN—GENTLEFOLK ONLY, and then to see two burly Prussian policemen beating a factory worker with the flats of their swords for disregarding one of these signs. There was little of that in Austria. In fact for all the Barons von This and Edlers von That, the Habsburg officer corps in my day was a solidly middle-class body, probably more so than its British equivalent. I had once accused my Second Officer the Freiherr von Meszáros de Nagymeszáros-háza of being a Magyar landowner. He was hugely amused by this.

"What?" he had said. "My old man's an official in the Hungarian Ministry of Railways. We sold the estate to the Jews back in 1874. The only land that we own now is in six geranium pots on the balcony of our flat."

But forgive me; I am wandering away from the story again. We could now carry a Third Officer, and we also had room for more engine-room personnel. Among these was one of the most remarkable people that I ever met: Elektromatrose Moritz Feinstein. The son of a well-to-do Jewish family, he had taken refuge in the Navy in 1914 after being thrown out of the Viennese Medical Academy on suspicion of helping to procure abortions. His nominal rank was that of Electrical Artificer, but in fact he served as medical orderly and general fixer aboard *U26*. Not only was it splendid for morale aboard a fighting submarine to have a near-qualified doctor among the crew, but Feinstein was knowledgeable about a great many other useful things not normally included in the curriculum for k.u.k. naval officers—like pressing trousers without an iron, desiccating binoculars and curing hangovers. I offered to recommend him for a commission—he had been a pre-war Einjähriger—but he declined, preferring to keep his head down for the duration in the hope that the charges pending against him would have been dropped by the time it was all over. Jews generally avoided the sea, I was always told, but Feinstein seemed positively drawn towards the U-Boat Service. Perhaps it was from a subconscious belief that the Procurator's Department would not be able to see him down there.

Our first cruise began on 27 January and lasted twelve days, covering 1,300 miles and operating in the waters east of Sicily. It was unrestricted war on commerce now: "Handelskrieg," the miracle weapon (Berlin assured our own reluctant government) that would starve England out of the war before the United States could come in against us. Our instructions were to sink all enemy merchant ships on sight, regardless of whether or not they were in military convoys and taking only "such measures as are thought practicable" to safeguard the lives of passengers and crew. It was a nasty business; but then so was the British policy of starving the population of Central Europe by total blockade. We bore no ill-will towards our fellow seafarers on the other side, and many of us had reservations about the wisdom of the new campaign, but we were determined, those who had been home on leave that winter and heard the grizzling of hungry children, growing up with rickets and brittle teeth; or seen harassed, grey-faced wives and mothers trying to make a family meal out of a kilo of frostbitten potatoes heated over balls of dampened newspaper.

It went quite well, *U26*'s first cruise. We stopped and sank the British steamer *Earlswood*, 2,900 tonnes, off Cape Passero on 30 January, then torpedoed and sank a French steamer of about four thousand tonnes, name unknown, in the same waters the following day. We were fired upon by coastal batteries near Augusta on 1 February, and ourselves fired two torpedoes—both of which missed—at a British destroyer south of Cape Spartivento on the 4th. But we had problems getting back through the Otranto Straits two nights later. Sea water slopped down a carelessly closed battery-venting tube as we dived in front of a patrol line of steam trawlers, and we were soon forced back to the surface by chlorine from the battery tanks. The outcome was a running battle with aircraft and Italian MAS motor boats in the early dawn. We got through though: casualties on our side were two men wounded by machine-gun fire and two affected by chlorine fumes. All things considered it was a promising start.

We looked to even greater successes on our next cruise, now that we could reach for that great artery of the British Empire, the steamer route from Port Said to Gibraltar. But the truth of the matter is that the Austro-Hungarian Navy had come into the business of commerce war when its best days were already over: those months in mid-1916 when the large, fast, well-armed U-Boats of our German ally could cruise for weeks on end in the central Mediterranean, sinking ship after ship for little more trouble than that of waiting submerged off a shipping lane, surfacing to stop and sink a victim with gunfire, then submerging again to wait for the next innocent passer-by. The Allies had not yet got around to organising convoys, but they had become wiser about routes, so that we had to use up time and diesel oil looking for our prey. They had increased the numbers of escorts, particularly the innocent-looking anti-submarine sloops known to us as "Foxgloves," after the name-ship of their class. Also they had taken to arming merchant ships, which deprived us of the chance to use our favourite sinking weapons, the gun and the explosive charge. If a merchantman seemed to be armed we had little choice but to expend one of our four precious torpedoes on it, for if we surfaced and were fired upon, even a single hole in our pressure hull would prevent us from diving again.

1917's most unpleasant novelty of all, though, was the depth charge, which nearly ended my career on *U26*'s third voyage. Numerous small anti-submarine bombs had been showered on us during the previous two years, but we took little account of them really. Sometimes they shook the boat badly enough to break a light bulb or two, but they were too small to do much damage. I think also that they must have worked with a time fuse, because the depths at which they exploded seemed quite haphazard. But dustbin-sized canisters of TNT were a different matter, especially when they were fitted with an adjustable water-pressure trigger to explode them at about our depth where the effect of the explosion would be greatest.

U26 first made their acquaintance off Malta at the beginning of May. It was early morning, and we had sighted a British *Russell*-class battleship escorted by four destroyers and a steam yacht. My suspicions should have been aroused by the sight of so large an escort for such an obsolete old tub; but a battleship, standing up there huge and grey on the horizon like some floating cathedral, is an irresistible target to any self-respecting submarine captain, so I pressed forward to the attack. *U26* got to within seven hundred metres without the escorts apparently noticing our presence, but just as the torpedo tubes were being cleared to fire I suddenly saw a cluster of signal rockets arch into the sky from the nearest destroyer. Then they all turned as one and headed straight for us, guided (I suspect) by very good hydrophones. I got the periscope down and went deep, then turned away, but I could not shake them off. We went down to thirty metres. Then there was the most fearful thunderclap: a triple detonation so violent that we were thrown off our feet as light bulbs popped and plates crashed down from the galley shelves. Our ears sang from the noise as I took the boat to forty metres; but then came another salvo of explosions, even worse than the last and prefaced a split-second before by that most hateful of sounds, the faint but audible click as the depth charge's trigger snaps shut to fire the main charge. Soon we were struggling to keep our footing on the oil-covered deck as fuel lines fractured above us and the boat pitched and rolled like something at a fairground. We had never encountered anything like this before, and I suspect to this day that we had walked straight into a trap set by a specialist U-Boat-hunting group, with the battleship as the bait. But somehow we managed to evade them after about four hours, when they were perhaps running low on depth charges and had deafened their own hydrophone operators in their enthusiasm. They were some of the longest hours of my life though, like being strapped into a dentist's chair and having a sensitive tooth drilled with a slow, very loud drill. Anyway, we escaped to make our way back to Cattaro battered—shaken and deafened, but at least wiser now about the need to treat escorts with more respect in future.

Such incidents aside, though, and despite the growing difficulties, *U26*'s war against commerce went well for the rest of 1917, during which time we sailed seven offensive patrols out of Cattaro, sank six merchant ships totalling twenty-eight thousand tonnes, and damaged a destroyer.

The attack on the destroyer was a most peculiar business, so perhaps you will bear with me if I tell you what happened. It was on the evening of 3 June, west of Cephalonia. We had sighted a three-funnelled destroyer of unfamiliar type a few hours earlier and given chase, but a sea was building up and we lost her. Then, about 8:30 p.m., running on the surface, we sighted the destroyer again to westward, steaming at about fifteen knots back towards us. We dived and closed to attack-range. The sea was so heavy now that only the target's funnels and masts were visible through the periscope, silhouetted against the setting sun. I could see well enough though to estimate his speed and relative bearing. Both torpedoes were fired at four hundred metres' range, and shortly afterwards there was a loud bang. We surfaced twenty minutes later and made for the place. It was nearly dark now. A few pieces of wreckage were being tossed on the waves. Suddenly Fregattenleutnant d'Ermenonville tapped my shoulder.

"Over there Herr Kommandant—I heard someone shouting." It seemed safe to use a shaded spotlight, and as its beam traversed the waves about us it picked up a figure swimming in the sea, waving frantically. We brought the boat about and got to windward of the man, then threw him a rope. To our amazement though he failed to catch it: in fact tried to swim away from us in obvious terror. In the end we had to manoeuvre the boat alongside—no easy feat in near-darkness and heavy seas—so that Grigorović could fish him out with a boat-hook. At first sight we seemed to have rescued a child, but a child who struggled and fought like a cat, scratching so fiercely that in the end it required four men to overpower him and get him below. It crossed my mind that perhaps we had picked up an escaped lunatic, but as they got our unwilling guest down into the control room I saw that he was an oriental: a tiny, slant-eyed, brown man dressed only in a singlet and shorts. He was defiant, but plainly terrified out of his wits, spitting and swearing at us in some strange tongue. Then it dawned upon me: we had picked up a Japanese. I didn't know the language of course, but I had spent a month in Japan many years before and recognised the sound of it. He seemed to calm down after a while and consented to eat some risotto left over from supper. We gave him dry clothes and a bunk in the engine room. I also appointed an off-duty rating to look after him and keep away the crew, who could scarcely have shown more interest in our visitor if he had fallen from the moon.

All went well until the next evening, when a shout of alarm brought me running to the engine room. "Der Japanerl" had nearly bled to death after cutting his wrist with a stolen razor. Feinstein bandaged him up, and from that time until we reached Cattaro he was kept under close guard. We handed him over at Gjenović when we arrived, but that was only the start of my troubles. Bureaucracies hate nothing so much as an exception, and here was an exception with a vengeance: Austria-Hungary's only Japanese prisoner of war. Under the terms of the Hague Convention he had to be given separate accommodation, a special diet, reading matter in his own language and regular visits from the Red Cross—in fact virtually a prisoner-of-war camp all to himself. I was left in no doubt that the officials considered this all to be my personal fault for having rescued him. A professor of oriental languages was brought down from Vienna to interview the man: Probationary Seaman Second Class Takeo Ikeda, a fisherman from Iwakuni on the Inland Sea. The little man proved to be quite an amiable character, once he had stopped trying to kill himself. He said that he had been aboard the destroyer *Tachikaze* that evening, in a working party on the fo'c'sle deck, and had suddenly found himself swimming in the sea. He could not tell us whether his ship had sunk, but we learnt later that she had been beached on Cephalonia, then patched up and towed back to Malta where a Japanese destroyer flotilla was working on convoy escort. The professor told me later that Seaman Ikeda had asked to be allowed to stay in Dalmatia after the war and ply his trade as a fisherman. It appeared that in his view, by being captured and allowed to live, he had automatically become a subject of the Austrian Emperor.

U26 did not escape without loss herself, in those summer months of 1917. In those days before radar, locating our victims was a matter for human eyeballs aided by binoculars, constantly sweeping the horizon for the tell-tale plume of smoke. Even so, seeking our prey could often become rather a bore, especially on the less busy steamer lanes like the one from Port Said to Salonika by way of the Kasos Straits. In fact, rather than waste fuel zig-zagging across the steamer route day after day waiting for a ship to appear, an idea struck me: why not use the island of Antikafkanas? I knew this place, about four miles east of the steamer route, from my pre-war yachting days. And I knew in particular that although it might appear to be a single island, and was shown as such on the charts, it was in fact two rocky, barren islets, kidney-shaped and separated by a channel just deep enough for us to lurk in, invisible except from above, until something interesting came along. The only problem was that if they could not see us, neither could we see them. So I asked for two men to go ashore to act as look-outs. There was no shortage of volunteers: we had been at sea for ten days now and everyone was desirous of space and the opportunity to stretch their legs, even on a barren rock-pile like Antikafkanas. Two men were duly rowed ashore in the folding dinghy, carrying a telescope and two signal flags. We waited most of the day, until one of the look-outs began semaphoring to us: "Smoke cloud bearing 230." Within minutes *U26* had slid out of her lair and submerged to wait.

Our victim turned out to be the cargo steamer *Clan Findlay* of Glasgow—8,650 tonnes, armed with a large gun on the poop deck and laden with a cargo of Army tents and general stores en route from Bombay to Mudros. We sank her with a single torpedo in the engine room, killing her Second Engineer and a stoker. It was a good hour and a half before she went though, sliding stern-first into the depths of the Aegean amid a welter of foam and wreckage, giving a last melancholy howl as the trapped air escaped from her fo'c'sle hatches in a blast of coal-dust. Having expended a torpedo on her, you may well imagine my feelings when we saw her "gun" suddenly bob to the surface amid the hatch covers and empty casks. We surfaced to marshal the lifeboats and even out the number of men in each, then gave them their position and sailing directions for Crete, but not before we had taken off the ship's Captain, Mr Whitaker of Hartlepool, since our orders were to detain merchant captains whenever possible. Then it was back to Antikafkanas to hide once more for the night in our cleft in the rocks. Captain Whitaker was morose at first, which I suppose was understandable, but in the end he took some supper with us in the tiny alcove that served as a wardroom.

Next morning at dawn I sought volunteers for another day's look-out duty. Once again, there was no shortage of candidates. In the end I selected Maschinengast Heinz and Torpedovormann Bjelić. They were rowed ashore and scrambled up the rocky slope, carrying with them a haversack containing zwieback, two tins of meat, some cheese, a flask of water and their day's wine ration. They had barely reached the summit when Bjelić was seen wagging his flags at us. It was an entire southbound convoy—at least five ships.

Things did not go quite so smoothly this time. The convoy had a weak escort—only a "Foxglove" and two armed trawlers—but something was wrong with our torpedo when we fired it at the largest of the merchant-men. It turned sharply to starboard, then began leaping out of the water like a dolphin. The escorts were down on us immediately, and there began a day of running southwards underwater, first with the "Foxglove" and the trawlers after us, then with a French destroyer on our tail as well. They seemed to be well supplied with depth charges and they were extremely persistent, because every time we tried to surface to recharge our failing batteries there would be a whirr of propellers overhead and then a mighty crash near by. It was not as bad as the hammering which we had taken off Malta a few months before, but it went on longer and only stopped when night fell. I must say that I felt most sorry for Captain Whitaker, sitting there bolt-upright and tight-jawed, knowing that his fellow-countrymen were unwittingly trying to kill him.

We surfaced at dusk and recharged our batteries—and were nearly run down in the dark by another convoy, larger this time and also southbound. We followed them until dawn, hoping to attack at first light, but they attacked us instead. There followed another tedious day of hide-and-seek as we tried to get at the convoy and the escorts tried to get at us. Evening found us a good hundred miles south of Crete.

Now I began to worry about Heinz and Bjelić back on the island. They had food and water for two days at most, and the two days were already up. I determined to make all speed back to them. But then, about midday as we headed northwards, we sighted a lone steamer heading north-west across our bows. She appeared unarmed, and we had only two torpedoes left, so I decided to take a risk. *U26* surfaced a few hundred metres off her quarter and fired a shot across her bows as a signal to stop. Then I took the speaking trumpet and ordered her crew to abandon ship. We sank her with eleven or twelve shells through her waterline plating amidships. She was the *Redesdale* of 3,200 tonnes, in ballast and bound for Piraeus. I called her master aboard, and as the lifeboat backed towards us with the Captain standing in the stern sheets I saw his face darken with anger.

"Oh, it's you is it then, you bugger?"

I was just about to tell him that while I understood his feelings, I felt that this was no way to address an Austro-Hungarian naval officer who had just put his own ship and crew at considerable risk in order to save his enemies' lives. But then I saw that the remark was not addressed to me but to Captain Whitaker, who was standing behind me on the conning tower taking the air. He merely looked disdainfully at the new arrival, uttered the words "Midden tin!" and went below. It transpired that our new captive, Mr Hargreaves, came from Hartlepool as well and was in fact Whitaker's brother-in-law; also that the two men hated the sight of one another.

The next two days were very trying. *U26* was attacked again; this time bombed by a seaplane. Not only that, but trouble with the tail clutch on the port propeller shaft kept us crawling along at four knots on one engine while Lehár and his men struggled to carry out repairs. Also there was the worry of our look-outs marooned on Antikafkanas. But really the worst of it was trying to prevent our two prisoners from coming to blows. It appeared that years before there had been some dispute over a will, with the result that the two men had become extremely bitter towards one another. Now they seemed entirely to forget the war and the recent sinking of their ships in their joy at being able to resume the quarrel. Worse still, once they discovered that I spoke English they evidently regarded me as having been sent by Providence in the role of independent arbitrator.

All the first day Mr Whitaker sulked in the fore-ends while Mr Hargreaves poured his complaints into my ear. Then all the next day, whenever I was off watch, Mr Whitaker would plead his case before me while his brother-in-law sat glumly in the engine room, refusing food and being generally disagreeable. I hope that I am a fair-minded man, but after forty-eight hours of this I would cheerfully have marooned the two of them on Antikafkanas and left them to fight it out between them.

We had been away nearly five days by the time we got back to the island. I scanned it desperately through my binoculars as we drew near, but there was no sign of life. We edged into the channel, and before our anchor hit the water the little dinghy was being rowed frantically across to the shore. We found nothing until a shout from Béla Meszáros brought us scrambling down to the seaward side. It was the haversack, lying above the water's edge and stuffed with the two men's clothes. Their shoes and the telescope lay alongside, arranged as if for a barrack-room inspection. We found a pencilled message inside the flap of the haversack:

10 July 1917

To Whom It May Concern

We, Maschinengast Othmar Heinz and Torpedovormann Anté Bjelić of the Imperial and Royal Austro-Hungarian Navy, were left on this island as look-outs on 5 July by our ship, the submarine U26. We fear that our boat was sunk on the morning of the 5th while attacking a convoy about five miles west of here, because she has not returned. We have neither water nor food left now and no shelter from the sun, so we have decided to try to swim to Crete while we still have the strength. We think it must be about sixteen miles. In the event of our not making it, would whoever finds this haversack be kind enough to inform our government and families of our fate?

We were back aboard within five minutes and raising anchor. All afternoon and evening we scoured the sea for our lost comrades, zig-zagging to and fro across their likely course until the light failed. In the end though we had to admit failure and set off sadly for home. Bjelić and Heinz were reported missing, presumed dead, as soon as we reached port. They remained a weight on my conscience for months afterwards; that is until early 1918, when the Marineoberkommando received a telegram from the Swiss Red Cross. The two men had been spotted late on the afternoon of 10 July by a British seaplane about four miles off the coast of Crete. The aeroplane had landed alongside them, taken them on to its floats and taxied with them to safety, thinking them to be survivors from a sunken ship. They were faint and delirious with exhaustion, but they had still been very annoyed at not being allowed to complete their swim "so that they could say they had done it." Both were made prisoners and came home in 1919.

Such picturesque incidents aside, life aboard a U-Boat on patrol was generally a rather humdrum business: whole days or even weeks spent scanning an empty horizon. Each hour at sea was perhaps fifty-nine and three-quarter minutes of tedium to fifteen seconds of excitement or fear. But at least life was not as grim for us as it was for the Germans up in the Atlantic and the North Sea, who had atrocious weather to contend with as well as a vigilant and well equipped enemy. In fact I have some quite pleasant memories of those errands of murder and destruction, peaceful days cruising the dark blue Aegean, or sitting on deck in the evening calms to escape the stifling heat below. I was very concerned to keep up morale and prevent boredom, so I formed a sort of Viennese Schrammel trio on board to provide musical entertainment. Feinstein was quite a good violinist, and we already had an accordion and a guitar, so our off-duty hours were diverted by a selection of the syrupy popular melodies of our Imperial and Royal Fatherland. A particular favourite (though not with me, I must confess, after about the fiftieth hearing) was "Mei' Mutterl war a Wienerin." We also possessed a very nice Decca portable gramophone, found along with a box of records in a drifting lifeboat off Sicily. There was a magnificent recording, I remember, of "Il Mio Tesoro" from *Don Giovanni,* by the Irish tenor McCormick. This proved so popular that I had to ration it to one playing a day. I heard it on the wireless one Sunday morning some weeks ago. Even now it evokes those last months of 1917—the lap of the waves and the smells of diesel oil, goulash and stale sweat.

God only knows though, there was enough to depress morale, given the opportunity. Temperatures below decks were appalling, frequently in the mid-forties. Condensation trickled from every surface and oil dripped from the reserve torpedoes on to the men lying in their cramped bunks underneath. The whole boat stank of unwashed humanity as we went about unshaven, with dandruff-clogged hair, in torn and oil-stained clothing. Also the boat proved an ideal breeding-ground for vermin with its tangle of pipes and its thousands of inaccessible crevices. Bedbugs, fleas, lice, cockroaches—we had them all in abundance, even an epidemic of crab-lice at one stage, acquired in the course of what was delicately described as "contact with the civil population" in the Bocche. Constant cleanings-down and fumigations seemed to make little impression, least of all on the cockroaches—animated plum stones dipped in stale vinegar which proved immune even to Feinstein's supposedly infallible remedy of mashed potato mixed with borax. Our most effective means against them in the end turned out to be a small tabby cat called Petra, rescued after the sinking of a French steamer. She developed quite a taste for the vile insects and would crunch them up by the dozen with every sign of relish.

At least the rations were an improvement on those available earlier in the war. Austria might be sinking into starvation and the surface fleet might now be messing on dried turnips and polenta, but at least the authorities had realised that the U-Boat crews could not be expected to face two-week voyages with only zwieback and Manfred Weiss tinned food for sustenance. Some good-quality tinned food (Swiss I believe) began to come our way; also dehydrated potato slices, tinned sardines and other such luxuries. We were even issued with bottles of Teplitzer mineral water. We also had a properly trained cook aboard for the first time: a Hungarian gypsy ex-safebreaker with the unlikely name of Attila Bárabás.

There were other small consolations too. At least the water was warm, so we could take a dip from time to time if we were sufficiently far from land not to be bothered by aircraft. Mostly we would just lie in the wash on top of the diving tanks, but if the boat were stopped for any reason the better swimmers would strike out a few hundred metres for the sake of exercise. That is, until the day when Maschinengast Souvlička was suddenly seen thrashing about in the water, waving his arms in panic. When we got him back on board, his face the colour of paraffin wax, we saw that he was streaming blood from a semicircle of wounds in his backside. He had been attacked by a shark: not a very big one—perhaps about two metres long—but aggressive. However, by the time Feinstein got him below to dress the wound Souvlička was in a high good humour, remarking that he would be stood free beers for the rest of his life on the strength of being the only man in Prague with a shark-bite scar. After this I took to posting a sentry armed with a rifle atop the conning tower whenever the men were swimming, and sharks were fired at on a couple of occasions. I once read that they can live to a tremendous age, so I suppose that somewhere in the world's oceans there may still be a venerable shark whose dorsal fin carries a hole made by an Austro-Hungarian rifle bullet nearly seventy summers ago.

Another small solace was the fact that we now had a decent wireless apparatus. Transmission was still rather uncertain, but on the surface at night we could raise our collapsible mast and make our report to Castellnuovo, then listen in to the news bulletins from Grossradio Pola and Nauen. It was on one such evening, late in February 1917 off Sicily, that Telegraphist Stonawski came to me with a freshly decoded signal. I have it here now: a sheet from a signal pad with the message

K.u.k. Marineoberkommando Pola congratulates Lschlt the Ritter von Prohaska of S.M.U. 26 on the birth of a son, Anton Ferenc, on 25th inst. Mother and child are both reported to be in good health.

16

THE IMPERIAL CITY

PRINGTIME IN VIENNA: "Im Prater Blüh'n wieder die Bäume" and so forth. Well, I have seen a hundred springtimes now, but never one as devoid of hope as that spring of the memorable year nineteen hundred and eighteen. It was a curious situation in which we found ourselves in the embattled Central Empires at the start of that year: rather like being sole occupants of a palace, yet starving to death amid the gilt, damask and velvet curtains. On paper, Austria's position had never been more favourable: Serbia crushed; Russia collapsed in defeat and revolution; Italy all but knocked out of the war at Caporetto the previous autumn. The troops of the k.u.k. Armee stood everywhere on conquered soil. Meanwhile on the Western Front our German allies were driving the exhausted British and French Armies back towards Amiens. It still seemed possible that we might win before the Americans arrived.

Yet in reality all was dust and ashes, for we were in a desperate state that cold, windy April of 1918: the towns and cities of Austria on the brink of starvation. Everywhere hunger, cold and misery haunted the streets: no coal, no gas or electricity, few trains, no trams or buses, no meat or milk and barely enough adulterated bread or rotten potatoes to keep people's hearts beating. Everywhere one heard the dry cough of tuberculosis and the dreary clacking of wooden-soled shoes on the muddy pavements; smelt acetylene lamps and lignite and cigarettes made out of dock-leaves; saw pallid, exhausted faces filled only with longing for it all to end—this war which was devouring their world like some crazed mincing machine. The currency was out of control; while as for our vast, venerable Habsburg bureaucracy, it was in the last stages of senile dementia, increasingly unable either to supply the fighting front or to administer even the most elementary rationing system behind it. Things were nearly as bad in Germany, but at least there they still had discipline and the hope of victory. In Austria, people had woken up at last to the terrible truth: that whatever happened now, our country would perish. If we lost, the Allies would break up the Monarchy; if we won, then we would be absorbed into a Greater Germany that already stretched from Zeebrugge to Baghdad. January brought a wave of strikes as the bread ration was reduced yet again. Then at the beginning of February the sailors mutinied at Cattaro, no longer able to endure the boredom and the miserable food aboard their steel prisons swinging at anchor in Teodo Bay. Yet, strangely enough, this general mood of sullen hopelessness was slow to percolate through to the men in the front line. In the frozen Alpine trenches and the battery positions in the marshes of the Veneto, ragged, hungry and short of ammunition, somehow that great patchwork army of ours still held together.

And we U-Boat sailors still put to sea, risking mines and depth charges in the cause of a dying empire. But even so, our task was not getting any easier in the spring of 1918, because at long last the Allies were convoying all merchant ships. This may not sound much, but I assure you as one who was there that it was a crippling blow to the U-Boat campaign; such an obvious thing to do, in fact, that it amazed us that the British had not thought of it sooner. Before then, all that we had needed to do was to get through the Otranto Straits—never a very difficult task—and then make our way into the central Mediterranean. Once there we had a choice of shipping lanes: Malta to Salonika, Port Said to Salonika or, most rewarding of all, the Gibraltar–Suez route. Then it was just a question of zig-zagging along the steamer lane until we sighted smoke, which nine times out of ten would come from an unarmed, unescorted, unsuspecting merchantman.

Convoys made our lives much more difficult. Our area of search was a circle about twelve miles across, so the likelihood of our sighting a convoy was not much greater than that of sighting a single ship. Whole weeks would be spent wandering fruitlessly across an empty sea. Then if we did sight a convoy and close to attack, the results generally ranged from disappointing to alarming. We could not surface to use our gun, so it had to be two torpedoes—and two only, for by the time we had reloaded the convoy would have swept past us. There was usually no second chance for an attack; and anyway, the convoy escorts would be down upon us like buzzards upon a carcass once they had seen the torpedo-tracks. Hours of depth-charging were the usual sequel. They were even intimidating to look at through a periscope: the solid front of camouflage-painted merchantmen advancing three-abreast like the avenging army of God with the destroyers and escort sloops fussing along on their flanks.

Also there was wireless to reckon with now. Back in 1916 very few merchantmen had been equipped with transmitters, but now they all seemed to have it—and not clumsy old spark sets either, but proper radio telephones, so that we only had to be sighted by one ship for the air to be filled with messages—"Hallo-Meldungen" we used to call them—giving our position and warning others to stay clear. Night after night we would sit glum-faced by the wireless receiver listening to Liverpool, Glasgow and Cockney voices exchanging information about the last known position of "that fucking Hun sub."

In January *U26* sank a large cargo steamer, about six thousand tonnes, which had fallen out of a convoy north of Derna. In February we torpedoed an oil tanker in a convoy south of Crete; then in March, east of Malta, we hit a steamer of about two thousand tonnes—again, a straggler behind a convoy. On neither of the last two occasions could we even stay around long enough to confirm that our victims had sunk. This was all depressing enough, but when we compared notes with our German allies back at Cattaro we found that even they, in their much larger and faster boats, were finding it increasingly difficult to sink ships. No one said as much, but gradually, insidiously, a suspicion began to grow that we were losing the war. The newspapers told us that Britain and France were on the edge of collapse and that the U-Boat campaign had cut the lifelines to America; our eyes told us a different story, as my men dived into the water after a sinking to rescue sides of Iowa bacon and sacks of Canadian flour to be shared out and taken back to starving families at home. For every ship that we sank, two more seemed to spring up in its place.

The blockade and the endless shortages—by now mostly total absences—not only made life hungry and miserable; they were even beginning to affect our ability to fight. Our wireless set was wired with aluminium wound in gummed paper and insulated on porcelain knobs; valve-wheels that would once have been made of brass were now cast from a horrid greyish alloy, which soon broke out into a white rash in the damp, salt-laden air, then became brittle to a point where it would suddenly snap off in the operator's hands; rubber seals were replaced by a sticky black compound called Kriegsgummi, made of hessian impregnated with pitch and God alone knows what rubbish. Our conning-tower hatch seal had perished and been replaced with such a substitute just before we set off on a voyage in mid-March 1918. I was not happy with this; and even less happy when, on our return passage through the Otranto Straits, we surfaced and opened the hatch to find that the seal had stuck to it and been torn in two. The boat was not watertight, so we could no longer dive. The result was a running battle for most of the night as *U26* made her way through the straits on the surface. At one point, around 3 a.m., we were engaged in a gun duel with two steam trawlers at a range of about eight hundred metres. It was a very near thing, star shells bursting above us as we tried to fight our way past them. I saw Grigorović cranking the traverse wheel of the Skoda gun as one of the trawlers closed with us. The loader thrust a round into the breech and clanked it shut. The trawler fired at us, kicking up a fountain of spray in the water alongside. Our gun roared and leapt, then as the smoke cleared I saw that we must have hit something: probably a pyrotechnics locker, because the trawler had turned away from us with a brilliant conflagration taking place on her fo'c'sle, rockets and flares flying everywhere as our machine-gunners raked her with fire. I remember shouting, "Well done!" to the gun crew—then feeling a curiously gentle sensation of being lifted off my feet as the night dissolved in a firework display of a radiance that quite eclipsed the blaze aboard the trawler. The noise, I remember, was rather like that of a gas jet being lit. They extricated me from the ruins of the conning tower a few minutes later, clothes in tatters and with a damaged ear-drum but otherwise unharmed. Steuerquartiermeister Patzak standing beside me had not been so lucky: he had been blown overboard and was lost. We made it through the straits to a point where our aircraft could come out from Durazzo to provide cover, but the conning tower of *U26* was a wreck. I spent a week on a hospital ship, then set off on a fortnight's leave while the boat made her way to Pola for repairs. The Dual Monarchy's railways were now in such a state that there was no question of my travelling to Poland to be with Elisabeth and our baby son. I had been summoned to the War Ministry in Vienna, so Elisabeth arranged to leave the child in the care of my cousins and travel to Vienna to stay with me at my Aunt Aleksia's flat.

"Es gibt nur ein Kaiserstadt, es gibt nur ein Wien," they used to sing in the wine-shops, back in those pre-war days that now seemed to have been in some previous life—"There is only one Imperial City, there is only one Vienna." Well, Vienna in early April 1918 was a city frightfully changed from that elegant, bustling capital of four summers before. Not that the difference was apparent at first glance: the trees still blossomed on the Prater; concerts were advertised at the Opera and the Musik-vereinsaal; people still read the newspapers in the coffee-houses. Yet it was a façade of cardboard, and thin cardboard at that, for hunger and despair lurked around every street corner. It was not famine in the African fashion of distended bellies and skeleton limbs: if one merely glanced at them, people still seemed well-covered enough. It was when one looked closer that it became apparent that this was in fact the pasty, greyish-white puffiness of exhaustion and hopelessness and years of meagre, bad food. Their feet dragged as they walked. Even on the warmest day people shivered with cold. The old and the sick tottered and fell dead in the street from heart failure. The grey-faced children were too listless to play and their bones were anyway brittle from lack of vitamins. On every weary face there was the unspoken plea, "When is it all going to end?"

Elisabeth and I went to the Theater an der Wien to see the Lehár operetta *Where the Lark Sings*—Tautenhayn and Louise Kartousch if my memory serves me right. The show was in the afternoon because there was no public transport any longer and no gas to light the pot-holed streets in the evenings. The performance was more like a requiem mass than an operetta, playing in front of acetylene lamps to a cold, half-empty house of soldiers on leave from the Italian Front—many of them no doubt watching their last show. We sat wrapped in our overcoats, saddened rather than anything else by the determined, desperate gaiety of the performers. When it was over we walked home in silence, along bedraggled grey streets littered with a scurf of plaster fallen from the buildings. As we passed along the Mariahilferstrasse we paused to look into the grimy shop-windows: either empty, or with their nakedness rendered all the more dreadfully apparent by a display of tooth-powder or a few items of clothing made out of wood-pulp. A fiacre or two crawled past, pulled by nags so ill fed that it was a wonder they could stand up, let alone draw a cab. An Army lorry trundled by, rumbling on wheels bound with tyres of hemp. It was all deeply depressing.

That evening in bed Elisabeth and I were talking.

"Otto, we've got to get out of this place."

"I know; Vienna's in an awful state now. But the war's got to end one day. Surely it can't go on for ever. Things must get back to normal some time."

"How do you know that this isn't normal? No, Otto, not just out of Vienna: I meant out of Austria—out of Europe even, once the war's over. This whole world of ours is dead now—not just dead but decaying. I don't know what will follow it, but I know it's going to be something ghastly, something that will make people look back on even this as tolerable. No my love—let's get out of it: to America, Canada, Brazil even."

"Liserl, I love you, but sometimes I think you're quite mad. I'm a career naval officer of the House of Habsburg: I know no other trade."

"Then perhaps we madwomen sometimes see things more clearly than career naval officers. Why not emigrate? You're clever and you know English well, and I speak French and Italian. You could always become an engineer while I train as a doctor. Surely there must be other places than this in the world."

"You're as crazy as you're beautiful. What life will there be for us and the little one away from Austria?"

"And what life will there be for us in Austria? More to the point, will there be an Austria left to live in a year from now?"

I was to present myself next day at the Marine Section of the k.u.k. War Ministry, dressed in my best frock coat complete with black-and-yellow sword belt. But before that I had another errand to carry out: visiting a flat in the 16th District to present the condolences of his shipmates to the widow of Steuerquartiermeister Alois Patzak. Patzak had been a reservist of the 1885 class and worked in civilian life as a foundryman at the Westbahn railway workshops. His home was a one-room flat at Solferinogasse 27, one of those vast, dreary tenement blocks built in the Viennese suburbs about the turn of the century.

I often think that it would be a good thing to take the popular lyricists of "dear old Vienna"—most of whom probably never got nearer the place than Long Island—and show them one of those dismal workers' barracks from the days when Vienna was to tuberculosis what Rome is to the Catholic Church, and when its slums ranked in squalor with those of Glasgow and Naples. Certainly Solferinogasse 27 would have done nicely: a typical "Durchaus" in which a tunnel-like passage led in from the street to courtyard after evil-smelling courtyard. As I neared the entrance to the tunnel I noticed a crowd at the corner of the street. A covered van had run away and smashed a wheel against a granite bollard on the corner, spilling its load into the street. It was a load of coffins. One of them had opened and a thin wax-white arm hung limply on to the cobbles. I saw that the reason for the accident was the sudden death of the horse, which had evidently found the slight rise too much for it. The creature lay on the pavement with a thin rivulet of blood and froth dribbling from its mouth and along the gutter. The driver was an undertaker's man from the City Corporation.

"I do a load a day in this street now," he informed me. "Dying like flies they are, especially the old ones. No coffins either, or even shrouds, on account of the war. We take them to the cemetery in these boxes, then tip them out and come back for another lot."

"Dreadful," I said.

"Yes, it's dreadful right enough: and it's not going to get any better, I can tell you. They say there's a new sort of fever starting to kill them over in Florisdorf."

With this cheering intelligence still ringing in my ears I made my way into the tunnel to find the appropriate courtyard and staircase. Grubby, thin children stared at me with evident hostility as I passed. Old women made loud remarks to one another about the Herr Admiral who was honouring the place with a visit. At last I found the dark staircase and made my way to the third floor, then along a greasy black corridor to Flat 329. It was only by striking a match that I was able to read the number on the door. I knocked. A listless voice from inside said, "Bitte." I entered to find myself in a seedy room lit by a single, dirty window. Its only furnishings were a bed, two chairs, a table and a stove. The occupants were a worn-out, young-old woman of indeterminate age and a soldier in shabby field-grey. A child, about five years old and obviously very sick, lay deathly still beneath the patched blankets on the bed. The room was saturated with the smell of boiled potatoes and misery. The woman looked up at me with dull eyes.

"Yes, what do you want?" I could tell from her accent that she was a Slovak.

"Frau Patzak? Permit me to introduce myself. I am Linienschiffs-leutnant Prohaska, Captain of the submarine *U26*. I have come to offer you my condolences and those of my crew on the gallant death in action of your husband." I began confidently enough, but her steady, empty gaze drained the meaning out of my words as I uttered them. I meant it—we all meant it: Patzak had shipped with us for three years and had been liked by everyone. But the dreary room and her stare made it all sound as fraudulent as the official communiqués in the *Armee Zeitung*.

"Thank you, Herr Leutnant," she replied, "but keep your condolences, when the Navy's taken my husband and left me here with four children to keep on fifty Kronen a month."

"Yes," added the soldier, "just you try living on that sort of money. It was a pittance even in 1914, and a cat would starve on it now. If it wasn't for me looking after Alois's wife and kids they'd all be dead by now—though looking at the little one we may have a mouth less to feed before long." He spat. "You officers and your precious war."

"Where's your unit, soldier, and why aren't you with them?"

His reply took me aback. "Obediently report that it's none of your business, sailor: I don't know where my unit is and I don't care. I was a prisoner in Russia for three years and I only came home in February. They were going to send me off to be killed in Italy, so I bade them goodbye and kiss my arse. Here, look at this." He held out his Army overcoat for me to inspect. It was made out of some coarse, harsh material rather like low-grade sacking. "Know what that is? Nettle-fibre. And look at this belt they gave me—impregnated paper. No, the end can't be far off now, not when the bastards are giving us rubbish like this to die in. I've seen the future coming in Russia and I can tell you, it won't be long before we've made an end with Kaisers and Generals and Herr Leutnants once and for all." Then, seeing my anger, he smiled. "Oh, don't take it personally. Alois always wrote that you were a good sort and looked after your men. But the day's coming fast now, and my advice to you is to get rid of that sword belt of yours: that is, unless you want to end up hanging from it."

"Thank you for your advice," I replied, "but what's to stop me from going out now and reporting you as a deserter?"

He gazed at me in amusement with his steady, bright blue eyes—very much Patzak's brother, I thought.

"You can report me to the Emperor himself if you want: they'd never catch me. There are hundreds of us around here now, soldiers who've gone on strike from the war. The gendarmerie daren't come after us. In fact they say that out in the country the deserters are going around in bands, with machine guns some of them, fighting it out with the police and the military when they come after them. No, Herr Leutnant, you're obviously no fool: you must see that this bosses' war is coming to an end."

I took my leave, staying only to promise Frau Patzak that I would do everything I could to see that she and her children got help from the Archduchess Valerie's Widows' and Orphans' Fund. Then I made my way through the courtyards back to the street, being narrowly missed on the way by the contents of a chamber-pot emptied from an upstairs window. When I reached the Solferinogasse I saw that the dead horse had disappeared. In its place was a smear of blood and scraps on the pavement, with a horse's tail lying forlornly in the gutter. It seemed that in less than fifteen minutes the dead animal—bones, hooves, hide, guts and all—had been torn to pieces and carried away by the crowd. I shuddered slightly, and set off on the long walk to the Marine Section of the War Ministry on the Zollamtstrasse.

Inside the temples of the Imperial and Royal bureaucracy little had changed after nearly four years of war. There were the same ushers, the same endless, echoing parquet corridors and staircases, the same hushed voices and the same trolleys bearing their loads of official files bound with tape of the appropriate colour: black-and-yellow for joint k.u.k. affairs; red-and-white for Imperial-Royal Austrian; red, white and green for Royal Hungarian. It was a world sufficient unto itself: serene, meticulously ordered, light years distant from the trenches and the U-Boats and the hungry tenements of Ottakring. My interview was with Linienschiffskapitän the Freiherr von Manfredoni-Forgacs: a fine specimen of the desk-bound naval administrator. It concerned my next posting.

"Now, Prohaska, I suppose that you must have wondered why you are still a Linienschiffsleutnant when you should have been gazetted Korvettenkapitän the year before last in the normal course of seniority." I confessed that I had wondered. "Well, it's like this. According to the Dienstvorschrift 13/85 MNV24b of 7 March 1909 a submarine is classed as a torpedo-boat for administrative purposes. This means that it cannot be commanded by anyone over the rank of Linienschiffsleutnant. So you see, if we had promoted you we would have lost one of our best U-Boat captains." I said that I did see.

"Still, enough is enough. We're going to send you on one or two more voyages aboard *U26,* until we can find another commander, and then you'll be promoted and sent to the new U-Boat Training School at Novigrad." I expressed mild surprise that the Navy should be setting up a U-Boat school; after all, it had never given much attention to training before, so why start now?

"Ah, my dear Prohaska, we intend to expand the Imperial and Royal U-Boat Fleet quite substantially over the next three years. By 1921 we will have at least sixty and possibly seventy boats in service instead of the present twenty—all of the most modern type as well. The Marine Technical Committee assures me that the designs being produced by Professor Pitzinger and Engineer Morn are far in advance of the U-Boats being built in Germany. Anyway, as I'm sure you appreciate, all this is going to mean a huge increase in our requirement for trained officers. That's why we are setting up the school at Novigrad and why we intend making you Chief Lecturer in U-Boat Tactics."

I cannot help admitting that this news was not altogether unwelcome. Thirty-two was rather old for a U-Boat commander, and I had been engaged in this curious trade for exactly three years now. My judgement was as good as ever, but my reflexes were getting a little slower and my nerves a little more on edge with every voyage. I was still an officer of the House of Habsburg, unconditionally willing to follow my oath through to the finish. But I began to feel now that I had done my duty, and that younger men should soon take over from me.

Even so, my interviewer's grandiose vision of Austria's future submarine fleet still seemed wildly at variance with the awful realities of the world outside. Any doubts on that point were dispelled soon after the meeting when I bumped into my old acquaintance Toni Straussler. He had received a head-wound while commanding *U19* off San Giovanni a few months before and had been posted to the Marine Sektion while convalescing. Perhaps the knock on the head had cleared his vision, but he was depressingly frank with me later over the infusion of dried raspberry leaves advertised as tea.

"Manfredoni? Stupid old windbag. Sixty new U-Boats indeed! Do you know how much steel Austria is producing each month now? I'll tell you: less than half of what we were producing in 1913. They laid the keels for some of these boats at Fiume in 1916, but they still aren't ready for launching. If it isn't shortage of steel plate it's shortage of labour, and if it isn't either of those it's lack of engines and batteries and piping and a thousand and one other things. I saw some of the papers yesterday. One of the boats is seventy per cent complete, but they still held up work for three months because they couldn't get mahogany for the seats in the officer's lavatories. 'No reduction in pre-war standards—No cutting corners with paperwork,' that's our motto—even if it means no U-Boat at the end of it. I tell you, if we could build ships out of paper, Austria would rule the oceans."

I made my way back to my aunt's flat. I was to return to Pola the next day. But there was still an evening to be spent with Elisabeth. The birth of our child and all the privations of the war had done nothing to lessen her enthusiasm as a lover, which had always been a matter of delighted wonder even to me, who was no novice in these matters. I can still see her now as if it were yesterday; how she let her nightdress slip off just before she got into bed and stood there in the pallid light of the acetylene lamp, glorying in the lithe elegance of her body as she spun round to show me her profile: her small, neat breasts, her slender waist and the soft curve of her hips.

"There," she said, "see how I've looked after my figure for you. Remember me like this when you're at sea—and think of me waiting for you when you come home again."

Yes, I do still remember her like that. She would be—what?—ninety-two now, nearly as withered and bent as I am. It was not to be. But at least to me she will always be as she was then.

Then came the morning: the platform at the Südbahnhof in the grey early light, and an agonised, tearful parting. It would only be one or two more voyages, but who knew? Perhaps one would be one too many. She ran along beside the train as it hissed away from the platform.

"Goodbye my darling—look after yourself and come back safely. Think of me and the little one . . . I'll always love you."

The journey back to Pola was not enjoyable. The carriage was crowded, and badly dilapidated by nearly four years' service in troop trains. Windows were broken; doors were missing; even sections of the roof had gone, so that lignite soot showered over us in every tunnel. Onwards we trundled, through Graz and Marburg and Laibach, the worn-out axle boxes squealing like a thousand piglets in their death agony. The only compensations for me were that Fregattenleutnant Meszáros boarded the train at Graz, where he had been on leave with yet another lady friend, and that at Divacca a flat-wagon with a regimental field kitchen was coupled on to our train. It belonged to a field artillery regiment moving to Pola, but the cooks kindly agreed to start cooking goulash for the rest of us once we had pooled our rations. It was mostly potatoes and dried turnips with scraps of horsemeat, but it was better than nothing.

Our locomotive from the junction at Divacca was in an even worse state than the one which had pulled us from Vienna. We came to a gradient about ten kilometres down the line, and the spavined engine simply jibbed at the slope like a horse at a hedge. We were all obliged to get out and walk beside the line as the train wheezed painfully up the incline. It was a glorious spring morning, with catkins out on the willow bushes and the gorse in full bright yellow flower among the bare limestone karsts beside the track. A pair of aeroplanes wheeled lazily in the pure azure sky above. An officer of the k.u.k. Fliegertruppe was walking beside us. He stopped and gazed upwards, shading his eyes against the sun.

"It's all right," he said, "they're ours," then picked up his bags and began to trudge up the slope once more. Suddenly he stopped, and looked up again.

"Quick—everyone take cover!" We dived among the rocks as first one plane then the other swooped down out of the heavens like a pair of falcons. There was a dreadful pause, then they came over the brow of the hill at a few metres' height, screaming straight down the track towards us. Machine-gun bullets cracked and whined off the rocks. Then CRUMP! CRUMP!—two bombs fell among the carriages. I had a sudden glimpse of a boot with a piece of white shin-bone protruding from it, curving through the air with a puttee unwinding behind it like a festive streamer. Then they were gone as quickly as they had come. We got to our feet and went to inspect the damage. The locomotive was all right, though pock-marked with bullet-holes. It also seemed that all but one of the carriages had survived, their dilapidation not noticeably worse than before. But our hearts sank as we saw that the flat-wagon with the field kitchen and our dinner had taken a direct hit. As for the two cooks, there was scarcely anything left of them to gather up. Then a call from Béla Meszáros drew us to the trackside where the wreck of the field kitchen lay. One cauldron of goulash was only half spilt. I think it says much for the state to which four years of total war had reduced us that we scrabbled among the rocks with our spoons and mess tins, scooping up as much as we could before it went cold. Then we sat and consumed what was left of our dinner while the engine-drivers tried to get the train moving again. The Fliegertruppe officer was very apologetic: said that they were Bristol fighters from the British squadrons based near Venice.

"Sorry fellows, but there's not much we can do. It's like that all the time now—too many of them and too few of us."

"Cheer up," said Meszáros, "fortunes of war and all that. It's not so bad if you live from day to day and take it as it . . ."

He paused, his face the colour of putty, gazing down into his mess tin of salvaged goulash. An eyeball was staring up at him from the bottom.

I reached Pola Naval Dockyard to find that repair work on *U26* was progressing like a fly wading through honey. Materials were hard to come by and the dockyard workers were sullen and unhelpful. An air of weariness, of things drawing to a close, hung over the wharves and slipways. In the end it was only by press-ganging workmen and soldiers that we got the boat ready to put to sea and proceed down to Cattaro, seven weeks behind schedule.

When we arrived in the Bocche though we found things to be in no better case. Everything was in short supply: not only food but all the thousand items necessary for a submarine to operate. Diesel oil was scarce. Torpedoes were rationed out two to a boat and were often faulty (we suspected) from deliberate sabotage at the Sankt Polten torpedo works. Battery acid, spares of all kinds, even distilled water became hardly obtainable. Clothing issues practically ceased: a fertile source of grievance aboard the U-Boats, where a two-week voyage reduced even the stoutest clothing to grimy rags. At last, when a supply ship arrived from Pola, it was found to be carrying five thousand sun helmets, an item never before issued in the k.u.k. Kriegsmarine, even in peacetime. By June our German allies had given up patience with the crumbling Imperial and Royal supply system: they took steps to set up their own, and promptly reserved all stocks of diesel oil. The result was that our own patrols were now reduced to Durazzo and back.

Then on 9 June *U26* was given a full complement of four torpedoes and ordered to put to sea. Our new Commander-in-Chief, the Hungarian Admiral Horthy, was going to lead a battleship raid on the Otranto barrage. Our part in this operation was to lie off Brindisi and wait for the French and the Italians as they came out in pursuit. We took up station on the evening of the 10th and waited all night without seeing a thing. Then, just as we were about to submerge next morning, we received a wireless message from Pola. We were to return to port: the raid had been cancelled. It was only when we got back to Cattaro that we learnt how the previous night, as the raiders steamed southwards past Premuda Island, an Italian MAS boat had torpedoed and sunk the mighty super-dreadnought *Szent Istvan*. As far as the k.u.k. battle fleet was concerned, this was effectively the end of the war.

The war went on for the U-Boats however—more or less. June and July were strangely quiet months as I recall them: almost like peacetime summer manoeuvres, except for the odd Italian air-raid on the Bocche. Austria's great last-gasp offensive on the Piave had come to nothing, apart from adding another two hundred thousand or so to the pyramid of skulls. Now a kind of uneasy hush settled over everything, rather like the quiet in a sick-room in that pause between the high-point of the fever and the patient's death. Somehow it meant very little to us: far less than the daily battle to scavenge enough food and diesel oil and spares to keep the boat and its crew seaworthy. Late in July Béla Meszáros returned from leave.

"I met Galgotzy on the train," he reported.

"Oh, how is he?" I enquired. "I heard that *U13* got mined off Cáorle a few weeks back. I hope he's all right."

"Yes, not too bad. He managed to get the boat to the surface and run her aground just before she sank, off the seaward end of our lines. Anyway, he said that just as he was getting his men on deck to go ashore, who should come wading out to the wreck but a gang of soldiers."

"What on earth did they want?"

"Food. They held him and his crew up at rifle-point while they ran-sacked the provisions lockers—stripped the boat clean in minutes."

"Good God. What did he do?"

"There wasn't a lot that he could do, not with a Mannlicher stuck up his nose. He threatened them with court martial for offering violence to an officer and theft of government property, but they told him to go hang himself: said that they'd had no rations for a fortnight, and not much more than that for months before—sometimes a lump of cheese and some raisins, sometimes just bread, sometimes only fresh air. They told him half their battalion had already deserted and were living on berries and mush-rooms in the woods."

Fregattenleutnant Meszáros was not with us when *U26* sailed from Cattaro on 16 August. The Spanish Influenza was now sweeping Europe, and my Second Officer had been one of its first victims at Gjenović. His place was taken by Franz d'Ermenonville while the berth of Third Officer was filled by a young wartime Lieutenant called Friedrich Heller, a border-Austrian from Linz. Heller thought and spoke of himself as "a soldier of the German Reich" and seemed to have very little time for the

Austro-Hungarian Fleet of which he was nominally an officer. He had tried to get posted to an Imperial German U-Boat, and after being refused he had taken to wearing a German badge on his cap. I ordered him to remove it—the only time in three years that I had ever given one of my crew a telling-off for being improperly dressed.

Neither d'Ermenonville nor I cared very much for Heller, but we had not the time to be choosy. *U26* had been given four torpedoes and a full load of diesel oil and sent out into the Mediterranean on a mission of the greatest importance. Naval Intelligence believed that a large troop convoy would leave Port Said about the 21st, bound for Genoa and carrying a complete Japanese Army corps who would then be sent by rail to attack our hard-pressed forces on the Piave Front. Our orders were to seek out this convoy and attack it with all the means at our disposal: that is to say, four 45cm torpedoes, a 7.5cm Skoda gun, a machine gun and five rifles. It was an idiotic assignment: either the convoy would turn out to be a chimera (as proved to be the case), or if it existed and we found it, it would be so massively escorted that the puny assault of a single slow, poorly armed coastal U-Boat would be dealt with as summarily as a beetle's assault on a steamroller. But there, orders were orders, and if we were not prepared to risk our lives for Emperor and Fatherland now, what had we been doing for the past three years? We cruised to and fro along the Malta-Suez steamer route until we sighted Port Said on 25 August. Then we turned and cruised back the other way further to the north. During the whole of this time we sighted scarcely a fishing caique, let alone a giant military convoy. Then in the small hours of the 28th I was roused from my bunk by Heller. The horizon to north-east of us was lit by a tremendous, flaring red glow which seemed to be getting nearer. I sounded action stations and we moved towards it, whatever it was. It turned out to be a petrol tanker, steaming along at about ten knots, blazing like Vesuvius from stem to stern and leaving a mile-long trail of burning petrol on the sea astern of her. There was no point in wasting time on this floating inferno, evidently the victim of an earlier attack. We let her steam away northwards out of control until she disappeared over the horizon. We crossed her tracks about dawn. The air still reeked of petrol. Then the look-out reported a drifting object. It was a cork life-raft, charred and still smouldering. As we drew alongside we saw an arm hanging over the side. I think that he may have been a Chinese, but there was no way of telling: in fact we could hardly tell which side of him was which. There was nothing we could do for him, poor wretch; only dribble a little water into the blackened hole that had been his mouth, then stand aside to let Feinstein end his sufferings with a double injection of morphine. We had just cast the life-raft adrift when a submarine surfaced about three thousand metres abeam of us. We exchanged recognition signals. It was one of the large German commerce raiders, *U117,* twenty-three days out from Cattaro. She was commanded by a Berliner called Max Dietrich whom I had come to know and like very much over the past year. He had that rarest of qualities in a German, a sense of proportion, and he also seemed rather to like us Austrians. We came alongside and exchanged greetings.

"Good morning, Dietrich. Were you the perpetrator of that blaze last night?"

"Yes. Do you have any idea of her name and tonnage? I thought you might have come across survivors."

"We did come across one a while ago, just before you surfaced. But I'm afraid that he was in no condition to tell us anything."

Dietrich avoided my eyes. "Don't tell me, please. I'd rather not know. Filthy business, this war—it's made murderers out of us all."

Since it now seemed that our Japanese troop convoy was a figment of the Marine Evidenzbureau's imagination, and since neither of us had anything better to suggest, we agreed to head back towards Alexandria, spaced out to be just within sight of one another. At least in this way our radius of search would be extended by six miles. Thus we cruised along for a day until, just before sunset, a signal lamp started to blink from *U117*'s conning tower:

"Large smoke cloud in sight, bearing 190°. Turning to close." It was a convoy: evidently not the one we had been sent to look for, but still a convoy.

Dietrich and I had held an impromptu conference that morning on the tactics to be used if we met a convoy. We had agreed that with her slow speed and mediocre armament, *U26* would be best employed in drawing off the escorts while *U117* tried to get in among the merchantmen with her two heavy guns and her powerful battery of torpedo tubes. We had also agreed that our best mode of attack would be to get as close as we could on the surface, so as to cheat the hydrophones of the escort vessels, then dive at the last moment. I asked Dietrich how he proposed getting past the screen of escorts.

"I shall dive deep. The boat's tested to seventy-five metres, but I think we can safely go to a hundred without the hull collapsing. Depth charges take time to sink and the Britishers never set the firing mechanism to more than sixty metres in my experience."

The convoy was a slow one: about eight knots. We watched from just over the horizon, then about 1 a.m. we went in, relying on the darkness and our low silhouettes to avoid being seen. There were four or five escorts, I think: two destroyers, a "Foxglove" and two armed trawlers. I went for the leading destroyer, fired one torpedo at him, then dived just as a star shell burst brilliantly overhead. The torpedo missed, but we reloaded as we turned away from the escorts. Then began four of the most unpleasant hours of my life: diving, being depth-charged until the fillings in our teeth rattled, then surfacing for a few moments as parachute flares burst overhead, always trying to lead the escorts away. We fired a second torpedo at the "Foxglove," on the surface at a thousand metres. It may have found its target—or at least hit something else, for there was a torpedo explosion about half a minute afterwards. This brought the lot of them down on us as we dived again. We had to get away, fast. I yelled for full power ahead on both E-motors. The telegraph lever was pushed forward—and immediately there was the most fearful bang inside the boat and a vivid blue flash which sent deckboards flying into the air in the crew compartment.

Before we could think, the inside of the boat was filled with acrid white fumes. It was all that I could do to scream, "Breathing apparatus!" before I fell to spasms of coughing, my eyes streaming. Someone thrust an escape apparatus into my arms: a bottle of compressed air with a mouthpiece, a nose-clip and a pair of goggles. I struggled into them, choking, and felt the vast relief as my lungs filled with clean air again. But worse was to come. Men were busy with fire extinguishers in the crew compartment, but there was also a violent commotion aft in the engine room and the boat was getting heavy by the stern. I left d'Ermenonville to handle the boat and struggled to the bulkhead door. To my horror I saw Lehár and his men already up to their knees in water. The pressure hull had been holed. Choking, Lehár called to me:

"Shut the bulkhead door—for God's sake shut the bulkhead door!"

I snatched the breathing tube from my mouth. "Come on, Lehár, get out of here—quick!"

"Don't worry—we can take care of it—just shut the door and run the bilge pumps full speed!"

So, feeling more like a murderer than I have ever felt in my life, I shut and locked the watertight door to the engine room. Lehár was going to fight his own battle while I got on with handling the boat.

We were in an awful predicament: being depth-charged at intervals, and at the same time groping about in the rapidly flooding, smoke-filled interior of a stricken U-Boat. The pumps were working at full speed, but the inrush of water into the engine room was evidently gaining on us. The only way to keep the boat from sinking was to blow high-pressure air into the main diving tanks: a doubtful expedient since the boat became violently unstable as the water slopped backwards and forwards in the tanks. Soon we were wrestling with the diving rudders to try and keep the boat even as she pitched and reared like a terrified horse. Also we had only one E-motor, for whatever had happened had put the port propeller shaft out of action. Conflicting thoughts rushed through my head. I had no wish to suffer the dishonour of surrender, but we had surely done as much as duty required and more. To continue fighting now would merely be to sacrifice eighteen men's lives in what might well be the closing months of a lost war. Certainly we were done for if we tried to stay submerged. No, enough was enough. I took out the mouthpiece. My voice sounded comical with the steel clip on my nose.

"D'Ermenonville, get the code-books ready and stand by to blow all tanks. We're going to surrender."

Just as I spoke there was a most stupendous bout of depth-charging somewhere in the distance: a great rolling peal of thunder which seemed to go on for about half a minute and which must have contained at least twenty separate explosions. Then there was an awful silence. D'Ermenonville sprang to the hydrophone table and put on the earphones, then motioned me to come over. I listened. I think it was the most hideous sound that I ever heard: a tortured, squealing, grinding agony of metal, as if an ocean liner's boiler were being crushed slowly in the jaws of some gigantic vice. We were listening to the last moments of *U117*.

17

AFTER ARMAGGEDON

W E WERE CERTAINLY IN A PRETTY MESS as we surfaced in the first light of dawn that morning of 29 August, about 120 miles north-west of Alexandria. The boat had lost half her power, the interior was filled with smoke from a battery fire, the pressure hull had been holed, and it was only with the greatest difficulty that we had got her to the surface. I opened the conning-tower hatch and clambered out, carrying the wardroom tablecloth to signal our surrender. D'Ermenonville followed with the lead-bound signal code-books under his arm, ready to throw them overboard. The plan was to get everyone on deck until the British came alongside, then open the flooding valves and sink *U26* beneath us. They might have us, but I was determined that they should not have our ship, even if I had to stay below and go down with her. I half expected to be shot to bits as I emerged into the air. But there was nothing there: or at least, almost nothing. A tremendous commotion was taking place about two miles to westward—rockets and flares and depth charges—but it seemed that the convoy and its escorts had moved on and left us, perhaps thinking that a third U-Boat was attacking them. We limped along after them on one E-motor at about three knots, intending to give ourselves up, but before long they disappeared into the thin half-light of morning. We were alone: alone aboard a sinking submarine with nothing but empty sea about us.

I went below to open the watertight door to the engine room and get Maschinenmeister Lehár and his men up on deck with the rest. They were up to their knees in water and had been badly affected by the smoke, but Lehár was cheerful once we had half carried him into the fresh air and he had regained his breath.

"I don't know what it was that did it, Herr Kommandant. Suddenly, bang!—all the port-motor net fuses blew and the water came rushing in. But we've stopped the worst of it now, what with shot-plugs and stuffing hammocks into the holes. The bilge pumps can cope now I think. I tell you though, I thought we were done for."

Once we had cleared the smoke and pumped out the engine room we found that it had all begun with our port propeller. Pitted and fissured with corrosion, the adulterated wartime bronze had flown to pieces like a fragmentation bomb when the motors went to "Full Ahead," sending jagged lumps of metal through the pressure hull like fragments of shrapnel. We found an entire propeller blade lying in the engine-room bilge. That was bad enough; but unknown to us, three battery cells had lost most of their electrolyte because of perished rubber seals and depth-charging. The batteries were connected in parallel for normal running underwater, but there was a second net to connect them in series for short bursts at full speed. The sudden, heavy load on them had caused them to explode as the plates melted.

Still, this did not help our case now as we crawled through the thin early-morning mist. The sea around was littered with dead fish and stained yellow with TNT residue. Then, quite suddenly, we found ourselves in the middle of a rapidly spreading patch of oil. The sea was boiling beneath it like a cauldron of some ghastly, stinking soup: air bubbles, chlorine, oil, blood and sewage all welling to the surface from the crushed remains of *U117* and her crew, still drifting down towards the sea bed two thousand metres below. We gazed in fascinated revulsion at the debris being spewed to the surface: crushed wood, pieces of white-painted cork insulation, a leather jacket, a locker door marked VORDERER PRESSLUFT in Gothic letters, a photograph of a small girl with her hair coiled up in braids. Even now I see it in nightmares: a man's heart and lungs bobbing past us in the filthy oil-scum, a sordid obituary notice for some unfortunate who had been blown inside-out as the pressure hull collapsed. Anyway, there was no time to mourn Dietrich and his men, or even to collect wreckage. A brief log entry marked their passing: "29 August 1918, 4:26 a.m.: German *U117* sunk by convoy escorts approx. 32° 46′ by 28° 17′. Large oil slick, air bubbles and wreckage. No survivors." Then it was back to trying to save ourselves.

The boat could crawl along on one diesel, but she was still leaking badly and certainly in no condition to dive if attacked. Also we were well over eight hundred miles from Durazzo and something like four hundred miles from Beirut, the nearest large port on Turkish territory. No, there was no question about it: we had to steer towards Alexandria and surrender to the first Allied ship that we met on the way. The sail was set to assist the starboard diesel, and off we went.

But in the same way as there is never a policeman to be found except when you don't want one, we were conspicuously unsuccessful over the next two days in our attempts to surrender. We met an armed yacht that afternoon, about five thousand metres off, and waved our white tablecloth for a good ten minutes. They took no notice whatsoever and sailed on past us. Then the next morning, a more promising candidate appeared: a British "Foxglove" sloop. She approached to within three thousand metres, then turned away. We fired signal rockets and waved our white flag as we limped along after her. I picked up the signalling lamp and winked out the message: "Please stop—we wish to surrender." There was no response. I made the same signal again, and got the reply: "Sorry—cannot read your signal." There was a pause, then boom! shriek! splash! A shell from their stern gun burst some way to starboard as they steamed away from us at top speed. It was all so preposterous that despite our plight we fell about with laughter.

In the end, by the evening of the second day, we had changed our minds a little. A favourable breeze was helping us and no one seemed disposed to take the slightest interest in us, so why not try for the coast of Palestine after all? I doubted very much whether *U26* could be repaired without a drydock, but if nothing else we could get back home overland by way of Constantinople. Thus it came about that the evening of 31 August found us just outside the minefields in front of the port of Haifa, introducing ourselves in French to a highly suspicious young Army Lieutenant commanding a Turkish patrol boat. It is not a pleasant feeling, to find yourself looking up the barrel of a 6cm gun with three Turks at the other end; but somehow I managed to establish our credentials as allies of the Ottoman Empire, and we were duly led into harbour.

Haifa in those days was nothing like the great city of today. In fact it was little more than a Levantine fishing village of flat-roofed white houses nestling under the mighty bulk of Mount Carmel. However, it had a stone quayside and some warehouses and the beginnings of a harbour mole at the end of the railway from Damascus. Most of the population were Lebanese and Greek, but there was already a good number of Jewish colonists, many of them Austrian Jews led out here in the late 1900s by the visionary Theodor Herzl. Across the bay was the crusader castle of St John of Acre, scene of a notable landing operation by British and Austrian sailors in 1840.

But however splendid its setting, however marvellous its prospects for development, Haifa had little to offer a crippled Austro-Hungarian submarine in the early days of September 1918. Our Turkish hosts took no further interest in us whatsoever, once we had moored to the quayside: they had troubles enough of their own on the crumbling battlefronts to southward. As for our German allies, their presence in Haifa was limited to an airfield outside the town and a rusting merchant steamer, the *Uckermarck,* which had taken refuge here in 1914 and was now a floating depot. The Germans were sympathetic, but could not offer us much help other than the use of a workshop aboard their ship. I telegraphed Vienna immediately we arrived and requested a new port propeller for *U26.* At that stage of the war however, I might as well have asked them to send us the Apostolic Crown of St Stephen. I doubt whether they even received the telegram.

We busied ourselves meanwhile with repairing the damage to the boat's pressure hull. There was no drydock of course; but in the end, after infinite labour, we got *U26*'s stern up out of the water by lightening the after-ends as much as we could, landing batteries and everything moveable, then flooding all tanks forward so that her bows rested on the harbour mud. We foraged some steel plate and the Germans lent us an oxy-acetylene welding torch, so at least we were able to patch the holes made by the disintegrating propeller—not elegantly, but enough to make the hull watertight once more.

The propeller looked like being an insuperable problem. That is, until one morning after we had been eight days at Haifa, when Elektromatrose Feinstein appeared at the quayside with a late-middle-aged man in tow: a tubby, bespectacled person of almost grotesquely Jewish appearance, and wearing a yarmulke on his head, but otherwise dressed like a Viennese doctor on holiday at Bad Ischl. He was introduced to me as Herr Mandel, a one-time foundry proprietor from Mödling bei Wien who had sold up in 1910 to become a farmer in Palestine, then gone back into metal-working as a contractor to the Haifa-Damascus railway. It appeared that he had a small foundry here in Haifa . . . We rowed him around in the dinghy to inspect the starboard propeller. He took measurements and made notes in a little leather-bound book, and scratched his bald head and sucked his teeth a great deal, muttering to himself. I stood on the quayside holding my breath as Grigorović lifted him up out of the dinghy.

"Well, Captain, do I take it that you would like a left-handed copy of that propeller?"

"Yes, we would like one very much if it were possible. Can you do it?"

"Captain, I spent thirty years casting statues for the Academy of Fine Arts. I see no great problems with a ship's propeller. It will take time to make the model of course, and I must take detailed measurements first. But as I have said, I see no problem—provided that some of your sailors can help me, because there is only my son now at the foundry."

"You can have the lot of us, myself included, for as long as you wish. But what about payment? Would you accept . . ." He waved his hand.

"Herr Leutnant, I may live in Palestine but I still regard myself as a loyal German-speaking Austrian. A promissory note on behalf of the Austrian Ministry of Finances will suffice. Anyway, I owe a debt of gratitude to the Germans here. Their men rescued my wife and me when the Turks were smashing our house up in April. But tell me, what about metal? I cannot give you marine bronze . . . Wait a minute though, I have an idea. Would you mind coming along to my shop with me?" We made our way to his foundry, about a kilometre from the harbour.

"The Germans have requisitioned every scrap of copper and brass from the English Channel to the Yemen," he said as we entered a dim wooden shed, "but I rescued this because I thought that the British might pay me good money for it one day." He rummaged beneath a large mound of rags and assorted rubbish. Suddenly a man's face emerged, a face about twice the size of my own, with old-fashioned side-whiskers and a noble, straight nose. The head echoed dully as Herr Mandel tapped it.

"There, Captain—Admiral Sir Robert Stopford KCB, GCMG, victor at St John of Acre, 1840. It stood over in the old castle. The Germans got me to remove it three years ago and melt it down for transport to Germany, but I hid it here and they forgot about it. It's not phosphor bronze, but it should do well enough if we mix it with some bazaar brass and that propeller blade you rescued."

So we set to work. Herr Mandel made a wax model of the new propeller, based on the starboard one but opposite-handed. This took us five days. Then he coated it in a pudding of foundry clay which was baked in the furnace until the wax melted and ran out. Meanwhile my men were at work with hatchets and hacksaws, butchering poor Admiral Stopford and reducing him to pieces small enough to be melted down in the great foundry crucible. Then, on the afternoon of 21 September, there came the moment that we were all secretly dreading. With Herr Mandel shouting instructions to us in thick Wienerisch German, we sweating sailors tilted the heavy crucible to let the glowing stream of metal pour into the mould. We sat waiting all night in an agony of apprehension, hardly able to doze, until Herr Mandel judged the propeller to have cooled sufficiently for us to start attacking the rough clay with hammers. Nothing happened for the first five minutes or so. Then, all of a sudden, the mould fell to pieces . . . and when our hearts had started to beat once more, we saw it lying there amid a rubble of foundry clay, gleaming golden-red in the early morning sun like a phoenix risen from the cinders: a perfect ship's propeller, one metre in diameter. It was covered in the thin metal straws left by the air-venting holes in the mould, and it was a little rough in places, but in all other respects it was the *beau idéal* of a propeller. I set Lehár's men to work at once with chisels and hand-files.

We had not much time left now, as we carried the propeller down to the quayside on a trolley and set up the derrick of telegraph poles that was to lower it on to the bare propeller shaft. Guns banged in the distance, then the noise turned into a steady, constant grumbling of artillery. Aircraft began to appear overhead—quite patently not German or Turkish aircraft. The Germans aboard the *Uckermarck* started to burn papers on the dockside. Then towards evening on the 23rd the first Turkish fugitives began to appear on the streets—not disciplined bodies of men but refugees from a disintegrating army: some with their rifles, most without; sick and wounded; men and officers alike drifting through the streets of the town like straw blown before the desert wind.

"It looks like trouble," I remarked to Franz d'Ermenonville as he stood beside me on the quayside. "For heaven's sake let's get that propeller fitted and put to sea. The British will be here within the next day or two by the looks of it, and I certainly don't intend that we should be part of the welcoming committee."

"No," he said, "and I don't much like the look of our Turkish allies either. They're said to be murderous enough at the best of times, so God only knows what they're like without their officers to keep them in line."

We toiled by the light of hurricane lamps to lower the propeller over the end of the shaft, easing it down centimetre by centimetre with an elaborate system of blocks and tackle. We got it into place about midday on the 24th and began to tighten the two lock-nuts that had held its predecessor in place. As we sweated with an enormous spanner borrowed from the *Uckermarck* a cry went up: "Aeroplane in sight!" The air shuddered with a deep throbbing roar as a very large, twin-engined biplane came lumbering into view across the ridge of Mount Carmel. It was big, and very obviously British, but at first we did not associate its arrival with ourselves—until its shadow passed over us and the air was suddenly filled with the scream of bombs. There were four I think—heavy ones. Two of them landed in the harbour, drenching us with muddy water, and one burst on the quayside about fifty metres from the boat, sending splinters of stone whistling over our heads as we lay on the ground. The fourth demolished one of the stone warehouses where we were sleeping while *U26* was being repaired. The bomber had missed the boat this time, but we had reason to suspect that he might come back. But for the moment there was no time to let that worry us. We worked several hours longer. At last though Maschinenmeister Lehár stood before me, weary and dirty but smiling.

"Obediently report that the propeller is on. Once we've got everything back on board we can put to sea."

That night and the next day were taken up with the back-breaking task of reloading the boat. First it was the iron ballast weights, passed down from the quayside by a human chain. Then came the heavy battery cells, each one lowered down through the engine-room hatch with the utmost care to avoid spilling acid. Then fuel and lubricating oil and drinking water were pumped back into the tanks from the oil drums which had held them on the quayside. Finally we loaded such food as we had been able to procure in Haifa—mostly rice and olive oil. Meanwhile the guns raged away, perceptibly nearer now than the day before. It seemed that the minefields extended far enough out to protect us from attack from seaward, but our bomber friend might soon be back. I had the machine gun set up and the Skoda gun made ready. The latter had been designed as a balloon-cannon and could thus be elevated almost to vertical, but it had no anti-aircraft sight and no suitable shells beyond the five shrapnel rounds in the ammunition locker. It was better than nothing; but not much.

Fregattenleutnant Heller had seemed to lack enthusiasm as we re-loaded the boat. Finally, late that afternoon, he came up to me without saluting.

"I'm going."

I looked up from my work, checking the battery electrolyte. "What do you mean, you're going, Heller? Where?"

"With the Germans, to Galilee. Some of the soldiers and a few of the men from the *Uckermarck* are going to strike inland this evening, to try and link up with our forces by Lake Galilee. There's a Major Höflinger down there—he says that it's all prophesied in the Bible: that after the battle of Armaggedon the Germanic races will meet the Antichrist in battle at Galilee and defeat him, and then go on to conquer the world. It's all to do with sacred numbers, apparently. The Germans are the twelve tribes of Israel and the Jews are the Children of Cain who drove them out and pushed them into Europe. Did you know that the Garden of Eden was really in Silesia, near Oppeln?" I edged away nervously. Surely the sun here was not that strong . . . Then I realised that this young man was serious. Certainly his imagination was too weak for him to have worked out all this nonsense for himself.

"But Armegeddon—isn't that supposed to be some time well in the future?"

"No: it was the day before yesterday, not thirty kilometres from here, at a place called Megiddo. All the prophesies are being fulfilled."

I lost patience. "Very good, Heller. If you leave us you are guilty of desertion in the face of the enemy, in which case a book of ancient writings called the *K.u.K. Dienstreglement* prophesies that you will be tied to a post and shot. However, I have no wish to sail with men whose hearts are not in this venture. You may come with us back to Durazzo if you wish. If not, then away with you and the Germanic race is welcome to you. Think carefully though: the Arab allies of the English are reported to be none too conscientious about taking prisoners."

The last I saw of Heller he was making his way along to the *Uckermarck* to join the other would-be fulfillers of prophecy. He would indeed have done better to have stayed with *U26*. I worked briefly in the War Graves section of the Austrian War Ministry early in 1919, just before I was discharged, and I found out what became of Major Höflinger and his force. They had made their way up the road towards Galilee that night, under the moon, until they bumped up against an Australian cavalry unit. Taking them to be the advance guard of a Turkish counter-attack, the Australians had levelled their lances and charged before the Germans could so much as unsling their rifles. Those who stood were skewered and those who ran were sabred down to the last man.

As Heller left I became aware of a figure standing over me. I looked up. It was a tall, lean man in German uniform, wearing a leather flying helmet and leaning on a stick as he smoked a cigarette. He introduced himself as Hauptmann Uchatius of the Imperial German Flying Service. It seemed that he had been with the German squadron up at the airfield, flying an Aviatik artillery-spotter.

"Actually," he drawled, "I was a fighter pilot in France with von Richthofen—until last year. Crashed an Albatross near Douai and broke my leg in about eight places, hence the walking-stick. The doctors patched me up and then they sent me out here to Palestine. But it looks as if it's nearly over. The fighters have gone, and they've left me behind to set fire to the planes in the repair sheds before the English get here. Then I'm supposed to fly the old artillery bus up to Beirut."

"It's a pity about the lack of fighters," I observed. "That big English twin-engined bomber nearly hit my boat yesterday."

"Yes, it's a Handley-Page. The British have got two of them down at Beersheba. We've been trying to get them for weeks, but they're very big and well armed. I tried it myself on a couple of occasions, but an artillery-spotter's not really designed for that sort of thing."

"Well, cheer up," I said. "At least you'll be back in Germany before long."

He thought for a while. "Between ourselves, old fellow, I wouldn't much mind if I didn't get home. There's not going to be a lot for an ex-pilot back in Germany if we've lost this war. This blasted leg of mine gives me a lot of trouble—trapped nerve or something. And anyway, you know what they say: 'Born in the war, died in the war.' After the past four years anything else in life would be a let-down." He looked at his watch. "Well, can't stand here jawing all day: the English gentlemen will be here before nightfall. Auf wiedersehen." He limped away in the direction of the airfield.

We continued loading the boat. The diesels were thundering away now, charging the batteries. Soon columns of black smoke were seen rising from the direction of the airfield. But another diversion was to be provided for us before we sailed, one that we would infinitely rather not have seen. It appeared that the Turks were holding a last-minute jail clearance. There was a railway signal gantry about three hundred metres down the quayside. One by one, civilians with their wrists bound were led out beneath it and hoisted into the air to kick and struggle their lives away. Feinstein said that they were nationalists—Jewish and Arab alike—whom the Turks had rounded up a few months before. Most of them had died in jail from typhus and cholera, and now the Turkish Army was applying more direct means to the ones who had survived. Soon eight or nine bodies were dangling from the gantry. I considered intervening, but the Turks were still nominally Austria's allies, beside which there were eleven or twelve armed soldiers with the hangmen, quite capable of starting a brawl which might prevent our sailing. Anyway, our own army had not behaved a lot better in Serbia in 1914 if reports were to be believed. We got on with our work and tried not to look; that is, until another victim was led out to have a noose placed around his neck. It was a boy of about ten. This was too much. I was on the conning tower, where Grigorović was standing sentry.

"Grigorović," I growled in disgust, "do you think that you could hit that Turkish dog at this range?"

Before I realised what I had said the big Montenegrin had raised his rifle to his shoulder, rattled the bolt and fired! No second shot was necessary: the hangman flung his arms in the air with a howl, staggered a few paces and fell on his face in the dust. Grigorović lowered the smoking weapon and slapped the butt smartly in salute: "Obediently report Herr Kommandant that yes, I could hit that Turkish dog at this range."

It was an idiotic thing for me to have said to a man from Montenegro, where shooting Turks had been the national sport for centuries. And it looked for a few moments as if my folly might have serious consequences, as the execution party levelled their rifles. Luckily though, Preradović and Szabo had the presence of mind to man the machine gun and train it on our erstwhile allies. They glared at us for a while, then turned and shuffled away, leaving their latest victim standing beneath the gallows with the noose about his neck, frozen with terror. I sent Feinstein running over to take care of him. They disappeared together, and half an hour later Feinstein came running back to report that the child, both of whose parents had died in jail, had found refuge with Herr Mandel and his wife.

Evening was drawing near. *U26* would have to escape under cover of darkness tonight or not at all, for rifle and machine-gun fire was crackling away now on the outskirts of Haifa. If we delayed we might suffer the most ignominious of all fates for a warship: that of being captured by land-troops. There was also that bomber to be thought of. Surely the British would try again before nightfall rather than let us escape. Others were making their preparations too. About 5 p.m. there were two muffled explosions, and the *Uckermarck* began to sink at her moorings. The drift of fugitive Turks through the streets had now become a flood. Then a group of figures emerged from the crowd and made its way down the quayside towards us: two men, carrying a third man on a stretcher, and two women. All were haggard with fatigue and lack of sleep. I saw also, beneath the caked dust, that one of the men and the younger of the two women were in uniform. The man saluted wearily after they had put the stretcher down.

"Herr Kommandant? Permit me to introduce myself: Oberstabsarzt Dr Veith of k.u.k. Field Hospital Unit No. 137, formerly based at Nazareth. This" (indicating the younger woman) "is Krankenschwester Odelga of the same unit, and our civilian companions are Herr Professor Dr Wörthmuller and his wife, who were carrying out archaeological work near Nablus but were imprisoned as spies by the Turks. We have been walking these past three days ever since our unit was overrun at Megiddo. We picked this poor man up outside the town. We think he may be a German, but he's certainly very ill. We came because we heard that there was an Austrian submarine here at Haifa, about to sail."

"Yes, Herr Stabsarzt, but we are not a refugee transport organisation. Space is very limited aboard, and food is short. Why not wait here? The British will be here before morning and I am sure that you can rely upon them to treat you honourably."

He looked doubtful. "Without question, the British would. But I am worried about their Arab allies—and the Turks. Two of our companions were robbed and had their throats cut on the way here, and Nurse Odelga says that four nurses from her unit were raped and killed by Turkish deserters a few days ago."

I thought. We were one man down now that Heller was gone, and we could always fit the two women into odd corners as we had often done with passengers in the past. The sick man though—it looked like typhus. It was a hard decision, but in the end we had to make him as comfortable as we could and leave him in a warehouse with a note asking the British to look after him.

We were nearly ready now as the sun sank towards the sea horizon. Then a shout went up: "Aeroplane in sight—thirty degrees port!" It was the Handley-Page, no doubt about that, coming in from seaward this time at about a thousand metres' height. The men scrambled to the guns. The barrel of the Skoda gun was cranked to point skywards as the fuses on the shrapnel shells were set. The aeroplane was coming straight towards us, past the shoulder of Mount Carmel. But the sun was in our eyes. We waited until we thought the range was right, then opened fire. One after another, puffs of shrapnel smoke burst in the sky—without any visible effect on the bomber's menacing, steady course. Then there was a shout from d'Ermenonville:

"Look—it's another aeroplane! I think it's a German!"

A milk-white biplane had appeared over the ridge of the mountain. The black crosses beneath its wings were visible as it closed with the lumbering bomber. D'Ermenonville, who was watching through binoculars, said afterwards that its pilot waved down to us. We heard the dry clattering of the bomber's machine guns above the noise of its engines as it tried to swerve, but it was too late. The Aviatik met it head-on, shearing off its starboard wings and one engine. The great aeroplane lurched, then began to spin downwards like a broken moth. It vanished behind a mountain spur and there was silence for a moment; then the roar of exploding bombs and a great mushroom of burning petrol erupting into the sky. The wreck of the Aviatik crashed into the mountain slopes further on, and it too burst into flames. Hauptmann Uchatius of the Imperial German Flying Service had achieved his twin ambitions of bringing down the Handley-Page and not surviving the war. In all likelihood he had also saved us.

Dusk fell at last: a twilight riven now by gun flashes and the rattle of musketry on the slopes of Mount Carmel. Stray bullets plopped in the water beyond us as we prepared to slip our moorings and head out into the middle of the harbour, where the water was just deep enough for us to submerge. The warp-handling party was already on the quayside, crouching nervously as bullets buzzed like cockchafers in the semi-darkness. Suddenly there was a blaze of light from the end of the quayside, then a hail of shots rattling off the conning-tower plating and ricocheting from the stones. An armoured car had appeared between two warehouses about three hundred metres distant and had us in the beam of its headlamps. The men fumbled desperately with the mooring lines as machine-gun bullets whined around us. D'Ermenonville and Tauchführer Névesely sprang down from the conning tower towards the gun and motioned frantically to the warp-handling party to lie flat. Névesely loaded a shell into the breech as my Second Officer trained the gun round. It roared, and when the smoke cleared we saw that although he had missed the armoured car, he had demolished a corner of one of the buildings so that it blocked the roadway. This seemed to put our enemies off their aim: the warps were cast off and *U26* began to move away from the quayside as the men leapt down on to the deck, dragging Elektroquartiermeister Lederer with them. He had been hit, but it was too dark to see how badly. Before long we were safely submerged in fifteen metres of water and edging out past the end of the harbour mole. I was not altogether happy about navigating my way out of Haifa submerged. I had a chart of the minefields drawn up for me by a German naval officer aboard the *Uckermarck,* but I had reason to suspect that the Turks had not been at all methodical about keeping the swept channels clear. But in the event we made it, after an hour or so cruising at two knots and straining our ears for the tell-tale scrape of a mine cable. We were able to surface before midnight and then proceed under diesels, leaving the battle for Haifa behind us as a confusion of bumps and flashes over the horizon.

There was one last duty to perform the next morning. Lederer had been shot through the back on the quayside at Haifa—a gaping, ragged wound from (I suppose) a ricochet. There had been little that we could do for him, and he died about 8 a.m. The funeral was, in its way, what the people of Vienna used to call "ein schöne Leiche": as grand a ceremony as our limited means would allow. Elektroquartiermeister Otto Lederer, aged twenty-four, from Kaschau in Slovakia, had shipped with us from the beginning and shared all our discomforts and dangers for three and a half years, so we were determined that not even Radetzky himself should have had a finer send-off. We were not morbid by nature, but we were all conscious that when our own hour came there might be no time for ceremonial. D'Ermenonville and I shaved and put on our best whites. All the off-watch hands turned out and stood with bared, lowered heads as I read out the Office of Burial over the blanket-wrapped corpse lying on the stretcher. I got to "Anima ejus, et animae omnium fidelium defunctorum per misericordiam Dei requiescat in pace . . ." The sailors raised their rifles and three volleys cracked into the empty blue sky. Then Névesely gave a tug at the slip-knot about the dead man's chest. The bundle slid out from under the red-white-red ensign and plumped into the sea, weighed down by an iron ballast weight. It bobbed astern for a few moments as the air seeped out, then it was gone.

The next ten days contained little that was worthy of note, as *U26* rumbled her way back towards Durazzo at a steady six knots, propelled by two worn-out diesels and a reconstituted British Admiral. Convoying might keep ships out of the way of U-Boats, but at least it had the advantage now of keeping U-Boats out of the way of other ships; provided that, like us, they desired nothing more than to make their way home as unobtrusively as possible. We saw only one other vessel: a small schooner sighted in the distance south of Cephalonia. In fact it was all rather like a sort of pauper's yachting party for most of the time, cruising along in the autumn sunshine as we repaired our tattered clothing and cooked our sparse meals. I have a photograph here of myself on deck with Lehár, Dr Veith and the professor and his wife: "30 September 1918, south of Crete." Frau Wörthmuller was in a poor state when we got her aboard. She had nearly died from typhus in the prison at Nablus, and the walk from Megiddo had quite exhausted her. But rest, sea air and a change of clothes—even sailor's overalls—did wonders for her. We rigged up a canvas screen to partition off part of the fore-ends for her and Nurse Odelga.

I can only say that I wish Nurse Kathi Odelga could have given my crew some privacy in return, but she had other ideas. She was a firm-minded young woman of about twenty from Wiener Neustadt: short, but quite pretty once we had hosed the dust off her. She was tired out for her first couple of days on board, but she regained her strength remarkably quickly, and soon set about trying to reorganise *U26* on the lines of a base medical unit, nagging the crew to make up their bunks with hospital corners and so forth. We all spent most of our time on deck: the temperatures below were awful as usual. Before many days were out I began to notice that Fregattenleutnant d'Ermenonville was spending a growing proportion of his off-watch time with Fräulein Odelga, instructing her in basic navigation, the rudiments of the sextant and other such skills likely to be useful on a hospital ward. I resolved to keep matters under observation.

It was a peaceful enough time out there on the Mediterranean, in the dying weeks of the World War. In truth though, there was little enough for us to be serene about. We raised the wireless mast every night and listened in to the news broadcasts from Nauen and Pola and Malta; even after making due correction for the distortions of propaganda, one thing began to emerge beyond any possibility of mistake: we had lost the war. Every night came news of further battles in France—first, west of the "impregnable" Hindenburg Line; then to the east of it. The pregnant words "United States troops" occurred now with increasing frequency. Bulgaria was reported to be suing for an armistice and British bulletins said that the Turks were on the point of doing the same. Everywhere in the German communiqués that eloquent phrase began to crop up: "Planned and orderly tactical withdrawal to prepared positions."

But even as our world collapsed around us, certain parties aboard my boat were preoccupied with matters of a more personal nature. It was on the morning of 1 October that my Second Officer appeared in front of me in my tiny cabin, where I was savouring a tin mug of coffee (at least we had managed to procure some real coffee beans in Haifa and roasted them inside a tin can with the aid of a blowlamp). He saluted smartly.

"Herr Kommandant, I obediently report that I wish to make an urgent request."

"Go ahead then, d'Ermenonville."

"I wish you to marry Nurse Odelga and myself: today if possible."

He had to slap me hard on the back to bring up the coffee that I had inhaled. When I had done with choking and regained my voice I informed him curtly that he was off his head: the grounds for this opinion being (i) that as a mere Fregattenleutnant he required the permission of both the War Ministry and his commanding officer in order to marry—unlikely to be granted even in peacetime, and which would take months to obtain even if it were forthcoming; (ii) that both he and his fiancée were under twenty-one, and would therefore require the permission of both fathers—same remarks apply as foregoing; and (iii) that although I had never given the question any thought, I doubted whether k.u.k. submarine captains were empowered to conduct marriages, either today or any other day.

"In any case," I concluded, "why do you want to marry her now? We'll have to run the Otranto Straits in two days' time, and we might well get blown to bits on the way."

"Precisely, Herr Kommandant: that's why we want to be married now."

I thought for a few moments, remembering Elisabeth and myself a couple of years ago, one morning on a mountainside in Transylvania. . . . In the end, in view of his exemplary conduct during our escape from Haifa, I promised to see what could be done. A wireless message was duly tapped out to Castellnuovo that evening, as we passed west of Crete. Meanwhile I scoured the *K.u.K. Dienstreglement* for any mention of solemnisation of marriages by Linienschiffsleutnants. As I suspected, it said nothing; so I concluded that in this case the law and custom of the sea would prevail. Then the miracle happened, next evening—the small miracles that do occasionally happen amid the chaos of falling empires. A message was received from Castellnuovo. It read:

To S.M.U. *26,* at sea

Regarding wireless request of 1st inst., k.u.k. War Ministry, Marine Section, grants permission for marriage of Freglt Franz d'Ermenonville and Krankenschwester Katherina Odelga. Both families also consent and send best wishes.

The marriage was celebrated next day on the gun platform of *U26,* with Dr Veith and Tauchführer Névesely as witnesses and with a pipe-compression seal as a token ring. My only stipulations were that bride and bridegroom should continue to berth in opposite ends of the boat until we reached port, and then take all possible steps to have the marriage properly solemnised by church and state.

Our passage through the Otranto barrage that night was far from easy. The moon was out, full and bright, and there seemed to be an abnormally large number of steam trawlers at work. At one point, about halfway through, I thought that we had run into a net; but whatever it was, we managed to free the boat by running the E-motors full astern, then went on our way. We surfaced soon afterwards, but were immediately forced back down again by a swarm of Italian MAS boats who showered us with depth charges for the next two hours—fortunately with more enthusiasm than accuracy. Finally, as we attempted to surface north of Saseno, a British *Weymouth*-class cruiser opened fire on us and obliged us to submerge once more. Just after dawn though, north of the straits, as we raised the wireless mast to inform Durazzo of our arrival, we picked up the following message:

"To all U-Boats—Durazzo evacuated by k.u.k. forces 3 October. Port no longer useable."

This was nice news: now we had to run a further thirty miles up the Albanian coast to San Giovanni, which was still presumably in Austrian hands. We arrived there about mid-morning, but as we approached an umbrella of smoke was sighted over the horizon to northwards. Soon a mighty thundering of heavy guns was shaking the air. I dived the boat and crept closer for a look, drawn by curiosity as much as anything else. Soon the masts of two large ships were visible over the horizon, then those of a good eight or nine smaller vessels. A shore bombardment was in progress, being administered by two Italian *Regina Elena*-class battleships and a force of destroyers and light cruisers. I had the torpedo tubes cleared to fire. We had two torpedoes left, and we had been very conscientious even while we were at Haifa about hauling one of them back out of its tube each day for inspection. We closed to two thousand metres undetected. Certainly our land troops in San Giovanni were being given a day to remember as the guns of the battleships rained shells upon them. But we gave the Allies something to remember as well: a last souvenir of the k.u.k. Kriegsmarine. The destroyer screen was heavy: far too heavy for me to think of getting through it. But then a British *Birmingham*-class light cruiser at the tail of the line did a very rash thing: swung round the end of the destroyer line and raced along outside it, probably trying to get upwind of the smoke that was now obscuring the target. The range was long—about a thousand metres—but I waited for the deflection angle, then fired: only one torpedo, because the firing mechanism on the upper tube jammed until it was too late. We waited a minute or so, and felt a sudden shock through the water as a column of white spray leapt up beneath the cruiser's stern, rising almost as high as her masthead. I knew that it was probably too far aft to sink her, but none the less the effect on the morale of our enemies was quite marvellous. Within five minutes the whole bombardment force had broken off the action and fled, the damaged cruiser zig-zagging along behind them like a snake with a broken back. We had done our duty for Old Austria, even as she lay on her deathbed.

I stepped back from the periscope as a cheer rang through the boat—only to be set upon by Nurse Odelga (or the Gräfin d'Ermenonville as she now was), who burst into the control room from the fore-ends, where she had insisted on helping the torpedomen. Her eyes were blazing with anger.

"Captain, I insist that you pursue those brutes up there!"

"But my dear young lady," I protested, "they are steaming away from us at top speed. We couldn't get near them now even if I considered it worthwhile to do so."

"Rot. You men are all the same—utterly spineless. We still have one torpedo left, and we could always sink another of them."

"Madam, please control yourself. I am in command of this vessel and you must trust my judgement. Besides, if I may say so, I find your desire for the enemy's destruction more than a little unseemly in a nursing sister . . ."

Suddenly she elbowed me aside and seized the handles of the periscope, applying her eye to the viewfinder. "Stuff and nonsense! Nursing sister be damned—those beasts up there would have killed my husband given half a chance."

In the end my Second Officer had to be called to put an end to this embarrassing scene. As he led her away, his face the colour of a plum, I gave him my views on the matter.

". . . And if you can't keep her in order," I concluded, "you had no business to be marrying her in the first place."

We reached the Bocche on the evening of 4 October, low on fuel and with the port diesel giving trouble. The Graf and Gräfin d'Ermenonville departed for their delayed honeymoon in the Gasthaus Zur Post at Baosić, while I was called to the Admiral and congratulated on our escape from Haifa, and also for routing the Allied attack on San Giovanni di Medua. A baronage was spoken of, and promotion by two ranks to Fregattenkapitän. I sensed however that Imperial favour was now likely to be a cheque drawn on a failing bank. One hardly needed to be a clairvoyant to see that things were moving to a close.

18

HOMECOMING

WAITING, WAITING FOR SOMETHING TO HAPPEN. It was a curious time, those last weeks of thousand-year Austria. Rather like waiting outside a sick-room for an elderly relative to die. Or perhaps like waiting in the condemned cell, drumming one's fingers on the table and wondering whether the hangman has missed his train. Despite our escape from Haifa and the torpedoing of the British cruiser there was little enough to celebrate once *U26* returned to the Bocche, for in our absence a new actor had come on stage to help bring down the curtain on this play which had run on too long. It was the Spanish Influenza, which had made its first appearance in the spring, but which was now scything down the exhausted, starving inhabitants of the Central Empires with a ferocity which made the efforts of mere men look half-hearted. I believe that in four months it killed more people in Europe than the entire four years of fighting. The hospital ships floating in Teodo Bay were packed with the sick, while as for the warships, they were now frequently hard-pressed even to muster anchor-handling parties. The atmosphere in those still, warm days of early October was that of a deathbed: Old Austria so far gone now that only a mirror held to her lips could detect any sign of life. We went through the daily rituals like clockwork toys: hoisting the flag at 8 a.m., lowering the flag and blowing the Last Post at sunset, holding Divisions and Captain's Report, detailing sentries and so forth, but the life and purpose was fast trickling away from it all.

On 17 October there was a bustle of activity aboard the German U-Boats over at Pijavica. As they made ready to put to sea, we learnt that Berlin had called off the U-Boat campaign preparatory to requesting an armistice. The smaller boats were to be scuttled outside the Bocche; the larger ones would try to make their way back to Germany as best they could via the Straits of Gibraltar. So we waved them goodbye, those formidable allies of ours who had been the terror of the seas for the past four years, whom we had admired and envied, but never much liked. Most of them managed to reach Germany; some were sunk on the way; a few simply disappeared.

Next day, about noon, there was a sudden mighty commotion in Teodo Bay: guns banging away aboard the ships at anchor and in the emplacements on the surrounding peaks; the wailing of ship's sirens and the thunder of aircraft engines; the whole fearful din multiplied a hundredfold as it echoed back and forth between the sides of the mountains. It was another air-raid: seven or eight Italian Capronis this time. We waited for the bombs to come shrieking down, but instead they dropped canisters that burst open in mid-air, showering the whole bay with leaflets. One of them fluttered gently down onto the jetty at Gjenović, almost at my feet. I picked it up. It was in Serbo-Croat and read:

SAILORS OF THE AUSTRO-HUNGARIAN FLEET!

The day of freedom is at hand!

Why do you go on risking your lives for the crumbling Habsburg corpse-empire and its German masters? Liberation is near. A government of the Serb, Croat and Slovene State has already been formed on Corfu and is ready to move to Belgrade. Germany and Austria have lost the war, so throw down your arms and join your brothers.

LONG LIVE YUGOSLAVIA!

I showed it to two of my sailors, Preradović and Baica, both Croats. They smiled, and looked steadily at me with their calm, grey eyes.

"Obediently report, Herr Kommandant, that we don't take any of this stuff very seriously. They talk of the South Slavs, but those were Italian planes up there, and we know that the Italians really want the coast and the islands for themselves, from here all the way up to Trieste. Why should we want to exchange rule from Vienna for rule from Rome?"

"Yes," said Baica, laughing, "at least the Emperor in Vienna is a long way off. The King of Italy is a lot nearer."

All very *kaisertreu* still; but, I wondered to myself, what do they really think?

Down here in the fjords of Cattaro, hundreds of kilometres from anywhere and walled in by the mountains, the rumours bred like white mice: that the Germans had occupied Vienna and deposed the Emperor; that Hungary had broken away from Austria and changed sides; that the French had entered Bavaria. I continued to perform my duties as an officer of the k.u.k. Kriegsmarine much as I had always done: filing reports, filling in forms, seeking write-off authority from the Ministry of Finances for a sailor's underpants, lodging a complaint with Budapest because two of my men going on leave across Hungarian territory had been plundered of food by customs officials. Yet I sensed that slowly, gradually, the stiffness of death was setting in. Orders no longer came from Pola. The telephone lines ceased to work, then came back on again for no apparent reason, then went dead once more. Mail stopped arriving, while every day more and more men were reported overdue from leave. Supplies failed to reach us, so that those aboard the ships who were not down with influenza had to spend a large part of each day out in the boats fishing, or hunting for small game in the forests around the Bocche. Professor Wörthmuller and his wife had stayed at Gjenović ever since we brought them back from Palestine. He stood with me one morning on the quayside, watching the bluejackets set out on their day's foraging.

"You know, Herr Leutnant," he remarked to me, "have you ever thought what a strange sight we are witnessing? I worked for two years in the Jordan valley, excavating a Palaeolithic hunter-gatherer site from about 12,000 BC. Yet here we are, in the twentieth century, watching as wireless operators and naval fliers revert to that mode of existence. It's curious; all very curious."

• • •

Even so, dying war and moribund Empire could still throw an occasional spasm. On 28 October, her tanks only half full of diesel oil, *U26* was ordered to put to sea to investigate possible Allied landings near the Drina Estuary. Our orders were to observe only, and not to engage the enemy unless fired upon. We cruised off Albania for the next four days, seeing nothing except a few aircraft and a French destroyer. Then the Spanish Influenza hit us in earnest: five men down with high fevers and terrible cramps. There were now too few of us to manage the boat easily, and anyway there seemed little point in continuing the patrol since our wireless set had broken down. We set course for the Bocche and reached Punto d'Ostro early on 4 November. A light drizzle was falling. On shore, all was silence. The forts failed to answer our signals, and no boom defence vessels came out to escort us through the minefields. In the end we lost patience and went in on our own—no great risk, since the swept channels had not been changed for months past and the net barriers had been left open. A couple of men watched us in silence from Fort Mamula, refusing to answer our hails.

The scene in Igalo Bay was very odd indeed. Warships' boats were plying to and fro through the Kumbor Narrows, arriving full and going back empty, and the railway station at Zelenika was surrounded by a sea of dark blue speckled with grey. At first I feared that another mutiny was under way, but when I inspected the crowd through my binoculars I saw that they all seemed orderly enough, in the curious, milling way that a swarm of bees is orderly. I saw though that the picket boats landing men at the jetty were flying an unfamiliar flag: horizontal stripes of azure, white and red. The same ensign also flew from the jack-staffs of the warships at anchor in Teodo Bay. When we reached the quay at Gjenović the U-Boat station seemed deserted. Four U-Boats were moored at the jetty, flying the same curious flag but with no one aboard. The crew tied up our boat in the grey November half-light while Béla Meszáros and I went up to the Stazionkanzlei building. It was empty and shuttered, like an abandoned railway station. The door was locked and a postcard was fixed to it with drawing pins. It read:

> 2 November 1918
>
> All ex-k.u.k. U-Boats are to be handed over to representatives of the Serb, Croat and Slovene State. Non-South Slav personnel are to make their way home by whatever means are available.
>
> signed G. v. Trapp
> for the Emperor Karl

We both stood silent for what seemed like several minutes. So this was it at last: the end of the war and the end of Austria. Like a man who has just had a leg cut off, but still seems to feel his toes, it was only gradually that it dawned upon me: that this was also the end of the Imperial and Royal Austro-Hungarian Navy in which I had made my life.

We walked back towards *U26* at the quayside, silent, wrapped in our thoughts. But as we rounded the corner of the Kanzlei building we ran into a squad of armed sailors led by a Fregattenleutnant. It was Anton Brokwitz, Edler von Podgora, Second Torpedo Officer of the light cruiser *Novara*. He had served under me as a Cadet when I was commanding a torpedo-boat before the war.

"Good morning Brokwitz," I called, "good to see you. Would you be so good as to tell me—" He cut me off in mid-sentence, replying in Croat:

"I'm sorry, but I don't know German." I was too surprised to reply. Then I saw that the sailors behind him had removed the K.U.K. KRIEGS-MARINE ribbon from their caps. In its place was a ribbon with the simple legend JUGOSLAVIJA in white paint. I recovered from my surprise and answered in Croat.

"I see. And might I enquire in what circumstances Fregattenleutnant Anton Brokwitz von Podgora has forgotten how to speak German?"

He smiled benignly. "I know of no such person. I am Captain Anté Brkovec of the Yugoslav Navy. But more to the point, Lieutenant, I have come to request the surrender of your submarine to the authority of the South Slav National Council in Agr . . . sorry, Zagreb. I assume that you have seen the notice." I agreed that I had seen the notice, so in the end I consented to hand over *U26* and its South Slav crew members—six in all—in return for a signed receipt made out on the back of a blank leave pass. As we walked down to the boat Brokwitz/Brkovec informed me that Admiral Horthy's order to dissolve the Imperial and Royal Fleet had been given on 31 October, but had not reached Cattaro until two days later. The warship crews were now being landed at Zelenika to make their way home as best they could.

"Between ourselves, though," he confided, "I would advise you and your remaining men to get away from here while the going's good. The French are preparing to land here, and since we're now supposed to be their allies there isn't a great deal that we can do to stop them. If they arrive I imagine that they'll simply round up all remaining Austrian personnel as prisoners of war." I thanked him for his advice, but requested that once we had packed our belongings I should be allowed to make a brief address to my ex-crew. He agreed, so a quarter of an hour later I was standing on the conning tower of *U26* with the men gathered on the quayside below me, kitbags at their feet. There were thirteen of us in all, the five sick men having been transferred to a hospital ship with Feinstein, who had volunteered to remain behind and look after them. I intended to keep my remarks brief: I was never much of an orator, and anyway time was pressing.

"Well," I said, "this is how it all ends. We have risked our lives for Old Austria, fighting a lost war for a fatherland that has crumbled away behind us. We offered everything; and on several occasions we nearly gave it. Yet at the end all we have to show for it is defeat. But always remember this: that we lived and fought together, sailors from eleven different nationalities, and that we can still say when we are old men that we fought together for . . . for the only fatherland worth fighting for; for one another, aboard this boat of ours. Nothing can ever take that away from us. Go now and take up your lives again. For my part I promise you that if I live to be a hundred I shall never forget any of you. That is all I have to say." I turned to Grigorović, standing behind me on the conning tower—and saw to my surprise that tears were in his eyes.

"Grigorović, lower the ensign."

Really there was not much lowering to be done, just lifting the staff of the red-white-red flag from its socket at the back of the conning tower. But as Grigorović grasped the flag-staff a voice came from the quayside.

"No, Herr Kommandant, not like that. Old Austria may be gone, but the flag's still not a dishcloth. Let's do it properly."

So Grigorović dipped the flag slowly to the deck as we sang the "Gott Erhalte" for the last time. I had heard Haydn's beautiful old imperial hymn a few thousand times before, I should think, but never as movingly as on that grey November morning on the quayside at Gjenović, accompanied on a piano accordion by the Hungarian gypsy Attila Bárabás. As the last note died away Tauchführer Névesely snapped to attention and called out: "Crew, dismiss." There were last handshakes among the thirteen ex-shipmates. Five minutes later we were hurrying along the road with our belongings on our backs, making for the railway station at Zelenika.

It was not easy, that journey from a lost past to a highly uncertain future. For those seven of us who remained from the crew of *U26* our aims were, firstly, to get ourselves away from possible Allied captivity and, secondly, to disentangle ourselves as neatly and honourably as we could from the ruins of the Habsburg armed forces. This may sound odd—why not simply go straight home? you will say—but remember that, so far as we knew, the war was still in progress, the Emperor still in the Hofburg and our oaths of loyalty still in force. The note on the door at Gjenović, after all, seemed to have discharged only South Slav sailors from the Austrian service. And anyway, we were no conscript rabble running away from the war: we were the remainder of the most successful of Austro-Hungarian U-Boat crews, and the last one to strike its colours. No, we had to get to Pola to obtain our formal discharge, or failing that, to Vienna itself.

The train of cattle trucks clanked away from Zelenika station on the evening of the 4th, taking us up the narrow-gauge line towards Sarajevo. It was scarcely luxury accommodation, even for men used to the cramped squalor of U-Boat life. The worn-out wagons rattled and jarred their way through the barren mountains of Herzegovina as we tried to make ourselves comfortable, with barely enough room to sit down and constantly irritated by the vermin that infested the dirty straw. But at least the fleas did us one service: they kept us awake to guard our meagre belongings from theft by our fellow-refugees. They were mostly k.u.k. Armee troops from the Albanian Front, many of them ill with influenza and malaria. They had coagulated into national groups, like milk gone sour, and occupied different parts of the wagon as they eyed one another suspiciously. The wagon ahead of ours was occupied by German U-Boat sailors from one of the last boats to arrive back at Cattaro. They were still dressed in their leather overalls and were heavily armed, with a Bergmann sub-machine gun among other weapons. They had little to do with us, apart from promising to shoot anyone who tried to board their wagon.

The Germans were also on their way to a very dubious tomorrow, in a defeated and starving homeland racked by revolution. But at least they had an identifiable country to return to. If Austria-Hungary had now fallen to pieces, where were our new homelands? I was a Czech by birth, but I had served for nearly fifteen years in the Habsburg officer corps, where one left one's nationality behind at the door, so to speak. Was I now automatically a citizen of this Czecho-Slovak Republic that was reported to have been set up in Prague, or was I an Austrian until such time as I elected to be something else? People nowadays speak of "Austria losing her Empire" in 1918 as if it were the same thing as Britain or France losing theirs a generation later. But it was not like that at all. Old Austria was a dynasty, not a country; the Empire had really been nothing but the dynasty's estate; and the woebegone little stump of a country that was now forced to call itself "Austria" was merely the German-speaking parts of that estate, plus its capital city—rather as if London and the Home Counties had been amputated from the rest of England, named "Britain," and ordered to make their way in the world as an independent state. Somehow, even then, Austrian nationality hardly seemed an attractive prospect. It was with uncomfortable speculations such as these that I occupied the hours to Sarajevo, then the two weary days from Sarajevo to the junction at Sissek in Croatia.

The journey from Sarajevo was not much easier than that from Zelenika. As was usual in those days, the train was not only grossly overloaded but also worn out and drawn by a decrepit locomotive burning lignite. The result was that any sort of gradient, of which there were plenty in that mountainous land, involved getting out to walk alongside the track, or even to push the engine uphill. Winter was coming on now in those bleak limestone mountains of Bosnia. Sleet and chill winds cut through our threadbare clothing as our seaboots struggled for grip on the mud and ballast beside the tracks. We finished what little rations we had brought with us from *U26,* then tried to barter for food with the peasantry along the line. Things had changed now though. This was the Serb, Croat and Slovene State. Austrian money was no longer accepted, and we refugees from the ruins of the old Monarchy were not welcome. Transparent as ghosts, we were merely tiresome vagabonds to be disposed of as quickly as possible, sometimes by the most direct of means. It was early morning near Kostajnica, on the borders of Croatia, as Meszáros, d'Ermenonville and I trudged wearily with our baggage up another incline, this time ahead of the asthmatic locomotive. Yet another corpse lay ahead of us, slumped across the rails. Tired as we were, we still had some residual scruples about letting the train run over the dead man, so we bent down to drag him off the track. He was a large man in an officer's greatcoat. A staff-pattern shako lay beside the line, and the hilt of a trench dagger protruded from a dark patch on his back.

"Nice overcoat," said Meszáros as he grasped the dead man's sleeve. "Pity about the knife. They might at least have had the consideration to knock him on the head." We turned the body over and saw the face, its eyes goggling blankly. It was Artillerie Oberst von Friedauer, late husband of the sumptuous Frau Ilona.

We reached Sissek on the evening of 7 November. There was no direct railway line to Pola, so we intended to catch a train down to Fiume and then travel by sea for the remaining eighty or so kilometres. But on the crowded railway platform stood a blackboard chalked with a message in Magyar. It read:

BY ORDER OF THE HUNGARIAN PROVISIONAL GOVERNMENT

All ethnic Magyar personnel of the former k.u.k. armed forces are to proceed from here to Hungarian territory by way of Zagreb.

Budapest, 6 November 1918

"Well, that looks as if it means us," said Meszáros with a sigh, " 'The Call of My Native Land' and all that. Come on Bárabás, my Tsigane friend, pick up your accordion and let's go home. Perhaps you will consider teaching me how to blow safes, because I'm damned if I can think what else a career naval officer is going to do in a country without a coast."

"Look after yourself, Meszáros," I said, shaking his hand, "and thank you for shipping with me these three years."

He smiled. "Oh, I'll be all right, don't you worry. I was officially declared to be a creature without honour back in 1914, so perhaps I'll find this new world easier to cope with than you decent, upright fellows. Goodbye."

He and Bárabás and a Slovak sailor disappeared into the field-grey crowd on the Zagreb platform. I never saw him again, but I believe that he did manage in that chilly post-war world. At any rate, I saw a brief obituary notice in *The Times* in 1961 recording the death in Rio de Janeiro of "Baron Béla Meszáros, the world-famous confidence trickster." It appeared that among other exploits he had once sold the Statue of Liberty to an Argentinian millionaire. May the earth lie lightly upon him, dear comrade.

We neared the port of Fiume while it was still dark the next morning. Then the train clanked and shuddered to a halt. Rifle fire was spattering fitfully up in the hills behind the town. There was a half-hour wait, then armed civilians came along and commanded us to get out "in the name of the Croat provisional government." There was no alternative but to pick up our haversacks once more and trudge along the railway line across the River Rjecina and into the town. Some of our field-grey companions left us there, but about forty of us continued towards the waterfront through the tunnel that ran beneath the highest part of the town. Gunfire still crackled in the darkness, punctuated every now and then by the sound of a grenade. D'Ermenonville and I were leading the column as we emerged from the tunnel. We stopped. About five metres ahead, in the cutting just outside the tunnel entrance, was a platoon of sailors drawn up in two ranks with levelled rifles, one standing and one kneeling as depicted in all the best drill-manuals. They were dressed in brass-buttoned pea-jackets and immaculate white gaiters, with little white caps on their heads like upturned dog-bowls. A petty officer stood beside them with a drawn revolver, pointing it at my chest with obvious lethal intent. There was an awkward silence as we stood facing one another, a silence in which I remembered uncomfortably that some of our party were still carrying their rifles. In the end I spoke.

"Please excuse us, but we are not your enemies."

"OK Bud, so who the hell are you then?" The American accent was unmistakable.

Ten minutes later I was being ushered into the main lounge at the Palazzo Lloyd Hotel on the Riva Szapáry, down by the harbour. I must have cut a strange figure among the velvet and gilt brocade: unshaven, unwashed, bleary-eyed and still dressed in my U-Boat clothes, with only my canvas cuff-rings and oil-stained naval cap to show that I was not a common vagrant. I looked out of the window and saw two destroyers moored to the quayside. One I recognised as a British *V* class. The other was a four-funnelled, flush-decked ship of a kind hitherto unknown to me. Then a deep voice caused me to turn round.

"Good God, it's Otto Prohaska. What on earth are you doing here?"

It was a tall, thickset Royal Naval Commander. His face looked familiar. Then I realised: this was Charles Grenville-Hammersley, who had been appointed my guide twelve years before when I had been at Portsmouth and Barrow-in-Furness studying British submarine construction. Despite our four years as enemies he seemed pleased to see me.

"What have you been doing with yourself?" he asked. "I must say you look pretty rough."

"Oh, fighting a war, like yourself I suppose—except that as you see, we lost. But if you will excuse my asking, what brings you to Fiume?"

He laughed. "You're an Austrian, Prohaska, so I was hoping perhaps you would tell me that, because I'll be buggered if I can make out what we're supposed to be doing here, us and the Yankees. I was in command of a light cruiser until last month, HMS *Colchester*. We were bombarding your chaps at a place called San Giovanni di something, down in Albania. Then some damned Hun submarine blew our rudder off with a torpedo and sent our Italian friends running for home. Wish I could get my hands on the blighter, I'd wring his neck for him . . . Anyway, the ship's in drydock at Brindisi and they sent me over here in a destroyer just after the armistice. Seems that as soon as peace was declared the townspeople started going at one another hammer and tongs for control of the place. My men and the Americans are trying to keep the two sides apart. By the sound of it though your chaps were bloody lucky not to have been shot on sight, coming out of that tunnel. Anyway, where are you bound for?"

"For Pola, to get ourselves properly demobilised. We finished the war at Cattaro."

He stroked his chin. "Pola? I'd steer clear of the place if I were you, old man. There's been trouble there as well I believe and the Italians have moved in. If you arrived there they'd just nab you as a POW and stick you behind the wire with the rest. I'll tell you what though," (he lowered his voice) "there's a train leaving here in an hour's time, evacuating Austrian civil servants and their families. It's not supposed to carry military person- nel but . . . but well, you're an old friend, despite the war, and I can get you and your men on to it if you hurry. It's only going up as far as the Vienna-Trieste line, but it'll get you clear of the wops."

Before we left the Lloyd Palazzo, Grenville-Hammersley was kind enough to allow the four of us—myself, d'Ermenonville, Lehár and Telegraphist Stonawski—a quick wash and a cup of hot, strong English tea. Poor Stonawski made a very strange face at this drink, but he was courteous enough to finish it with a pretence of enjoyment. Then we were off again. As the repatriation train clanked along the chestnut-lined waterfront it passed the k.u.k. Marine Akademie: my old Alma Mater, scene of so many youthful dreams, now almost as grubby and dishevelled as myself. We passed the shipyards at Cantrida, then the train slowed as the track turned inland and began to climb over the shoulder of Mount Ucka. Soon we were rumbling up a deep cutting in the mountainside. Something made me turn around to look back down the narrow defile. There behind me lay the Adriatic, like a steel-blue curtain hung across the end of the cutting, gleaming in the weak November sunshine, its smoothness broken only by the humps of Veglia and Cherso Islands. Then the train-wheels squealed on the worn rails as we began to negotiate a bend. The sea disappeared, blocked out by engine smoke and the high limestone walls of the cutting. The train turned back a little, giving me one last glimpse of it, then it was gone for good as we entered a tunnel. Somehow I knew that my life as a sailor of Austria had ended at that moment. It was only later that I realised it must have been at that same place all those years before that I had caught my first glimpse of salt water as we arrived for our family holiday at Abbazia.

The next four days passed like episodes in a fever: nothing quite real and every scene melting into the next. First was the station at Divacca, which we reached after yet another weary fifteen-kilometre trudge: like Freudenau on a race day in about 1913, except that the runners here were monstrously overloaded trains, and the crowds made up of a solid mass of field-grey humanity, still caked with the mud of the trenches. In fact the station and its environs were so thronged with soldiers that the trains could barely get to the platform through the mass of bodies. The flood of men back from the Italian Front was now in full spate: hundreds of thousands of those who had managed to evade capture a few days before as the Padua armistice came into effect. They were all on their way home now, returning to the half-dozen new and (for the moment) very hypothetical fatherlands that were emerging from the ruins of the Dual Monarchy. I think that it would have brought a lump to the throat of the bitterest of our enemies, to see the state to which the Imperial, Royal and Catholic Army had been reduced: an amorphous throng of weary, defeated, hungry and often sick men in ragged uniforms, struggling and jostling to hang on to the doors and sit on the roofs of battered cattle-trucks. The multinational army of the Habsburgs had simply fallen to pieces, like the state which it had once defended. It was nearly nightfall now, and there seemed little prospect of getting aboard a train, even hanging on to the outside. We were just beginning to reconcile ourselves to a night camping out in the rain when we heard voices calling and saw someone waving from the door of a moving cattle-truck. It was Toni Straussler and the crew of *U19*. They dragged us and our belongings inside as we ran alongside the train. They had come up from Pola: walked up the railway line out of the town as the Italians arrived. One of their number had been shot dead by a sentry as they scrambled past a road-block near Dignano. Then they had managed to get aboard a train to Divacca.

"Thank you Straussler," I said, "it was good of you to keep us a place."

"Don't mention it: we U-Boat men must stick together. But is this all that's left of you?"

"Yes, only four. We left five men sick at Gjenović and one to look after them. The six South Slavs remained behind, then Meszáros and two others fell out at Sissek. So what you see is the crew of *U26*. We're making for Vienna now, then home."

"And you?"

"My wife and son are in Galicia, near Cracow. I've got an aunt in Vienna, so I can stay with her for a few days while I see what the War Ministry wants to do, then try to make my way up to Poland."

He was silent for a while. "You needn't have bothered, old man: the Emperor released us from our oath of loyalty a week ago."

The rest of our travelling companions in that cattle-truck were Bosnian Muslims: dark, hatchet-faced men in grey fezzes who, even in the last hours of the war, had still been frightening the daylights out of the enemy in the trenches on the Monte Grappa. A nice irony, I thought, that the last fighting soldiers of Catholic Austria should have been followers of Islam. But murderous as the Bosnians might have looked, at least we were tolerably safe in their company, which is more than could be said of those further down the immensely long train as it laboured up towards the Adelsberg Pass. The train stopped, and we got out once more to walk beside the line. Shots could be heard further down, then a grenade exploded with a puff of smoke.

"Who is it? What are those idiots down there playing at?"

"It's the Magyars having a go at the Slovaks."

"No, it's the Reds and the Monarchists. They say they're going to declare a Workers' Republic when we get to Vienna."

"Rubbish—it's the Poles and the Ukrainians."

"Mad bastards," Lehár muttered to me as we trudged along. "God knows how many million dead in this rotten war and they still haven't had enough killing."

We entered the first of the Adelsberg tunnels. The entrance was littered with the dead bodies of men scraped off the roofs of passing wagons. Brains and hair were smeared on the stone archway. We tramped up the echoing tunnel, then squeezed ourselves to the walls in the dripping darkness as a train thundered past us, going the other way. Then there was a squeal of brakes in the distance. We heard later that it had smashed into the middle of a brawling mob of Magyars and Slovaks, too engrossed in their tribal dispute to notice its approach. It had killed about twenty of them and maimed as many more. The general verdict was, "Serves them right."

The rest of the journey to Vienna was slow, but relatively uneventful, apart from an exchange of shots in Cilli when soldiers from the Isonzo Front tried to steal our locomotive, then another trudge across the Semmering Pass. Towns and cities passed like dreams as we read or played cards in the straw. My chief recollection is of the central park in Laibach, with dozens of ex-artillery horses wandering disconsolately and browsing the trees and flower beds where their two-legged masters had abandoned them. But that was what it was like, the end of the black-and-yellow empire. Old Austria was not overthrown: it just collapsed like an old barn with dry rot.

We arrived at last in the capital just after dawn on the morning of 11 November. Needless to say there were no brass bands and bouquets of flowers for Austria's returning warriors: instead we were summarily pushed out of our cattle-trucks at the Matzleinsdorf goods yard, to disperse like phantoms into the early-morning gloom of the bedraggled, starving city that had now become the dustbin for all the human debris of a vanished empire. Some made their way back to homes where they would be just another mouth to feed; others set out on the next leg of their journeys to Lemberg and Brünn and Cracow. But before we dispersed for the last time, the remaining crewmen of *U26* had a piece of business to conclude. I saw a figure in a naval greatcoat standing some way off with a pencil and clipboard. He had a Fregattenkapitän's rings, so I decided that we would make our final report to him. I felt in my breast pocket after the receipt for *U26*. Then the four of us formed up in front of him and I saluted. He looked up at us and grunted.

"What d'you want?"

"Obediently report, Herr Fregattenkapitän, that we are the remaining crew members of His Imperial and Royal Majesty's submarine *U26,* surrendered on the orders of the Naval C.-in-C. to representatives of the South Slav State at Cattaro on 4 November. I have the honour to be her Captain, Linienschiffsleutnant Ottokar, Ritter von Prohaska." He looked at me in bewilderment, this bedraggled survivor from a sunken world. His reply was simple.

"Bugger off, sailor."

It was then that I saw that the sleeve of his greatcoat—probably stolen—bore a red armband marked VOLKSWEHR.

We said our farewells as Lehár and Stonawski set out for the Franz Josefs Bahnhof en route for Prague and Teschen. I asked Lehár what he was going to do now. He smiled.

"Oh, settle down on shore I think. The Merry Widow sold up the business in Pola and bought us a place in Olmutz—or Olomouc now. Her last letter said that the local brewery is looking for a plant engineer, so I think we'll manage. Please remember that you and your lady and your little boy will always be honoured guests with us. Anyway, goodbye, and I hope to see you again some day."

It was only as he departed that I realised something: for the first time since we met we had been speaking in Czech. I hope that Lehár got his job with the brewery, because I would like to think of him old and full of years, some time in the late 1960s, sitting in the garden with a mug of good Czech beer beside him and his great-grandchildren about his knees, telling them of his adventures in the U-Boats in that long-forgotten war: how we brought the camel back from Libya; how we nearly perished when we were stuck on the bottom off Chioggia; and how we escaped from Haifa in the last weeks of the war with the British Army on our heels.

Franz d'Ermenonville took his leave of me, promising to see me again shortly, since he lived just outside Vienna. I did meet him again as it happened: in London in the year 1942. He had been conscripted into Hitler's Kriegsmarine in 1939 and made Second Officer of a U-Boat which was later sunk by the RAF off the Shetlands. He had been rescued, but wounds and his age had put him on the list for an exchange of prisoners. Before this took place though the British Intelligence Services—to my eternal shame, using me as an intermediary—managed to inveigle him into a half-baked plot to assassinate the Führer. The Gestapo knew of it in advance, of course, and shadowed him for a year before they arrested him. The sequel is not pleasant to think about. At any rate, I have spent the past forty years trying not to think about it.

But compared with the pressing concerns of the moment, the distant future was of little importance to me that morning as I made my way along the Wiedner Hauptstrasse. I was just coming within sight of that huge, ugly block of tenements called the Freihaus when two figures sprang out at me from a doorway. Before I had time to think I was being held up against a wall with a rifle muzzle poked into my belly while one of the men searched me, taking my pistol from my trouser-belt, then rummaged through my belongings. He stood up and demanded my papers, which he examined by the light of an acetylene lamp.

"So, a sailor back from the sea. What's your unit, pig?"

"The U-Boat Service. Who the Devil are you?"

"People's Militia, toe-rag. And button your lip if you don't want to be shot for resisting arrest." The two men were in Army uniform—or rather the remains of Army uniform—and like the "Fregattenkapitän" at the station, they wore red armbands.

"All right, let him go," said the man with the lamp, "but first let's have a little equality. Here, let's have your cap." So the Imperial crown and cipher were ripped from my cap with a clasp knife, then the rings were torn from my fraying cuffs. I was too tired and dispirited to resist. What did it matter now?

"Has he got any food or tobacco?"

"No; only this sword belt. Won't need that now, will he?" He flung the black-and-yellow belt over a wall.

"Right then, send the bastard on his way."

So I set off once more, no longer carrying arms, or even the outward marks of k.u.k. officer status. Strangely enough, despite this unpleasant encounter and my unenviable situation, I felt a sudden, curious sense of relief—as if the ripping-off of my last remaining officer's distinctions had at least relieved me of the remnants of a dead past; rather as an amputation, though painful, gets rid of a shattered and gangrenous limb. I had no idea what the future might hold for a career naval officer without a navy in a country without a coast. But there; I was still alive, nearly four years in U-Boats had made me resourceful, and with Elisabeth by my side I was confident that we would sort ourselves out somehow. Perhaps it was just the light-headedness brought on by fatigue, but I even began to sing to myself a little as I tramped through the bleak streets of that defeated city.

I arrived at my aunt's flat on the Josefgasse. The flat staircase, once so elegant, was now grimy and smelt of poverty and damp. The place was cold and silent as a tomb. I rang the bell. No one answered. I rang again. At last there was a scuffling within and the sound of bolts being drawn. The door was opened by Franzi, my aunt's mildly half-witted housemaid. She stared at me with her great china-blue doll's eyes, then her face fell in horror, her jaw working soundlessly. I sensed at once that something terrible had happened.

"Herr Leutnant . . ."

"My aunt, Franzi—What's the matter?"

"Oh, Herr Leutnant . . ." she moaned, "we tried to send a telephone, but they don't work no more . . . they come and took her away . . ."

"Oh God—where have they taken her? Which hospital? How bad is she?" Then it was my turn to stare in amazement. My aunt had appeared in the hallway: pale and haggard, with her grey hair hanging down in strands, but indubitably my aunt, and seemingly in good health. She looked at me for some seconds, then fell to sobbing hysterically on Franzi's shoulders. Slowly, slowly, I heard a ringing hiss in my ears; felt an awful sensation of an ice-cold skewer being run through my heart . . .

"Otto . . . Oh Otto . . . the Gräfin Elisabeth . . . She came here from Cracow to meet you . . . She must have had the influenza already . . . She died yesterday morning."

I have no recollection whatever of how I came to be standing at the end of the Ringstrasse by the Aspern Bridge. It must have been about midday I suppose. My head felt as if it were being crushed in a steel tourniquet. It was like waking up from the most ghastly nightmare imaginable—and then realising that it is all true. I must have wandered through the streets like a sleep-walker, jostled by passers-by, until a lorry nearly ran me over. But however I had got here, here I was now, with the Danube Canal in front of me. The first thing that my faculties were able to grasp at as they emerged from the catalepsy of shock was a black-and-yellow poster, freshly pasted on the wall of a building. A small crowd had gathered in front of it. It bore the Imperial eagle and was headed INSTRUMENT OF ABDICATION. Beside it was another poster, red and white this time. It read PROCLAMATION OF THE REPUBLIC OF GERMAN-AUSTRIA.

The Volkswehr guards had taken my pistol when they searched me, otherwise I would not be speaking to you now. There I was: a refugee from a lost war, homeless, bereft of my life's career, a servant of a fallen dynasty—and now a widower as well. All I had left to live for was a baby son, whom I had seen only once. What did he need me for now? I knew that my cousin and her husband in Poland would bring him up as one of their own children. No, Prohaska, I thought; better make a clean end of it now, like some servant of an oriental despot drinking poison at his master's funeral. I looked around. The road had been dug up in front of the Urania. I selected two granite paving blocks, placed one in each pocket of my tunic, then walked on to the bridge. A fine drizzle was falling, stippling the eddying, rat-coloured waters of the Danube Canal. The current was strong now from the autumn rains, and anyway, people would be too preoccupied with their own miseries to notice my departure. I had faced that last gulp of water too many times over the past four years for it to frighten me now. I prepared to clamber up on to the parapet.

Then something caught my eye. It was at the corner of the street, where it met the Franz Josefs Kai. There was a large government building there, with its entrance right at the angle where the two streets met. Two bands of armed men were making their way towards it from opposite streets—invisible to one another, but both visible to me. I saw that one group wore red armbands; both were obviously intent on capturing the building. I paused to watch as the two gangs bumped into one another on the corner, recoiled like two cats, then stood staring awkwardly at one another, wondering what to do next. The matter was resolved by the building's door-keeper, who came out and evidently gave them a good telling-off. They milled about for a while, then merged, and dispersed with every sign of amity. Such was the Viennese "revolution" of November 1918. I thought grimly to myself that whatever else, Vienna remained Vienna: nothing ever done in earnest either for good or for bad. Then I turned back to the task in hand.

But somehow the moment had passed. I stood irresolutely by the parapet, gazing down at the water and trying to summon my resolve to climb over and jump. Then I had a vision. I tell you this even now with some hesitation; not least out of professional pride, because submarine commanders who are in the habit of seeing things tend not to last very long. But I saw my Elisabeth there before me. I cannot explain how it was—not an apparition in a burst of gilded plaster rays, like the Annunciation of the Blessed Virgin behind the altar in the Church of St Johann Nepomuk, but still a vision: the only one that I have ever had, until they started coming again a few months ago. It was as if she was superimposed on reality, neither inside my head nor outside it, yet infinitely more real than the drab misery around me. She looked anything but a shadow from another world as she spoke in that gentle, slightly accented voice of hers.

"And what do you propose doing now, my love?"

"Drowning myself. What sense is there in living, now that you are dead?"

She laughed. "Oh really, Otto. Don't be a silly idiot. Just fancy—surviving three and a half years in the U-Boats and then drowning in the Danube Canal: it's just too ridiculous. Couldn't you go and jump in the Stadtpark boating lake if you really want to be a laughing-stock?"

"Why in God's name did you die on me at a time like this, just when I needed you most?"

She sighed. "Yes, I'm sorry my dear, truly I am. But there's been a lot of untimely death about these past few years. It was stupid of me to come to Vienna, but how was I to know? I wanted to bring you back to Poland with me because I'd arranged you a job in Cracow. Believe me, I didn't want to die: I fought for six days to stay alive, but they couldn't find me a doctor and it was just too much for me in the end, when it turned to pneumonia. Be brave and try to carry on, darling, for the child's sake. He needs a father still. I said that I'd always love you, that last time I saw you, on the platform at the Südbahnhof—and I always will. Be patient: you'll come to join me soon."

"How long?"

She smiled. "Not long, not long, I promise. Just be patient."

Then she was gone.

Well, that was sixty-seven years ago now. I never even knew where they buried her. There were so many dying in Vienna that winter that they just tipped them into pits in the cemeteries, and no one could remember where they had taken her. I married again, many years later, but it was not from love, just a marriage for friendship between two elderly people. The memory of her faded and grew dim with the years, and the struggles of the years, and the onset of old age. But then as I sank into extreme old age, and the bodily decay in which you find me now, a curious thing began to happen: somehow the memory of her began to grow bright and fresh once more—of how it was when we were young in those twilight years of the old Monarchy. I even began to remember things about her that I had not consciously noticed when she was alive: the way she held her pen when she wrote, the way she used to unpin her thick black hair at night. It was like the imperious ocean spending half a century covering a sandbank with metres of grey mud, then changing its mind and stripping it all away again in a few weeks to leave the sand shining pure and golden as ever in the sunlight. Perhaps she is waiting for me after all: I cannot say. I was never a religious man, you see, just a naval officer, so I am quite unqualified to tell you what lies on the other side of the door: that door through which I must pass before long.

Anyway, the box for these little cassette things is full, so I had better shut up, now that the autumn gales are lashing sea-spray against the window panes. I don't know where I have found the strength to go on spinning these yarns over the past few months, these tales of a world that must seem so far off, but really was not so very long ago. But I am glad that I have lived long enough, and hope you have enjoyed them: perhaps even believed about ten per cent of them. If you think I am lying, though, just ask yourselves: could I possibly have made it all up? No, I have told it to you as I remember it, without excuses and without pleading. I am glad to have lived the life that was given me to live, and proud that for as long as she needed me I did my duty by Old Austria—perhaps not the best of causes to have fought for, but certainly by no means the worst. But there, enough is enough: I am an old man, monstrously old, and I tire easily nowadays. I hope that you will excuse me, but I must put out the light now and sleep.

EPILOGUE

OTTOKAR, RITTER VON PROHASKA, last surviving Knight of the Military Order of Maria Theresa, died at Plas Gaerllwydd early on the morning of Monday, 23 February 1987, less than two months short of his one hundred and first birthday.

He had been taken ill with bronchitis just before Christmas. Father McCaffrey was called and Extreme Unction had been administered, but the old man got better and seemed to make a good recovery. Then, at about tea-time on Sunday 22 February, he began to complain of dizziness and shortness of breath. He was helped up to his room and put to bed at 7 p.m. Sister Elisabeth remarked afterwards how he had leant on the end of the bed for several moments, gazing into space, then smiled and said "Wart' noch einen Moment Liserl, ich bin noch nicht ganz fertig"—"Wait just a moment Liserl, I'm not quite ready yet."

"I think this is strange," she told Dr Watkins next morning, "because though he speak with me German sometimes, he never call me 'Liserl' before."

The doctor estimated the time of death at about 4 a.m. and wrote down "Coronary thrombosis" as the cause of death.

"But he always have the good heart—very strong," Sister Elisabeth had protested.

"Ah, Sister, I'm a doctor. I didn't train for seven years to write 'Stopped living' on a death certificate—even if it is true. It's just not expected. But I'll say one thing: he was a tough old boy—doesn't look a day over eighty."

The old man's worldly possessions—some clothes and a few books—

were dispersed among the other residents or left out for the dustmen. A small box of medals was sold for £10 as a job lot to a coin-dealer from Swansea; except, that is, for the most pricelessly valuable of them all: a small, white-enamelled cross with its red-and-white watered-silk ribbon still folded Austrian-style into a triangle. Sister Elisabeth stole this the evening before the funeral, then crept down to the chapel early next morning and tucked it into the folds of the shroud before the undertaker's men came to screw down the coffin-lid. As she removed the medal from its case a yellowed slip of paper printed in Gothic letters had fluttered out. She smiled as she read it:

> This decoration remains the property of the Grand Master of the Military Order of Maria Theresa. On the death of the recipient it must be returned to the Chancery of the Order, Vienna 1, Minoritenplatz 3.

As befits a penniless refugee, it was a pauper's funeral: the very cheapest that the Swansea and West Glamorgan Co-Operative Society could offer. The coffin was borne down the muddy lane to the little churchyard of St Cadog, beside the sea, where the winter storms drench the gravestones with salt spray. The church is kept locked most of the time now. The parish has no parishioners, and the Poles from the Plas are the graveyard's only new customers these days. Sister Elisabeth evicted a colony of mice from the bronchitic harmonium and played a hymn as the coffin was borne from the church after the funeral service. It was Haydn's "Glorious Things of Thee Are Spoken, Zion City of Our God," the tune of which had sentimental associations both for herself and for the deceased.

She and Kevin were the only mourners, standing in the late winter drizzle as Father McCaffrey tossed his handful of sandy soil on to the lid of the coffin. Later the undertaker's men put up a creosoted wooden cross at the end of a row of such crosses. It bears an enamelled metal plate with the simple, misspelt legend: OTTOKAR PROCHASKA 1886–1987 RIP.

And there he lies, in that place where the Irish monk built his wattle hut fifteen centuries ago, when the Germanic and Slav tribes were first jostling against one another in the forests of Central Europe. The metal plate is already beginning to rust in the salt air. Ten years from now it will be indecipherable, and twenty years from now the cross will have rotted and tumbled over into the dune-grass, as some have already done at the other end of the row. Nothing but a low hummock in the ground will mark the place where he lies, only a stone's throw from where the great ocean waves crash ceaselessly on the shore.